BODIES IN THE WATER

BODIES IN THE WATER

AJ ABERFORD

This edition produced in Great Britain in 2022

by Hobeck Books Limited, Unit 14, Sugnall Business Centre, Sugnall, Stafford, Staffordshire, ST21 6NF

www.hobeck.net

A CIP catalogue for this book is available from the British Library.

ISBN 978-1-913-793-71-5 (pbk)

ISBN 978-1-913-793-70-8 (ebook)

Cover design by Spiffing Covers

www.spiffingcovers.com

Printed and bound in Great Britain

PRAISE FOR BODIES IN THE WATER

'I thought I knew everything about murders in the Med – not so – this series is a fantastic read!' Robert Daws, bestselling author of the *Rock* crime series

'What a fantastic debut thriller from AJ Abeford! *Bodies in the Water* gives the real lowdown about crime and corruption in the Mediterranean, in an adventure that ranges from the tourist enclaves of Malta to the war-torn deserts of Libya and weaves together an intricate tale of murder, human trafficking, money laundering, terrorism and organised crime. In the centre of it all is Detective George Zammit, an intriguing new character on the crime thriller scene who is sure to become an instant fan favourite. Meticulously researched by someone who clearly has a deep understanding of the subject matter, *Bodes in the Water* rattles on at a supercharged pace, leaving the reader waiting expectantly for the next novel in what is destined to be a hugely popular new series.'
J.T. Brannan, bestselling thriller and mystery author

'I am definitely a fan of George and 100% will look forward to reading the next in the series.' Alex Jones

'… a cracker. Organised crime, people smuggling, run ins with ISAL and the hapless Detective George Zammit. Tricksy as a Zen novel.' Pete Fleming

'Highly emotive and gripping.' Louise Cannon

'I really enjoyed it. The writing was crisp and flowed well. The characters were strong and it was interesting how their paths crossed. The pace was excellent.' ThrillerMan

'I enjoyed this book immensely … very exciting and unpredictable.' Sarah Leck

'What started as a cross between *The Godfather* and *Midsomer Mysteries* soon developed into a twisty thriller, full of humour and coincidence where you can't help but root for unlikely hero, Inspector George Zammit.' Angela Paull

AUTHOR'S NOTE

Although the plot points are inspired by the political circumstances and certain events at the time of writing, the story is the product of my imagination and not intended to be an accurate account of any such real-life events or a comment on any of the people who may have been involved in them.

Malta is a small island and three-quarters of the population share the same one hundred most common surnames. As a result, there's a chance I have inadvertently given a character the same name as someone alive or maybe dead. If that is the case, I apologise. The events, dialogue and characters in this book were created for the purposes of fictionalisation. Any resemblance of any character or corporation to any entity, or to a person, alive or dead, is purely coincidental.

ARE YOU A THRILLER SEEKER?

Hobeck Books is an independent publisher of crime, thrillers and suspense fiction and we have one aim – to bring you the books you want to read.

For more details about our books, our authors and our plans, plus the chance to download free novellas, sign up for our newsletter at **www.hobeck.net**.

You can also find us on Twitter **@hobeckbooks** or on Facebook **www.facebook.com/hobeckbooks10**.

For Nick and Margaret, Marisa, Doris, Brenda and Hazel. A generation whose time with us is now over.

PROLOGUE

NORTH OF KANO, NORTHERN NIGERIA

THEY CUT THROUGH THE VILLAGE, on their motorbikes, AK-47s swinging from their shoulders. The sun was going down and the dusty streets were filled with the sound of children playing. Families were making the most of what sunlight remained, busy indoors after a day working in the millet fields. The elders sat on their haunches, outside their single storey, one-roomed dwellings that made up the village.

Their target that day had been the military base, some kilometres north of Kano, Nigeria, where they could steal arms, ammunition and vehicles, but they had underestimated the resolve of the Nigerian Army who had repelled and humiliated them. They landed in the village as mean and vengeful as a dozen angry wasps.

Standing just off the central square of the village, the Apostolic Church of Christ was a simple chapel with whitewashed wooden panel walls and a corrugated iron roof. It regularly held services for up to fifty worshippers and had long been an irritant to the ISIL-affiliated jihadis. That afternoon, as a consolation for their earlier disappointment at the military base, they had decided to burn it down and kill anyone who tried to stop them.

Two brothers, Abeao and Mobo, were helping Christ's work along, replacing some corrugated iron sheets on the roof, when they heard the bikes entering the village. They knew immediately what that sound meant. When they were young teenagers, they had witnessed their own village being burned and their parents slaughtered, all for the sake of their Christian beliefs. Now, only ten kilometres away, it was about to happen again.

They saw the first wave of villagers from further up the main street running, grabbing children and bolting down the alleys between the houses to hide in the scrub beyond. The old could do little more than retreat inside their houses and pray that lives would not be lost and the danger would soon pass.

The brothers jumped down from the roof and pressed themselves behind the fencing at the side of the church. They watched two very young militia soldiers dismount from their Honda bike and untie two plastic jerry cans from the rear rack. They shouted to each other in Hausa, as they splashed petrol around the wooden structure. From their hiding place, the brothers saw the first flames begin to climb up the frame to the roof. The brothers spoke mainly Yoruba and a little English, but they understood enough Hausa to know those kids were armed and high as kites on heroin or opioids.

It was Mobo, the younger of the two, who reacted first. He broke cover and grabbed one of the youths, seizing his automatic weapon. As they struggled, the gun discharged a burst of fire, hitting two militia youths, who were standing nearby watching the flames crackling against the side of the church.

Mobo and Abeao were both big men in their late twenties. When they were not fishing on Lake Chad, they hired themselves out as builders. They were strong from years of manual work. Abeao quickly leaped to his brother's aid, wielding his roofing hammer, puncturing the scalp of the jihadi with the gun, before dragging Mobo away from the burning church. They fled through the back streets, followed by shouts and shots.

They hid, panting and shaking, under the floorboards of a house built on low stilts, at the edge of the village. There, they listened to the sound of automatic gunfire and the screams of those villagers not quick enough to escape, or unwilling to leave the old or the young behind.

Later, as nightfall came, they heard the low revving engines of the motorbikes in the lanes and saw their headlights scouring the buildings. The murderous youth cruised up and down, stoned on weed and drunk on *Ogog'*, the nasty local home-distilled palm liquor.

The brothers lay still, pressing their faces into the dirt, ignoring the insect bites and the smell of the garbage that lay rotting beneath them. Eventually, the shouts and sounds of the hunt faded away and the animal cries of the night took hold, undisturbed. Most villagers remained in the scrub until dawn, shrouded by the smoke of their burning homesteads.

As the cry of the first cockerels announced the start of another day, Abeao took his brother back to the small outhouse they rented and went into their patch of garden. There, under the bougainvillea hedge, they dug up the rusted tin box containing all the money they possessed. Abeao gathered a mobile phone and a few items of clothing and pushed them into a small ruck-sack. He turned to his brother.

"It's time, we've got to go. They'll be back. We're a danger to them all now." He waved his hand towards the village. "These people won't protect us."

Mobo looked tearful as he raised his bulk from the plastic beer crate that served as a stool.

"Europe, brother? It's far."

"Yes; to Niger, then north to Libya. There's a man who'll take us, but we must go now."

It was a plan they had discussed many times, so both knew what they had to do and what lay ahead of them.

Outside, they mounted the small motorbike, which buckled

under their combined weight, and Abeao pointed it northwards, towards the border with Niger. As they left their home, a small groups of silent, unsmiling neighbours watched them go, the acrid smoke of their smouldering houses hanging in the air.

CHAPTER 1
INSPECTOR GEORGE ZAMMIT
GRAND HARBOUR, MALTA

MALTA IS SOMETIMES REFERRED to as the 'Jewel of the Mediterranean', but those standing anxiously at the rails of the ship sailing into the island's magnificent Grand Harbour could have been forgiven for not fully appreciating the compliment. The fortified limestone walls of Valletta's bastions rose high above them to their right while, to their left, the centuries-old forts of Ricasoli, St Angelo and St Michael stood guard, as they had done across the ages.

The *Samaritan* was old, built forty years ago in Germany as a salvage vessel, but its recent blue and yellow paint job made it a distinctive sight. The ship weighed about four hundred tonnes and was forty metres in length. It belonged to the charity Medical and Rescue at Sea and the hearts of many frightened and abandoned migrants had beaten faster at the sight of the bright coloured boat ploughing across the southern Mediterranean towards them.

Observed from the high walls of Valletta, the decks seemed jam-packed with people, most of them dark-skinned, all wearing bright orange life jackets. Some were women, some children or babies, but the majority were young men; all of them anxious, hungry and exhausted.

Although the *Samaritan* had been on patrol for ten days, those currently on deck had spent a week longer at sea, on rafts, adrift in the Mediterranean. Their food had run out in the first few days and their water a few days later. When the drone from the *Samaritan* first confirmed the specks on the horizon were indeed drifting inflatable boats, it was already too late for six souls, who lay in body bags on the floor of the small mortuary in the hold of the ship.

While making the turn to port, had the skipper of the *Samaritan* looked up to the opposite quayside, he might have noticed a short, stout figure, shielding his eyes from the sun, watching the ship's arrival.

George Zammit was an inspector in Malta's *Pulizija*, who had just received a call telling him the clear blue waters of the Grand Harbour had been fouled by the discovery of a floating corpse. He had driven to the western end, onto Victoria Quay, where a workman was waving and pointing over the side, summoning him to look down into the water which shimmered in the early morning sunlight.

He had been walking over the dusty concrete deck, hands in pockets, to take a look, when he had spotted the *Samaritan* making its way through the Grand Harbour. As an inspector in the Immigration Department, he would generally be required to help process the new arrivals but, given the growing heat and humidity building on the quayside, he was happy to leave that laborious task to whoever had been caught lounging around the office in Floriana.

As the *Samaritan* slowed and headed in towards Boiler Wharf, he turned his attention to the oily waters lapping round the pilings, spotting the body immediately. It was lean and male, the arms outstretched, the feet shoeless. A thin white T-shirt rode up over the loose jeans, revealing the waistband of a pair of branded pants. From above, the body was hanging as if suspended in flight, weightless; its head gently knocking against the concrete pillars. His first thought was that it did not seem to be a Maltese; possibly one of the many migrants that worked in the docks, hard to tell.

It was only a few months ago that he had been promoted to the rank of inspector, much to his surprise. It had also raised the eyebrows of his colleagues, as he had never been a 'man to watch' in the promotion stakes. He noticed the looks and heard the comments, but pointedly ignored them and made sure his new, silver epaulette badges were polished bright every morning.

The promotion had moved George out of the Criminal Investigations Team, which caused him few regrets. Investigating crime in Malta was always fraught with problems. The Maltese were few in number and a small-island people. They lived in tight communities, where anonymity was a luxury few enjoyed. Families were large and extended. Causing offence to one member, inevitably offended others. A careless word or deed could cause ripples that spread across the whole community.

While the Maltese were devout Catholics and pious at prayer, they could hold grudges that passed down the generations, sometimes spilling over into arguments and even violence. No inquiry was ever straightforward. Here politics, family, business and crime all rubbed along together.

Hoping that this investigation might avoid such complexities, George worked through what had to be done and reached for his mobile to phone the Marine Section.

"Inspector Zammit here, *mela,* we have a body in the Grand Harbour." Like all Maltese, George used the all-purpose word '*mela*' hundreds of times a day, in gaps in speech where he would otherwise just take a breath. "Yes, on Moll ta' Victoria, Victoria Quay, at the south-west end between the tug and fishing vessel berths. Yes, yes, it's up against the wharf ... yes, an easy lift."

A rag-tag of fishing vessels were berthed in that part of the harbour, their decks tangled with nets, lines, floats and other tackle. Assorted washing hung like bunting from the masts and aerial rigs. The marine supply vessels and the orange tug fleet also tied up there. On the northern side of the harbour was the Waterfront, where the massive cruise liners berthed, spilling their cargo of aged tourists to wander the streets and struggle up the steep stone steps of Valletta. On the south side were the fancy marinas of the Three Cities. The enormous super yachts hung on their mooring ropes, idle for months on end, their crews filling time by washing down the high gloss hulls and polishing the stainless-steel fittings.

"Who is he? Do you know?" A Maltese voice spoke up behind George.

A small crowd of workmen had gathered, shuffling around in twos and threes. They were talking amongst themselves and peering over the edge of the wharf for a glimpse of the spectacle below.

George turned to face the speaker, the same man who had first pointed him towards the corpse; a squat overseer from one of the nearby, stone-built warehouses.

"How do I know? He's lying face down in the water, isn't he? He could be anybody. Did you ring this in? Any of you boys know who he is?"

Silence.

"*Mela*! We've got a body here, some help, please. Anyone, any ideas?"

George watched them – casual labourers paid by the hour. Most were from the open camps in the south where the new arrivals from the *Samaritan* would end up. There, they would swell the pool of cheap and unregulated labour that helped fuel Malta's booming economy.

The Mediterranean has a small tidal range and the western end of the harbour was washed and rinsed by waters from Marsa Creek, not the tide itself. Either someone had dumped the body where it was floating or he had fallen in and drowned. Peering over the side of the wharf, George spotted a galvanised steel ladder embedded into the concrete, almost within reach of the floating corpse. He realised, with a touch of irritation, this was not someone who had accidentally fallen into the water and could not find a way up.

The sound of vehicles caught his attention and he turned to see two squad cars pull up. A small team of *Pulizija* tumbled out and sauntered over towards him. At the head of the group was Sergeant Major Chelotti, a man who specialised in making George's life difficult.

"Now then, it's the 'use it or lose it' inspector! So, George, what've we got here?"

Following an unplanned retirement, an inspector's post in Immigration had become vacant and rumour had it that the superintendent was told to appoint somebody immediately or lose the post in an upcoming budget review. As George was the longest-serving sergeant major, the post became his by default. That was how his good fortune had come about, as well as the taunting nickname, the 'use it or lose it' inspector!

George was not a physically imposing man, but he puffed out his chest, ran a hand across his thinning, light brown hair and yanked his belt over his pronounced paunch, rising to his full height of 1.75 metres.

"I'm glad you've remembered I'm an inspector, Chelotti; kindly address me as such. I'll do the same for you, when the time comes." He paused for a moment to let that sink in. Then a thought occurred to him. "Actually, I'm not sure I need you here. Why don't you leave the others and go down to Boiler Wharf to help process the arrivals on the *Samaritan*?"

Chelotti had only been a police sergeant major for a few months less than George and was deeply resentful of his colleague's promotion.

"Off you go, sergeant major. To Boiler Wharf, please."

George turned his back to hide a smile, as Chelotti glared at him, then stalked off across the quay, muttering under his breath.

Before long, an ambulance arrived, its blue lights turning and, moments later, the Marine Section motor launch appeared through the shimmering heat haze. The Marine Section sergeant and diver had brought ropes, hooks, a retrieval net and a black body bag.

While the diver slipped into the water to secure the body, George gazed around the Harbour. For the first time, he considered the two ships moored further down the quay. Running his hand through his damp hair, he realised he would have to pay them a visit. The thin man in the water might have been a crewman who took a fall, returning from a late-night shore excursion. That would give a quick and easy answer to the question of identity.

The Marine Section sergeant recovered the corpse using a green cargo net. He and the diver, both perspiring in their marine garb, had climbed up the ladder and managed to heave the body onto the wharf. It lay in a small pool of water that spread across the hot concrete.

Once the body was disentangled from the retrieval net, George looked at it closely. He was now certain it belonged to a North African. The corpse had darker skin than the Maltese locals, with thick black hair and the sparse moustache of a young man. He was slightly built; his cheap clothing well-worn. He had obviously been a working man. His eyes were open, pupils dilated, but death had stopped the blood flow and they had the blue-white haze of a long-dead fish.

At first sight, there were no obvious marks on him, but it was difficult to tell, given the skin was already becoming bleached and wrinkled. The corpse was also starting to swell slightly around the abdomen.

George knelt and felt inside the trouser pockets, his fingers brushing against the cold damp skin. He recoiled slightly. The marine sergeant stood by, watching, making sure the body was thoroughly searched. No wallet. No phone. No papers.

Next to poke about the body was the medical officer; all bustle and officiousness. They all stood back to let him do a preliminary examination. After a few minutes, he turned to George and said: "On first inspection, I can tell you he didn't drown and I'd say he's been in the water for up to twelve hours. I'll get back to you after the postmortem to confirm, but you shouldn't be writing this off as an accidental death. I think you've got yourself a possible homicide."

"Why's that?" George could not hide his surprise.

"Well, the fact he was dead before he hit the water, for one. If he'd drowned, his lungs would've filled with water and he would've sunk. This corpse is floating around like a lost football! Also, there's a hint of bruising on the arms and neck, look, here," he pointed, "and a contusion to the head. Might be nothing. Could've happened when the body was in the water, banging up against the concrete, but the water's calm enough at the moment. We'll see. I'll try and get this done in the next day or so."

"If you think there's foul play here, we'll need you onto it quickly," George said, in a rare burst of authority.

The examiner shrugged, unimpressed.

"Protest noted."

George saw him looking at the bright silver epaulettes.

"And, yes, congratulations. I'd heard you'd made inspector. Must've been a nice surprise for you?"

George stood expressionless as the examiner gathered his things and left.

The paramedics chatted as they bagged and labelled the corpse, then lifted it into the ambulance. The puddle on the dock-side had already started to disappear, the last trace of the body's imprint evaporating away. With all corporeal evidence removed, life on the wharf returned to normal.

George ambled down towards the two ships, stepping over the heavy-duty lines that bound them to the bulbous cast-iron mooring bollards.

As he approached, he noticed movement on the larger, second vessel, moored some seventy metres or so away. He spotted three men, leaning low on the stern rail, who seemed to be watching proceedings on the quayside. He squinted into the intense sunlight to get a better look at them. As he got nearer, they all suddenly turned and moved away from the rail, ducking low, trying to keep out of sight, as they moved back inside the vessel, one slowly closing a bulkhead door behind them.

CHAPTER 2
ABDULLAH BELKACEM

MARSABAR, LIBYA

MARSABAR WAS A MEDIUM-SIZED COASTAL TOWN, midway between Tripoli and the Tunisian border, home to about thirty thousand people. From his terrace, Abdullah Belkacem could look across the parched brown fields at the thin crops of wheat, barley and groundnuts. He could also see the sprawl of the town's grey and white, low-rise cinder-block houses, a few kilometres away. Two cranes, necks bent like giant grazing giraffes, marked the port, while the pale blue and white tip of the minaret echoed the colours of the late-spring sky.

To the east of the town, the refinery's flare stack, storage tanks and distillation towers rose above the skyline, blackened and ugly. Beyond that, the deep blue ribbon of the Mediterranean stretched along the coast. The extensive bay curved from northwest to southeast. The wide, sandy beaches drew visitors into the town during the spring and autumn, when the warm air from the Sahara met the cooling air from the Mediterranean.

Abdullah Belkacem's farmhouse stood at the end of a long, compacted, dirt track. The high stone walls boasted two guards at all times. In Abdullah's business, he always had to take precautions. He enjoyed a good life and did not intend to lose it through carelessness.

He was sat on the terrace, enjoying the onset of evening, watching his three children playing in the dust of the large compound. They were fighting with sticks, squabbling and teasing the dogs. His wife Rania, her sister and their mother were chatting outside the door leading into the kitchen. The low evening sun, still strong, was turning the sky black and orange, throwing deep shadows across the yard.

The next day was his eldest son's twelfth birthday party. The women had been busy making date-filled biscuits, deep bowls of spiced rice pudding and piles of savoury breads. Tomorrow they would grill chicken, fish and lamb, and it would be a good day for all the family.

Abdullah was with his elder brother, Tareq, enjoying a tray of tea. Neither of them was saying much; happy in each other's company, each lost in his own thoughts. Early evening was always Abdullah's favourite time of day. He was a tall man, a little under two metres, with a thick, oiled, black beard and lively dark brown eyes that were rarely still. His hair had kept its dark colour, despite him entering his middle years, and was usually bound with a cloth turban. He was slim, with an athletic gait and huge reserves of energy. Respectful of his Muslim faith and Berber heritage, he favoured wearing the traditional North African *djellaba*, a hooded, calf-length, loose-fitting cotton robe. He saw it as a symbol of his connection to his religion and his culture.

His older brother, Tareq, was totally different. He was shorter and more powerfully built. He had thick forearms and calves, while his shoulders were broad, from years of working in the unyielding fields of the family's farm in the nearby hills. His beard and curly hair were streaked with grey, and his pock-marked skin was the colour of roasted walnuts. Tareq dressed in modern Western clothes: jeans, T-shirts and sweatshirts, with logos and slogans speaking of places he would never visit.

Tareq had been born with a strength that was respected across the district and in the town. As a young man, he had wrestled in the village festivals and even spent some time in a wrestling-focused gym in Tripoli, before homesickness brought him back. Abdullah had broader interests so, while both had tilled the soil and herded animals, it was Abdullah who had regularly attended the madrasa at the local mosque and completed his education.

His parents were farmers, but that life was hard. He believed his own family deserved better than the precarious existence the land could provide. So, he had moved his young family, to the coastal town of Marsabar, where Tareq had soon joined them. Abdullah would rise early for prayers and then start about his business, continuing until the late afternoon. He bought and sold: land, cars, petrol, water ... anything that was in demand. He and Tareq also sold people and transported them across the Mediterranean to a new life in Europe.

His was a complicated business, but one that had brought rich rewards. He traded with the dollars he kept in the strong room, buried in the limestone cellars beneath his villa, and with the guns and the muscle of his extended family.

In the far corner of the compound, he watched three Somalian 'bodies', as he referred to his stock-in-trade, wrestling with a large rectangular frame made from scaffold poles. They were tying a huge sheet of thick PVC to the frame to form a swimming pool for the children. A tanker with 10,000 litres of fresh water was due to arrive the next day and the makeshift pool would be filled. Then the fun would begin. Abdullah knew that wasting precious drinking water like that was a sin but, for the pleasure of hearing the children's shrieks and laughs, it was one he could bear.

In 2011, Abdullah had watched the overthrow of the Tunisian government, only a few miles down the Coastal Road. The protests in Tahir Square in Cairo soon followed, spreading to Morocco, Syria, Yemen and elsewhere. He had known it was the right time to break the yoke in Libya, so he had taken some men from Berber families and other trusted farmers, leaving the coast for the Nafusa hills to the south. Word had soon spread that they would rid Marsabar and the villages of Gaddafi and his jackals, and find a new way to be. More men had joined them.

As had four French soldiers from Special Forces, who brought trucks of weapons from Egypt and France and taught his new militia how to use them. It was a wonderful time, full of excitement and purpose, but they had to act fast. With their crops in the fields, they only had a few weeks, otherwise their families would have gone hungry later in the year. When they returned to their homes on the coastal plain, they were a strong force of over a hundred men who were able to teach others how to maintain a machine gun or fire an RPG.

Abdullah had been talking with Tareq about the war being played out on their doorstep and how the Egyptian and Emirati backed warlord, General Boutros, was encroaching on the capital, Tripoli, only one hundred and twenty kilometres down the coast to the east. Tareq was concerned and spoke more to reassure himself than from conviction.

"Well, if the militias come from the east, we can push them back down the Coastal Road. We did it to Gaddafi's soldiers and I know we can do it again."

Abdullah paused before he answered. This was a conversation they had had many times.

"You know, last time, we only won because the town rose with us. Had they hidden in their houses and locked their doors, we would have been standing in front of Gaddafi's guns with our pants down, showing our arses. If anything happens, we must have the town behind us."

"But how were you so sure they'd stand and fight with us last time?"

Abdullah tapped his nose, joking with him.

"Because I know everything, brother!"

Tareq smiled and turned away to watch the deepening sunset.

They had fought three skirmishes in the town against the government garrison. The people had rallied, bringing such weapons as they could find. A crowd of over a thousand had stood behind them. It had been a gamble, but the inhabitants had turned out, prepared to fight.

Before Gaddafi's thuggish troops pulled out, they had used heavy weapons and artillery against the people and their homes. There were many casualties and several deaths. This had incensed the townspeople so many more had joined Abdullah and his men in chasing the soldiers down the Coastal Road. Abdullah and his militia had subsequently become known as the defenders of the town – *'The Defenders of Marsabar'*.

Revenge and anger had driven them forward: farmers, shopkeepers, teachers and fishermen. Gaddafi's army had eventually retreated thirty kilometres to Sabratha, to defend the huge refinery at Az-Zawiyah. Eventually, Gaddafi had left Tripoli and gone west, as far as Sirte, a coastal town on the road to Benghazi. NATO planes bombed his convoy and, in the end rebel militia found him hiding in a drainage pipe, from where they dragged him to nearby wasteland and beat him to death.

Clans were like families and, in the desert, were stronger than any government, Imam or occupying army. Abdullah's clan were Berber people. These days, most of them no longer lived in the desert but in the vicinity of Marsabar. They scraped a living from the poor soil, worked in the town or took what they could from the sea, but, in their hearts, they remained a strong and independent people.

Tareq took a toothpick from the tray and began to worry his teeth.

After the victory, when all was chaos, Abdullah had tried to bring order to Marsabar. For a few years, the people had made him the town's mayor and he had led the municipal council. He took money from local businesses to rebuild the school. The national bank gave the town loans and grants to repair and improve the port. He raised local taxes from the refinery, from visiting traders and ships that berthed in Marsabar. He looked after his Berber clan and those who had fought with him on the Coastal Road.

As time passed, he realised that this interlude could not last. Things had got worse in the country as a whole while the death of Gaddafi had sparked yet more confusion and unrest. He needed to stay strong to make sure Marsabar remained safe from the bandits and militias of Tripoli, as well as those in the east. Others were trusted to govern the town while Abdullah focused on its safety and security. His men and his family had kept their weapons. He fed them all, paying them from the profits of his several enterprises.

The Marsabar militia made it their job to ensure trade between Tunisia and Tripoli happened without interference. His men caught, then punished, bandits and smugglers, while taking over their businesses. Abdullah started buying cheap fuel from the refineries and sold it on to the fleets of wagons making their way to and from Tripoli. He took control of the petrol stations and sold cheap petrol and diesel. He also managed the market for *mazout*, the heavy oil used in domestic generators. He sold not just to the locals, but also smuggled large quantities into Tunisia, just across the border. Business was good.

As the two brothers sat talking, they noticed a rising plume of dust, black and red against the setting sun. A vehicle was approaching the compound, down the long unpaved track from the Marsabar Road. They watched it carefully until it became clear it was their own Toyota minibus. Abdullah turned to Tareq.

"Are we expecting arrivals this evening?"

"Possibly. Khaled was picking up north of Debdeb. It looks like him. If it is, he's made good time; it's a long drive."

"So, Debdeb: Malians, Nigerians, West Africans?"

"Most likely. Should be only ten or twelve bodies today."

The minibus, covered in a rich, ochre dust, eventually stopped outside the main gate and waited, engine idling. The driver hung his arm out of the window. It was a rule that the bodies were not allowed inside the homestead, unless it was to work. Tareq rose from his chair and went downstairs to talk to the driver. The Somalian workers peered through the security gate, searching the faces of those in the bus for family or friends.

The brothers Abeao and Mobo sat on the back seat, cramped and sore from the days of travel. They tried to stretch their tired limbs. They were anxious about what awaited them. They looked up towards the big house, through the orange-red desert dust that coated the windows of the van, and saw a man with a blue chequered turban, sitting on a plastic chair on the terrace, legs casually crossed, his loose white djellaba luminous in the gathering dusk. He had a long black beard and his white hood hung loosely across his shoulders. Despite his stillness, they could sense his latent power and authority.

Uninterested in the cargo in the van, Abdullah watched Tareq and the driver for a few moments. Tareq peeled dinar notes from a roll, pushing them through the window. The driver took the money, waved to Abdullah, raised the window and revved the engine. As the van pulled away, Tareq caught a glimpse of the faces of the migrants in the van, pressed against the windows, eyes wide and fearful.

He rejoined his brother.

"Six with money to go to the compound waiting for the boats; seven with nothing, so they'll go to the construction sites tomorrow.

Abdullah nodded his approval.

As the number of men needed to keep Marsabar safe grew, so had the need for money to arm and feed them. For years, the Berbers and other tribal groups of the Sahara had used migrant labour to help grow the crops. African migration was nothing new and nobody could cross the Sahara unaided.

Without money, all a body could offer was their labour. In recent times, those from the Middle East had joined the oppressed and dispossessed from the Sub-Saharan countries, the Sahel and the Horn of Africa. All of them wanted to cross the sea to Europe, to feel safe and do right for their families. Abdullah understood that.

Those who arrived without money to pay their fare had to work in local construction, on farms or, if they preferred, selling themselves for the pleasure of others. If Abdullah did not have use for a body's work, he might sell it on to someone who did. It did not always end well, but at least it gave a chance to those who had nothing and had travelled far.

The countries of Europe preached against this trade, but they lacked clean hands also. When they were hungry for labour to fuel their growing economies, they had encouraged arrivals from their former African colonies and beyond. But when enough was enough and they tried to turn off the tap, that was not so easy. Migration was a dream of escape and, one way or another, people still made their way towards the cities of Europe.

As the numbers had continued to grow, so had migrant deaths at sea. In 2013, the EU had the Italians launch a rescue mission, *Mare Nostrum*, Our Sea, that in twelve months brought one hundred and fifty thousand migrants safely to Europe. That was good for business, as even more hopefuls arrived on the coastline of north Africa.

It was true Abdullah's boats were the best equipped in Libya. He was proud that many passengers survived their journey in them. Illicit sea crossings were never safe and nothing was guaranteed, but they had a better chance with him than with most of the other bandits who operated up and down the Libyan coast. Those who travelled with common traffickers risked death through drowning, thirst, illness or violence. Fighting was common on the boats, where there was a desperate struggle for water, food and space.

Abdullah knew the good times moving migrants across the Mediterranean would soon be over. The governments of Europe were sick of the refugees and the business could suddenly stop. He watched CNN, Al Jazeera and the BBC – the fast route to Italy would soon be closed.

People were tired of the migrants. In Europe, everyone cried and complained at their suffering, but they were not prepared to share their houses, medicines or schools. A new wave of European politicians had seen their countries change around them and did not like it. The migrants were poor, had no useful languages and little education.

Without work and as unwelcome guests in foreign lands, the new arrivals soon discovered that the riches they had promised their families and the money lenders were nowhere to be found. There was no way back, not without more expense, more debt and the shame of failure. So, they lied to their families about the good life in Europe, while they scraped a living as best they could.

Abdullah had watched all of this, which was why, for many months, he had been working on a new business that would change things for him and for Marsabar. He had plans; big, exciting plans.

He had looked around and saw oil everywhere. Only two hundred metres from his fence, he could see the pipelines taking the crude from the oil fields of the south, across the scrubland, to the refinery on the coast. At night, he would watch the intense blue flame from the flare stack that burned the gas high into the purple sky. He had seen the coastal tankers come into the port to load the fuel oil, despite the sanctions on banks and oil sales. There was money in all this, big money, and it did not weep, bleed or drown in the water and pollute his shore.

CHAPTER 3
NICK WALKER
CASTELLO BONNICI, MALTA

NICK WALKER DROVE his soft-top sports car northwards, up the Malta coast road, enjoying the rare opportunity to put his foot down and feel the car's acceleration push through his spine. His blond hair was thick enough to keep its style, despite the back-draft, and his skinny-fit expensive blue suit was appropriate for his slim frame. His fair colouring and smooth complexion made him look younger than his years and a recently grown beard was not quite enough to dispel the boyish appearance he was trying hard to lose.

That morning, he had woken with a gnawing sense of unease deep in his gut. He had known for some time that there was something untoward going on in the business he ran. For too long now, he had chosen not to mention his suspicions, as he was pretty sure the owners were deliberately holding back the truth about what was going on. Today's meeting with them would change all that. He was determined to find out where exactly the flood of money that was swamping his business was coming from and to whom it belonged.

He drove past the shabby resort of Buggiba on Malta's north-eastern coast and took the car up onto the limestone ridge that bisected the island, following the winding road through the hilltop village of Il-Wardija. A small sideroad led to a secluded eighteenth-century *palazzo,* or *castello.* A prominent sign read: *'Castello Bonnici, Private, No Access Without Appointment'.* The three-metre gates and stone wall surrounding the extensive property ensured both privacy and security.

Nick had been there several times before and stopped his car at the huge matt black, steel gate, designed to fit the fortified feel of the place. He pushed the button on the entry phone and the gates slowly swung open. Inside, a range of expensive cars were parked around the gravel turning circle, in front of a large columned portico. Adjoining, was a small private chapel, with high gloss, varnished wooden doors. At the top of the chapel's small stone tower, a tarnished, green, brass bell hung patiently.

A man stepped forward from the shelter of the portico and stood tight to the driver's door. It was Simon, Head of Security at the *castello.* He was heavily built, with his head shaven and muscles straining under his tight black suit. He spoke in an East European accent.

"Nick, good morning. Please, you're expected. I'll do the parking."

"Thank you, Simon." Nick smiled and gently lobbed the keys to him, mindful that the gesture should not disrespect the powerful figure in front of him.

With an exaggerated display of deference, Simon extended an arm to usher him into the house. Nick knew he could just as easily have chopped him down, bundled him in a car boot and thrown him off Dingli Cliffs.

Simon walked ahead, his large muscular frame swaying from side to side. He assumed Nick was following and there was no small talk. The entrance was through a pair of huge double wooden doors, studded with ancient iron nails, which led into a cool, darkened hallway. Nick was always impressed by the grand double staircase. Separate flights from the same central axis reached either end of a magnificent gallery that wound its way around the first floor.

Tapestries hung on the unplastered stone walls, dating back to the seventeenth century, showing the triumphs of the Knights of St John. The floors were polished stone flags, with hues of pink and green. Suits of armour stood to attention along the corridor that led to the reception rooms, between which, heavily framed paintings portrayed scenes of biblical mayhem and saintly sacrifice. The place smelled musty and stank of old money.

Nick entered a study and saw the two men waiting for him. A quick glance at his watch assured him he was neither early nor late. Floor-to-ceiling bookcases, filled with antique leather-bound books, lined the room. The whole place had an oppressive atmosphere, filled with heavy, antique furniture. At the back of the room, full-length doors opened onto a terrace, spilling light into the gloom.

Marco Bonnici rose to meet Nick, extending a hand. He was an unassuming-looking, middle-aged man with a full head of greying wavy hair and a thin angular face. He wore half-moon glasses and a cream cardigan to match his crumpled chinos. The look suited his mild urbane manner. This was his place and Nick still found it strange that anyone could look so at ease in the antique *castello*.

"Nick, how good of you to come! Welcome. Please, come in. Let me introduce you to Sergio Rossi."

The second man wore a crisp white shirt and black trousers; looking every inch the Sicilian that he was. He was in his late forties and the opposite of Marco Bonnici: short and stocky, with his wavy steel-grey hair gelled back so it curled behind his ears and over his collar. The top two buttons of his shirt were unbuttoned, revealing a mound of grey chest hair. Nick knew that Rossi represented an established Milanese family that, together with Marco Bonnici, owned the business Nick managed. Rossi was standing against the open doors to the terrace, holding a cigarette outside, with a pronounced show of courtesy.

He welcomed the visitor, flicking the cigarette across the

terrace and giving him tobacco-smelling kisses on both cheeks. Nick responded, in the Italian way.

"Nick! *Benvenuto*! So pleased to meet you finally! Marco has told me so much about you."

Nick ran an online i-Gaming company called BetSlick.com, based in a high-rise office block in Paceville, the seedy entertainment area of Malta. He had founded the business four years earlier and it was in the money from day one. But, to his surprise, it seemed that level of success had not impressed Marco, Sergio and their friends.

A little over eighteen months ago, Nick had been in the office minding his own business, making money as usual, when he had taken a call from an English lawyer, a partner in a boutique City firm in London. He had said he had a proposal that would change Nick's life. As it turned out, that statement was not an exaggeration.

The lawyer had flown to Malta the following week and taken him to lunch in one of the top hotels in St George's Bay. As soon as the coffee had arrived and it was time to talk business, the lawyer put a cheque on the table. It was a six-figure sum, which he explained was a non-returnable, goodwill payment, just for him agreeing to enter into discussions. Nick could not believe it. It was crazy! Money for nothing! He had picked up the cheque and put it into his wallet; then sat back to listen.

The identity of the lawyer's client was to remain a secret, he was told. Not only was he offering Nick a huge capital sum for the business, he would also receive a chunky salary and a sizeable bonus if he agreed to stay on and continue to run it. The sums involved were enormous. It was an easy decision. However, nothing in life is ever completely free and, before long, Nick realised he should have taken the cheque, thanked the lawyer for lunch and walked away. He accepted he had been greedy and stupid. But by the time he began to suspect what he was really involved in, he also knew that walking away was no longer an option.

It was true he had had serious reservations about the deal from the off, but the fancy car, the use of a fast cruiser moored in Msida Creek and the new five-bedroomed villa with its infinity pool had all helped him to put his doubts to one side. An added bonus was the company of the woman, the so called 'housekeeper', who lived in the apartment to the side of the main house.

Marco gestured for Nick and Sergio to go out onto the terrace.

Nick made sure he sat in the shade, while Sergio was happy to put on his sunglasses and bask on the sunny side of the table. They settled down to business. Nick was on high alert. He intended to listen carefully to every word that passed between them.

"So, Nick, how's it all going at BetSlick? I hear good reports."

"Well, Mr Rossi, I've got to say, first, it's great to meet you, and second yes, I think it's going really well!"

Sergio's head suddenly and theatrically jerked back.

"Whoah, Nick! No! I'm Sicilian. Touch your balls at once!"

Nick looked at him, confused.

"I'm sorry? Touch my balls?"

"You're tempting fate! Just touch your balls – for luck! Do it! It's a Sicilian thing! God, I hate their superstitions, but this thing … touching your balls, well … it works!"

Marco started to laugh.

"Nick, ignore him, he is being crude. He thinks it is funny!"

He turned to Sergio.

"Please, do not offend our guest. He is an Englishman. They are sensitive and have manners!"

Nick pulled himself together and grabbed his crotch, giving it a good shake, in that over the top, unabashed Sicilian way.

"OK, there, are you happy?"

"*Si*, bravo!" The Sicilian laughed and slapped his thigh. "Now we can talk business and you can call me Sergio!"

"OK, great! Well, as you asked, we're in good shape and I think we're ready to do the extra business Marco's been talking about. I can't see why not. In the last twelve months, the platform has received twenty-five million pounds in gross income. We could move to double that over the next twelve to eighteen months, with some support for advertising and sponsorship opportunities. All the player accounts stand up to scrutiny and we're nearly ready to talk about receiving funds in virtual currencies. I know that idea interests you. It'll definitely speed things up!"

Nick took a deep breath before continuing.

"My only concerns are the compliance issues I mentioned to Marco. I assume you're aware of them?"

Nick looked at Marco, who gestured for him to continue. Sergio sat back in his chair and folded his arms across his chest. Nick noticed the change of body language.

"Tell me about these ... compliance issues."

"Well, it seems to me the business is being used by outsiders who're legitimately signing up with us and depositing large amounts of cash into our player accounts. We're talking about big sums – tens, sometimes hundreds of thousands. They make a few small bets and then close the accounts. We return the cash to them and then, if they're asked, they can claim it's gaming winnings. I've mentioned it to Marco a few times now."

Marco nodded in agreement, but said nothing. Nick continued.

"Sergio, it's classic money laundering and they're using your company. We've got software in place to identify unusual betting patterns and there's no way these punters don't know that we know. It's as if they don't care! They're taking the piss, excuse my language."

Nick knew exactly what was going on and so far had managed to hide it from the firm's compliance team and other senior colleagues. He needed this conversation to move from a situation where he was expected to feign ignorance, to one where he was firmly in the loop.

Sergio smiled and sat in silence for a moment, while Marco polished his spectacles. Finally, Sergio spoke.

"Shall we get this out in the open? D'you think we would pay you the sort of money we do to take a few bets on an online game of pontoon? Get real, Nick. You're a clever boy. You were paid a fortune for the business and you've a package that any CEO of an operation ten times the size of yours would wet himself for! You understood what you were getting yourself into."

Marco was watching for Nick's reaction. He knew the Englishman had been suspicious from the get-go, but had brushed his concerns to one side, focusing primarily on the cash and the benefits. Sergio glanced at Marco, who subtly nodded to him. Sergio pushed himself forward in his chair, leaning across the table to bring his face closer to Nick's.

"Let me tell you something, Nick, something you need to hear. We're well into a big project and BetSlick is an important part of that. We're gonna make you the CEO of one of the biggest i-Gaming businesses in Europe. For that to happen, we need you to get with the programme."

Sergio pushed his chair back, rested his crossed arms on his chest and said, with a smile: "So, how about that?"

Marco put his glasses back on and looked at Nick intently.

"We have faith in you. We would not include just anybody in our arrangements. In many ways, you should see it as an honour that we have brought you into our trust. We have been in business for longer than you can imagine. We protect ourselves and all those who join us. You need not worry about this."

Marco paused.

"Do you know about the Queen's shilling?" he asked.

Nick shook his head. In his heart of hearts, he was not surprised by this development. Marco continued speaking.

"Well, in Queen Elizabeth's day, and I mean the first Queen Elizabeth of England, if you accepted a shilling from her, it meant you had contracted to serve her."

Sergio raised his hands and pulled a face at Marco to show he was confused.

"Bear with me, Sergio, this is relevant. Often, press gangs in the naval ports would look for sailors to man Her Majesty's ships. They would offer to buy the sailor a beer and secretly drop a shilling into his tankard. Once he had taken a drink, he had accepted Her Majesty's shilling and he was in, like it or not.

"You, my friend, have drunk from the cup."

Nick breathed deeply and saw the two men looking at him keenly. It was his move.

"OK, I'm not stupid. I've known what was really going on for a while now. I understand, but I needed to hear it from you. What d'you want me to do next?"

CHAPTER 4
INSPECTOR GEORGE ZAMMIT
THE GRAND HARBOUR, MALTA

THE MIDDAY SUN was throwing a shimmering haze of heat across the concrete wharf. Although the deep blue water in the harbour looked cool and inviting, in reality it was not far off ambient temperature. George often thought the worst part of the job was having to work outside in the middle of summer, longing for the air conditioning of the car or the office. The sweat ran down your nose, your back, along your wrists, blotting your paperwork. The Maltese always did their best to walk, or even drive, in the shade but, sometimes, the job at hand was over there, on the bright side of the street.

The two vessels were tied up to the quayside. The first was a new supply vessel that ran back and forth to the ships anchored on Hurds Bank. The Maltese police made a point of not getting involved in activities out there. It was an area of shallow water, just thirty metres deep, allowing ships to anchor. At fifteen kilometres offshore, it was outside Malta's territorial waters which meant there were no fees or charges payable. The *Pulizija* had no jurisdiction out there and what happened at sea, stayed at sea, in their book.

Shipping used Hurds Bank as a free maritime parking lot. There was nowhere else like it in the Mediterranean. Visitors arriving in Malta by plane would fly right over the flotilla of anchored ships on the final approach for landing. Vessels there waited for crew changes or for orders about their next job. Some sat full of crude oil from the Gulf, waiting for the spot price to change. Others were rusty old tramps, waiting to dash off to the more obscure Mediterranean ports at a moment's notice, to carry something to somewhere.

All sorts of villainy went on in those shallow waters. Russian tankers from the Black Sea made ship to ship transfers of oil to bigger vessels bound for sanctioned Venezuela. Ships full of subsidised, tax-free, Libyan petroleum waited for fuel smugglers to collect their cargo, to be illicitly sold into the European market. Even Russian naval vessels, barred from most Mediterranean ports, refuelled on the banks, all under the nose of the Maltese coastguards and the indifference of the *Pulizija*.

George had never been out there. He did not much like the sea; its endless horizons always made him anxious. He had never learned to swim, a fact that had often held him back when he was younger. Many times, on the beaches of the north, friends and family would spend hours messing around on the sands, throwing balls in the waves, swimming off the beach. Meanwhile, he would sit in his shorts and T-shirt, on his towel, pretending to laugh and enjoy himself.

Come the hunting seasons, however, George became a different creature. He and his father, Peter, lived for shooting birds. In the spring, his father would wake him way before dawn and they would rush down to the fishing village of Marsaxlokk, where they would borrow a friend's small wooden fishing boat and motor the required three kilometres away from the coastline. As the dawn broke, watching intently through binoculars, he would set them up with their guns to welcome the migratory birds approaching the islands from the deserts of Africa. At sea, they had first shot at the incoming echelons, ahead of the dozens of guns waiting on the cliffs.

For twenty days in April, it was the quail-hunting season and

George and Peter keenly hunted the small, plump, ground-dwelling birds. Despite his bulk, George was light on his feet and would quietly stalk the birds through the limestone landscape of the national parks, ready to fire when they fluttered up from their nesting places. Like many Maltese, his father had a bumper sticker on the back of his rusted Datsun that read – 'If it flies … it dies!'

At an early age, George became a marksman and, when he joined the police, spent many happy hours on the range at Pembroke. In his early days in the force, he had been a regular medallist in both bullseye and rapid-fire classes at the annual *Pulizija* shooting competitions. He still liked the sport and had a naturally steady hand and a good eye.

He paused on the quayside to consider the first vessel. It was painted an orange shade of red and was a Malta registered bunkering vessel, which meant it ran fuel to ships either at anchor in the port or out on Hurds Bank. Called MT Santa Helena, George saw at once it was not going to give him any answers. It was tidy, the gangway was down and a chain saying 'No Admittance' hung across the entrance. More to the point, he spotted a friend of his cousin's on deck, whom he knew to be a solid, reliable type; not the sort to get mixed up with floating bodies in the Grand Harbour.

The second ship was a different prospect. It looked as though it had had a hard life. The protective paintwork on its hull and sides was scuffed and damaged by scrapes and bumps, that, in itself, was not unusual for a scrappy tanker or a tramp. A tattered blue flag with a yellow sun hung on its rear flagstaff confirming the ship was registered out of Palau, a country 500 kilometres east of the Philippines, with a ship's registry that asked few questions of the owners. On its mainmast, it flew Malta's national flag. It was a normal mark of respect to fly the flag of the home port. With a shake of his head, George noticed it was hanging upside down.

A pale ribbon of diesel fumes was coming from the exhaust in the funnel. The generators were humming, but there was no gangway from the ship to the quay. The afternoon heat was sitting thick and heavy over the wharf. George felt his shirt sticking to his chest. He shouted up to the rail, expecting someone to be on deck.

"Hey, *Pulizija*! Immigration!"

At his third attempt to hail the crew, a man peered down, leaning over the rail, a cigarette hanging from his lips. He was stripped to the waist, a North African type, looking at the policeman with a blank expression. He might have been one of the men hanging around the stern of the vessel earlier, George could not be sure.

"*Pulizija*! Speak English? *Italiano*?" George held up his police identity badge, but the crewman just looked on, with no reaction. George repeated the speech. He expected at least some attempt to engage: a shrug, a few words of something, but, no – the crewman said and did nothing.

"Your Captain ... *Capitano*! Where is he? *Dov'è*?"

The man gave the hint of a smile. Then he had the cheek to flick his cigarette butt over the side and disappear. George's temper flared at his insolence.

"I'm coming back! You can't think that's the end of it! *Ritorneró!* Bastard!" he hissed under his breath.

Stomping to the stern of the ship, George wrote its name in his notebook. *Malik Albahr,* Arabic for *Sea King,* was stencilled in both Arabic and Roman script. Standing on the quayside, he made a call to the Harbourmaster's Office, asking them to email the ship's papers and any information they might have on its port of origin and destination.

Walking back down the quayside, he thought about the thin man in the water. It could not just be a coincidence that they found him floating one hundred metres from what looked like an Arab-crewed tanker. What was it they said? That thirty per cent of apparently drowned bodies turned up within five metres of where they entered the water. It was odds on there was some connection. He needed a team, with ladders, a translator and a warrant. Then, maybe when it was a bit cooler, they could get down to the quayside and board the tanker.

CHAPTER 5
NICK WALKER

CASTELLO BONNICI, MALTA

AFTER MARCO CLOSED off further discussions about Nick's concerns, their meeting moved on to the more practical details of BetSlick.com. Nick found himself joining in the planning for the expansion of the set up and the upgrading of the IT system. Both Sergio and Marco were working on the assumption that business volumes would increase significantly and Nick was careful not to ask where this new business might be coming from.

After another hour, Sergio had heard enough. He stood up, slapped the table and announced he was hungry. They stayed on the shaded terrace overlooking St Paul's Bay, but moved to a new table, set with a white table cloth and heavy silver cutlery. A small pasta starter was followed by turbot fillets, accompanied by a delicate floral white wine from Marco's small vineyard in the valley beneath them.

Nick enjoyed the food but Sergio complained about Marco's thin and acidic wine, suggesting a fuller bodied Sicilian variety would have been a better match! Marco took the joshing with good humour, saying in future he would not waste the best of his cellar on someone who knew so little about good wine.

A gentle breeze blew across the terrace, rippling the ivory-coloured voiles shading the table and making the whole occasion almost pleasant.

They took a short break before coffee was served and, while Sergio smoked and made some calls, Marco showed Nick around his gardens. The Bonnici estate included olive groves and vineyards, but he left those to the gardeners, who were more like farm labourers than horticulturists. They were not trusted with the wellbeing of his more exotic specimens.

Over the years, he had gathered species from as far away as Central Chile, California and the Cape. He also had an extensive range of plants from the Mediterranean basin. However, the special feature of the garden was his collection of succulents and cacti from the dry terrains of America and Africa. The cacti, in particular, did exceptionally well in the fast draining Maltese soil. Some, he had bought when they were already mature and were up to two metres in height. They were a work in progress and would survive him, he hoped, slowly growing to a great height.

"They are very slow-growing plants but, with luck, these saguaro cacti, for instance, could reach up to fifteen metres tall. It will not happen in my lifetime – it could take as much as two hundred years! But I will make sure their early years are all photographed and documented for posterity."

He turned to Nick for a reaction, but saw he was looking down the valley, oblivious to the wonders of the cactus garden. Marco laughed ruefully.

"I am sorry, Nick, we gardeners get carried away. We think everybody shares our passion. I spend hours here, you know. Gives me a sense of proportion. Peace, even."

Marco paused, gathering his own thoughts for a moment, then led Nick back to the table where Sergio welcomed them with a broad smile underneath his designer sunglasses. A new guest had appeared and was sitting at the table, coffee cup before him. He was long and lean, with thin, receding silver hair, brushed back from a high forehead. He wore a white shirt and striped tie and his grey pinstripe suit was buttoned tight, despite the strong early-afternoon sun. He lifted himself part way out of his seat as Sergio made the introductions.

"Nick, please let me introduce you to the big cheese himself, Assistant Commissioner Gerald Camilleri, Organised Crime and Anti-Money Laundering Command."

Nick felt the blood drain from his face.

"We thought it'd be a good idea for you two to get to know each other – you'll have much in common. Come on, Nick, sit down, he's not the Big Bad Wolf! Sit down, sit down. Now, Gerald, tell us what's happening in your world."

Nick was speechless and sat silently, while Camilleri ran through the work of his department: relationships with the Financial Services Authority and the Gaming Authorities; proposed changes to the licensing regime and the problem of new upstart operators brazenly ignoring the anti-money laundering legislation.

Sergio rounded off the conversation by saying that Camilleri was there to help and if Nick had any questions or problems, he should go straight to him.

He said:

"Gerald has the knack of making problems go away. You should consider him your friend and confidant. Isn't that right, Gerald?"

Camilleri made an effort to smile.

"Quite so, Sergio."

CHAPTER 6
INSPECTOR GEORGE ZAMMIT

BIRKIRKARA, MALTA

HOME FOR GEORGE was about three miles from the end of the Grand Harbour, where they had found the unknown man, although nowhere was very far from anywhere in Malta. Birkirkara was a crowded suburb, on a crowded island. George lived an ordinary life there with his wife, Marianna, his teenage son, Denzel (Marianna had insisted!), and daughter, Gina.

He had been lucky. They lived in his parents' ground-floor apartment, which came to George when Peter passed. It was part of a traditional building: square, three storey, built of local limestone.

George had met Marianna over twenty years ago at the Festival of Santa Maria, in the square by the church. He had been fresh into uniform and was drinking some beers with people from the neighbourhood. Tinny music blared from the stalls along with the usual cannonade of fireworks that showered the silhouette of the church spire with a multi-coloured sparkling cascade. They had been standing around, talking about one thing or another, when George had spotted a group of girls on the other side of the square. Marianna was the ringleader, talking to her friends, quickly and loudly. She noticed the rotund, but attractive young officer looking at her and stopped her chat, returning his gaze with interest.

Telling her friends she had business across the square, with a show of resolve, she had slowly walked towards him, her gaze never leaving his. Her friends followed her slow and deliberate walk. George had been enthralled, but nervous at the same time. He had never had much confidence around girls. A friend had pushed him in the back, so he had taken an involuntary step forward towards her. The beer helped him put his shyness to one side. He remembered hooking his thumbs down behind his thick duty belt and demanding to know why she was out so late. He had asked her why she was not with her boyfriend and whether her parents would be worried that she was out alone after dark.

She had stood coyly beside him and said she had no boyfriend, that she was frightened of the noise made by the fireworks and there were so many drunks, she did not know how she would get home safely! She had rolled her eyes theatrically as she said it, looking back at her friends, who were holding each other up, as they giggled themselves silly.

George had offered her his arm and she had linked hers around it. The walk home had been perfect and, at midnight, they had said good night to each other on her doorstep. He remembered how their fingers had brushed and, at that moment, he would have married her there and then. As it was, they waited three months to get engaged and, two years later, they were married.

By then, Peter had been dead for over a year, so Marianna had moved into the family apartment, with George and his mother. Intergenerational living was very common in Malta, so it disturbed George when, after less than twelve months, his mother left to live with her sister in Gzira. He knew some strange battle had been fought during those months, out of his sight and beyond his understanding, and that his mother had lost. Mother had claimed she had to go and look after Rosa in her widowhood, as she was getting old, but it had not rung true.

George felt Marianna was never the same after his mother moved out. She had Denzel shortly after and immediately moved her own mother into the house to help with the baby. Of itself, he understood that but, twenty years later, Silvia had still not returned to her apartment in lower Valletta. She had become a faint presence in the house who, most days, sat at the kitchen table and quietly sipped soup.

Gina, George's daughter, was sixteen – a pretty, round-faced girl with thick black hair, large dark eyes and a loving nature. Marianna never encouraged her to get the most out of school and, despite their many arguments, Gina preferred to spend her time in the house, helping with jobs and running errands. George suspected she would marry a local boy, become a Maltese wife and mother, and realise, too late, that other opportunities had passed her by. She spent far too much time with Marianna for his liking and he noticed the knowing smiles and looks that constantly passed between them, as the girl started to shape herself on her mother's last.

Denzel was two years older than Gina and worked in a motorbike repair shop. He lived and breathed rock music and motorbikes, and flying around the island on a high-powered Suzuki machine, terrifying motorists and pedestrians alike. There were few roads where you could take a bike to any real speed, so Denzel compensated by endlessly revving the engine and accelerating in the short distances between the queues of traffic.

He worked hard and was a popular boy in the neighbourhood. He played football to a good level and, to George's surprise, had become an ardent supporter of the Maltese Labour Party. Denzel and George got on well and they quietly let the women run the house, whilst they went off to watch football or sometimes to the local social club to play bocci, the Maltese version of boules. George did not worry for Denzel; he was confident he would find his way in life.

In the kitchen, Silvia was sipping a cup of chicken soup at the table and the dirty dishes told George the family had already eaten. Marianna was standing in front of the sink watching the television in the corner of the room.

"George! I thought you weren't coming. It's late."

"I know. Trouble at the Grand Harbour. Some Arab got himself drowned."

"Really? Rabbit pasta in the pan; just warm it up. I'm going to lie down. I've had a terrible morning getting Mother's medication. I had to wait hours at Farrugia's."

"Hmm."

George gobbled down the tagliatelle with rabbit and peas. Afterwards, he took a small espresso out into the backyard where he sat comfortably in his well-worn wicker armchair.

The herbs in their pots gave off a pungent green scent and the shade had lowered the afternoon heat to a more tolerable temperature. The chatter of the TVs and the sounds of the neighbours from the open windows provided a soothing background of white noise. Insects buzzed around and he knew that, if he sat very still and breathed very slowly, they would not bother him.

When he woke up, warm and satisfied, he was surprised at how stiff he felt and the coffee was stone cold. He could easily have closed his eyes again and continued the pleasant reverie, but a glance at his wrist told him it was 15:30. He had slept for over an hour.

George jumped to his feet, grabbed his jacket from the kitchen chair and cursed Marianna for letting him sleep so long.

Fifteen minutes later, he drove through the arch of the imposing, stone-built Malta Police Headquarters in Floriana, just outside the main gate to the city of Valletta. Reaching for his jacket and papers, he noticed a long black BMW 5 Series pulling into the car park, three spaces to his right.

He sighed. There was never a good time to meet the tall, slender figure in the double-breasted, pinstripe suit. Assistant Commissioner Gerald Camilleri had just returned from his meeting at Castello Bonnici. He rose from the back of the car, smoothed his thinning silver-grey hair and, like a praying mantis, slowly unfurled his long legs. It was rumoured that, on the quiet, he ran the police department and had links high up, beyond the Commissioner himself.

"Good afternoon, George. I hear you have been doing a little fishing in the Grand Harbour today?"

"*Mela*, not much to tell yet, Assistant Commissioner. No witnesses, no ID, no reported missing persons. We're just getting started. Probably doesn't even belong in the Immigration team."

Camilleri fixed him with his hooded eyes.

"Well, that is how it goes, George, is it not? Wrong place, wrong time. I suspect the enquiry is all yours. Good luck with it. Anyway, keep me in the loop. You know how it is? Everything around here ties in with everything else, eh? Unexplained bodies in the Grand Harbour? Hmm, bad for business."

Camilleri flashed his trademark humourless smile, all tight mouth and raised cheeks, with no teeth showing and a perceptible narrowing of his eyes. It was a wellknown fact that no one in the force had ever heard him laugh. With a glance back at his driver, summoning him to follow with the briefcase, Camilleri calmly walked up the stairs into the HQ.

George followed. As soon as he entered the reception area, his sergeant, Alfonse Romano, came bustling up to him, rushing him up the stairs to an urgently called meeting with his Superintendent.

George checked his shirt for rabbit tagliatelle stains and licked his teeth to make sure no telltale signs remained. He paced himself up the four flights of stairs, so as not to arrive flustered and out of breath. Sergeant Romano flung open the door, to usher George through. As luck would have it, the door hit a chair, sending it skidding across the parquet flooring. When George walked into the large briefing room, all heads immediately turned towards him.

"Zammit, late lunch, eh? Where have you been? Nobody could get hold of you. Well?"

George looked helplessly around the room. Superintendent Farrugia had crammed most of the Immigration team into the space in front of the raised dais, while he glared down from above, particularly in George's direction. The rest of the team had clearly enjoyed his shambolic entrance and all heads were turned down to conceal supressed laughter.

"Sorry, sir, I was out following up a few things and my phone was out of charge. Apologies. What do we know, sir?"

"Nothing, George," barked the Superintendent. "That is the whole point. You were the one who was there, not me! The question is, what do *you* know?"

"Sir, it's not obvious that this is actually an Immigration Section matter. I thought the operational guys would take the case. It might not be an illegal. There might not even have been a crime committed. There were no obvious signs of violence on the body."

"That is because you did not look hard enough, George. First news from the mortuary is that someone had tied the man's hands and he was dead before he hit the water. We will know more later, but this is most likely a murder and our victim is an undocumented Arab found floating between some rust buckets in the Grand Harbour. It is ours because the Assistant Commissioner says so. We have a head start in the investigation because you were first on the scene and got the ball rolling. God help us! What did you learn from the ships?"

"Well, there was a Maltese supply vessel. All present and correct. The second was an old bunkering tanker, say one hundred metres long, registered in Palau. Called …" To buy time he fumbled through his notebook. "… *Malik Albahr*. It means the *Sea King*. They weren't very helpful, I'm afraid. We'll need to go back with a warrant and a boarding team."

"So, you did not go on board? Was nobody there? No engines running? No signs of life at all?"

"Sir, there was a crewman, but he didn't speak Maltese, Italian or English. He didn't seem to understand me. There was no gangway; nobody afforded me access."

"Nobody afforded you access? What the hell does that mean? George, this is a murder enquiry, they damn well will 'afford you access'. Get your team together, get your warrant and get down there now. Find out what is going on."

"Sir?"

A young Detective Constable looked up from his laptop.

"The latest update from the Port of Valletta website says the *Malik Albahr*, or the Sea King, left well over an hour ago. She might still be in our waters, but only just."

For a moment, there was total silence. All eyes moved to the Superintendent, whose mouth had twisted and brow furrowed, as he tried to contain his anger.

"For God's sake, George! Did she run?" he asked the young officer.

"Could be. She seems to have left ahead of her scheduled departure time." His eyes peered at the screen.

"Holy Mary, Mother of God! You just let her sail out from under our very noses! Did you not think of putting a uniform on the dock to watch her until you got a warrant?"

George coloured up badly and began developing a nervous sweat across his top lip. He turned to the constable with the laptop: "Can we track her?"

"If she's got her automatic identification system turned on, the satellites will spot her," the smartarse said, "but, if she's dodgy, she could have turned it off by now."

George watched Superintendent Farrugia slump in his chair.

"Briefing over, get out, all of you! George, wait behind, please!"

The room cleared. George stood by uncomfortably, holding the door open for his departing colleagues.

"Find me something on this body and this ship by 1800 hours. I am meeting the Assistant Commissioner then and need to update him or I will look pretty stupid! Now go!" Farrugia ordered.

George gratefully stepped out into the cooler, fresher air of the long corridor. Romano was waiting for him there. He looked at George with a well-practised insubordinate smirk.

"That went well!"

George could only shake his head, as he tried to stifle a belch.

CHAPTER 7
NICK WALKER
VILLA BIANCA, MALTA

It was only when Nick got back into the car and started his short drive back to his villa that the anxiety about the morning's events returned. If the introduction to Camilleri was supposed to make him more confident about the BetSlick arrangement, it had only set more alarm bells ringing. He felt confused and there was no-one he could really talk to about his strange day.

He had never thought of himself as a loner but, in reality, he was. He had no close family, apart from his mother, who lived in Finchley, North London. He tried to see her once or twice a year, but the visits were tedious and she had as little to say to him, as he had to her.

Before going to Malta to start up BetSlick, he had begun his career in the gaming business in Gibraltar. Previously, he had worked in an international shipping business in the City, but the work was predictable and boring. At times, he felt the absence of a partner, a friend even. It was probably this that had led to the start of his relationship with Natasha, the so-called 'housekeeper' who had the apartment to one side of the villa.

Marco had told Nick the villa came with a housekeeper, a good friend of the family who, in exchange for accommodation, looked after the staff and kept an eye on the place. Marco stressed, she was not there to do chores or run errands – there were staff for that. He had added, with a laugh: "You can always try, but I do not give much for your chances!"

Nick had given it little thought, until he saw her on his first day, when he had arrived with two cases and half a dozen boxes of belongings. She had appeared, walking up the stairs towards the pool deck, to introduce herself.

Nick had actually caught his breath. At first, he could not look her in the eye. He was fearful his expression would betray the intense, immediate fascination she aroused in him. She was tall, 175 centimetres at least, with a mass of dark brown hair piled into a rough knot on top of her head. Her skin had an olive tone, with a glossy sheen, and her body was lean and firm. She wore a loose crocheted cotton top and tight denim shorts. She needed no make-up – she looked fantastic just as she was.

After he had got over the shock of seeing her for the first time, he found they got on well together. Natasha was smart and sassy and she seemed to want to get to know him better. Gradually, he started to relax around her and lost the awkwardness he had felt at their first meeting. In the following weeks, they would occasionally meet for evening drinks on the terrace and, early on in their conversations, she had asked if he minded her using the pool and the terrace, as it was the best place for the evening sun.

Nick tried to push her for her story, but she was always quite evasive. Over time, he learned she was a friend of the Bonnici family and had known Marco as well as some of the people in his business, since she was small.

She told him that, as a young teenager, her family had brought her to Malta to stay with Marco at the *castello*, so she could improve her English at a language school in St Julian's. When she was at university, she had returned to work at one of Marco's hotels during the summers and, since leaving London, did a bit of bookkeeping work for him. She had come to like the island with its ancient history, thriving population and strong

Italian vibe. As she grew older, she had gravitated back to Malta and had come to think of it as home.

She told him she was taking some time off between proper jobs so, when the chance came up to take the apartment in exchange for keeping an eye on the place, she had jumped at it.

Gradually, Nick had started to bring small plates of snacks out onto the terrace in the early evening and, while the sun disappeared over the hill behind them, they would sit drinking a glass of wine and picking at olives, salamis and cheeses. She was a beautiful woman – no doubt about it – and Nick was happy to enjoy her company. He was not going to push anything, that was not his style, but he had to admit he was increasingly attracted by her and often found himself rushing back from work, to be sure he did not miss the chance of sharing an early evening drink.

Before long, Nick found himself talking to her about BetSlick and, to his surprise, she seemed genuinely interested in his work. As she was the only person he could share his day with, he appreciated her interest. She would always remember their conversations and follow up, sometimes asking technical questions about his projects and the work he was doing to grow the business. She asked about his relationship with Marco and about other people in the company. Nick found it helpful to unburden himself and share his ideas and thoughts.

So, it was not unusual, when he sat down with Natasha that evening, over a bottle of local chardonnay, that the conversation should turn to his meeting with Marco and Sergio.

"Were you up at the *castello* today?"

"Yeah – how d'you know that?"

"I saw your car heading that way out of St Paul's. I couldn't think where else you might be going."

"Very observant. Yeah, it was a bit of a weird day, to be honest. There was this guy there called Sergio Rossi. D'you know him."

"Yeah, I do. I've known Sergio for years. He and Marco are in business together. Construction, property, that sort of thing. I heard they started in telecoms, back in the early days. I think they might even be cousins or something. Sergio's often at the *castello*. I've met him quite a few times over the years."

"What do you think of them?"

"Who, Marco or Sergio? To me, they're both good guys. I don't know what they're like in business. But they're your bosses, and Marco is my landlord, so I'd better be careful what I say! But, no, they're respectable, obviously rich, connected – well, I know Marco is. He seems to know everybody that matters on the island. Sergio's a bit more, Sicilian – d'you know what I mean? But I like them both. Why, what's the problem?"

"Nothing, really. There's some funny stuff going on at work, that's all. I'm not sure I'm one hundred per cent happy about it. I brought it up and got my wrists slapped."

"What sort of funny stuff?"

"Well, I can't tell you, you know that, but in the gaming business, there're all sorts of ways you can handle cash. They were suggesting some things I wasn't that comfortable with. D'you understand what I'm saying?"

Natasha smiled knowingly and nodded her head.

"Look, Nick, listen to me. I'm not totally surprised, to be honest with you. This is Malta – not London. The place is swimming in cash. Libyan cash, Russian cash, Azerbaijani oil money, Angolan diamond money … and the rest!" She paused to take a sip of wine. "If you work in Malta, it's different from other places, you're going to come across this stuff. Marco and Sergio have been around the block a few times, they know how the game's played. If they ask you to do something, I'm sure it's OK."

"As simple as that? I think it's a bit more complicated. They also say they're into something big that's going to impact the business. They wouldn't tell me what and it sort of freaked me out a bit."

"Personally, I think you should just trust them and you'll be fine. You work in a cash business, which they own, and you've already told me you get paid a fortune, so it doesn't surprise me that they expect, umm, a little help from you now and then. Don't fall out with them or ... well, you might have to kiss goodbye to your boat and your Porsche ... and this!"

She waved her hands to indicate the pool and sun terrace.

"True, true. But listen to this. On top of everything else, this police guy turned up. It turns out he's the Assistant Commissioner in charge of Anti Money Laundering! I nearly died!"

"Oh, you met Gerald? I think he's a useful man to know, especially in your line of work. And, you see, that's exactly what I mean – how can there be any problems when he's on your side?"

"Bloody hell! Does everybody know everybody on this island? "

"Look, I don't know him personally, I know *of* him. I think he and Marco both went to St Edwards – not at the same time – but there's a strong old boys' network there.

"Listen, if you want my opinion, I think you've got it good, Nick. In your business, you can't be a stiff. It's not the Maltese way and it really isn't Marco's and Sergio's way. They're big-time guys. From what I know, you're lucky to be working with them. You could learn a lot."

"Yeah, that's more or less what they said."

"Well. I'm right then, aren't I?"

He turned away from her to look out over the glass panels on the edge of the deck, running his hand through his hair. The sea was a deep blue, stippled with fine lines of white foam. As usual in the early evenings, out in the distance, a flotilla of small boats and pleasure cruisers ploughed their furrows south, returning from their day trips, to the marinas and ferry terminals of Sliema and Msida. Nick knew she was right and, more than that, he had known what he was getting into the minute he had picked up the cheque at that restaurant in St George's Bay.

He was conscious that Natasha was watching him.

"What're you thinking?" she asked him.

"Nothing much. But you're right. I've got to learn to be a bit more trusting. It's good to talk to you. And, I'm enjoying the evening all the more for you being here. I do like being with you, you know." He turned to smile at her.

She laughed, taking her sunglasses off and putting them on the table.

"Well that's nice to hear." She paused, looking directly at him, and leant across to take his hand.

"You know, I thought I might stay here tonight. If that's alright with you?"

CHAPTER 8
INSPECTOR GEORGE ZAMMIT

PORT AUTHORITY, VALLETTA WATERFRONT, MALTA

From HQ, George drove the short distance down through the high walls fortifying Valletta, to the quayside. The Harbourmaster's Office was a matter of ten minutes away. The heat and humidity had built up during the day and the rushing around was making him perspire, heavily.

The office was part of the larger Port Authority building and had the run-down, utilitarian feel of most Maltese public offices: faded, duck egg blue gloss paintwork, sheets of grey floor tiles, filthy aluminium framed windows. An overweight clerk sat in the accumulated heat of the day, seemingly perfectly comfortable in his heavy woollen sweater. He showed George into the Harbourmaster's Office. George introduced himself and started to interrogate him: "*Mela,* the *Malik Albahr,* what've you got for me?"

After a moment it dawned on him that the Harbourmaster was Joe Mifsud. Many years ago, they had been at the same school, although the Harbourmaster was a year or two older than George and had not acknowledged the connection.

The Harbourmaster was busy staring at his screen.

"She arrived a week ago from Marseilles pending sale inspections. No cargo, no passengers, nothing else significant. A new crew arrived three days ago. There was some issue with visas, but that was sorted out," he read on. "New ownership registration papers were filed and we scheduled her to leave tomorrow. But then, it seems we allowed that to be brought forward to today."

"Why did you do that? You knew there was police interest in the ship. Normally you need forty-eight hours' notice of a departure, don't you?"

"Well, we were only waiting for an updated crew list, with customs clearance, and that came in this morning. She asked for permission to go early this afternoon, which was OK by us. Traffic in the harbour was light and we didn't see any harm in allowing an early departure. I didn't know there was police interest. All you asked for were the papers."

"*Mela!* For God's sake! Didn't you think there might be a reason for that? Were all the crew on board when she left?"

"According to the system, apparently so."

"So where was the ship heading to?"

Mifsud looked at the screen again.

"Annaba, Algeria."

"But we don't know if that's where she's actually going?"

"Well, no. After your colleagues called, we tried to find her, but her transponder was off, so that's it. The Coastguard's onshore radar might give you some idea of the bearing she was on, but she could be nearly thirty kilometres away by now. It'll be difficult to pick her up in all the traffic and that's a lot of ocean."

"It's not normal to switch off the AIS, is it?"

"No, it's against the regs for a ship of that size, when at anchor or underway and especially when entering and leaving port. It's an anti-collision tool."

"Anything else?"

"Nope," said the Harbourmaster. "You don't think that body came from the *Malik Albahr*, do you?"

"Don't know. But I think they might've got spooked and

decided to leave before we could question them, which has to tell us something. I'll need all your paperwork – particularly the details of the shipping agent who handled the sale inspections. Who was it, by the way?"

"Well, it was my brother's firm, Mifsud's. I've called him. He says he knows very little. The owners changed on the sale, obviously. Ownership is now with some offshore company in Turks and Caicos. All he got was a couple of emails from an office in Tunis, one appointing him and one thanking him. When the inspections went through, he reported back, and that was that. They filed the usual paperwork, paid money into the account for fuel and fees. That's it. Nothing unusual at all."

"*Mela*, I'll go and see him."

As George prepared to leave, the Harbourmaster looked up at him and said: "Didn't you go to St Aloysius Sixth Form College?"

George nodded. The two years there had not been the happiest time of his life. He had been bullied and never settled into the place.

"I remember you," the other man carried on. "Didn't they call you '*Pastizz*'? Not kind, but then kids aren't, are they? Anyway, doing all right for yourself now, eh?"

George glared at the smiling Harbourmaster. The nickname still rankled. *Pastizzi* was Malta's favourite street food, so it was like being called a pasty. George had to admit he was heavy for his height at school, but not massively so. Still, it was enough to be self-conscious about it. Soon after he arrived at the school, a gang of older boys found him in an empty classroom, stuffing his face with a bag of four *pastizzi*. They stole the food and threw it around the room, shouting, '*Pastizz! Pastizz! Pastizz!*' The name had stuck.

When Marianna was in one of her more spiteful moods, she would sometimes call him: 'You big *pastizz*.' She knew it still upset him more than it should.

Ignoring Joe Mifsud's gibe, he picked up his papers and

walked out into the heat, dust and noise of a late Valletta afternoon.

The Assistant Commissioner was in a difficult mood and George left for home after their briefing, feeling tired and despondent. He had definitely had better days.

As he swung the car into the narrow road that led to the garage under the apartment, he almost collided with Denzel's red Suzuki, as it flew up the ramp and out onto the street. Denzel's helmet was loose and a cigarette was hanging out of his mouth. He was in a T-shirt, jeans, and flipflops. He braked sharply and the bike bucked on the front suspension. He stuck his head into the driver's window.

"Hi, Dad! You OK?"

"Yeah, but listen, you can't take the bike out like that. Look at you! What if you come off? How can you even change gear in flipflops? It's just stupid and dangerous."

"It's OK, relax! If I get stopped, I'll tell them to talk to you! I'm not going far. I'll be back in an hour for dinner. Tell Mum."

"You getting stopped is the least of my worries. Don't be late back! You know how it winds her up!"

Denzel laughed, revved the bike and shot out into the late-afternoon traffic.

CHAPTER 9
ABDULLAH BELKACEM

MARSABAR, LIBYA

ABDULLAH SAT in the passenger seat of a Toyota pickup, as it rattled down the broken tarmac road from his house, heading to Marsabar. There were four trucks in the convoy, all carrying armed men. Abdullah knew the second-to-last vehicle was always the safest in case of attack. An attacker's instinct was always to hit the front car first; a miss would give a second shot at the following car and a strike could leave the wreck blocking the road, helping the ambush. Abdullah thought about these things a lot; it was why he was still alive.

Since the death of Gaddafi, the modern, democratic state he had hoped for during the Arab Spring had failed to materialise. He had no nostalgia for the Gaddafi days, but the country remained a battleground between a myriad of rival militias and political factions.

The UN-backed government in Tripoli was weak and its rivals in Benghazi, to the east, were growing stronger. General Boutros, the Libyan-American, enjoyed significant backing from Russia, the UAE and Egypt which had enabled him to mobilise a large militia. In reality, it was a naked power grab of the country's oil resources, which would inevitably lead to civil war.

Boutros and Abdullah did agree on one thing – the most

dangerous and unpredictable of the new insurgents were the ISIL jihadis who had gradually started to appear across the borders from Chad, Sudan and Niger. Abdullah's Islam was not the same as theirs and, although there was communication between the two, their relationship was uneasy.

Abdullah called them the 'Beards'. In the south, they fought the local Tuareg and Boutros's militias. They also blackmailed the oil companies by interrupting supplies and kidnapping their workers. Their trips north were all about taking money and buying weapons. Abdullah considered them bandits, pure and simple.

He put those angry thoughts out of his mind, because today was a happy day, one to be enjoyed. He, Abdullah Belkacem, had bought a ship. A real ship, nearly one hundred and twenty metres long, with a real captain and crew! Now people would see, he was becoming somebody!

He knew he had to be careful, though – things like that did not happen in Marsabar every day and news would soon spread across the district, as well as beyond. Questions would be asked about what he was up to and jealousies would be stoked.

His convoy travelled at speed, bumping down the rotted tarmac and stretches of compacted dust roads. They were heading towards the biggest of their coastal compounds on the east side of the town, beyond the refinery. As those inside recognised their boss's approach, the high sheet metal gates slid open.

The compound was the size of a football pitch, surrounded by a three-metre block-built wall with wire fencing above that. On the right, several Portacabins sat on concrete bases. These accommodated a toilet block, stores and an office. A further steel framed unit was used as a boathouse. A concrete slipway ran through another high metal gate, across the beach and into the water. Tareq and some other family members came to greet Abdullah.

Tareq embraced him and smiled.

"Today my brother becomes an international oil man! We had

better watch out or you will leave us to go live in Texas, with the Americans!"

They all laughed. Abdullah looked around the compound. The heavy, pungent reek from the dozens of people cooped up in the cheap warehousing units filled the air. Like chickens, they were kept indoors, away from prying eyes. Although Abdullah's business was no great secret, there was nothing to be gained by making it too obvious.

In winter, conditions were worse. The average stay was longer, because of the poorer weather and the heavy air failed to lift the stench that clung to the cold mud. He could hear the bodies from where he was standing. A low frequency rumble of voices, whispering and drifting around the large, dark, airless shed. When his men opened the doors, the noise instantly dropped and, apart from the children, there was silence.

Inside the shed, he saw preparations were being made for a boat to leave.

"Tareq, why is a boat leaving in daylight, eh? The Coast-guards are about."

"We've got good weather for the next few hours, so the boats can get clear. Then we're expecting strong north-westerly winds, which are no good. They'll blow the boats back to shore. Better to go now and to trust Allah."

One of Abdullah's young relatives began scanning the bodies with a barcode reader and pushing them into a line, where the excited and anxious passengers sat on the dirt floor. Each body had a laminated barcode hanging from a lariat around his or her neck. This provided all the details the operation needed: name, age, how much they had paid, how much remained to be paid, other family members, where they had worked. These passes were also shown at mealtimes and each body was scanned and charged accordingly. The database told them if anyone was working for someone else, had run away and they could also tell who had died or otherwise disappeared. Each body was issued with a passage number that identified who was next to leave and when. The bodies did not know that. It would only cause trouble and encourage queue jumping, bartering or worse.

When the long-anticipated moment arrived and they were ready to take their place in one of the many boats, their names would be called, their cards taken and their data deleted. As far as Abdullah was concerned, they were no longer his responsibility; his job was done. They were in Allah's hands from that point on.

"Where is the ship, Tareq, how far out?"

They both instinctively looked down the beach, as if the vessel would magically appear, coming over the horizon.

"It's an hour out, brother. We'll join it as soon as the RHIB is ready."

A tractor was reversing a trailer down the concrete slipway, hidden beneath five centimetres of sand, to conceal it from the drones and spy planes that polluted their skies. Every morning, a team would shovel and rake the windblown sand back into position to keep it hidden from above.

The trailer carried the white RHIB with a twin rig of 200cc engines, capable of speeds above fifty knots per hour. It was for the use of family members only. Next to it, a compressor was inflating a less sturdy fifty-person dinghy, which would shortly carry the line of refugees sitting expectantly inside the compound.

The slipway was the starting point of the nightly journeys, where the bodies climbed into the inflatable boats that left the beach. Each boat had a satellite phone with prepaid airtime and a compass. Once it had sailed twelve hours from the beaches of Marsabar, one of Tareq's men would call it and provide the telephone numbers of the Italian Coast Guard in Lampedusa and one of the action lines, manned by the NGOs. By that time, they would have passed the EU-funded Libyan Coastguard patrols, which searched every night for departing boats. Tareq paid the Coastguards handsomely to ignore their rafts but, still, they often made mistakes.

Apart from death at sea, the worst outcome for the migrants was to be picked up by the Libyan Coastguard. If that happened, they would be returned to one of the hellish government camps, where they could be sold, enslaved, tortured or locked up for years.

Lampedusa was an Italian island lying between Libya and Malta; the gateway into Europe. The Italian Navy and EU naval patrols would take the lucky ones to a reception centre where they would be processed and then shipped to camps in Sicily and the mainland, where the Italians would consider their requests for asylum and resettlement. It only worked for as long as the Italians were prepared to pick up the boats and their wretched occupants.

The Maltese had washed their hands of the 'Mare Nostrum' so-called rescue programme, claiming that Malta had already taken its fair share of immigrants and could not accommodate further arrivals. Malta was a devout Catholic country, but its government, and people, showed the migrants all the humanity of a cold-hearted priest.

The business of migration was nothing new; it had been happening for hundreds of years. Coastal Libyans had always profited from the stream of migrants and refugees coming from hopeless situations in Africa to find a better life in Europe. Abdullah was proud of his operation, never sending his boats out into stormy weather, making sure the phones were charged and even providing a spare battery. The compasses and GPS were always in working order and the boats were never overloaded.

On top of that, there was enough food and water for each body, for at least a week. They even got a new orange life jacket each. Business was business and the bodies paid for everything they were allocated, but it made the crossing as safe as possible. People in Europe called the traffickers murderers but, to his way of thinking, they were simply business people.

They always tried to nominate a captain, from amongst the

bodies, who had at least some experience of boats. That body travelled for free and agreed to take responsibility for the raft.

Once the RHIB was ready, he swung himself onto it and settled into one of the rear bucket seats. Six of his men climbed in and weapons were handed to them from the beach. He had bought the ship that was approaching Marsabar. It was his! Well, at least he had paid two million dollars to a shipbroker in Indonesia. It had taken time and effort to get half the money to his partners in Malta, who had deposited it in a Maltese bank that did not ask too many questions. He had borrowed the other half from the same partners, who were to be repaid from the proceeds of their lucrative new venture.

The twin motors of the RHIB rapidly accelerated and he hung on tight, as it lurched and crashed against the whitetops. Abdullah did not like the water and he did not enjoy the high-speed rides in the RHIB. Tareq saw his brother grimace and, sensing his discomfort, put an arm around the helmsman's shoulder, shouting: "Slow down, we don't want the weapons getting wet!"

The speed relented a fraction.

" We're not expecting trouble, are we?" Abdullah asked, grimly holding onto the stainless-steel roll bar.

"No, as you said, Samir and three others are on board as crew. They joined in Malta. They've told the skipper to expect us. So, no, not really. But always best to be ready for surprises".

Tareq slapped the stock of his American M4 carbine, grinning.

CHAPTER 10
NATASHA BONNICI
CASTELLO BONNICI, MALTA

Ever since Natasha was small, she had been a worry to her father, Marco Bonnici. She was a self-contained child, with a mass of thick, curly, dark brown hair and large brown eyes. Adults thought her a very serious and slightly strange child, while other children were somehow attracted to her quiet confidence and her independent nature. Natasha, however, had little interest in them. At times, she could be remote and never went out of her way to make or retain friends.

As a little girl, she was unresponsive to her father, especially after her mother's death. She never answered when spoken to and went through periods of rarely making eye contact. She seemed happiest in her own company. At her eighth birthday party, she had spent the whole time under the dining table, alone, drawing, while the other children ran excitedly around the gardens, enjoying the organised games. Eventually, adults who knew the child stopped trying to bond with her, coming to the conclusion that, despite her good looks and privileged upbringing, there was something about her that seemed just a little bit 'off'.

As a teen she developed what her school called 'anger management issues'. She was handy with her fists and had a wicked tongue which, at first, Marco had put down to the absence of a mother's guiding hand. The answer turned out not to be sessions with an educational psychologist or the school counsellor, but to follow the suggestion of the school's athletics coach and enrol her in a judo class.

At fourteen, her wiry physique had suited the sport. She did well at it and moved through the competitive grades for her sex and weight. She still followed a martial arts regime as an adult, but was finished with rolling around on a judo mat. As she got older, she had got more into the mindful side of the sport.

As a young woman, Natasha never had a long-term relationship with a man or a woman. She enjoyed brief affairs with both sexes, but never saw the point of investing in anything more permanent.

Contrary to what she had told Nick, she had left the Università di Roma to do a master's in Business Analytics at Stanford, California. She had studied the intersection of data and business, which fed into her interest in maths and systems. On leaving with a master's degree, it was only natural that she should be attracted to a trainee programme with one of the top investment banks.

Marco had fully supported her choices and was happy to see her settle in London, after winning a place with Schapiro's, the prestigious international American bank. He also thought it a good idea to steer her towards a flat share with the widow of his friend and business associate, Pierre, who was also living in London, following the death of her husband the previous year.

Pierre had been younger than Marco, but his wife, Inès, was younger still. In fact, she was only a year or two older than Natasha and also worked in the city.

It seemed the ideal arrangement. Inès could support Natasha on her arrival in a city where she knew nobody, while Natasha could help Inès get over the shock of her bereavement and provide company, as she readjusted to life after Pierre.

What neither Marco, nor Inès, realised was that Natasha had

no intention of being shackled by any such moral obligation and was quite capable of finding her feet in any new situation. She quickly fitted into the work hard, play hard life of the bank and Inès soon realised that Natasha was never going to be the friend and confidant she had hoped for. In fact, Inès rarely saw her and most of the time Natasha was in the flat, she spent catching up on her sleep.

For the first twelve months, things went well for Natasha and she felt she had found an environment in which she could thrive. Her natural affinity with numbers and her technical expertise were matched by her love of the game of making money. There was rarely a trick she missed or an opportunity that slipped passed her.

However, things took a nasty turn one March night, following a celebratory drink and some flirting in the back of a taxi with one of the bank's vice-presidents. Knowing Inès was away in France for a few nights, Natasha had invited Charlie Witton up to the flat and he was more than eager to follow her into the lift, where he had grabbed her and forced her against the rear wall, pushing himself against her.

Once inside, what Natasha first thought was his excitement and enthusiasm, rapidly turned into something else.

She had tried to calm him, as he grabbed and groped her.

"Charlie, slow down, not like this!"

He had responded by yanking at her blouse, tearing the buttons and scratching her breast, a fact the police had later thought significant.

She had tussled with him, but could not seem to stop the assault. At one point, he had forced a laugh. Still with a fierce grip on her wrists, he had said: "Come on, it's fun! You can't say no now!"

There had been a look on his face that had told Natasha there was only one thing on his mind and he was not going to stop until he got it.

"Charlie, get off me! Stop it, leave me alone! I mean it!"

They were both panting heavily, something that had only seemed to excite him further. He had managed to turn her around, wrapping a forearm tight against her windpipe, while his other hand had pushed her skirt up around her waist.

Realising she was running out of energy and that Charlie's superior strength would eventually win out, she had sunk her nails into his forearm and, with one last effort, managed to get her teeth far enough into his arm to taste his blood.

Charlie had wrenched his arm away and taken a step back, examining the teeth marks on his wrist.

"You bitch, what was that for?"

Natasha had felt a cold fury building inside her.

She had lunged at him, grabbed his shirt at the bicep and spun him around, pulling him towards her. The move threw him off-balance and she used his weight against him to roll him over her shoulder, sending him crashing head first through Ines's all glass, designer coffee table. Had Charlie stopped there, maybe nothing more would have come of it and they could have written it off as the consequence of a few drinks too many.

But he had struggled to his feet and said: "What the fuck d'you think you're doing? You're mad! You fucking crazy bitch!"

With an inhuman shriek, Natasha had flown at him, landing a rabbit punch at his throat. As he slid to his knees, one hand on his throat, trying to regain his breath, he did not see Natasha grasp a solid brass table lamp from the sideboard and pull off the shade. He was aware that she had come to stand over him, her whole body shaking and her eyes blazing with fury, but never realised she had hit him across the head, as hard as she could, several times, with the heavy brass base.

The ambulance crew later found Natasha, sitting in an armchair, her blouse torn, breast scratched, knees held tight against her chest. She had her eyes fixed on Charlie, who lay semi-conscious on the floor in front of her.

Neither Marco nor Inès had time to get to London before the police took samples of DNA from Natasha's fingernails, photographed her bruised face and torso, and interviewed her at length. The crime scene seemed to support her story of attempted rape.

One blow to the man's head could be explained by her pushing him backwards onto the coffee table, but Natasha was unable to elaborate on Charlie's numerous other serious head injuries, apart from saying she remembered, at one point, beating her fists against him. There was no sign or mention of the brass lamp.

A few days later, Marco and Inès were sitting in the flat's lounge, with Natasha and the inspector in charge of the case. After making preliminary enquiries about how Natasha was doing, he had shifted position and turned to the real purpose of his visit.

"Natasha, Mr Witton will suffer long-lasting impairment due to his head injuries. Doctors say he's unlikely ever to recover his full faculties. On the one hand, we can't work out how he sustained those injuries from the account you gave us. On the other, he's unlikely ever to be able to help us with our enquiries at any point in the future. So, is there anything further you'd like to add?"

Marco had heard his daughter's account of the incident and believed every word of it. He faced the police officer, seething with anger.

"My daughter is already severely traumatised by this whole incident. Why are you pursuing her to go over and over it? You are not here when the tears come, every night. That man has destroyed my daughter's confidence, her new career … this ends now with her would-be rapist being charged and Natasha being allowed to put her life back together – yes?

The inspector carefully interlocked his fingers, silently wishing this over-protective father elsewhere.

"It's legally possible for us to try Mr Witton but …"

He sighed and turned to address Natasha.

"Given that the man who undoubtedly sexually assaulted

you, has serious brain damage and is unlikely to recover, Natasha, do you really want to press charges? He'll be represented by a legal guardian and lawyers. They'll ask you in detail how he came to be so badly injured and will point out that self-defence has to involve only a reasonable use of force. Do you want to go through all that? Do you want those questions raised?"

Inès sat on the edge of the couch, elbows on her knees, listening carefully and studying her flatmate. She was surprised by the suggestion that Natasha had been traumatised by the whole episode. To her, Natasha did not seem to have been affected by it in the slightest. There was also the not unimportant matter of yet another arrogant, entitled male who had shown no qualms about taking what had not been freely offered.

"Natasha, you can't let him get away with it! He was a menace at the bank, people have told me, and, for every Charlie Witton, there're a dozen more out there. Think about this carefully."

It took Natasha no more than five seconds to decide.

"No, the inspector's right. Let's end it all here. Thank you, I won't be pressing charges.'

Inès shook her head in disappointment.

Natasha snapped: "What're you complaining about? It wasn't you who got attacked. And if you think I'm going back to work at Schapiro's, where everyone knows I was almost raped, you're wrong. I don't care if I never set foot in that place again."

An uneasy peace descended on the flat in the days after the inspector's visit. Marco was staying at a nearby hotel and Natasha was frequently out with him. Inès felt that Natasha was avoiding her and few words had passed between them. Inès could not help wondering what had really happened that night and how Charlie had ended up so badly hurt. The more she thought about it, the more wary she became of her flatmate.

One evening, Inès went to the small cupboard in the hall, looking for a spare light bulb. To her surprise she saw the brass lamp that had previously been on the sideboard, peeking out of a paper carrier bag, at the back of the cupboard. The satin shade was bent and the lampholder had snapped. She took the lamp out of the bag and, to her horror, noticed the bottom was coated in a sticky brown resin-like substance, with clumps of hair stuck to it.

Her scream brought Natasha running from her room. As Inès sat in the corridor, tears running down her face, she looked wide-eyed at Natasha, who coldly returned her stare. Natasha picked up the lamp, replaced it in the carrier bag and put one finger to her lips.

"Shhh," was all she said. It sounded more like a warning than a request for silence.

The following day Inès sought out Marco and met him at his hotel to explain to him what had happened. He listened without interrupting. As Inès finished her story, Marco leaned forward in his chair. His head dropped into his hands and he felt his stomach shrink with shock and alarm. His daughter, his only child, had done this …

Finally, Inès said: "I'm scared of her, Marco. Really scared! You have to do something."

His mind raced.

"Inès, I am sorry I got you involved. I thought living together would be good for both you and Natasha, but I am devastated by what has happened. Please, for the sake of our relationship and my friendship with Pierre, say nothing about this and I will make sure my daughter leaves London. I can see how much this has upset you and I understand."

"But you're asking me to cover up something terrible."

"It is a broken lamp, Inès. The rest is pure conjecture. You are covering up nothing. At worst, Natasha hurt a man who was trying to rape her. She has never denied fighting him off."

Now Marco knew what had happened, he felt shaken to his core. Regardless, he knew he would always defend Natasha. It was his duty as a father.

That night he had taken Natasha to dinner at his hotel. To his surprise, she seemed to have anticipated the conversation he intended to have with her and pre-empted it.

"Dad, I know Schapiro's is a fantastic opportunity and things were going so well, but I don't think I can stay there now. Everywhere I go, I'll be known as the girl Charlie Witton tried to rape. Or, be the bitch who put him in a wheelchair. If I stay, I won't be able to get past that. The men there are pigs, they won't let me."

Marco reached across the table and took her hand.

Natasha continued with such sincerity, Marco almost found himself believing her.

"The other thing is Inès. You don't think it's unfair to leave her by herself, do you? She relies on me a lot. She's very vulnerable at the moment."

"I think you have done all you can with Inès. She says you have been a great help, but you have to think about yourself for a change."

"I just feel so guilty running away and leaving her like this."

"Listen, I have an idea. There is a property, a nice place, on the island, that is being taken by a new guy in the business. There is a separate apartment there, so maybe you could take that? We want to keep an eye on our new arrival, make sure he settles in and is doing all the right things. We really need someone we can trust to watch over things, but it would be helpful if he did not know the direct relationship between you and me. He is a young Englishman and, if I am any judge, not a bad looking one."

"Dad! I'm done with men, especially Englishmen, so don't even think about it."

For the first time in a week, they both managed to smile. Natasha thought about her father's unexpected suggestion for a moment, but only a moment.

"Well, it's not how I saw my career working out but, if I can help you, of course I will. It sounds great!"

Natasha was not at all sure what to expect on her return to

Malta. But, she soon realised her proximity to Nick and his willingness to share the details of his work, was a real opportunity to have him unwittingly teach her the business of running a large, international, online gaming company. As the months went by and she understood more and more about how BetSlick fitted into the structure of the Family's business, it became apparent to her what her next move should be.

CHAPTER 11
DENZEL ZAMMIT

BIRKIRKARA, MALTA

Denzel sped off, clearing the suffocating traffic of the densely populated central belt, and hit the Malta coast road on the eastern side of the island. Once there, he dropped his visor and opened the throttle. The wind whistled around him as his speed picked up and he swung the bike around the curves in the road, enjoying the thrill.

Denzel filled his evenings helping some friends making deliveries around the island. He had met them the previous year at an all-night outdoor club in Rabat. They seemed impressed that he was a policeman's son and, when he bragged he could go anywhere on the island and never get stopped for speeding or racing, they were even more so. They were a cool crowd, with good clothes and nice cars, a cut above the greaseballs who worked at the garage. Denzel thought the new crowd were much more his sort of people.

The first time he had got a call to make a delivery, it was an urgent document that had to go to a guy's house in the south of the island. His friend had said his car was being serviced and asked if he could help. Denzel was honoured and immediately grabbed his helmet, and raced round to do the favour. He was surprised when he received fifty euros for his trouble.

His friend explained: "It's a sort of executive service, for top-class people. When someone rings, we drop everything and packages are delivered within the hour. We're paid well. We just need one or two reliable and discreet couriers. What could be simpler? Easy money, Denzel. Of course, we respect client confidentiality. We don't know what's in the packages and we don't want to know. That way, there's never any problem. Get it?"

Denzel got it all right! It thrilled and excited him. He was soon picking up five or six deliveries a week, which accelerated to two or three an evening. He began to wonder why he even bothered going to work during the day.

He had also started spending some of his money having fun with his new friends in the clubs around the island. Drugs were easy to buy and his new smart friends were happy to share lines of coke and MDMA – nothing serious.

Tonight was his favourite drop of the week. There was a whitewashed villa on a low ridge overlooking the coast, with high gates and an entry code. The patio at the side of the house led to an infinity pool and entertainment area. It belonged to the boss of one of his friends, an English guy called Nick. He ran one of the many gaming businesses on the island and was loaded. According to Denzel's friends, he fuelled his gaming activities with a steady supply of cocaine. He was always discreet when buying though and did the business in the garage under the house, with the doors lowered against prying eyes.

The reason Denzel was so interested in the drop was Nick's live-in girlfriend. That woman was beautiful! Dark-haired, tanned, fit … and never quite fully dressed. In the late afternoon, she was always hanging around the place: lounging on the patio with files and papers stacked on the table in front of her, tanning herself on the sun lounger, or gently swimming up and down the pool.

Whenever he arrived at the place, she would turn her head towards him and raise her sunglasses to let him know she was looking at him. He loved the way she would gather her hair to one side, to show her high cheekbones, and there was always that half smile at the corners of her full mouth. It was a crush, he told himself, but there was no harm in it. On that particular evening, he pulled into the drive but could not see Nick's car in its usual place. Denzel sensed she was alone and felt a tingle of excitement.

CHAPTER 12
ABDULLAH BELKACEM
MEDITERRANEAN SEA, NORTH OF LIBYA

After twenty minutes of bouncing over the waves, they saw the low-slung profile of a tanker appear in the distance. The men shouted and cheered, like a coachful of schoolboys. Abdullah could never have imagined a day such as this. He took the binoculars from the cockpit. The ship looked small and insignificant, as it rolled through the white tops of the waves. Wide streaks of brown rust ran down the hull beneath the anchor lockers. A proud owner had once painted its sides red but, over time, it had become an earthy shade of brown. He had seen numerous photographs of it, even a video, but they must have been taken many years previously. His excitement turned into mild disappointment, but he hid it with an approving nod. The ship was plodding along at a steady twelve knots. He put down the binoculars.

"Well, Tareq, that is what two million dollars buys!"

Tareq looked at him, doubtfully.

"It's beautiful, brother!" he exclaimed, though his expression suggested otherwise.

"Well, maybe it is not so beautiful, but we do not want to attract attention, eh? It is better this way. It is the same as you and that Mercedes. People get jealous and then we stop being one of them."

Tareq was his brother and he knew him better than anyone. Abdullah glanced sideways and caught Tareq giving him a sly look.

The two brothers studied the vessel as the RHIB flew around the sides and across its bows. Written in large faded white lettering across the stern, in Latin and Arabic characters, was its name: *Malik Albahr*, the 'Sea King'. Abdullah mouthed the name of the ship to himself, trying it for size. *Malik Albahr.* Yes! At that moment, he felt a surge of pride that a humble farmer, a man who had started with nothing, could have achieved so much!

Several faces appeared at the rail and two of them raised their hands in greeting. The ship had cut its engines and had slowed in the water. The RHIB pulled alongside and a crewman unrolled a rope ladder with wooden rungs. Abdullah had not considered how we would get from the RHIB to the ship, but the churning green waters caused a sense of dread to rise inside him. He motioned to Tareq: "You first!"

"Ha, I forgot, the big man doesn't like the water! Maybe there are sharks waiting to bite his ankles? Better send his big brother first!"

Tareq slung the carbine over his shoulder, grabbed the ladder and, laughing, swung himself onto the rungs with ease. One by one, the team climbed the ladder. Tareq leaned over and beckoned to Abdullah. Heart pounding and short of breath, he leaned out from the RHIB, grasped the rope of the ladder and made the climb. The boat pulled back and headed back to shore.

Once aboard the ship, Samir, a distant cousin from Tripoli, greeted them. He had fallen out with a militia group in the capital and had made a hasty departure. He had come to see Abdullah looking for work and, so far, he had been a useful addition to their numbers. He took Tareq and Abdullah up to the bridge, where they met the nervous Egyptian skipper, Amr Warda. Amr was a small, thin man with greasy, black wavy hair that needed a trim, and a prominent moustache. He was wearing a crumpled blue short-sleeved shirt and stained grey trousers.

The Maltese partners had introduced a crewing agent to help find a skipper and crew. The agents had recommended Amr as an experienced captain who did not want a high salary. Abdullah had asked whether he could read the weather, navigate, load a ship, fix the engines and *'all the other ship things'*. The agent had laughed at this, telling him Amr had worked his way up with the big shipping lines as a junior officer, then first officer and finally as a master. To command a ship, he had to be able to do all those things. Abdullah had been impressed.

Abdullah mumbled a few words of prayer to himself, for good fortune, both for him and the future safety of the *Malik Albahr*. Then he turned to her captain.

"May peace be with you."

"And with you."

Amr shook his hand and Abdullah waved away the offer of drinks. There was business to discuss.

"So, Captain, now you work for me, eh? Life with me is good. Ask Tareq and Samir. Do as I ask and we will always be friends and maybe you will become rich too! But anger me and things will not be so good for you. I am a fair and just man so there is no reason all should not go well with our business.

"Tomorrow we talk about the expenses, the crew, and other business things. We work out of Marsabar and we see how things go, Allah be willing. *Inshallah.* Tonight, when you finish your work, you come and eat with my family, eh? We get to know each other, yes? Now, I want to look around my ship!"

As he turned to start the inspection, he noticed Samir standing just outside the bridge talking to Tareq in low but urgent terms. Abdullah immediately knew something was not right and went outside to join them. Tareq saw him and took his arm.

"Let's walk over here, brother. Samir has news. Tell him."

Samir was wide-eyed and jumpy.

"Abdullah, terrible news, I'm afraid. Someone killed Mahmoud Mansour in Malta. The police have found his body in the harbour, so we had to leave early, before they ask questions."

Abdullah looked at him, expressionless. How could that have happened? It was a simple job to go to Malta and board a ship. Mahmoud was his wife's sister's boy. He was family! Tareq saw the look on Abdullah's face and knew they needed somewhere private to talk.

"Let's find somewhere below. I'll ask the skipper where we can go. I hope you've not bought a cursed ship!"

Amr led them to his dirty and chaotic cabin, which smelt of diesel, sweat and tobacco, but at least it had a small desk and two chairs.

"This is good for you? I did not expect to have guests."

Tareq waved him away.

They settled into the cabin and, once Amr had backed out and closed the door behind him, Abdullah turned his attention to Samir.

"Your story better smell sweeter than this cabin."

Samir shook his head regretfully.

"I'm sorry, Abdullah, it isn't. We drove to Tripoli and took a plane to Catania, then a bus to Pozzallo. All good. We had no problems in Sicily and travelled straight through into Malta."

It was Abdullah who had told them to take a circuitous route to Malta, to make it look as though they had arrived from Sicily. He knew the level of scrutiny the border guards and Europol paid to groups of young Libyan men entering Europe, so had thought it best they make a detour before arriving at their Maltese destination.

"We did as you asked, we made sure nobody talked to us or followed us. We went to the port, found the ship and talked to Amr. But he said we had to have visas and paperwork to join the crew and we couldn't leave without them."

"So, what happened? How did this lead to my nephew being left behind, dead in the water?"

Abdullah was angry. The stupid boy did not realise how much trouble he was in. He had raised his voice and that did not happen often.

"We told Amr just to leave Malta, get going, but he said it was impossible; we needed customs permission. So, he phoned someone and then told us that our papers were no good. But, for one thousand euros, he could fix them and we could leave. So, we waited outside a warehouse on the wharf and hand over the money. They say papers will go to the Harbour Office the next day. Then, they attack us, looking for more money. I ran, Mahmoud also, but they followed. They caught and beat Mahmoud. When I got back, I couldn't find him. The next day, we saw police pulling a body out of the water."

"Stop! I do not understand. A man you have just met makes a call and tells you to give money to somebody you do not even know, who promises you he will send papers somewhere, and then they attack you? Tareq, does this make sense to you?"

The story was stupid and made Abdullah furious. He swung his arm and crashed the back of his hand against Samir's face. He crumpled over, hands cradling his nose.

"Have you learned nothing? If it is the truth, which I do not believe, you think that was a good plan, eh?"

Abdullah waited for the young man to drop his hands and look at him. There was anger in his eyes when he did, and Abdullah was pleased to see blood leaking out of his nose.

"Go on – how did Mahmoud die?"

"I'm not sure. I didn't see him. He must've fought, so maybe they put a cord around his neck. They took the cash and left him in the water. That's all I know. I swear!"

Abdullah's anger flared. Such a story did not ring true. Why would a customs man or port official, meeting for a pay day, kill for money he would be getting anyway? Why take the risk? There was no sense to it. The Captain knew who he had telephoned, so the identity of the murderer would not be a secret for long.

Tareq looked at his brother. They were both thinking the same thing. Tareq stood up, already on his way to fetch the hapless Amr.

"Tareq, stop! Let us think a minute."

Tareq turned back towards his brother.

"If we beat the Captain, or if we kill him, as he richly deserves, who will take my ship into the harbour? We are nearly there. Be still. We will talk more with him tonight. Until then, he will do what he is paid to do."

CHAPTER 13
NATASHA BONNICI
VILLA BIANCA, MALTA

NATASHA HAD LIKED Nick from the first moment they met. He was certainly physically attractive: cleancut, athletic-looking and always well dressed. His gentle and considerate manner was a pleasant change from the macho egotism she had become familiar with at the bank. She had started sleeping with him, but that did not really mean anything. However, as the months had passed, she found herself becoming rather fond of the self-contained Englishman.

She watched Nick closely and studied his moods and behaviours. Lately, he had seemed happier in the business and was spending more time at work than previously. The expansion he had talked about some months earlier, was underway and more staff were arriving by the day. The business had taken additional floor space, as well as bigger, faster telephony and IT systems.

She had encouraged him to put his doubts aside and press on with growing the business, telling him she was sure it was what Sergio and Marco would expect. At times, though, his natural reticence and caution frustrated her. She could see what needed to be done, but was unable to persuade him to push on and do it! Sitting and watching from the sidelines was not her style.

There were moments when she regretted the move back to

Malta. The pace of life was slow and she yearned to get back to the cut and thrust of working life. It was not the company she missed, but the excitement of doing a deal, chasing the business, winning approval. She knew she was smarter than most people she met. She was competitive and competent, but she needed to find a way of expressing it.

The one thing about Nick that had surprised her, was his coke habit. It had taken her a while to work out what was happening. She had never felt the need for drugs of any kind herself, so had little experience in spotting users, and Nick was discrete. Nevertheless, the realisation annoyed her, as it meant he could not be entirely focused on the job of growing BetSlick.

Once she had realised what was happening, it had not taken her long to notice that he had acquired a weekly caller; a young, local guy on a bike, who was very full of himself. He would arrive, wave and grin inanely at her, then disappear with Nick into the garage for a few minutes. Later, she would find small Jiffy bags in the recycling bin. He was obviously Nick's dealer. She could not think of any other explanation and, if she was right, she was inclined to put a stop to it. It would not serve Nick well in the long run if his habit started to interfere with his work. There was too much at stake, for Nick himself and, of course, for her father and Sergio.

So, when the boy on the bike turned up one Friday and Nick was not at home, Natasha saw her chance to interrupt his supply. More fool Nick for forgetting to cancel the delivery.

She felt her heart start beating a little faster. There was a side to her that enjoyed such adrenaline-fuelled situations. When she had to, she could keep those feelings in check, but sometimes it was fun just to run with them. The devil in her knew she was going to enjoy this little encounter.

She raised herself from her lounger, adjusting her bikini to make sure it skimmed her body. The wide-eyed boy did not miss a single second of the display. Draping a flimsy thigh-length coverall round herself, she pushed her sunglasses high onto her head and gathered her hair to one side. Then she slipped into her wedge sandals that lengthened her legs even further and made her way off the deck. Denzel soaked it all up. She gave him her best smile. When necessary, she had no hesitation about using men's own stupidity against them. She was enjoying her little performance. She had the boy exactly where she wanted him!

"Hi, I'm sorry, Nick's not in."

The idiot grinned and looked down the drive.

"I know, his car isn't here."

"Just wait there, I'll be back in a minute."

Natasha walked past him to go into the house. His eyes followed her as she climbed the stairs from the deck. She glanced back, coyly. Once upstairs, she hurried round to her apartment and grabbed a brown leather shoulder bag. Then, taking a black case from the bedside cabinet, she entered the PIN code, opened the lid and took the small Ruger lady's handgun. Tucking it into the bag, she returned to the deck.

The boy was standing exactly where she had left him.

"So, what d'you want with Nick? If you've got something for him, you can give it to me, you know?" She smiled at him and raised her eyebrows.

"Is he going to be long?" So far, the young visitor was enjoying the encounter.

"I don't know," she replied, suggestively. "I don't think he'll be back any time soon."

The boy grinned back at her. She took two steps towards him, closing the distance between them, hoping he would smell the coconut-scented sun cream that made her skin glisten in the low afternoon sun.

Keeping her eyes on him, she beckoned with her head.

"Come over and sit down on the deck for a bit. It's lovely this time of night. Let's have a look at what you've brought in that brown bag of yours. Maybe we can try some – to make sure it's all good and does what it's supposed to. You know Nick buys it for me, don't you?"

They sat down on some teak chairs at a glass-topped table and Natasha pushed her work papers to one side. The boy reached into his satchel and handed her a Jiffy bag. Making sure she never took her eyes off him, she opened the bag, took one of the small sealed plastic packs and popped a finger nail through it, dipping it into the powder. Then she put it into her mouth and rubbed her tongue around the soft flesh.

He watched, his eyes round and mouth hanging slightly open.

"By the way, who do you work for?" Natasha asked him.

At first, he was taken aback but, after a slight hesitation, he went off on a ramble about an executive courier service and deliveries within the hour. He really was that clueless, so Natasha reached into her bag, by the side of her chair, and pulled out the Ruger, smiling all the while.

Suddenly, she dropped the innocent look, staring at him intently. The muscles in her shoulders tensed; she was ready if he tried anything stupid. She raised the gun and pointed it straight at him. The boy's expression was a picture – his whole face dropped and his pupils dilated. He leaned back, scraping the legs of the chair, his mouth slack and speechless.

His excitement and arousal drained away, so Natasha pressed home the advantage of surprise and pushed the gun hard into his groin. He recoiled and instinctively raised his hands, looking at the gun, then at Natasha, terrified.

"Listen, you horny little shit. You ever come around here again with your hard on, I'll have you killed, d'you understand me? Now, I asked you who you work for? If you don't tell me, I'll shoot you here and now. Then I'll ring the police and tell them you're a scummy dealer who forced his way into the house. You found me out here, dressed like this, and tried to rape me, so I shot your balls off in self-defence. How's that for a story?"

Then, she let out a mock sob, opened her eyes wide and said in a little-girl voice: "I can be very convincing!"

She dropped the act before continuing in a cold, hard voice:

"If you contact Nick again, I'll find you. Tell your bloody executive courier outfit that they're in fucking big trouble. They obviously don't know who they're dealing with. If they want to get off the island, which I'd strongly recommend, tell them to do it now."

She jammed the gun hard into his balls, just to emphasise the point.

"They're going to be coming for you and your shitty little operation. Now, before you fuck off and give them the bad news, tell me who you work for?"

He stammered out such names and addresses as he knew, all of which meant nothing to her. She pushed a pen and a notebook at him from her pile of papers.

"Write them down, then get out of my house!"

Denzel jumped up, shaking, not daring to turn his back on the woman. Grabbing his satchel, he threw it over his shoulder and started to back away, before leaping down the deck stairs as fast as he could.

Panic-stricken, his stomach churning, he mounted his bike, fired it up and shot down the short drive, out through the open gates. Turning left onto the dual carriageway, he went up through the gears, tears of shame and shock running down his face. He could not process what had just happened. His primal instinct was simply to flee. God, she had pulled a gun on him. The crazy bitch! Actually threatened him with a real gun. He was shaking. He had never known fear like that before and it completely overwhelmed him.

The bike picked up speed. He swung out to avoid tail ending a slow car in the inside lane but over-steered as he moved into the outside lane. At the speed he was travelling, he could not straighten his line in time. His front wheel clipped the opposite curb and the rest was down to speed, mass and gravity.

The bike took off and, for a moment, Denzel managed to keep hold of the handle bars. Suddenly, he saw his legs in front of him as he was somersaulted forwards to smash onto the tarmac.

There is a reason motorcyclists wear leathers and boots – Denzel's flipflops, T-shirt and jeans provided no protection as a large area of his skin and two of his toes disappeared into the hot asphalt. The landing and the flips fractured his ankles, pelvis and left leg, leaving his left tibia poking through the front of his jeans.

The ambulance and police found him unconscious, but alive. The medics performed a triage assessment, gently removing his helmet, to make sure his skull was still intact. They splinted and dressed the leg with the compound fracture and strapped him to a stretcher, driving him to Mater Dei Hospital, with full blue lights.

Two police motorcyclists had happened to arrive on the scene moments after the impact. They had secured the site, diverted traffic, and examined the contents of the biker's satchel, to check for ID. Opening his wallet, they soon recognised his name and address and realised who they were dealing with.

One of the patrol officers called Assistant Commissioner Gerald Camilleri, saying they had found George Zammit's son, half dead, after a bike accident on the coast road. That was bad enough, but they wanted to know what to do about the few thousand euros worth of cocaine, MDNA and methamphetamine in his satchel. Camilleri told the patrol man to keep the satchel safe and said he would send someone to collect it. He stressed that it was a sensitive matter and told the officer not to say anything to his superiors or anybody else. His help would be noted and he would be thanked in the usual way.

CHAPTER 14
ABDULLAH BELKACEM

MARSABAR, LIBYA

DINNER WAS LATE THAT NIGHT. It was well past ten by the time Abdullah sat down with his men at the long wooden table inside the farmhouse. Getting the *Malik Albahr* into port had taken a long time but, finally, the ship was secured and they were able to sit down and eat.

Tareq, Samir, Amr and more relatives who worked with Tareq in the migrant business were all at the table. They ate spiced lamb, smoked cigarettes and watched Juventus playing on the big flat screen TV. The women sat in the kitchen with the children, around a smaller table, eating their lamb and rice on plastic plates. A game show played in the background.

"We eat well here, Amr, eh?" Abdullah did not look at him; he was watching the game.

Amr smiled, his greasy mouth filled with lamb, and raised a hand in salute. He was quiet and said little. Abdullah could tell he was nervous but was trying to fool them by constantly nodding his head and an inane grin on his face.

Amr wanted nothing more than to go back to his dirty cabin, to the warm comforting smells of oil and diesel. He had noticed Tareq and Samir furtively glancing at him from time to time and he knew something was up. What it was and how it involved him, he had no idea.

Abdullah turned to look at him.

"Tell us, my good friend, where else have you eaten such good lamb, eh?"

Amr swallowed hard and struggled to answer. A piece of lamb was still packed in his mouth, but retained the fixed smile, with one cheek bulging.

Without warning, a high-pitched wail came from the kitchen. A second voice joined the first in its anguish. It was like cats in the night. Abdullah recognised his sister-in-law's cry, accompanying the first one. Then another voice started its keening. It was his wife, Rania.

Abdullah pushed his plate aside and stood up to grab the TV remote and turn up the volume. There was silence around the table and the Italian commentary dulled some of the weeping noises coming from the kitchen. They had eaten enough and he could sense the tension building among the men. The commotion in the kitchen had killed everyone's appetite, anyway.

His sister-in-law had obviously just been told that her eldest son, Mahmoud Mansour, was lying under the waters of the Mediterranean, his body swollen and skin slack. Although it was not true, what did it matter where his body was? He was dead. Rania was always good in these situations, but Abdullah had a duty to offer comfort, prayers and, usually, money. All three would be needed that night.

He went through to the brightly lit kitchen, where the children sat quietly on a bench, their eyes large and watchful. The other women stood embracing Mona, his wife's sister, in her spasms of grief. Abdullah had previously told Rania the terrible circumstances that had led to a fatal blow to Mahmoud's head; a shifting load of cargo on a rough sea, crates falling from a broken pallet. A terrible accident, but at least it was quick and there was no suffering.

He changed his expression as he entered the kitchen. It was

the picture of despair, tears glistening in his eyes. Approaching Mona, he held her at arm's length, looking into her face. He needed her to listen; not to grab him and weep and wail. The women could do that together, later. Mona was in her fifties and Gaddafi's men had killed her husband in the fighting on the Coastal Road. He had been an honourable man and quick to join Abdullah in the early days. Since his death, her son had been her sole provider and now he was gone. Abdullah had to remember to add her to the list of pensioners in his care.

He began to utter his words of sympathy.

"Mona, listen to me. It is the worst thing that could happen to a mother. It brings me to tears to think of the grief you feel. The loss of a son is the most terrible thing. But, Allah be praised, he died instantly. There was no suffering. This, at least, is something. They washed him, Mona, they did everything properly. They wrapped him in a white shroud and said prayers over him. His injuries were serious and not good to look at. It was best we buried him at sea; there was no other way.

"But listen, it was proper and it is allowed. As soon as I heard, I spoke to the Imam at the mosque to make sure everything was correct and done right. There was nothing more we could have done for him. He is with Allah now, Mona. Mahmoud was a good man. He looked after me and, in thanks for this, I will look after you. Remember, we all belong to Allah and to Him we return."

Mona sniffled and sobbed, but she looked at Abdullah and nodded in agreement. That was good. She had understood and there would be no trouble in that direction. One day, he would have to pay for all his lies; but not just yet.

He glanced at Rania, who was resting against a cupboard, her arms folded, eyes reddened, and she nodded her approval. She came forward to comfort her sister and he was released, his duty done.

Abdullah was satisfied his words had calmed the women, so he returned to the dining room where Juventus had just conceded a goal. The men were muttering and complaining about the referee's decision.

He took the remote and, without looking at anyone, switched off the TV. He turned to Tareq.

"It is time."

Abdullah went to the door and lit a cigarette.

Tareq and the others stood up, extinguishing cigarettes and grabbing phones. Amr looked around, unsure what was happening. Samir stood behind his chair and suddenly lifted him to his feet, pulling his wrists together behind his back, whilst slipping on a cable tie. He yanked it tight.

Amr had turned pale and his eyes were blinking wildly, trying to make sense of it all. The men dragged him outside and bundled him onto the floor of a flatbed truck waiting in the compound, its engine running. A work boot came down hard on his head and wedged him to the floor. He found it hard to breathe, with his lungs compressed and his arms twisted behind him. The journey was a short one, less than five minutes.

Abdullah was the first to arrive, in his Land Cruiser. Behind him, they dragged Amr out of the truck and into a low outbuilding, leaning against a rock face. Agricultural tools were piled against the walls but, at the back, there was a steel door that led to a narrow passage hewn out of the rock, which was lit by bulkhead lights. After a few metres, it started to descend, ending at another steel door which was thrown open. They pushed Amr inside. The first thing he saw in the vaulted limestone cave was Abdullah, lighting a welding torch. It flared, then roared, as he adjusted the flow of gasses to the flame. His heart missed a beat when Abdullah turned to face him, the corners of his mouth downturned in a cruel grimace. At that moment, there was nothing he could do to stop the stream of warm urine from trickling down his leg.

CHAPTER 15
INSPECTOR GEORGE ZAMMIT

BIRKIRKARA, MALTA

Mater Dei Hospital was the pride of the Maltese public health system, with a thousand beds, sprawling over a massive site, in the middle of the Central Belt. It was a mess of double-parked cars and ad hoc buildings, crammed onto a site much too small for its needs. In the car, on the way over, Marianna was nearly hysterical: "I told you, you should never have let him have that stupid bike. I knew this would happen … I just knew it! Tell me what they said again."

George had never known such a feeling of dread; he was shaking with fear. He saw Denzel as a small boy: a happy child on his little tricycle, always laughing; playing football for the Spartans; sitting at the dinner table, arguing with his sister. He could not imagine what he would find when they got there. George gripped the wheel of the car, urging it on through the evening traffic, the flashing blue light stuck on the roof.

Marianna wailed all the way there. He was thankful the hospital was only a matter of minutes from their house and it did not take them long before they were screeching into one of the police parking spaces outside A&E.

They spent the next two hours waiting and following a drugged, unconscious Denzel from A&E to X-Ray and then to the ICU. When he eventually came round, Marianna shrieked, grabbing the boy and hugging him, to his obvious discomfort. Amongst other things, a compound fracture of his tibia needed surgery the following day. The pain relief was strong, but Denzel managed a smile and said a few words. It looked as though he was drifting off to sleep but, at one point, he fought the drowsiness and reached out to seize George's wrist.

"Dad, is my bag here? I need my bag." His voice was weak, his eyes flickering.

Marianna laughed and said, "Denzel, don't worry about your silly bag. You've got everything you need for tonight. Tomorrow, after the operation, I'll bring some more things in for you."

George looked in the cabinet and around the bed.

"No, son, I can't see it. But don't worry, the paramedics or police will probably have it."

Denzel started to grow agitated. He tried to sit up, but moaned and slumped back onto the bed.

"Dad, please talk to the ambulance people, whoever … I need that bag back!"

His eyes locked with George's and he nodded, to emphasise the point, then dropped his head and disappeared into a deep, opioid-induced sleep.

George thought for a moment, while Marianna continued to stroke Denzel's hair. He had an uneasy feeling that the bag might be important, but he could not figure out why. It worried him that, despite Denzel's condition, he was going on about it so much. He took a final look at Denzel and then at Marianna.

"He's sleeping, Marianna. Thank God he's going to be alright. *Mela*, let's talk to the doctor about what happens tomorrow. Then we should go."

"Go? No! I'm going to stay for a bit longer. You go if you want. I'll ring you later or get a taxi back. I can't just leave him like this."

"OK, I'll try to find out more about what happened and see

where his belongings are. He seemed really worried about his bag."

A&E had nothing but Denzel's helmet and one flipflop to offer. The doctors had cut his jeans from him and binned them. His T-shirt had been a blooded mess and had also been disposed of. Even though it was late, George went back to the office, into the Traffic Division, to find out who the officers at the scene had been. They were off duty now, but they had not logged any bag. He checked on the roster and saw that they were both on an early shift the next day. The bag had definitely been around Denzel's shoulder when they had spoken outside the garage. The most likely explanation was that it had been thrown aside somewhere during the crash and perhaps overlooked. He shuddered at the thought of it. He decided to talk to the two officers the next day and then go to the scene, to check the roadside scrub for himself.

Later, Marianna had phoned to say she was back in the house, having met a neighbour and taken up the offer of a lift. It was late when he finally made it home, feeling drained and a little emotional. He was just about to turn onto the ramp down to his garage when a parked car, facing him, flashed its lights.

Glancing around, he could see there was nobody else in the road. It was dark. There were no streetlights, only the glow of lights behind curtains casting patches of yellow light onto the road. Slowing, he drew parallel to the car and lowered his window. It was a dark BMW. As he came to a stop alongside it, he saw the occupant through the lowered window on the driver's side. Assistant Commissioner Gerald Camilleri was smoking. He dropped the cigarette out of the window, between the two vehicles.

"George, listen, sorry to hear the news about your boy. Thought I would come straight round. Will he come through it OK? Must be a dreadful shock for you and your wife."

George was dumbstruck. What the hell was this man doing here, offering him sympathy at eleven o'clock at night?

"Yes, thank you, sir. He's got some fractures and needs surgery in the morning, so it'll take time, but he's alive and it looks like he'll be fine, thank God."

"Good, good. We should be grateful for that. Well, anyway, once he is better, you will have to transfer your visits to Corradino."

George paused, confused, and looked at Camilleri for a clue as to what he was talking about. Camilleri merely focused his gaze on some point straight ahead of him and sat back in his seat.

"Assistant Commissioner, sir, what are we talking about here? I appreciate your concern, but what has my son got to do with Corradino?"

Corradino Correctional Facility was a hell hole of a prison on the outskirts of Valletta, built by the British in Victorian times, where drugs, violence, rodents and suicides were rife.

"Do not worry for now, George. First, we have to make sure Denzel gets better. But he has been a naughty boy, I am afraid. The traffic officers found his bag and were so concerned about what was in it, well, they rang me straightaway. I know you and Marianna have enough on your plate right now, so I have taken the bag into my protective custody. The two officers agreed that its safekeeping should be entrusted solely to me; so, do not worry about them."

"*Mela,* what's the problem with the bag? What was in it?"

George did not understand what the AC was talking about.

"Your son's bag contained several thousand euros worth of cocaine, MDMA and other narcotics. I am sure you knew nothing about all this, but it seems your boy was a dealer and, by the looks of things, a busy dealer, at that. We all know that this is going to put Denzel in a bad situation and I am sure Internal Affairs will want to speak with you too, to make sure it was not a family affair. Let us hope we can manage to sort it out."

Camilleri turned towards him and smiled.

"Do not worry about any of this just yet, George. Concentrate on helping Marianna and Denzel get over this ordeal. It must have been quite an evening for you, quite a day, in fact!"

George felt sick and found his powers of speech had left him. For a moment, he had to put both hands on the steering wheel and hold on tight, to prevent himself spinning off into some other universe.

Camilleri, happy with the impact of their chat, raised his window, started his engine and motioned for George to pull forward and let him move out.

CHAPTER 16
ABDULLAH BELKACEM
ABDULLAH'S CAVE, MARSABAR, LIBYA

Abdullah told Tareq to put the bastard captain on the wooden chair. He turned off the welding torch and sat down on a stool at the back of the cave, staring at Amr the whole time. Tareq smiled and cut the plastic cable tie on Amr's arms.

"Take those pissy pants off!" Tareq shouted.

Amr loosened the belt, undid his pants and stepped out of them. Tareq kicked them across the floor and used his foot to push them into the side of the cave. Amr started shaking. He had not said a word since they had lifted him from the dinner table; not a protest, not a plea, not even a cry for mercy.

Everything in the cave was designed to instil fear. It was true, they had sometimes hurt people in it, but mainly they used it to slaughter sheep and goats. The cool of the rock preserved the meat until they could take it to the freezers. There were no flies and the rock floor was easy to hose down with water from the well. Most people who were brought there were so panic-stricken, they could not see beyond the extent of their own fear. They thought it was a room from hell, the sort of place that existed only in nightmares and movies. More often than not, the room's visitors willingly told Abdullah everything he needed to know, without a drop of blood being spilt.

Tareq strapped the Captain's skinny arms to the chair with fresh cable ties. He sat in his wet, stained baggy Y-fronts, his stick legs jiggling up and down with terror. Tareq then got more cable ties to fasten his feet to the chair legs.

"No, Tareq, leave him. It is easier to cut his balls off when the legs are not strapped".

It was a joke they used every time and it still amused them all!

They were even more amused to hear Amr finally let out a whimper. In a small voice, he said: "What's happening here? What d'you want? I've done nothing!"

Abdullah approached him slowly and, taking a cigarette from one of his men who was lounging against the wall, drew in a long drag from it.

"You stupid man! Do you not know what you have done? You think I am stupid too? Are we all stupid here? Can you guess what we do to people like you down here? Can you?"

He waited to see if the Captain answered. Nothing!

"Let me show you what we have here. First, a nice water bath." He pointed to the far corner of the cave where an old bathtub stood in a wooden frame; a plank, with holes drilled to accommodate some stout nylon cords, resting half in and half out of some green, scummy water.

"Then, we have full power from the generator." He reached across to show Amr some heavy-duty jump leads which he swung under his nose.

"You can start a wagon with these – we have done it before, eh, Tareq?"

His brother nodded, making an effort to keep a straight face. He was enjoying witnessing the Captain's terror.

"They deliver a mighty punch! With these on your balls, you will never have children, eh? Oh, but no, maybe we cannot do this, because we have cut them off already!"

Tareq snorted a laugh and hastily put a hand over his mouth.

Abdullah continued speaking.

"Then, we have the blowtorch. I enjoy that; the smell lasts for days. Reminds me of Rania's lamb, no? Look, we even have a drain here so we can wash the blood and the tears down to the watercourse."

He paused, pushing his face right up to Amr's.

"I remember once, Tareq took someone to pieces down here. Cut bits off him till there was nothing left to cut. Jointed him like a chicken!"

Tareq looked at Amr and nodded in agreement, as if relishing the memory. Amr stared at the deep brown stains of sheep and goat blood all around the hole in the centre of the room. The shaking got worse. Tareq could tell he was going out of his mind with fear. All eyes were on him and he knew there was not a shred of pity in the room.

"We also have hooks in the roof," he glanced upwards, "and then we have the box."

A strong blackened, wooden trunk, about one metre by one and a half metres, lay in front of Amr.

"Show him the inside of the box, Tareq."

There were knowing smiles around the room.

"I can't," Tareq said, shrugging his shoulders, "there's still someone inside it."

"Open it!" Abdullah shouted.

Tareq took off the locks and unfastened the hasps. He lifted the lid so Amr could see into it. A bound, hooded figure was curled in a ball, elbows, head and feet crammed against the sides of the box. It twitched, but could not make any further movement. Tareq reached across for a bottle of water from a nearby shelf. He poured half the contents over the hood on the figure's head and then slammed the lid, as muffled sounds came from within. For good measure, Abdullah explained to Amr: "He's probably got about three more days left!"

Nobody else said anything, which made Amr's groan of

despair even more pronounced. Someone standing at the back of the room let out a small burst of laughter.

At that point, Abdullah jammed the lit cigarette into Amr's neck, just above the shoulder. Amr jumped and bucked, screaming hoarsely for several seconds. Then he collapsed into a fit of sobbing, rocking backwards and forwards against the cable ties. The burn hurt, but it was not serious; it was the fear of what might come next that was killing him.

It was usually at this point that tongues became loose and the talking started.

Abdullah took his stool and placed it in front of him.

"So, Amr, it is now your time to choose. Where do we start? The torch, the water, the knife, or the electricity and then the box? Everyone goes into in the box, eventually. That is what usually kills them. Hard to breathe in there, no water, pain from the injuries, blood loss – not everyone's heart can hold out, even for one day. Some go mad within the first hour."

Abdullah pushed him with his hand and he flinched violently, as if he had been prodded with the jump leads.

"So, what is it to be? Let me help you, Amr. Let me tell you what you have done and what I want to know. You set up one of my family, Mahmoud, and he was killed. My own nephew!"

Amr interrupted: "No, no, I didn't know what would happen, I didn't!"

"So, what exactly did you think would happen, Amr? Do not even think for a minute of lying to me."

Sobbing, he tried to get his story out.

"Look, the Harbourmaster's Office rang, saying he needed the crew's papers. The new crew had to be registered and they needed passports, with entry visas. I got all the papers to the agent, but he said there were no visa stamps on the passports. So, I rang the owner."

Abdullah stared at him in surprise.

"How did you know who the owner was?"

"There was a number on an email I saw. Please! Listen," he pleaded, "that's all I know. I beg you!"

"So what happened then?"

"I rang the number, a Malta number, and spoke to this guy – East European, maybe. I told him the problem and that the boys had no money. He got angry, but says he'll fix it and talk money later."

"What was his name, Captain Amr? What was this East European man called?"

"Steven, or Simon. He's Polish, or Ukrainian, or something. This Polish man, Simon, I think it is, rings me back. He tells me to go to the shipping agent and pick up an envelope with money and meet a passport guy at ten o'clock that night at the end of wharf. He says the guy'll make the paperwork good with customs the next morning and then we could leave. That's what happened! I did what the Polish man said."

Abdullah knew the truth when he heard it and he believed Amr was not lying. He looked at Samir, who was slouching against the wall. His eyes were looking at the floor.

"Well, Samir?"

Abdullah did not like the story so far and knew there was more to it.

Samir kept looking at the ground: "Yeah, that's what happened."

"What was the problem with the visas?"

Samir did not raise his eyes.

"We got visas for Malta from the Embassy in Tripoli, but we entered through Italy. That was the problem. We didn't know that – visas are visas, no? Anyway, it was a mess."

"So how did you get into Sicily with the wrong visas?" Abdullah did not understand.

"I don't know. They stopped us for a few minutes, took our passports away, then came back and let us go. No problem at all."

Something was still not right with this story. Abdullah could not see how it had led to Mahmoud's death. There was more to find out and he started to wonder if it really was the fault of the hapless, trouserless man, sitting in front of him, shaking in his chair, or of someone else.

"So, soon to die Captain, then what happened? How did you let my sister-in-law's only son get killed?"

Amr looked at Samir, whose eyes turned back to studying the floor. Abdullah caught the direction of the Captain's glance and how Samir quickly turned away.

"Samir? Maybe you can help, eh?" Abdullah said to him.

"I've told you! Amr said we needed to take the cash to hand over to the contact who would fix the papers, easy. We were supposed to meet at ten o'clock. Mahmoud said he'd do it."

"What! On the ship you told me you all went. You are lying to me! Tell me the truth, why did Mahmoud go by himself? Why did you not go with him, just in case of trouble? That is what we always do, you know that; one to talk, the other to watch."

A silence developed. Amr was sniffling, but the silence told Abdullah everything. There was a secret between Amr and Samir, something that remained unspoken, hanging in the stuffy cigarette fumes of the cave.

"They weren't there, that's why!" Amr finally blurted out. He was trying to jump up, pulling at the restraints. "Samir took them whoring in Albert Town and left Mahmoud to meet the contact by himself! Samir said he was still a boy and not old enough to go with them, so he had to do it!"

Amr's eyes flicked to the right, towards Samir, who jumped to his feet, alert and sensing danger. Abdullah saw that Amr was now more frightened of him than he was of Samir. That was how the cave worked and how they always discovered the truth in the end. Samir would have threatened the Captain, getting him to say that everyone had remained on board that evening. But Mahmoud had gone by himself to the harbourside meeting because Samir and the others were elsewhere.

Now Abdullah started to see the full picture. He turned to Samir.

"Tell me this is not true. That you let young Mahmoud go by himself to meet these strangers, while you went sinning with whores?" Abdullah's anger was rising.

Samir saw the game was up. He shook his head and fronted up to Abdullah. He was always a cocky one but, this time, he was in big trouble.

"What could go wrong just handing over a packet? They worked for the Port Authority; they were getting paid. Why would there be any danger? It made no sense that they would kill him. Anyway, we didn't go whoring. We just went to sit in the square in Albert Town, maybe smoke some weed and watch the people, I swear! Please, Abdullah, it's a mighty mess I know, but I seek forgiveness from Allah and forgiveness from you! I've let you down, and Mahmoud and his family. I'll make it right with them, by Allah, I promise."

"How are you going to make it right, Samir? Are you going to raise the dead?"

Tareq approached the young man with undisguised menace.

Abdullah held up his hand, a signal to Tareq to stay calm. He turned his own attention to the pathetic figure of Amr.

"My friend Amr, your first mistake was to let Samir frighten you. You should have been much more scared of me! Your second mistake was to hide his lies from me. I have killed men for much less.

"Tonight, I feel merciful and, because you did not know me when this happened, I will forgive you this one time. Now we understand each other, there will be no secrets between us. Is this agreed?"

The Captain nodded.

"Tareq, free his hands."

The Captain rubbed his wrists and gently felt the burn on his neck.

"Maybe we can let you finish your dinner? Tareq get him

some pants and lock him somewhere comfortable with a bed. Amr, I will speak to the Polish man and his boss, the owner, tomorrow and then we will have a talk about the future. You can see now, I am a fair and just man, eh? Tareq, let Khaled out of the box. Forgive me, Amr, we just wanted to scare you." He smiled at the Captain. "Sometimes we must dig a little for the truth, eh?"

Abdullah grasped Amr's forearm in a gesture of friendship and to show him he had not taken it badly. He needed him to sail the ship, after all. Amr tried to give him that nervous rictus smile, but could not even manage that.

Tareq lifted the lid of the trunk and pulled the hooded figure out, slipping the loose bands off his wrists. Khaled pulled the hood off, shaking his wet hair and grinning.

"Wow, it was hot in there! How long was I in for?"

He looked around and sensed the mood in the cave.

"What've I missed?"

Abdullah turned his attention to Samir. His men were all waiting for him to pass judgement. He weighed up the seriousness of the situation. He knew he had to make an example of Samir's dishonesty and, although he believed he was not directly responsible for Mahmoud's death, his actions had contributed to it.

As he approached Samir, the group became silent, waiting, eyes down, fearful of what might happen, but knowing that Samir could not go unpunished.

"I have said I will look after Mahmoud's mother and that means for the rest of her life. Now, I do not have to, because you will. If you do not want to do that, you can leave Marsabar before sunrise. It is your choice. If you do not support her or you let me down again, I will have Tareq kill you. That will be justice for Mona. But I must also punish you for your lies and deceit to me. You will take a beating from Tareq.

Do you agree that this is right, and I am being fair and merciful?"

"Yes, it is right, and you are being fair and merciful. I accept the punishment and will do as you say."

Samir knew he was lucky to be walking up the corridor and out of the cave, into the desert night, alive.

CHAPTER 17
MARCO BONNICI
CASTELLO BONNICI, MALTA

The Bonnici family history recorded that they had originally come from Amalfi and could trace their ancestry way back to the eleventh century. The library of Castello Bonnici contained papers that told of remote relatives who had even held counsel with the Holy Roman Emperor, Charles V.

For centuries, the Bonnici family had traded across Europe, gaining favour with popes, princes, lords, bishops and cardinals. Other families, with similar intentions, were also to be found in the shadows of the royal courts, governments and churches. These families were friends to all, buying influence and steadily accumulating wealth. In time, they formed their own unique guild based on the organisations of renaissance Florence and became known as the '*Familia Con Pane*', 'the Family With Bread', or, in more recent times, 'the Family Company'.

Over the last century, things had changed. The two world wars and the upheavals in Eastern Europe, had laid waste to years of work and riches. Marco's great-grandfather had seen it as his duty to fight with the Austrians, as an ally of the Ottomans, in the First World War. Following their defeat, the Bonnicis had scattered, with Marco's side of the family retreating to live quietly on their lands in Malta, which they had held since the time of the Knights of St John. The British, who ruled Malta up to its independence in 1964, presented no problem, welcoming well-mannered aristocrats, even those of Austrian heritage!

All those involved in the Family alliance had suffered and they were adamant that such a misfortune should never befall them again. The Family Company reinvented itself, becoming a tighter, modern, multinational organisation, operating between the lines of international and domestic laws. They had established a council of elders, called the Wise Men, who sat in Milan and oversaw the Family's wide-ranging and diverse businesses. Its legitimising imperative was to recoup the wealth that been disastrously squandered through the folly of others in the previous century.

Marco had gone to Catholic boarding school at Ampleforth College, in the UK, where the only thing worse than the food was the rugby. When he returned to Malta, it was decided that he should finish his education with the Italian side of the Family, in Milan. It was there he had first met his cousin, Sergio. They had liked each other at once. Marco had studied economics at the University of Bologna, while Sergio, for a short while at least, studied law. He had taught Marco to smoke, drink and charm women. Although he was a little younger and wilder than Marco, Sergio and he had become, and remained, firm friends.

While at university, Sergio thought it would be a good idea to establish their credentials within the Family and impress the Wise Men. Marco had worked out a scheme to 'sell' large volumes of trans-Atlantic telephone traffic and reclaim large amounts of VAT from the Italian government, with falsified invoices. An uncle of Sergio's had found out about it. After he had berated them and had them punished, he forced them to hand over the details of the scheme, refined it and made himself a small fortune!

Marco's father, Franco, had been responsible for rekindling the Maltese side's fortunes when, in the late nineteen fifties and early nineteen sixties, he had become involved in the rebuilding of the island after the war. The problem was that development cash was almost impossible to find, so Franco had gone to Milan to talk to his cousin Nico. They had started working together and Franco had helped Nico develop the cheap hotel model, first in Rimini and then all along the Mediterranean Coast.

In Milan, Marco had begun to understand the true nature of 'the Family'. It was one of the reasons his father had wanted him to spend time there. He had proved himself a creative and competent businessman and was duly encouraged to participate in the Family's projects. Eventually, he had been introduced to the Wise Men of the Family and, before long, had begun trusting him to run several more significant projects.

On reflection, Marco marvelled at the way the Family had conspired to take him in, supervise the final years of his education and integrate him into its wider business affairs. Then, they had introduced him to a daughter of another Family member, Sophia, and, as luck would have it, the two of them immediately knew they were meant to be together. It was suggested that, after they married, they should return to Malta, where Marco could help his ailing father and take his place running the Maltese side of the Family business.

Marco's father died shortly after seeing his son married, but before the birth of Natasha, a year after the wedding. All was well for several years, which Marco fondly recalled as his happiest time, until tragedy struck.

When Sophia had died, Marco had been so broken, Sergio feared he might choose to join her. It was only his devotion to Natasha that had kept him alive. He had only been married six years when the accident happened.

Natasha had few memories of her late mother, although she had seen pictures of her; a tall, vibrant-looking woman, with an intense stare and the dark mane of hair that she had inherited. She was aware her father had never recovered from the loss and, as far as she knew, had never again shared his affections with another woman. He was an attractive man, with wealth and position, but friends and family had soon learned not to match-make and respect his life choice.

Sergio was one of only two people who knew that Sophia had been pregnant with her second child when she had died. Marco and Sophia had told one other person the good news, and that was the five-year-old Natasha. Marco had confided in Sergio that Natasha had not been pleased to hear she was going to have a brother or sister. She had refused to eat or speak, except to throw tantrums, for two days, prior to Sophia's accident.

Marco had heard the screams for help and found Sophia lying on the narrow landing, midway down the marble staircase, clutching her stomach and had watched, horrified, as a dark red stain had crept rapidly down her legs. He knew the pregnancy was over and his wife had lost consciousness before the ambulance arrived. The haemorrhaging had killed her by the time they reached Mater Dei.

Looking back on the incident, he realised that, at the height of the panic, when the staff and he were busy telephoning for help and trying to see to Sophia, Natasha was calmly sitting on the top step of one side of the divided staircase, expressionless, her chin in her hands, looking down at the drama below. He had tried to ask her if she had seen what had happened, but she had offered no explanation whatsoever. She had remained silent on the subject for well over twenty years.

Marco felt a mixture of contradictory emotions whenever he saw his daughter, now a beautiful and talented woman, enjoying a good life, as if that awful day had never happened.

He should have realised that the existence of a well-educated, financially astute, independent-minded Bonnici daughter would not go unnoticed in Milan. Like all organisations, the Family was always conscious of the need to renew itself with trusted members from within. It had been suggested that, in these modern times, bringing a woman into the organisation might be something to be welcomed. Marco had nodded along sagely with the suggestion but, for some reason, had yet to discuss the possibility with Natasha.

It was early evening and Marco was on his knees, in the shade of an Aleppo Pine, examining the underside of a shrub, when his phone vibrated in his pocket. He wiped the soil from his hands onto his dirty cord trousers.

"Well, my friend, how are you and how is your beautiful new ship?"

"Why ask me about my ship when you have a corpse belonging to my family rotting in one of your fridges, eh?"

"If you want it back, I am sure that can be arranged." He wondered if Abdullah understood sarcasm.

"You joke with me, but I do not find it a good joke."

"I am sorry, a death is never funny. I never like to see a life wasted, my friend. I always think about what it might have become. But this was the fault of the stupid boys you sent, and I hope the lesson has been learned, so others do not find their young lives cut short."

"Hmm! Do not concern yourself about that! You can be sure lessons have been learnt! But, we must talk of other things. Now I have the ship, I can start to move the oil. We are nearly ready."

"That is good, we are ready to receive it in Malta. There is tank space reserved. I must tell you the demand for your oil is very high. I hope you can supply at least two tankers a week?"

"That might be difficult with only one ship. But, we can start with three trips every two weeks."

"Seriously, you need to start thinking about how we can increase the supply. This business will not be here forever, so we must make the most of the opportunity now."

"I will think further. There are others I am meeting soon, to help make us stronger, so we can supply more. The cost will come from my share, so you need not worry. I fear, once our project becomes known, there will be much interest. Libya is not like Malta, the streets are full of hungry dogs."

"OK, my friend. Tell me when you are ready to sail, then we can move the money to you as we agreed. Until we speak again."

"Until we speak again."

CHAPTER 18
NATASHA BONNICI
THE ALBANIAN BASEMENT, ST PAUL'S BAY, MALTA

Marco was on his way down the hill into St Paul's. He had arranged to meet Natasha at a hotel, just off the sea front. She had been insistent she needed to understand what was happening with the plans to expand BetSlick, if she was going to continue to keep an informed eye on Nick.

He arrived at the hotel earlier than expected and was waiting, as Natasha's Audi pulled into the car park. In one smooth movement, she swung her legs out of the car, raised the soft-top and strode over to greet him. Instantly, the black cloud that had gathered around him that morning evaporated, as he saw his daughter, so vital, confident and beautiful.

"Hi, Dad! Is this it?" She lifted her sunglasses and looked in the direction of a door, leading to the basement of the hotel.

"Morning, Natasha. Yes," he pointed to the door, "this is the Albanian Basement, so-called because it is a basement and it is full of ... Albanians!"

They walked down the ramp and Marco pressed the entry phone to speak to someone inside. He turned to Natasha and said: "This is where we are fuelling Nick's operation from. He knows the money is arriving thick and fast, but he does not know this is the source of it."

Marco raised his eyebrows at her conspiratorially.

There was the sound of locks shifting and a small skinny character in a singlet, with thick stubble and a cigarette hanging from his mouth, peered round the basement door.

"Yes sir, come in. All very busy."

As they entered, Marco introduced the guy to Natasha as Elbasan. She followed her father through the door, noticing Elbasan brazenly looking her up and down. She fixed him with a stare and he smiled at her, revealing stained, gappy teeth. He was probably in his forties but, when he smiled, he looked about sixty. She shot him a look of disgust, but he continued to leer.

"Very pretty, miss!"

She thought: *In your dreams, Elbasan.*

Marco swung his arm around to indicate the basement garage, an area large enough to take probably twenty cars. There were portable air conditioning units everywhere and over a dozen workstations, with a mix of people all plugged into headsets. Some of the women wore headscarves, but most were young men in jeans and T-shirts. They looked rough; cheap clothing, tattoos and shaved heads. Nobody looked directly at them, but Natasha was sure she and her father were both being carefully checked out.

Marco started to explain.

"The system is simple, yet effective. Elbasan and his family set up fake customers; nothing more than a few bytes of data. They use stolen or false personal details to open genuine bank accounts, buying lists of names and copy documents on the Dark Web. Then they mock up phoney IDs and utility bills to satisfy the bank's compliance checks. Once BetSlick has the bank account details, it opens Player Accounts for those customers. A Player Account is an internal account, managed by BetSlick, where a customer keeps his float and his winnings, if there are any.

"Elbasan and the guys then stoke the Player Accounts with large sums of cash that we supply, using prepaid credit cards, ewallets, cash transfer companies like Western Union, bureaux de change, Middle Eastern chits and other forms of non-bank transfers. We also have a small number of Family-owned, land-based betting shops that we feed with cash deposits which are then also transferred to BetSlick Player Accounts. So, that way, the money ends up with Nick, but there is no record of it having been paid through a customer's bank account."

He looked at her to check she was following it all so far. Natasha nodded to show she understood.

"All this cash comes from activities that the Family prefers to keep private, mainly for tax reasons. Nick places one or two bets on behalf of these 'customers', for the sake of good form, but the bulk of the cash in the Player Accounts is simply repaid to the original bank account. If anyone asks about the source of funds, it can be proved the cash is clean gaming winnings. Once in the bank accounts, the money can be moved into the Family's more legitimate enterprises. Classic money laundering!"

"Very creative!" Natasha was impressed. She already knew BetSlick laundered money, but it was interesting to see the Albanians printing piles of fake utility bills, sifting bank account opening forms and making calls with dozens of new, shiny credit cards laid out in front of them.

Marco was not finished yet.

"This is only phase one; we are now well into planning phase two. We have already established BetSlick as a well-founded business, making large profits from a host of fake transactions around the world. It has paid its Maltese taxes and carried its own expenses. But now, rather than repaying the money in the Player Accounts back to the original bank accounts, the fake punters suffer heavy losses and we push the cash through as our legitimate business profits, going straight back to the Family's accounts as tax-paid dividends – all legal and above board."

"How do we know this bunch aren't just stealing the money? You say they handle cash? Looking around, I'm keeping tight hold of my handbag!" Natasha murmured, leaning closer into Marco.

"It is all tightly audited. Everyone is searched going in and coming out. As a group, they are all educated – which is rare for Albanians. The exception is Elbasan. I do not think he has ever been inside a school, but he has other talents! We recruit them through his family and pay very well. To get a job here, they also have to put up a surety, like a bond."

"You mean a cash deposit of some sort."

"No. Most of them do not have a lot of cash. We usually recruit in pairs, from the same family. One works here and the other in Cyprus, in a mirror operation. So, if money goes missing here, it is understood we will have the Cypriots punish the sureties. If the Cypriot operation turns up short – this lot are for the chop."

"Dad! That's terrible!" she made herself say, inwardly admiring the elegance of their solution to any in-house chicanery. She put her hand to her mouth to hide a grin!

"It was Sergio's idea. Neat, yes? But I tell you what – we have not suffered any losses yet!"

"So, can I ask about the numbers?"

"We will process about two hundred million euro in cash this year. That is gross turnover. We are looking to quadruple that over the next two years, once the oil business comes online. We have plans to treble the size of this end of the operation."

They drove back up to the *castello*, Natasha following Marco's white Range Rover up the hill. Once back on the terrace, her father asked Katia to bring them coffee. Natasha noticed Marco had taken a seat in the wicker chairs he favoured when he was going to have one of his 'chats'. She sat down opposite him.

"So, an impressive operation, all in all, do you agree?"

"I do. I'm just staggered by how much money flows through it! What's the turnover of the Family as a whole? If you've got nearly a billion euros that you want to pass through BetSlick, it must be enormous!"

"In truth, I could not tell you. I doubt anyone could. The whole organisation is set up to be pretty opaque. The Wise Men say they know, but I have my doubts if even they know the full picture.

"Which brings me to what I would like to talk to you about. The Wise Men have taken an interest in your future development."

"Really? That's interesting."

Despite herself, she slid to the front of her chair, putting her hands on her knees and leaning forward, her attention levels immediately on high alert.

"There are not that many people in the Family with an MBA from Stanford and a Schapiro's Management Trainee Programme behind them! If you are interested, the Wise Men have asked me to invite you to come to Milan to have a chat."

Natasha had waited a long time for this moment, but was determined to play it cool.

"Well, that's very flattering, but I don't know. What have they got in mind?"

"Frankly, I do not know the details. Before this came up, I was thinking, if you are interested, there must be a role in BetSlick that would suit you. It would be a good thing to have you in the business, somewhere on the accounts side, in case there is any problem with Nick – not that I foresee one, of course. It would extend the current watching brief you have."

Natasha nodded along non-committedly. Working in the engine room of the BetSlick accounting team was something she had no intention of doing. She smiled to herself, at the thought that her father considered that might be the limit of her ambitions.

"The Wise Men were saying the affairs of the Family were getting too big and they were concerned about the control of the business as a whole. They are talking about setting up a 'Family office', to bring all the legitimate businesses, and some of the other activities, under one roof. They agree this is not a job for an outsider. It means working with a senior Family member, who would run the office."

"Now that is something I could do! Wow!"

"Well, yes, it is exciting but …"

"No, Dad, it's exciting, full stop!"

"There are down sides, you know? Once you are in the Family, there is no getting out. You will be privy to all the inner workings so it is a job for life. You will never be totally free again, you realise that? What you do, what you say, how you behave, will all be watched. How you spend your time, who your friends are, who you date and who you marry, how you bring up your children, everything will be scrutinised."

"I'm ready, Dad, I know how it works. I've been ready for some time. This is exciting!"

"OK, OK, calm down, nothing has been decided yet. There is still a long way to go. At some point I will take you up to Milan and you can meet one or two of the senior Family members."

"The Wise Men?"

"I cannot tell you that. Until you get to a certain level, you are not allowed to know who the Wise Men are. It is a bit of a joke, because people soon work it out! So, if you are sure?"

"Sure? of course I am! When can we go?"

"Well, maybe sooner than you think. I am due a trip up in a day or so. It might be a little short notice, but I will see who is available."

Marco looked at his daughter, pleased to see the enormous smile on her face, even though part of him wondered what he might have started.

CHAPTER 19
SERGIO ROSSI

VALLETTA, MALTA

IN VALLETTA, the summer was only just starting to take a grip on the city. The sun was shining and the humidity was rising. The tourists swarmed inside St John's Co-Cathedral, casting their inexpert eyes on the works by Caravaggio, or taking coffee in the narrow streets behind St George's Square, trying to find refuge from the heat.

Under the vast bastions that surround the fortified city lies a labyrinth of old tunnels, originally used to imprison the Turkish slaves whose forced labour had built Valletta in the sixteenth century.

One particular old low tunnel, built through the enormous limestone walls, led to a small garden with spectacular views over the Grand Harbour, where a restaurant had set out a few tables. Those in the know could dine well and in private, their conversations inspired by the magnificent views in front of them. Sergio and Marco had used the restaurant for years and, every once in a while, would meet there to enjoy each other's company and talk business, as old friends and allies.

Marco had reserved the last lunch sitting and told the manager no other late diners were to be admitted. Once they had eaten and the other patrons had left, they ordered one more bottle of Sicilian Grillo and had the large parasol adjusted to protect themselves from the afternoon sunshine.

Sergio had just returned from Istanbul and Madrid, where he was meeting petroleum traders to wholesale the tax-free petrol and diesel they were planning to take delivery of from Libya. In southern Europe, there were still a large number of non-affiliated petrol stations which were free to buy petrol from whoever they chose and the cheaper it was, the more they bought. The major oil companies did not have the same grip on distribution in the south, as they had in northern Europe.

"So, the Turkish brokers, how did that go?"

"Well, they're talking about at least fifty million litres a year."

Marco started tapping the calculator on his phone.

"That is a lot of product."

"Yeah, and that's just to start with!" Sergio confirmed.

"So, with the other territories, over time, this means we could have something like a billion-dollar business, if we can get the supply?"

"Marco, we're only just getting started!"

"Bravo! But we cannot get ahead of ourselves! We have got all the players in place and the infrastructure is there. So, for a turnover of a billion, we are going to need about one hundred and fifty million litres of fuel. That is a lot of hydrocarbons!"

"You know, these big Libyan refineries turn over twenty million litres of fuel a day – they're enormous. It's all down to the deal we do in Libya. There's a limit to the amount of oil your Libyan friend can steal or obtain by blackmail. But it's also possible to buy product under the counter, directly from the Libyan Resources Corporation, at subsidised prices; it's cheaper to buy oil from the LRC than it is to buy bottled water! And if you're not paying the duty, we can undercut anybody in Europe! One tanker isn't going to be anywhere near enough. We'll need more ships."

Marco shook his head, dismissing the suggestion.

"I know, I know. But we have to keep this manageable so we

do not attract too much attention. If we do those sorts of volumes, we will be filling the Grand Harbour with our ships and the game will soon be up. We have to be careful. There is a limit to how much we can channel through the Malta storage facilities. It is not the Persian Gulf, you know!"

"Yeah, yeah, I agree, I suppose. But, listen, this brings me to something else we need to talk about."

Sergio put on his serious face. Marco had seen it many times before.

"What is it, Sergio?"

"I've had a call from one of the Wise Men. They're worried about the Libyan end. I know you've worked hard to organise it, but this deal has got bigger and bigger. The Wise Men are concerned that your Libyan friend won't be able to handle it alone. He's got no experience. He's just a small-time local operator."

Marco leaned back in his chair, gazing upwards. He did not like the sound of what Sergio was saying.

"Look, Marco, there's nothing wrong with the plan but, I gotta agree with them, the Libyan side is a weak link, given what we've got going on. What other connections do we have over there?"

"To be honest, Sergio, I do not know. I will give it some more thought, but the upside of using him is, he is a true independent."

"Well, maybe we can use him for the first few runs and then drop him later, when we've found a stronger partner? It's such chaos on the ground there, it's difficult to know who to partner up with! It could all be different tomorrow."

"Exactly, Sergio. That is my point. Just so you know, I would not be happy about dropping him right now. It is a huge risk to the project. You tell that to the Wise Men."

Marco picked at the last of the dessert and poured another glass of wine. He felt mellow and a little sad that the neat arrangements he had worked so hard on were being dismantled.

It looked like Abdullah would soon be shafted in the interests of the Family's mounting ambitions. Things were changing in the Family's approach to business and, more and more, they seemed to be slipping out of Marco's control.

Sergio spoke again.

"So, apart from that, we're all looking good here in Malta?"

Marco pulled himself together and tried to shake off the effects of a bottle and a half of wine.

"*Si, si.* All looking good. The fuel leaves Libya, we transfer it ship-to-ship on Hurds Bank, off Malta, and the storage here is all booked – actually, over there, you can see it," Marco pointed to a series of storage tanks, nesting at the base of the Grand Harbour. "We also have capacity booked in the Freeport. We will draw up some purchase invoices and I have found an obliging man at the Chamber of Commerce who will give us Certificates of Origin, saying the fuel is Saudi Arabian!

"If we can do that, we can get it into the European supply chain and move it on to Turkey, Spain or wherever. We are all organised, so please remind the Wise Men to think carefully about upsetting the arrangements."

Sergio laughed.

"I'll have a think before I pass that message on!"

"I need to pay and piss."

Marco sighed, then raised himself from the chair and left the garden. Sergio was not a man to waste time, so he quickly grabbed his phone and accessed his contacts list. He picked a number and rang it. The call was answered almost immediately.

"*Ciao*, Danylo, it's Sergio Rossi here. Yes, all well, thank you. Busy. Busy for you too? Good. Listen, I might have some business to discuss. Where're you at the moment? When can we talk? D'you still have your friends in North Africa? Good, good. Send me your best phone number and we'll speak again privately this evening, you understand? Good. OK. *Ciao*."

Danylo Husak was a Ukrainian dealer in ex-military vehicles, arms, munitions and civil defence equipment, who traded across the Middle East and North Africa. Although it was not the Family's normal line of business, they had provided him with capital loans to fund his stock purchases. Some of his customers were the bigger militias in Libya. Sergio was hoping he might have some ideas about how they could buy in extra help.

CHAPTER 20
NATASHA BONNICI
SIGNOR BRUNO'S PALAZZO, BRERA, MILAN

MARCO WAS true to his word and, within two days of their conversation, Natasha found herself in a taxi with her father, threading their way the through the historic old town of Milan, heading to meet Signor Bruno, one of the senior members of the Family.

Natasha had fretted about what to wear for the occasion, her dressing room littered with discarded combinations of suits and blouses. Eventually, she had opted for an austere formal business look, pinning her hair back and choosing a plain white blouse and a fitted grey suit.

Signor Bruno's Palazzo was a small neoclassical masterpiece, built as a Jesuit college in the seventeenth century, with wide galleries around a central courtyard. It was situated just off Via Brera, in the elegant eponymous district, north of the famous Galleria Vittorio Emanuele.

They were met at the gate by Toni, a burly Sicilian, who introduced himself as Signor Bruno's 'driver'. He showed them into a large, book-lined study. As if she could not be any more nervous, Marco stressed Signor Bruno was famous for his razor-sharp mind and had, in his time, been a Deputy Governor of BankItalia – the central bank of Italy.

Signor Bruno must have been in his late seventies and seemed the embodiment of a courtly elderly gentleman. He had an old man's watery blue eyes and heavily veined hands with liver spots. His suits were handmade and classically styled, in heavy cloth from a mill in the Biella region, fifty kilometres to the north. Everything seemed oversized, as if he was gradually shrinking inside his heavy formal clothing. His skinny neck protruded from a stiff, white detachable collar and, like the English Royal family, whom he admired, he favoured the neat-looking 'four-in-hand knot' for his ties. When he spoke, there was a mischievous smile on his face. His speech was slow and deliberate, never wasting a single word.

Marco and he embraced and Natasha accepted Signor Bruno's flaccid, old man's handshake. After some preliminary enquiries about their journey, Signor Bruno turned to Marco and suggested he might like to explore the library, in the *sala nobile*, the grand drawing room on the first floor. Natasha could see her father was a little taken aback but, with a smile, he excused himself, saying he had often wanted the chance to explore what was on the shelves.

Once Marco had left, Signor Bruno's tone changed. He ceased to be someone's favourite uncle and set about dissecting Natasha's curriculum vitae with forensic skill. After an hour, he sat back and called for coffee, his tone reverting to that of the genial elderly gentleman. Natasha was not fooled. She had seen the steel in the man and realised that, despite the change of tone, she was still under the same level of scrutiny.

"Natasha, I must say, I am impressed by your qualifications and your experience. You have achieved a lot for someone so young." He sat back in his chair and paused for a moment. "I knew your mother, you know. You do remind me of her."

Natasha was momentarily stunned. It never occurred to her that he might have known her mother.

"Oh? I was very young when she died."

"Yes, it was tragic. I understand you were on the stairs when it happened?"

He looked at her, his head on one side, studying her reaction closely.

Natasha had no idea what to say in reply, so she remained silent. Signor Bruno continued.

"Sophia was a very strong-willed and highly principled person. She did not always approve of what we in the Family did. I hope you have a more flexible approach to our way of doing business?"

"As I said, the tools and methods I'd use here are the same as those I used at the bank, but I accept the risks we incur might, shall we say, be a little different."

"Indeed. You are aware, if you choose to join us, it is more of a vocation than an employment? You are joining a Family, in every sense of the word. Once you are one of us, you are stuck with us. I must make that absolutely clear. I do not wish to speak out of turn, but your mother did not see the world quite as we do and, had she lived, I think things would have become difficult for your father. Do you understand me?"

"I think so. Sometimes things turn out for the best. I was too young to know my mother, but from what you've said, you'll find I'm a very different person. I can assure you of that."

"This banker in London you grievously injured. How likely is he to regain full control of his faculties?"

For the second time, Natasha was shocked by the bluntness of his questions. Sensing her hesitation, Signor Bruno raised his eyebrows enquiringly.

"Though I did nothing more than defend myself, I don't think he will ever fully recover." She paused. "How d'you know about that?"

"You do not think we take people into our trust without investigating them, do you? If he shows signs of coming round, be sure to let me know. There are things we can do to prevent any future embarrassment.

"So, Natasha, I sense a level of ambition in you that I like. We need trusted people who not only have skill and drive, but also the appetite to push this organisation forward. All around us, there are inefficiencies; in government, markets, regulation and finance. Where there are inefficiencies, there are opportunities. And that is the nature of understanding risk. We will need you to turn from gamekeeper to poacher."

He smiled slightly. Natasha kept a straight face and said calmly, "I can do that."

"And can you work for me?" He paused to let the awkward question hang in the air. "You might do things with your father or your Uncle Sergio, but I want you to work in my interests at all times, no matter what. You take my meaning? You answer to me, no one else. We are all one Family, but I require a loyalty that supercedes everything else. If you can do that, I will ensure your interests are always protected and that your career is a success. None of us do this for money alone. We all have more of that than we could ever need. I think you could achieve a great deal – and I can see how important that is to you."

Natasha realised she had not drawn breath for over a minute and had to recover herself. He had criticised her dead mother, questioned her own presence at the scene of the fatal fall, intimated he knew the truth about what really happened to Charlie Witton and then said he expected her to place her loyalty with him, ahead of her father or Uncle Sergio. And she had said yes!

Over lunch, in what was known as the small dining room, overlooking the gardens to the rear of the *palazzo*, Signor Bruno was more relaxed. He chatted generally with Marco and Natasha and talked about how they would go about bringing together the Family's complex web of companies and trusts, pooling the cash and investments, so they could be handled more efficiently and generate better returns. He explained there were too many companies, in too many jurisdictions, and there was too much money sitting around not working hard enough for them. Their job would be to make sure that was put right. He said he expected Natasha to start thinking about this right away.

Natasha nodded along and made one or two obvious suggestions that seemed to be well received. As they were leaving, Signor Bruno gave her a linen business card with his private mobile number and email address on it. He held out his hand to her, which she accepted. He then grasped it, hard, in a formidable grip, causing her to wince with pain. Drawing her firmly towards him, he whispered in her ear.

"One last thing. I might be getting on in years, but please, do not ever underestimate me."

CHAPTER 21
INSPECTOR GEORGE ZAMMIT

PORT OF VALLETTA, MALTA

SCHEMBRI AND BORG, the two motorcycle officers who had been first on the scene of Denzel's crash, had been off-duty for the two days immediately following the accident and, since their return, George had struggled to catch up with them. He had concluded they were deliberately avoiding him.

Every day since their return, he had put a note in their electronic diaries, saying that he wanted to see them. Every day they seemed to have been called out, first thing, and were unable to make a meeting. George had had enough of their behaviour and was determined to track them down. He reckoned that their first stop in the morning would be for a quick coffee, before heading out into the traffic. There was a small café called Joe's on the waterfront, near where the high-speed catamaran to Sicily berthed. It was a favoured hang out for the traffic police, because of the long stretch of parking that was concealed from view of any passing superior officers.

Sure enough, he was not wrong. There they were, lounging under a large branded umbrella, smoking, stretching their legs across the narrow front pavement of the café. They spotted him, as soon as he got out of the patrol car. George knew Schembri by reputation; an insolent and idle type. He was banking on the fact that he was the one who had given Denzel's satchel to Camilleri, hoping for some future favour or payback.

George took a deep breath and walked towards the men.

"Gentlemen, I'm pleased I finally found you. I wanted to thank you for the work you did, when you found my son on the coast road last week. Assistant Commissioner Camilleri spoke to me and told me you'd been exemplary in performing your duties."

Borg looked at Schembri. Without a trace of irony, Schembri replied: "It was a pleasure to help, Inspector. I wish it'd been in better circumstances. Thankfully, I hear he'll recover. It looked bad when we pulled up, I can tell you!"

"Yes, his mother and I are thanking God every minute for that. *Mela,* I wanted to ask you about something that seemed to go missing from the scene, if you don't mind?"

Borg started to fidget with the spoon on his saucer, while Schembri stroked his short, tufty beard.

"Denzel had a brown leather satchel ... he took it everywhere with him. I've checked the accident logs and went to the scene the morning after the accident, but the satchel seems to have disappeared. Assistant Commissioner Camilleri told me he knew nothing about it, either. I appreciate his concern, but how the Organised Crime Command became involved in all this, I've no idea. Still, I thought I'd check. I don't suppose either of you remember seeing a brown leather satchel at the scene?"

Schembri shook his head, as if deep in thought.

"I've got no memory of any satchel or bag. Have you, Joe?"

Borg studied his boots and likewise shook his head.

"No, I don't remember seeing anything like that."

"OK," George ventured, "so, Assistant Commissioner Camilleri must be right then. There was no such satchel at the scene?"

Schembri shrugged. "It seems so."

George was happy that they had all reached a consensus and it seemed there was no immediate threat to Denzel. Changing tack, he pulled up a plastic moulded chair and sat down, checking to make sure the flimsy legs would take his weight.

"So, tell me, what d'you know about the crash? What do the witness statements say?"

Happier on safer ground, Schembri took the lead.

"Well, he joined the coast road two hundred yards before the crash site, already moving at speed it seems. The driver of a Golf said she saw him appear from nowhere, in her rear-view mirror, and then try to come round her right-hand side.

"Another driver confirmed he shot out onto the dual carriageway from a side road and went straight into the outside lane, hit the kerb and lost it. There was no other vehicle involved. It was all over in seconds. Cars swerved to avoid him and there was a minor collision between two of them, but nothing to worry about. We're looking at a careless driving incident, at worst. But given, nobody but Denzel was hurt, and in the circumstances ..."

Schembri shrugged and rocked his head from side to side, as if weighing up the trouble involved in bringing a prosecution, against the benefit of George owing him a favour.

"Anyway, we were already heading up to St Paul's so we arrived a few minutes after it'd all happened. A motorist had already called an ambulance. We checked his vital signs and made sure there was no airway obstruction, but thought it best to leave him where he was. We could hear the ambulance siren, almost as soon as we got off the bikes, and we don't touch injured victims unless we have to. It could've been a lot worse, believe me; he looked a right mess when we found him."

George nodded.

"Yes, quite right. You both did well." It was Schembri's turn to look at his boots. Borg was too stupid to detect the faint sarcasm in his voice.

"And that's it, Inspector. After the ambulance left, Victor did the accident report, had the bike removed and marked the road – all the usual stuff."

He thought about what he had just been told.

"*Mela*, one thing that puzzles me is where exactly Denzel joined the road? From memory, there's no junction on that stretch north of the roundabout?"

Schembri replied, almost too quickly.

"Well, Victor might've got that wrong. Maybe Denzel was at the road side and accelerated out into the traffic?"

George paused, thinking about the accident site.

"You said the driver of the Golf told you he joined from a side road, 'at speed'?"

"Well, maybe she's wrong about that, too. Maybe he soon picked up speed; those bikes can get from zero to one hundred kilometres per hour in a matter of seconds."

"OK, I can see that. Well, thanks for your time. Enjoy your coffee and thanks again for your help."

George rose, leaving them to it, and walked back to his car. He took a big breath and congratulated himself on how the conversation had gone. He was pleased they had been deferential, to his face at least. Even better, he could go to the hospital and tell Denzel he could relax. Dad had got it all sorted! But, not before he had a serious word about the stupidity of his son's behaviour and how close he had come to doing time in Corradino as a drug dealer, of all things.

George was busy for the rest of the day, so it was not until late afternoon that he had the chance to head north up the coast road to have another look at the site of Denzel's accident. The road opened out into a dual carriageway that twisted and turned, following the rocky bays and inlets of the eastern coastline. It was a favourite road for bikers, one of the few where they could test their machines, leaning into the corners and accelerating down the straights. The withered bunches of flowers tied to the crash barriers on the first long sweeping curve said it all. George passed the floral tributes, making the sign of the cross.

The most recent accident site was marked on the road with yellow spray paint, the road traffic incident number painted alongside it. Malta's roads were a patchwork of yellow squares and numbers, recording where collisions and accidents had taken place. He looped around the roundabouts and covered the stretch of road three times to make sure there was no other way Denzel could have joined the coast road.

The only entrance he could see came from a private villa, concealed from view behind some high metal gates. It joined at a right angle, so it would not even be possible to join 'at speed'. Visibility of oncoming traffic from that point was also poor. Nobody would drive straight out, the way the two traffic cops had described. On the third pass, George pulled into the drive, got out of the patrol car and pushed the intercom button.

After a short wait, it crackled and an Englishman's voice answered.

"Yes?"

"Inspector Zammit, *Pulizija*. A moment of your time, please, sir."

The double white gates started to swing open and George took his car up the drive. The villa was a luxurious residence; all white plaster walls, stainless-steel rails and glass panels. To the side, was an infinity pool, with superb views down the coast, to the towers of St Julian's, the water reflecting the low sunlight of early evening.

George walked up towards the front door. On the deck, a good-looking, dark-haired woman sat at a table, under a neutral-coloured parasol, working on a laptop. She raised her glasses to look at him, but her expression remained fixed.

An Englishman opened the door. He had ruffled blond hair and a cropped pale beard. He was dressed in a blue open-necked shirt and slim-fitting trousers. Despite his relative youth, the man had an assured, condescending air about him that immediately got George's back up.

"Thank you for your time. I've come about a traffic accident last Friday evening, just outside your gates, involving a motor-bike. A young man was badly hurt. Are you aware of it?"

The Englishman stepped back, holding the door open to let George enter the hallway.

"Well, yes. My friend," he gestured down towards the pool, "told me something about it, but it was all over by the time I returned home from work."

"Could I have your name please, sir?"

"Nicholas Walker."

George took out his notebook and made a note of it.

"Thank you. It seems from witnesses that the young man concerned might have left this house before joining the coast road. Could that be correct?"

George watched him register the question, but he seemed unsure how to respond. Interesting.

"I don't think so. What was the man's name?"

He made a show of checking his notebook.

"Denzel Zammit?"

The man blinked, but quickly recovered his composure.

"Denzel Zammit? I think I would have remembered a name like that! If he'd come up to the house, my partner might have dealt with him. Means nothing to me, I'm afraid, Inspector. I'm sorry. Wait a minute, I'll ask Natasha."

George watched him walk down to the deck towards the woman, who looked at him, raising an eyebrow.

Walker spoke to her, too loudly and obviously for George's benefit.

"It's the Police, Natasha. About the road accident last week. Any visitors Friday evening? They seem to think a motorbike may have pulled out from here?"

The woman shook her head and said something to him George did not quite catch. She then turned back to her laptop. George looked at the woman and had the distinct impression he had seen her before. She was striking and not the sort you would easily forget but, at that moment, he just could not place her. He had a good eye when it came to faces. If he thought he knew someone, he usually did. The Englishman returned.

"Sorry, Inspector. We can't help you. We don't know anything about it."

"Could you give me the name of your friend, please?" He held his notebook ready.

"Gimmondi ... Natasha Gimmondi." Natasha had been careful to conceal the Bonnici surname from Nick, a subterfuge that was more complicated to maintain than she had originally supposed. She had to be careful that letters, bills and bank statements in the name of Bonnici were promptly filed away. She had even asked the Family-owned Antayla Bank to set up a new account in the name Gimmondi and issue her with a new set of cards.

George pulled out a card from his wallet and dropped it on the glass console table. Walker was looking uncomfortable by now. George knew what Denzel was pedalling and these two definitely looked like potential customers to him.

"Memories are tricky things – they come and go," he commented. "Someone nearly died in that accident. Remember, all I want is to work out what happened to that biker. I've no interest in what he was doing here."

The Englishman did not make a move. He did not protest or concede any ground. George's suspicions were confirmed and he knew he had scored a point.

He drove home, mulling over his visit to the villa. There was something about the girl on the deck. He definitely knew her from somewhere, but could not quite put his finger on it. His thoughts were abruptly interrupted by his mobile ringing.

"George, it's Joe Mifsud here, Valletta Harbourmaster. You OK to speak?"

"Yes, Joe, I'm in the car alone, it's fine."

He was surprised to be getting a call from Mifsud who had not seemed like the helpful or communicative type. George thought perhaps he was feeling guilty about the *'Pastizz'* gibe he'd made when they last met. Maybe he regretted it now.

"You were asking about the *Malik Albahr*? I don't know

whether it's still of interest, but a colleague of mine heard a bit of gossip that might be of use to you."

"I'm interested in anything you've got. *Mela,* tell me."

"We get on with the navy down here and they often get intelligence from US sources. You know, satellite stuff? Well, it might well be nothing, but we put the *Malik Albahr* on the navy watch list. We recorded the destination the *Malik Albahr* gave us from the departure records as Annaba, Algeria but, according to our American friends, she didn't go there at all; she made a course to Marsabar, in Libya. I mean, you might just say 'So what?' but I thought I'd pass it on."

"Interesting. Marsabar. Refugees and oil, or something"

"Yes, that's it. I've let Naval Intelligence know you want to question the captain about the Grand Harbour body, so if it pops up again, we should get word."

"Thanks, Joe, that's great. Thanks for letting me know."

George rang off and pressed on home. The information was interesting, but he was not sure whether it was of any use. There was not much they could do if the ship had ended up in Libya. Anyway, it was well past dinner time, if Marianna had even bothered to prepare anything before her visit to the hospital. These days, he never knew when he would eat and when he would not. He thought that was exactly how a man could end up with a stomach ulcer!

CHAPTER 22
NICK WALKER
VILLA BIANCA, MALTA

NATASHA JOINED Nick at the top of the stairs to the house, watching the inspector take his car to the end of the drive and pause; no doubt assessing the layout of the villa against what they had said in their conversation.

She was furious. She had only just returned from Milan and was determined nothing was going to interfere with her opportunity to work with Signor Bruno.

"The policeman knows that dickhead was here, Nick. How stupid can you be, inviting a drug dealer into your home? In fact, how stupid can you be buying coke from the street in the first place? Look what you've done – you've brought the police into our lives!"

Natasha picked up the inspector's card and read it, throwing it back onto the console table.

"For God's sake, Nick! You're such an idiot!"

"How d'you know who he was and what he was doing here?"

"D'you think I'm stupid? Your lapdog turned up, like he does every Friday, so I spoke to him and scared him shitless. He spilled the beans. He must've sped out of here, pissing himself, and crashed his bloody bike. That's not the point though, is it?

"That guy's an inspector in the *Pulizija*. He's not some stupid constable – and he knows you were buying drugs. He's not here about some bloody bike crash; he's interested in something else and, at the moment, that's you and me. This is so fucked up! Christ! I have to do something about it."

Nick was shocked. He had never seen Natasha so agitated before. She started walking up and down the hall, chewing the end of the pen she had been using. He slumped against the wall, trying to work out why she had flown off the handle like that. He just did not get why she was so wound up by the policeman's visit. He knew nothing about the Milan visit and could not understand the overreaction.

Natasha took hold of his shirt and yanked him towards her.

"I've got to go now, Nick. I can't cover this up for you. You know I've got to tell Marco and it'll be up to him what happens next. You've messed up and you've let him down. I can't believe you've been so stupid!"

Her display of anger and aggression scared him. She paced the floor again, fists balled by her sides.

"Marco? What's Marco got to do with it? I don't understand what I've done that's so bad?" he protested. "I bought a bit of blow from a local – what's the big deal? And now what? You're going to run off to Marco and grass me up, are you? I get it, I always thought you were his snitch."

"You brought that local dealer here, to us, to *me*, you dick-head. I've got a position to protect too, you know. I'm not some bloody little servant girl who's good for a shag now and then! I've got plans and I'm damned if I'm going to let you spoil them.

"Marco needs to keep noise to a minimum at the moment. You don't know the details, but there's a big oil deal coming off and he doesn't need you stirring up trouble. Don't you get it? What if those dealers talk to the *Pulizija* and give up your name? Why d'you think Marco wants you to keep a low profile? Why?"

He had had enough of her ranting.

"Oh, fuck Marco, it's no big deal!"

Natasha's eyes blazed and she was nearly shaking, she was so angry. Her tone was deathly cold: "Sorry, Nick, it *is* a big deal. And don't you ever disrespect my father again."

He felt the shock of her admission hit him like a punch to the gut.

"Your father? What the … Marco's your father? You never told me that! Why on earth …?"

He stood there, stunned, trying to process what he had just heard. She looked at him with a defiant, intense glare.

"Really? You never guessed? It never occurred to you to wonder what I was doing here, sticking so close to you? Well, at least I know more about you now. A coke-head and a liar. Are you really the person who should be trusted to run BetSlick? I wonder what they'll say when they hear what I've got to tell them! How long d'you think it'll last, Nick? The way I see it, it could all be over for you!"

She had never raised her voice to him before, but there was something else about her that scared him; a smile around the edges of her mouth. It was almost a look of satisfaction at the way she was playing the situation. Right at that moment, Nick had no idea who she was.

He fell back onto a chair in the hallway.

"I can't believe you never told me. You've lied to me right from the get go. All this time, you've been reporting straight back to Daddy. Did he put you up to it? All those nights we had … the sex … what? You were just doing your job?"

He looked at her in disbelief. It was his turn to get angry, now.

"What the hell are you? Some sort of high-class whore?"

She stood still for a moment, looking at him scornfully.

"I'm going, Nick," she said finally. "Right now, I need to speak to my father."

"Natasha, wait! Can't we sort this out between ourselves? Surely we can work something out? This has all got way out of hand, don't you think?"

Without a word or a backward glance, she picked up her bag and went out to her car, leaving him sat there, dumbstruck, in the elegantly lit hallway. Natasha waited until her car had joined the coast road before she allowed herself a small, self-satisfied smile.

CHAPTER 23
ABDULLAH BELKACEM

NAFUSA HILLS, LIBYA

TAREQ HAD CAUGHT Samir just in time. He was at the family house, about to make a run for it. His mother had packed a bag for him and his father was preparing the truck, so he could leave the village by sunrise. He had made his choice. He could not stay with Abdullah, after what had happened. He had only recently arrived from Tripoli and had no intention of taking a lifetime's responsibility for Mahmoud's mother. Samir thought he could do better for himself back in Tripoli. There were plenty of militias he could sell himself to.

When Tareq found him, he had two of his men beat him with rifle butts and twisted electrical cable. Samir's father had rushed to intervene, but a solid strike from a rifle butt put him to the floor. After they were finished, Samir could barely see through one eye and nursed bruised, if not broken, ribs. Tareq had also smashed the rifle into Samir's left knee, resulting in a limp, that would be with him for many months. Tareq knew Samir would hate them from that moment on; a deep hatred, one that would smoulder in his bruised and battered body for a long time.

Abdullah stood with his brother on the roof of the house, looking out into the grey light of early morning.

"So, you taught the snake a lesson?"

"Yes, brother. Word will get around today about what happens to people who break our trust. His mother will weep her way around the kitchens, looking for sympathy. No one will give it. He should be gone by now. But we'd better watch our backs for a while. There was a look in his eye ..."

"He is no loss to me. Anyway, today we will check out the ship and then we have to drive to meet the Beards. It will take several hours to get to Al Jawsh, where we meet the guide. He will take us into the hills to meet Abu Muhammed."

The Nafusa Hills were the traditional lands of the Berber people. Abdullah always enjoyed his trips out there. His family used to live in one of the villages, deep in the ravines cut into the hillside. He often visited the hills, taking his family to attend weddings and other gatherings. Rania's family still lived in the area, raising goats, growing olives, grains, figs and apricots. It was a good and simple life and people there were rarely troubled by the chaos on the coast. The hills rose, fifty kilometres south of Tripoli and extended westwards, all the way to Tunisia. Travel was difficult and in winter there could even be snow on the highest points.

The tyrant Gaddafi had banned the name Nafusa, as it was a Berber word. He had renamed the hills the Western Mountains. Since his death, ISIL forward camps had appeared, taking advantage of the deep valleys and the high escarpment. The ISIL leaders often had the cheek to come into the towns and villages, even being seen on the streets of Tripoli or eating in cafés in Marsabar. They based their larger forces in the deep south of the country, in the Murzuk Basin, south of the Sharara oilfield.

From there, they could exploit the various oil-drilling sites that tooled the crude out of the ground. They would blow up facilities, raid the wells, kill or scare away the security, threatening or kidnapping workers. Their violence would shut down the wells, in the knowledge the oil companies would pay bribes and ransoms to get the black gold flowing again.

Tareq lit a cigarette and looked out over the rock-strewn brush that ran from the house down to the coast.

"I don't like it, Abdullah. I don't like the Beards. I don't trust them. And I especially don't like Abu Muhammed or the rest of the ISIL scum! I know they don't like us, either!"

"We have to bring them in, Tareq. They are ignorant people who have no honour and little courage but, if they are not with us, we cannot get or move the oil we need. We need their protection on the roads from the refineries near Tripoli. From the Marsabar refinery to the port is easy. But even then, Abu Muhammed has connections, protecting the pipelines coming into it from the Sharara and Wara fields. If we do not bring them in to the deal now, they will force themselves into it later on."

"I don't see why them. They're the worst of the worst. Why not talk to Libya Dawn in Tripoli? Ansa al Derna is a reasonable man; he's not a bandit. Al Derna wants a free Islamic Libya, not the Beards' Caliphate. He's a politician, but he's got men and he's powerful. Surely, they're better to deal with. They just want money. These ISIL preachers and Mullahs, they think differently to us."

"Tareq, we go to see Abu Muhammed exactly because he is the worst of the worst. If we bring him in, the others will not dare touch us. If he is killed, Allah willing, then we can deal with someone else. Until then, he and his army of foreigners are our friends. Anyway, with our new Italian connections, we can get Abu Muhammed what he wants most of all."

"Weapons?" Tareq asked.

Abdullah smiled.

"Not just weapons. The Italians give us access to Europe. We can sell petroleum, diesel and fuel oil there, but the money goes into European bank accounts in euros and dollars. All the Beards can do is blackmail the producers for soft money."

Tareq looked at him, raising an eyebrow.

"Leave the thinking to me, brother, eh?" He grabbed Tareq's arm. "So, how many trucks and men do we take?"

"We have eight trucks and about forty men. After Al Jawsh, we'll leave the main road and hit the tracks. There, we can put two flags on each truck; the green flag of Islam and the white flag of peace. I don't expect trouble; Abu Muhammed will be too interested in the deal we have for him."

"I think we should take two trucks with ten men," Abdullah replied. "Enough to handle any trouble on the road. We do not want to arrive looking like an army. All will be well today and let tomorrow look after itself. Just fly the green flag on the lead truck. We are not surrendering anything. In fact, take the Land Cruiser and put some of the men in it. You and I will ride in front of it, in the old red truck."

Tareq nodded. He understood the thinking. The new expensive Land Cruiser would be the obvious target for the first RPG or drone strike, should there be one. It would at least give him and Abdullah, riding ahead, a chance to evade a second strike or bail out of the vehicle.

Three hours later, the small dusty convoy bumped up a steep mountain track, dodging the bigger boulders strewn along the way. The rocks were dry and loose. There was little foliage and no cover from anyone watching on the steep cliffs either side of it. The green flag on the Land Cruiser fluttered and the high suspension ensured a smooth ride for those inside. The aircon was on full power and the temperature was positively icy.

In the red Mitsubishi, the windows were down, to coax some air into the stuffy cabin, and the rock-hard suspension jolted their very bones. Tareq looked at Abdullah as the movement of the truck repeatedly banged his head against the side of the door frame.

"Next time, I'll ride in the Land Cruiser and accept Allah's will, whatever it may be!"

"Watch out, brother! They are coming now!"

Behind them, they saw three rusty, battered Toyota pickups, with large-calibre machine guns mounted on the rear decks. The so-called 'technicals', laced with red sandstone dust, drove up from a side track and pulled out in front of the Land Cruiser. A squad of men jumped out of the trucks and fell to the ground, weapons trained on the vehicle.

The red Mitsubishi truck stopped about twenty metres further up the track. Abdullah grabbed the CB radio and spoke to the Land Cruiser.

"Everybody sit still, hands in sight. It is their move."

Other men took positions behind the cover of some rocks on the road side and Abdullah saw the bulbous ends of the RPGs pointing at them.

"Looks like we are close, Tareq," Abdullah said, with a smile.

A man got out of one of the trucks and pointed towards them in the Mitsubishi. One of the jihadis, who was wearing a flat Afghan-style *pakul* cap and a long woven waistcoat over khaki fatigues, started walking towards them, his Kalashnikov hanging at his side.

Abdullah opened the door and he immediately raised his weapon.

Abdullah lifted his arms to show he was unarmed and shouted out to all the men surrounding the vehicles: "May peace be upon you."

"And may peace be upon you, too," the Afghan replied.

He looked inside the Mitsubishi and addressed the driver, gesturing with his weapon.

"You, in the back!"

The Afghan then slid into the driver's seat, started the engine and pulled out, leading the Land Cruiser. The convoy moved off and they drove for another fifteen minutes, over rocky, unchartered terrain. They crossed a drystone riverbed at walking pace and then bumped up a tight ravine until they eventually arrived at a large, flat, open space, surrounded by cliffs on three sides. Massive sheets of camouflage netting formed a dappled canopy, strung across the ravine sides, many metres above them. A lattice of cables, screwed into the rock, secured the arrangement. This afforded the double benefits of concealment and shade.

Looking around, Abdullah guessed there were at least a hundred men operating out of the base. The ground was strewn with plastic bottles, cigarette cartons and other litter. Under the netting, there were a dozen Portacabins, all hooked up to power supplied by a diesel-powered generator, which chugged away in the background. A fleet of 'technicals' and trucks were lined up at the edge of the compound, some with machine guns mounted on their flatbeds. Many carried the large black flags of ISIL.

The guide led them to a Portacabin at the rear of the compound, where an air-conditioning unit strained and rattled. Inside there were several greasy, stained sofas and a cheap Formica-topped table with a kettle, some metal tea pots and a stack of glasses on top of it. A green glass shisha pipe sat in the corner. The surface of the table was thick with spilt sugar, in which ants scurried back and forth. Worse than that, were the oily remnants of a previous meal lingered on a pile of plastic plates, piled in a small plastic bowl.

Four middle-aged men were lounging on the sofas. Two wore military style uniforms in desert camouflage colours and, to Abdullah's surprise, they sported clean and fashionable Nike trainers. The older ones wore the more traditional black, loose-fitting cotton pants and black T-shirts, under long waistcoats. None of them spoke as Tareq and Abdullah entered. The room stank of sweat, stale spicy food and cigarettes.

Abdullah had never met Abu Muhammed, nor had he ever seen a photograph of him. He repeated the welcome phrase: "May peace be with you."

The greeting was met with a sullen silence. The men all stared back at him.

Tareq bristled, but Abdullah soon realised none of these men were Abu Muhammed.

He was proved right when a small bespectacled man bustled in, smiling and repeatedly bowing his head. Abu Muhammed was bald, with a large shiny forehead, emerging beneath a black turban that covered the rest of his head. His long, grey beard reached halfway down his chest, the left corner of it yellowed by intensive cigarette smoking.

"Salaam, Salaam!" he said, raising his arm across his chest.

"Not too bad a journey, I hope? The road is hard and uncomfortable – especially when you ride in the cart, not the carriage." Abu Muhammed grinned at his own joke. "We live safely here. So, a little hardship on the journey is not too much to bear. Please, let us have a prayer, that we might understand each other and work together in peace."

The little man impressed Abdullah. He was hopeful the meeting would go well.

Abu Muhammed was the notional leader of the western part of the ISIL caliphate in North Africa, called Wilayah al-Tarabulus. When the ISIL barbarians in Iraq had accepted pledges of loyalty from the warring Libyan Islamist factions, they had split Libya into three provinces. They all knew the war in Syria had exhausted their funds. After Assad's victory and the destruction of the strongholds in Iraq, the Libyan groups had to find their own money for food and weapons. Their aim was to link up with other ISIL units who wanted to create an Islamic State, stretching through Egypt, up into the Middle East and, then, Syria and Iraq. It was why Abdullah was sitting talking to Abu Muhammed who needed money for food, wages and guns, just like any other militia leader.

Abu Muhammed told him how his men were now being hindered by militia groups from the east who were not true believers, more interested in looting the government wealth and taking control of the oil. He said Boutros's eastern-based militias, with Russian, UAE, Egyptian and Saudi backing, were getting stronger and the fighting would soon be with Abdullah, in Marsabar. Abdullah hoped they would all kill each other someday in one enormous battle and leave them alone, but he knew that was not the way of things.

There was confusion everywhere and he cared neither for one side, nor the other. He wanted to be left in peace, in his home, to raise his family, protect his clan and grow old without fear. He was certain the time would come when he would have to turn against the mild-mannered Abu Muhammed, because he would never live in an ISIL caliphate with those people. Abu Muhammed had not realised it yet, but neither would any other Libyan militia leader. It all made Abdullah's head spin.

Since they did not wish to discuss their differences, the conversation quickly turned to business. Abu Muhammed did much of the talking, while the others in the room looked on, smoking. Abdullah knew they were listening, despite their studied indifference and, although they said little, they were Abu Muhammed's council and nothing could happen without their agreement.

One of them spoke to tell him what barrelage each refinery could produce; how much oil they could extort for free and what price they could expect to pay for the rest. A tall man, in the standard loose, black cotton clothing and a soiled fleece jacket, explained the pricing of the different grades of marine fuel, oil, petroleum, diesel, aviation fuel and how the protection racket in the southern desert worked.

Abu Muhammed opened the trading by asking for half of all the money they expected to receive for the oil. Abdullah had to explain that there were expenses for the storage and for the shipping. Abu Muhammed countered, telling Abdullah he had expenses too: guns, men's mouths to feed, bribes. They talked and argued and drank tea for four hours. At one point, Abdullah stood up, as if to walk away from the negotiations. Abu Muhammed was quick to concede, making him sit down, and the discussion continued. They were an Arab and a Berber, doing the ancient dance of buying and selling.

After several hours of hard talking, they agreed a complicated payment structure. One of the men in army fatigues produced a laptop and hastily wrote out the pricing principles in a Heads of Terms agreement, to avoid later arguments.

Abdullah agreed to pay the money in US dollars and provide

access to a European banking service, which Abu Muhammed desperately needed. He offered it confidently, while hoping his Italian partners could arrange it. Abu Muhammed pushed him on how his distribution of refined products would work, but Abdullah did not tell him who his contacts were or where in Europe they were planning to sell the product. He was not stupid.

"Your job, my friend, is to help me get the oil to the port of Marsabar and to the ships; mine is to get it to Malta and into the hands of the Italians. After that, we have no interest in what happens, as long as they pay us what is due. It is better this way."

Abu Muhammed promised the wells and pipelines in the Sharara and Wara fields would have his protection and guaranteed he would deliver the agreed volumes. The crude could flow to the refineries in Marsabar, which they could operate as they had done in the Gaddafi days. Abu Muhammed would help defend them against interference from any other militia or government troops. He would tell the refineries they would only enjoy his protection for as long as they provided an agreed amount of free product and sold the remainder at a discount to that set by the Libyan Resources Corporation, the government agency responsible for all legal sales of Libyan oil.

They then discussed the importance of keeping the other rival militias at bay, either through cutting them into the arrangements or through the use of their combined forces. Abu Muhammed probed Abdullah on the strength of his forces, reminding him that many men and much hardware was needed to fight the stronger militias of Tripoli and Boutros. Abdullah did not dare reveal how small his group was or how few weapons he had, compared to other more aggressive militias. He would never fight beyond Marsabar, but he promised they would prove to be a small and deadly opponent, if attacked in their own area. Libya was not a gentle land.

Once the deal was done, they shook hands, drank a final cup

of tea and returned to the vehicles. They bumped down the road to the highway, with three ISIL jeeps accompanying them for protection. This time, Tareq made sure they rode in the Land Cruiser. Abdullah was satisfied with the day's work. It was a step up. He was on his way to becoming someone!

When they reached the highway, the jeeps pulled back and Abdullah told the driver to go faster. He wanted to place a call to Malta and tell them the good news. The shipments would begin in a matter of days, so they had better be ready.

CHAPTER 24
ABU MUHAMMED

ISIL CAMP, NAFUSA MOUNTAINS, LIBYA

As the Land Cruiser and Mitsubishi pulled away, the tall man in the black cotton trousers and long grey waistcoat, who had sat silent in the corner, rose and stretched his long frame. He said nothing, tugged at his hennaed beard and went to the kettle to fill the teapot. The others sat watching in a respectful silence. He turned to the smaller, bespectacled man who had led the negotiations with Abdullah.

"You did well, Faysal. I could not have got a better deal, had I spoken with the godless Marsabar scum myself."

"Thank you, Abu Muhammed. So, will we trade with them?"

"Well, maybe, but not for long. I sat and I listened and I wondered: why we need them at all? They have connections in Europe and can move money, sure. This cannot be so hard to do. Our brothers in Iraq can help us. We do the real work: getting the oil, fighting the security, spilling blood. It is our job to get the oil to Marsabar, while their ship is just sitting there. We could just take it, no?"

The group all looked at each other and assessed Abu Muhammed's mood. They remained silent.

Abu Muhammed turned to Faysal Habib.

"Find out who they are working with. I will speak with the

brothers in Iraq. You speak to the bankers in Cairo and see if they know who might be helping them; how it might work. There must be a person in Malta who is a part of it, some Italian or, maybe, a Russian. I do not know. Ask the questions and see what comes back.

"When we are ready, we will make the Maltese and their money men realise their Marsabar friends are insignificant people. Once we find the right ears to whisper into, we tell them this will never happen, unless it is with us. You know, after losing the Syrian oil fields, money is short for us all. I am not letting those dogs get rich, when we have Allah's work to do."

CHAPTER 25
MARCO BONNICI
CASTELLO BONNICI, MALTA

MARCO DID NOT LIKE SURPRISES, so when Natasha arrived unexpectedly that evening, he immediately sensed there was a problem. He was even more concerned, once she told him what it was. It had all seemed to be working so smoothly, yet somehow it had suddenly fallen apart. Natasha had escalated the whole thing and blown her position with Nick, a situation in which they had invested so much. He knew immediately Nick would now feel alarmed and betrayed by everybody.

On top of that, he had assured Signor Bruno that she was ready to step into the Family's business and something like this would inevitably come to his attention, reflecting badly on both of them.

"Natasha, listen to me, weigh up the odds here, please. The police involvement is not such a big deal – trust me, we can handle that.

"Nick is not the first employee to develop a liking for cocaine. Sergio's uncle was a raging alcoholic, but ran the Family for twenty years, drunk most of the time! Yes, we need Nick to stop but, if the drugs do not affect his performance at work, or his wider reputation, then I could have let it go with a warning. But I am sorry that he knows about our connection. I am surprised you felt that was the right thing to tell him."

Natasha cast her eyes down, as he continued speaking.

"I agree Nick's involvement with this gang of locals is a problem. Do you have any idea how he came to be dealing with them?"

"They're just local. Strictly small time. I got the names from their runner."

"Well, I suppose it is one for Camilleri to look into."

Natasha paused and looked out of the window for a few moments. The sun was setting over the hills, the long shadows painting blackened patches over the buff and khaki fields. She turned back to him.

"Why always Camilleri? I don't like him; he gives me the creeps."

"Because he is good and he gets things done! Listen, you have to keep your head and stay calm. Let me handle this. You do not want Signor Bruno regretting his decision."

Marco looked at his daughter, trying to read her. As usual, he could never tell what was really going through her head. She looked tearful and upset, but he was struggling to decide whether it was genuine or not. All too often, he had seen events in which she was involved, escalate rapidly into serious conflict, and old worries he had about her made him uneasy about this new situation with Nick.

"Look, go back to the villa and at least calm things down. He will be in a panic and that is never good. We have to take a little time and work out a sensible plan, OK? Come on, you have done so well this past year. Can we not try to get over this and put things in perspective?"

"He called me a whore!" Natasha looked at him, her face pained.

"Why? Have you slept with him?"

"No, of course not!" she lied. "He annoyed and disrespected me, that's all. I won't go back, Dad. I can't go on with it. It was only supposed to be for a few months. Anyway, I'm tired of it now, all the lies and the endless charade. It's been thirteen months. It's not the life I want.

"I threatened the courier and he went and nearly got himself killed. It wasn't my fault, but it upset me. I can't concentrate on the other work you and Signor Bruno want me to do if I'm stuck at the villa and, in fairness, that's far more important than nurse-maiding Nick."

"Watching Nick is still important and you have a big opportunity doing the private office work for Milan. Mark my words – that will not have been decided without a lot of thought."

"I want to be someone in the Family, Dad – not just a babysitter or a company secretary filing papers and writing minutes. What Signor Bruno offered me is a start, and I am grateful for it, but I'm not stopping there. I've got way more ability than that and I want to be successful in my own right. Surely you can understand that? I want to build a future for myself and I'm not going to let Nick screw it up for me, just as I'm getting started."

Marco paused, letting her statement sink in.

"Well, that is a new and interesting perspective! Listen, sweetheart, you have to be careful; you are not on some graduate entry scheme anymore, you know. Things in the Family do not just happen because you want them to. Anyway, now is not the time for this discussion.

"But I agree, you have done what we asked you to. We will sort this out with him soon. But for tonight, you need to go back to your apartment and pretend you were just cross with him. We cannot have him doing anything rash. Just calm him down. To be honest, I am surprised you have let him get under your skin like this."

Natasha watched her father carefully for a hint of his reaction to the disclosure of her ambitions within the Family. She was pleased he had not laughed or dismissed the idea out of hand.

"OK, I'll go back, but just for tonight. I'll smooth it over tomorrow, but then I'm coming back here, until I decide what to do next. I'm going to take the Range Rover; the Audi is too low and the oncoming lights dazzle me at night. That OK?"

Marco put his hands to her cheeks and kissed her forehead

"*Brava*. We will talk again tomorrow."

Marco saw tears well up in her eyes, but she turned away to hide them from him. How he wished she did not look so much like her mother.

CHAPTER 26
INSPECTOR GEORGE ZAMMIT

MATER DEI HOSPITAL, MALTA

The Zammits were told Denzel only needed a few weeks of hospital care and recuperation to make a full recovery. Marianna fussed and cooked, spending every spare hour travelling up and down the road to Mater Dei. Her prayers became intense and emotional. There was also no end to the number of times she could tell the story, be it on the phone to distant cousins, visiting neighbours or even while accosting people she met queueing for the bus.

The morning after his conversation with the traffic cops, George called at the hospital on his way to the station to catch his son before Marianna arrived for her daily vigil. Denzel was awake and reading magazines, while listening to something on his headphones.

"Hi, how's it going? Pain better?"

Denzel eased himself up into a sitting position, the movement obviously causing him discomfort.

"No, it still hurts like hell and I hate it in here. The noise – all bloody night! It never stops."

George looked around him to make sure they could not be overheard.

"Listen to me. I'll make this quick, because your mother will be on her way. This could all be far worse; you could've been looking at five years in Corradino! So, don't complain to me about it being bad in here."

"I know, Dad, I'm really sorry. I was stupid. What's going to happen to me? I've been really worried."

"The bag has 'disappeared', so you don't need to worry about that."

"How? What about the stuff and the cash?"

"Money? How much?"

"About a grand."

That was news. Schembri and Borg must have forgotten to mention the cash to Camilleri.

"Whatever. It's all gone! You should be grateful there's not going to be any more police involvement – I've fixed that."

Denzel's head lolled to one side of the pillow. He shut his eyes and sighed deeply.

"I don't know how to thank you."

"So, these friends of yours, have you seen them recently? Have they been in?

"Yes, but Mum gave them biscuits and talked at them non-stop for twenty minutes, so they left."

"*Mela,* next time they show, tell Mum you want a drink from the café. Then tell them I was given the bag by friends of mine in the force, with your things, after the crash and I'm keeping it in the evidence room at the station. Tell them they're safe with me, but you're to be left out of it. Say the cash has gone to the Police Charitable Fund and if there's any trouble, and I mean any trouble at all, I'll make sure the police magically discover it ... in their car, at their house, at their parents' house. Make sure they understand that! I want them to know I'm serious and your association with them is over, Denzel."

"I get it. Thanks. I will, I'll tell them. I'll make sure they understand."

As George was leaving Mater Dei, walking through the car

park, a shadow passed in front of him and he felt a presence at his shoulder. He glanced around; it was Camilleri.

"George, what a nice surprise. Our paths certainly do keep crossing."

"Assistant Commissioner, always a pleasure to see you. All well, I trust?"

George was not at all surprised to see his superior; he had been expecting this approach with a mix of fear and foreboding. He knew there would be a price for the disappearing satchel, but he had not expected to have to pay it so soon.

"All is well, George, thank you. I was hoping to bump into you. I need a private word. Superintendent Farrugia and I were just talking about you today. I told Mario how highly I thought of you and that we should look for opportunities to develop your skills and experience."

Camilleri made his usual attempt at a smile – screwed up eyes and lips awkwardly stretched. George supposed it was as close as he could get to a benign expression. He listened without comment. He knew his boss had very little interest in developing a lowly inspector's *skills and experience*, and wholeheartedly believed that George's rank, as a 'use it or lose it' appointment, exceeded his abilities. It was something he had made clear to George on more than one occasion. So he braced himself for what was coming next.

"Have you heard of the International Organisation for Managing Migration?" Camilleri was holding his hands together in front of him like a priest. George could sense the supercilious smirk on his face, even though he was looking away. Camilleri did not wait for him to answer.

"It is UN-backed and a worthwhile enterprise. Very worthwhile indeed. They are organising a conference about how concerned agencies can work together more effectively: forming links, joined up thinking, inter-agency cooperation ... you know the score. Apparently, they would like a representative from the Maltese Police to attend. Well, I immediately thought of you! You are in the Immigration Department, so I did not hesitate to suggest it to Mario. It is a perfect opportunity for you. And do you know what? I think he is coming around to the idea.

"This could be a real feather in your cap, George. Useful to have a little upside in your career."

George said nothing, but alarm bells began ringing loud and clear.

"It will only be for a couple of days, so you can treat it as a little holiday. I might even suggest you take a day or two of leave afterwards, to do a bit of sightseeing. "

George racked his brain to try and guess what was happening. He knew he was being stitched up for something and there was nothing he could do about it. He had no choice but to play along and wait for the sting. He started to feel a chill creep over him.

"Well, that sounds interesting. Where's this conference going to be?" he asked.

"It is in Tripoli, Libya." Camilleri was no longer smiling; his expression had turned serious.

George's head whipped round to face him; his mouth fell open.

"Please do not gawp at me, George." Camilleri shrugged. "You know very well that is where the trouble is and where the migrants gather. The talks would hardly be in Portofino, would they? There are plenty of nice hotels there. Take a direct flight, spend a day or so at the conference, enjoy yourself. Who knows? You might even learn something! Then, I have a little private job that requires some sensitive handling. Might take another couple of days, but I will tell you about that later."

"What little job?" Here came the sting.

"As I said, I will tell you about it later. It is nothing much. You do not need to worry about it or mention it to anyone – not even to your lovely wife."

George pointedly raised his eyebrows to make sure Camilleri

saw his objection to this sarcasm. Camilleri carried on, oblivious to his reaction.

"Mario will send you the conference details and get someone to organise your travel. We would not want you getting lost, would we? Factor in two extra days after the close of the conference, when you book the flight. Despite everything, I hear Libya has a lot to offer the adventurous traveller."

The instruction was unambiguous. George had never been an adventurous traveller, preferring home comforts and familiar food. Apart from a few shopping trips to Sicily, on the high-speed catamaran, to the retail parks of Catania, he had never left the island. Libya! It was a war-torn country, where gun-toting militias kidnapped people at will and the rule of law was non-existent.

Camilleri turned around to walk back across the car park. "By the way, how is Denzel doing? Making a full recovery, I hope? He is a lucky boy to have a father like you – so far, that is!"

With that, he walked off and left George standing in the car park, slightly weak-kneed. What *private business* did Camilleri want him to take care of in Libya? As he walked away, George gathered himself and found that, much to his surprise, the prospect of Camilleri's offer, no, Camilleri's demand, started to grow on him. In truth, the last couple of weeks had been very stressful and the idea of a few days away, lounging in a five-star hotel, eating good food and watching TV, seemed quite appealing. He did not even have to leave the hotel if he did not want to. He could pop out to run Camilleri's errand and it should all be fine.

Hell, he might even enjoy it, and Marianna could not possibly object to such an important business trip. He had been chosen to represent the Maltese Police at an international conference. What an honour! In that moment, George thought things had started to turn a corner and perhaps it would all work out alright in the end.

His good mood continued when he returned to the hospital

that evening and found Denzel in good spirits, talking to Marianna and Gina.

His wife was chatty and excitable.

"George, come in. Look, we're all together, the four of us – must be the first time in weeks! This is nice! Denzel's friends have just left – here's your Coke, Denzel."

George looked over at his son, who smiled back at him and gave him a wink.

CHAPTER 27
NATASHA BONNICI

TONY'S BAR, ST PAUL'S BAY, MALTA

NATASHA DROVE down to the resort of St Paul's and pulled off the promenade road, past the Aquarium. A rough track led down to the waterside, ending at some cheap-looking beach-side bars and a row of lock up boathouses. Seasonal tourist cafés sprang up there, as soon as the spring sunshine appeared, selling drinks and snacks. The coastline in that area was unattractive, low-lying rock and the resort tried to make the best of the poor hand that nature had dealt it. Small patches of beach nestled in little rocky inlets and steel ladders gave access from the rocks to the warm blue waters of the Mediterranean.

It was early evening when she arrived. She parked up and walked to a bar that was little more than a chromium-plated caravan, surrounded by decking, littered with branded umbrellas and white plastic tables and chairs. A few tourists sat staring out into the darkness of the ocean that grumbled up against the jagged limestone. There, at a table on the edge of the decking, hair slicked down, in some pale blue trousers, new white trainers and a brown nylon shirt, was her date.

Natasha noticed his appearance and swore to herself. The dickhead had actually got dressed up for the occasion!

The man sensed her arrival and swivelled in his chair to give her a full toothless grin.

"Hey, pretty lady! You're very late. I was thinking you not coming."

Natasha smiled and sat down. She looked at him, as he ran his eyes over her body.

"You're looking very smart tonight. Well? For God's sake! Doesn't a gentleman offer to buy a lady a drink in Albania?"

Elbasan leaned forward.

"I buy you a drink, but you not a lady. You have the money?"

He made to stand up to go to the bar.

"Oh, sit down, Elbasan. The last thing I want to do is drink with you. Let's do the business and then I can tell you to fuck off. Nice shirt, by the way. Yes, I've got the money; have you got the paperwork?"

Elbasan pushed a white A4 envelope across the table and sat back, arms folded. Natasha reached across, opened the envelope and scrutinised the forms and statements, front and back.

He looked offended.

"All genuine. Account is active and money is there. This is what we do. Check on phone."

He pushed a smartphone towards her.

Natasha took his greasy handset and found the Bank of Malta app on the cracked screen. She opened the site and raised her eyebrows at Elbasan.

"445316."

She put in the PIN and studied the opening screen. She saw there had been no transactions apart from a deposit of four hundred thousand euro made three days previously.

"You see, pretty lady, all good. But, you know, if I want steal this money, it goes!" He clicked his fingers in the air. "Like that!"

She pulled an envelope from her bag and pushed it across the table towards him.

"That's the point, Elbasan. This money has already been stolen and it won't take Marco's people long to realise that!

"Remember who I am and what I said. Keep to the story and we'll both be OK. You've been paid well and this business is between us and only us. If this gets out, to anyone at all, I'll make sure your family is destroyed and those nice Cypriots rape your daughters. If anyone asks me what I know, I'll say I know nothing. If it comes to a choice between somebody believing me or believing you, what d'you think will happen?"

She stood to leave, throwing his phone back across the table.

"Be good, Elbasan!"

He took the envelope and his eyes flashed with pure hatred.

"Oh, and Elbasan ... brown and baby blue, really? It doesn't go!"

CHAPTER 28
NICK WALKER

VILLA BIANCA, COAST ROAD, MALTA

Once Natasha had disappeared down the drive, Nick went and slumped onto the livingroom couch. He tried to make sense of the argument, wrestling with what had just happened. One minute he was convinced it was all something and nothing, which would blow over by morning; the next, he tried to see it from Natasha's point of view. But no matter how hard he tried, he could not understand what had caused her to snap like that. She had changed right in front of his eyes, become someone he barely recognised; someone with the strength to physically attack him. There was violence in her. He had never seen that before.

He went to the bedroom and took his last few lines of coke, then flopped back onto the bed; he needed to be thinking in double time. He was fairly sure the policeman could not prove anything, unless the dealers shopped him, which was possible, but unlikely. Even if that happened, he was sure Marco could pull some strings to sort the problem out.

The next issue was Marco himself. What would he think about it all? He definitely would not be pleased, but surely Nick could not be the first employee to get himself into trouble with recreational drugs.

The comment about the Libyan oil deal was interesting, but

he knew nothing more about it than that. In fact, he was no wiser about Marco and Sergio's wider business activities than he had been when they had bought BetSlick. He now knew Natasha was involved somehow and, thinking about it, she had seemed particularly distracted over the last few days.

What worried him the most was the amount of money that seemed to appear in BetSlick, as if from nowhere. The sums were enormous, millions every month. This was big-league stuff and he felt vulnerable right in the middle of it all. He knew it was not just a question of losing his personal gaming licence, he could also spend years in prison. For that reason alone, he could not afford to fall out with Natasha or Marco.

Then there was Natasha herself. What was he supposed to make of her now? The woman had deceived him for over a year. She had willingly and enthusiastically slept with him, but he had to wonder whether that was just part of the deliberate deception. He felt like a fool.

He got up from the bed and walked out onto the deck, where the stiff evening breeze was warm and humid. He thought about all the interest Natasha had been showing in the business. Being Marco's daughter and obviously bright, it occurred to him that perhaps it had always been her plan to get rid of him, so she could take the seat. It was entirely possible. She could have set up the whole thing, precisely to force this outcome.

Nick considered making a quick call to Marco, just to tell him he had had enough and was out. But he knew better than that.

It was a cloudy and moonless night. He could taste the salty sea breeze and hear the rumble of the sea on the other side of the coast road. He could only just make out the faint lines of the surf, racing in towards the rocky shoreline. He took some deep breaths. He would often stand there in the evenings and listen to the sound of the waves, bullying the coastline. He loved the villa and had thought he had been happy there, but he had been deluded. He could not believe that he had missed what was happening right in front of him.

Nick had his mobile in his hand and had just decided ringing Marco was not the best idea, when he saw the white gates start to swing open and the security lights along the drive flare up. His heart jumped, expecting to see Natasha's Audi.

For a minute, he hoped she might have gone for a drive to clear her head, calmed down and had come back to sort things out. The anxiety started to drain out of him, only to kick back in when he saw Marco's Range Rover enter the drive and come to a stop, a little away from the parking area. The car lights dimmed, but no one got out. Nick stood back from the edge of the deck. He was at a height, so fairly certain he was out of the driver's line of sight. In the shadows of the drive, he could not quite make out who was inside. The car was stationary for several minutes, clicking and ticking as the engine cooled. Then, the security lights timed out and it all went dark. He heard the car door open and his panic was back with a vengeance.

If Marco had come to talk to him, he would not have waited until the security lights timed out. He would have just walked up to the house. Nick knew something was wrong. Marco had to be a pretty ruthless operator, although Nick had never seen any evidence of it. But why would he keep security like Simon around, if there was no need for it? It suddenly occurred to him that it might be Simon in the car. He was ex-military and looked capable of anything. For the first time, it flashed into his mind what extremes Marco, or Simon, might go to! At the end of the day, everyone was dispensable; he had heard that often enough!

He quickly decided to go back into the house, dim the lights and wait it out, pretending he was not there. Once the car had gone, he would definitely be leaving – and with no call to Marco. He could feel his heartbeat and his breathing quicken.

While Nick crept back into the house, Natasha sat in Marco's Range Rover, working out what to say to him. As the gates closed behind her, she realised the house was in near darkness, apart from a light in the lounge, which was unusual. The front door seemed to be ajar, which was also unusual. Nick was usually very security conscious. She felt a creeping anxiety. Something did not seem to add up. She wondered how Nick might have reacted to their argument. She was not sure. They had never really argued before. He might well have just walked out and left everything.

The dark house forced her to make her next move. It was an isolated property. The cars speeding down the coast road provided no sense of comfort and the ever-present rushing of the sea would drown any noise or cries for help.

She wondered what Nick might be thinking and smiled to herself. She had meant to frighten him, scare him off even. That had been the plan, but frightened people could be unpredictable. She noticed the lights in the lounge being dimmed until there was total darkness inside. For the first time, she felt vulnerable. She reached for her phone to ring her father, but stopped. She had already made a fool of herself once that evening. Anyway, she wanted to keep her options open.

There was definitely somebody inside; somebody had dimmed those lights. She thought it was most probably Nick. But she wondered why he would turn the lights down if he knew she was sitting in the drive about to come into the house.

Instinct took over. She slipped off her heels and started to look on the keyring for the key to the steel box Marco had fitted under the dashboard of the Range Rover. He kept a small handgun and a magazine of bullets in there. She took the subcompact Glock out of the case and slid the cartridge into the grip. As she left the car, she put both hands around the grip, holding the gun in front of her and keeping her eye sighted down the barrel. She felt safer with it in her hands.

Then a thought crossed her mind. What if there was an unfortunate accident? She could claim she had returned to find the door open and the lights out. She had gone inside and the gun went off …

Then she could phone Marco for help.

Nick had edged back against the wall and slid into the house, leaving the front door open, to avoid making any noise, but also so he could slip out again, once whoever was in the car had ventured past him. He could disappear round the side of the house and into the fields, and work the rest out from there.

It was all happening so quickly. The hall was already dark and all he could hear was the rasp of his own breath and his heart banging away in his ears. His breathing got faster and shallower. He cowered back as far as he could, against the lounge wall, near the front window, but hidden from view of the lounge door by a large display unit. If someone scanned the front room from the door, they would not see him

Then he saw her, through the lounge window, edging up the stairs towards the front door. Slowly emerging from the darkness, treading lightly in bare feet, her trousers rolled up above her ankles and her hair gathered back. Her arms were outstretched and … she was holding a gun!

Nick could not believe his eyes. He knew Natasha could handle a gun. She had said it was fine for men to talk about the dangers of handguns, but they were not the ones who got assaulted or raped. He saw her professional, purposeful pose, holding the gun straight ahead and moving with the lethal intent of a stalking cat.

At that moment, a thought flashed through his head – Marco must have sent her back to kill him! It might have been the cocaine or the fact he had worked himself up into a high level of anxiety, churning the questions around and around in his head, but his shock turned to anger. He was not going to stand there and be gunned down by that treacherous bitch. The only weapon within reach was a Murano crystal vase on the shelf unit beside him; heavy, nearly the length of his arm and the perfect size for his grip. Without thinking, he took it and held it in front of him, with both hands.

He sensed she must be inside the villa by now. He tiptoed through the shadows of the darkened lounge, careful his trainers made no noise on the tiled floor, and hid behind the door leading to the hallway. His breathing came in surges and gasps. He imagined her bare feet, soundlessly feeling their way down the cool marble floor of the hallway. He tried to look through the crack between the doorjamb and the wall to work out where she might be by the grading of the shadows.

Slowly, the shadows intensified as her body moved into the doorway. Then he saw a flash of her light-coloured shirt. He was sure she was edging around the door. He heard her call, tentatively: "Nick? Where are you?"

For a moment, he thought he caught a hint of her scent as she entered the room. He saw her foot appear on the lounge tiles, her painted nails and ankle bracelet; then, the outline of her calf. But still he held back, not sure what the hell she was going to do.

She was half in the room now, both hands extended in front of her, holding the gun in a combat-style grip. She was looking down the length of her arm, keeping the gun pointed along her line of sight. She was calm and collected.

"Natasha?"

She spun around, the gun swivelling towards him in one movement. Instinctively, he swung the vase from low right to high left, taking the impact through his wrists as it smashed against the side of her head. Her arms flew up as her head jolted sideways, sending the gun flying up, ricocheting off the ceiling, before clattering back down onto the tiles.

He stood perfectly still, letting the adrenaline run through him and waiting for calm to return. It did not happen. His pulse raced and he gulped in air, in huge mouthfuls. She had hit the wall and slowly slid down onto the tiled floor. She looked lifeless; her limbs sprawled in an unnatural position. Her thin blouse had ridden up as she fell, showing her tight, muscled torso. He bent down, his shaking hands feeling her throat for a pulse. He adjusted her blouse to cover her bra and studied her face. Her eyes were closed and he could not detect any breathing. She could have been sleeping, her distinctive scent prominent now. He pushed his face into her hair and breathed it in.

Then he reminded himself not to drop his guard; she was a killer. She had fooled him, used him and then tried to shoot him. He moved his foot to where the gun lay, not taking his eyes off her, and pushed it away, into the far corner of the room.

He replaced the vase on the unit, having wiped it on his polo shirt. God, Natasha was dead! It suddenly hit him hard, but he just could not process the sight of her lying there, in front of him. A small sob welled up in his throat. He thought of her in life; beautiful and exciting. He thought of their intimacy and what had passed between them. How she walked around the villa when she was working, oblivious to the pencils she had stuck in her pile of thick dark brown hair. He had heard her sing and seen her dance. They had shared plates of tapas, drank wine and watched movies together. Then, he had struck her down, making her lifeless on the cold tiled floor.

As if things could not possibly get any worse, a wave of fear swept over him. Nick realised that her death was only the beginning of something. They had not got him that time, but he needed to move. He could not even begin to imagine Marco's reaction when he found out his only daughter had been killed.

The first thing he had to do was get off the island. He went to his bedroom in a panic, grabbing a light rucksack, and threw in his passport, wallet, iPhone charger and a bundle of several thousand euros he kept in the bottom desk drawer. In his business, he had reason to be suspicious of banks and cash, so he had also converted a lot of money into gold. He would clear his bank accounts and open new ones, once he was off the island. When he was gone, he did not want Marco trying to raid his accounts, nor did he want to be traced.

He took the cellophane-covered rolls of Krugerrands and sovereigns, together with some heavy gold chains, from a small safe in the bedroom wardrobe. He also grabbed the watches and other items from Natasha's jewellery box that she kept in there, more out of spite than anything else.

On his way out through the door, he hesitated, just briefly, and for reasons he could not even explain to himself, he took the business card from the hall table, with the name and number of Inspector George Zammit. At some point, he might have to trade information with the police to escape the clutches of Marco and his cronies. Zammit was the only policeman on the island Nick knew, who had not been introduced to him by Marco.

He took one last look at Natasha, lying still, on her side, on the tiled floor. He could not believe she was dead. He touched her head and ran a finger down her face. The blood from the wound was pooling around her shoulder.

The white Range Rover was blocking the drive and he did not want to waste time moving cars, so he wheeled the small commuting scooter out of the garage and slipped on a helmet. It would be a lot less obvious than any of the vehicles in the drive and harder to find once the inevitable search got underway. He slung the rucksack across his shoulder, started the scooter and drove through the white gates and onto the coast road, heading south.

CHAPTER 29
ABDULLAH BELKACEM

MARSABAR, LIBYA

ABDULLAH WAS AT THE PORT, inspecting his fine new vessel. He was strutting around, letting everybody know this was his ship. He had decided they should paint it, as it was not a pretty sight. He told Amr he wanted it repainted in green and yellow; green, the colour of the Arab world and yellow for the sands of the desert. There was plenty of labour in his compounds and many would gladly hang from bosun's chairs to work towards a passage to Europe for their families. He imagined a net of ropes, swinging from the side of the ship, suspending a host of workers, busy with rollers and fresh clean paint. What a sight she would be when they had finished!

Amr was quick to explain that painting a ship was not like painting a house. It would not be possible and involved more than hanging some of his 'bodies' over the side rails. As well as time and money, he would need a drydock to do the job properly. The ship had to be washed clean, then blasted to remove rust, algae, barnacles and slime. Only then could it be sprayed with anti-fouling paint. A cheap cosmetic job, above the water line, would soon be noticed and raise suspicions about what failings lay below. It would also make the ship look half finished. He asked Abdullah whether he really wanted people to think he had just put lipstick on a camel?

Amr smiled.

"Why change her? She's beautiful as she is. For an old ship, the paintwork isn't too bad yet and she sails well. The engines are strong, the tanks are sound and she can carry all the cargo you could want."

So, like an ugly daughter, he had to learn to love her as she was.

Abdullah had grown to like the little Egyptian. After the episode in the cave, they were starting again; learning about each other and laying the foundations for mutual respect, if not friendship. Amr was supervising the loading of the first cargo shipment, a mix of marine fuel oil and petroleum product. Abdullah was no engineer and there was a lot to learn about loading the oil. The heavy, bunkering oil which dirty power stations and the big engines on ships burned, was warmed, so the viscous liquid could flow freely. That cargo was to be burned in Malta's old oil fuelled power station. A contract had already been arranged.

It was all new to Abdullah, but he was interested to learn that side of the business. He questioned the Egyptian with the naïve enthusiasm of an eight-year-old boy. The heavy tar-like bunkering oil came by pipe from the Marsabar refinery and filled four of the six cargo tanks. The other two tanks were being filled by a fleet of road tankers from another refinery, further down the coast. That was the fuel destined for the filling stations of Italy, Spain and Turkey. The road tankers each carried forty thousand litres of petrol, so it would take over fifty of them to fill the two empty tanks. There was a queue day and night on the dockside, as they pumped the fuel aboard under Amr's watchful eye.

An operation like that attracted attention and Abdullah had been careful not to overlook any local official, when making his payments. The promise of big rewards or simple petty jealousy could easily lead to trouble. Abdullah was also wary of another militia trying to muscle in on his new and highly lucrative scheme. Lookouts had been posted. Marsabar was Abdullah's home turf and, if he could not safely operate there, he could not operate anywhere. But, even if he could control his home territory, he still needed Abu Muhammed. His protection beyond Marsabar, in broken Libya, was essential.

Abdullah stood at the back of the ship, looking over the rail, making his calls. The last one was to the man in Malta.

"So, my friend, I am standing on the deck of a ship that is getting heavier and heavier by the minute, with fuel oil and petroleum."

"That is good to hear. Have you made your local arrangements? Is everything safe? How much did you have to pay?"

"Yes, that has all been done and all is safe. The cost of the deal is for me to know but, I will tell you, I had to pay a high price. There is nothing left for me, after I pay all the expenses. This business will leave me a poor man!"

"Then you must be a fool or a poor businessman! And I know you are neither." They both laughed.

"Be careful with the Islamists, they are not to be trusted. As a Catholic, I dislike doing business with them, or doing anything to help create their crazy caliphate. But I agree it was necessary. Just watch them."

"I am with you. The Beards are truly dangerous. They are strong, because they believe everything they do is blessed by Allah and, that way, they can do no wrong! It would be funny, if it were not so terrible. I will be careful, but I am glad you talk of money. This is what I need from you now.

"It is time to start the payments. I am not a rich man like you. Now, I have partners to keep happy, refineries to pay, officials to feed, a ship to fuel, provisions to buy and a tanker fleet to hire. I need the down payment we discussed. I need to have money now!"

"I will have the initial funds transferred to the account in Antayla Bank, but we will make all future payments after the ship-to-ship transfers have been completed. Until then, the risk is yours. You understand this?"

"Yes, yes, I understand. But I need the trusted names at the bank, paperwork, passwords, telephone numbers, access codes and the software to deal with the money. There is also the goodwill payment we discussed. It is time for me to receive this also."

"OK, I agree it is time. Within the next few days, you will meet our courier. He will bring you bank papers and the account details; four accounts in euros, US dollars, sterling and Saudi riyal. He will also bring you the software, so you can operate the accounts freely. One thing – we want the courier returned to us unharmed and he must know none of our business. That is important. He is just a messenger – nothing more."

"I understand. And the goodwill payment in gold?"

"Yes, we have not forgotten. The courier will bring five kilos of gold, as a down payment against the first shipment. We value this at about two hundred thousand US dollars. I understand that you Arabs like the touch and feel of gold! Will you be keeping it in your tent, with your camel?"

"You make fun of me? I am a Berber, not an Arab. We are not desert dwellers now. These days, we wear shoes, drive cars and have real toilets in our houses!"

They shared the joke.

"But, sometimes, a man's gold is all that matters. I can show it to win friends, use it to frighten my enemies and, if all else fails, I can put it in the back of a truck and drive it into the desert! So, if the courier arrives and there is no gold, I kill him, eh?"

"If that happens, send him back to me and I will kill him myself!"

They laughed again.

"The courier is nearly ready to leave. He will be with you in three or four days. We need to get him from Tripoli to meet you. I take it you will not go to Tripoli?"

"No, no, no! You do not understand the situation, my friend.

If I leave the protection of my clan, I am an easy target for any bandit I meet on the road.

"But I have thought about this. I have a man who is well placed in Tripoli. He can meet your courier and bring him to me here, where it is safe. We can do our business and I will have your man back in Tripoli the same day."

"So, I will tell the courier to wait to be contacted and then just follow instructions?"

"That is how it will be. You send me a name, a photograph and a place where we can find him."

"Well, everything seems to be going well. Unless there is anything else? Until we speak again."

"Yes, my friend, until we speak again. *Inshallah.*"

CHAPTER 30
NICK WALKER
MSIDA MARINA, MALTA

It was well after midnight when Nick arrived in St Julian's on the scooter. There, he used all of his bank and credit cards to take as much cash as possible from his accounts. Ten cards, at a maximum of seven hundred and fifty euros per card, plus the cash in his bag and the value of the watches and gold, gave him enough to put some distance between himself and the island. Nick banked with a tame Turkish bank that Marco had introduced him to. Their name came up regularly at BetSlick. He had a hunch that his Antayla Bank accounts would soon be frozen and, from then on, he would not be able to use ATMs. He was sure Marco and his connections would be tracking him.

He worked through all his options. He knew taking a flight out of the country would be too risky. Marco had the *Pulizija* in his pocket and he could well be dragged out of line at the gate to face the consequences for murdering Natasha. God, was that what he had done? As he rode through the chill of the night, he shivered and tried to think calmly. Running seemed like such a cheap move, but he was not sure there was any alternative.

The high-speed catamaran to Sicily did not leave until early in the morning and he could not be sure whether Natasha's absence would go unnoticed until then. Again, there was passport control on boarding and they could also pick him off when he disembarked in Sicily. All it would take was one phone call from Camilleri.

No, it was important to buy himself some time and do the unexpected. He had the cruiser, the Blue Cascade, moored at Msida Creek. It was a fifty-foot motor boat and its twin engines could cover the one hundred kilometres to Sicily in less than three hours. It was capable of getting to most places in the Mediterranean, given decent weather. At this time of year, the winds and seas were moderate and the morning's forecast had confirmed the voyage should be hampered by bad weather. Thinking it through, he realised that, if he tried to make a run for Sicily, they could easily track him and, again, pick him up on arrival.

He got to the Msida marina around three in the morning. It was not unusual for boat owners to arrive at that hour, to make preparations for an early start. He found the security guard dozing in his office and started chatting, telling him he was planning a passage to the east coast of Sicily.

Within an hour, he had stripped the covers off the boat, plotted a course and used his credit card to fill up with fuel from the self-service pump. Before first light was even breaking over the harbour, he edged off the pontoon; the gentle chugging of the low-revving engines reassuring him there might just be a chance of a future. The Blue Cascade moved through the black waters of the harbour. In the east, the sea ahead merged with the sky in the obsidian darkness of the moonless night. The only relief was the occasional navigation light, flickering green or red, marking the passage or warning of reefs and rocks.

The Blue Cascade picked up speed and he swung the boat north east, as if heading towards Sicily. As he tracked the coastline, the first tentative glimmer of sunlight started to push its way over the eastern horizon, slowly turning the blackness into the deepest shade of purple. Nick had no real sailing skills, but he knew how to work the course plotter and the GPS system. He was banking on daylight arriving, and soon.

It only took the Blue Cascade twenty minutes to motor north, past the lights of St Julian's and St Paul's. Up on the hill, between the two towns, Nick would be able to make out the villa, standing alone, with its whitewashed walls, where Natasha's body lay, still and quiet, cooling on the tiles.

He strained his eyes to see if the house was lit with *Pulizija* floodlights and the headlights of the squad cars. He imagined Marco pacing backwards and forwards on the paved driveway, shouting vengeful instructions to Simon down his phone, insane with rage. But there were no lights. The house remained in darkness, silent, holding on tight to the secret of what he had done to Natasha.

Once he got to the end of the island, it would be a short hop across the channel to the port of Mgarr, in Gozo. Instead, he turned west, striking out across the north coast of Malta, with the early morning sun starting to rise behind him.

When the land fell away on the port side of the boat, he changed course again, heading south-west, and plotted a course to the small Italian island of Lampedusa, about one hundred kilometres from the Tunisian coast. The plan, as far as he had one, was to reach Lampedusa, rest up for a day or so, then push on to Tunis. After that, it all became a little vague. He thought he could sell the Blue Cascade and take a flight back to mainland Europe, where he might be able to find a way of starting his life again. There were some big gaps in the plan, but at least he was on his way.

Before he got out of 3G range, there was one last thing he wanted to do. In the cabin below, he took his iPhone out of his bag and rang the number on Inspector George Zammit's business card. He thought kicking up a shitstorm would give them all something else to think about, another distraction. It might buy him some more time.

It was early and he was not even sure the inspector would

pick up. After a few rings, Nick heard his voice above the drumming of the engines.

"Zammit."

"Nick Walker here. You called at my house yesterday, about the motorbike accident? I've got some information for you."

There was a pause on the line.

"Mr Walker, I'm at home right now. Can we meet somewhere later, to talk about this in person?"

"No, I'm sorry, that won't be possible. I've left the island. I had to get away from some very dangerous people and I want you to know they're serious criminals. Listen, I know this sounds dramatic, but my life's in danger and I don't know who else to call. I haven't got time to tell you the full story, but I'll give you names and tell you where to look. The rest is up to you."

The inspector seemed less than enthusiastic about this line of conversation.

"OK. Well, I suppose, if you must. Where are you? You sound miles away."

"Where I am doesn't matter, just listen ..."

Nick told Zammit as much as he knew: how BetSlick was an international money laundering operation; how it was controlled by a criminal fraternity based in Milan. He identified Marco Bonnici as the king pin behind the Maltese operation and said Sergio Rossi from Milan was the one who pulled the strings. He also told Zammit they were planning on smuggling oil from Libya and it was going to happen imminently. The background noise of the boat's engines and the wind whistling around the cockpit meant Nick could not be sure the inspector heard everything he was saying. He pressed on, competing against the noise of the engines.

"Mr Walker, there's no proof for any of the things you're telling me," he heard Zammit's voice saying, faintly. "These are very serious allegations against some very important people. What d'you expect me to do with it all?" .

"I know. That's why I'm reporting what I know. What you do with it is up to you! You're the *Pulizija!*"

Then he heard a girl's muffled voice, shouting in the background: "Dad, let me in! It's getting late … the school bus goes in twenty minutes. Come on! "

The line crackled.

"I can't talk about this now! You've given me no evidence and say you won't even come in and talk about it face-to-face. I'm not sure what you think I can do. You're leaving the country, on the run, which isn't very helpful, is it? It doesn't look good. Come back and talk to some colleagues. I know someone who might help. He's the Assistant Commissioner and head of the Organised Crime Command Unit, Gerald Camilleri. This is more his territory – he'll know what to do."

"Look, Inspector, I'm on a boat and nearly out of signal range now. Just so you know, if you think Camilleri will help you, or me, you're wrong. He's involved in this, up to his neck. Camilleri is their protection in Malta. He's in Bonnici's pocket. Those guys want to kill me! They're racketeers and this oil thing – it's a big deal for them. I don't know anything else, but you've got your starting point. Believe nothing you hear about me. They'll try to discredit me. That's why I'm leaving and that's why I'm calling you. There was an accident involving the woman I lived with, but I'm not responsible for what happened. Inspector, I have to go. It's up to you now."

With that, Nick cut the call and then used the last of the signal range to call the emergency services, telling them that there had been a terrible accident and giving them the address of the villa.

CHAPTER 31
INSPECTOR GEORGE ZAMMIT

GEORGE'S HOME, BIRKIRKARA, MALTA

George's reflection stared back at him from the bathroom mirror. It was tense and worried. He had always tried his best to stay away from the political side of the job. It was common knowledge that favours were done by the *higher ups* for the business types on the island. Several senior officers had houses, cars and boats that were not affordable on their salaries alone, but George avoided such associations, turning away and letting them get on with it, without any help from him. Nick's call could thrust him right into that whole dangerous territory, with potentially serious repercussions.

Gina started banging on the door again.

"Dad! Get out! You can't hog the bathroom! And if you're going to talk on the phone, go somewhere else!"

He opened the door and his daughter pushed past, wearing her dressing gown, clutching a pile of school clothing. In the bedroom, he slumped back onto the bed.

While staring at the ceiling, it occurred to him that the best solution could be to have a quiet word with Camilleri, warning him of the nonsense being spread by Nick Walker. It would not hurt George's standing with the all-knowing Assistant Commissioner. It was a problem he would rather not have, for sure, but he knew it could not just be ignored.

The other thing that nagged at him was that name 'Bonnici', which struck a chord. He had been worrying about the political ramifications of the conversation, but he knew somewhere there was a connection to something that had been on his mind recently. And then it struck him! The girl with the Englishman at Villa Bianca had been Marco Bonnici's daughter. He knew of Marco Bonnici and, although they moved in very different circles, had seen pictures of the daughter in some of the gossip pages. She had even been Bonnici's plus one when, as a newly promoted Inspector, George was a guest of Camilleri's at the annual police charity dinner. Natasha had turned some heads that night!

What did Walker say – that there had been an accident at his villa? In a fluster, George rang the office immediately and, even though it was early, Alphonse answered. Ignoring some inane questions about who had said what to whom and when, George told his squad to grab a car and get to the villa as fast as they could.

CHAPTER 32
MARCO BONNICI
CASTELLO BONNICI, MALTA

THERE ARE few worse things than the death or serious injury of your own child and Marco had taken the assault on Natasha very badly. The good news was that she was alive, if unconscious; the team at Mater Dei had placed her in an induced coma, while they assessed the damage. She was in the care of a senior neurosurgeon whom Marco knew and trusted.

Driving home, with Natasha just admitted into hospital and Nick Walker nowhere to be found, Marco acknowledged something had gone terribly wrong. He knew he had to call Sergio and tell him about Natasha and about the mess with Walker. Not only had Nick created the problem with the local dealers and the police, but it appeared he had battered Natasha half to death and then fled.

As he had expected, the call to Sergio did not go well. He reacted with shock and anger, using a tone of voice that Marco had never heard from him before, in all the years of their friendship: cold, hard, angry.

"This is a mess, Marco. I'm not sure what to do. First, of course, I will pray for Natasha … whatever happens, you know that. Secondly, we need to find that sonofabitch Walker and do what we have to do! I'll organise it, but you've got to help me with the locals."

"Sergio, listen to me. At this point, I am not sure what this man has done but, if it is what it looks like, he is not getting away with it. As God is my witness, I will follow him wherever he goes and, when I find him, I will kill him myself."

"Marco, you focus on Natasha and the business. Leave Walker to me. When we have him, you'll be the first to hear. This is what I do. In the meantime, keep the gaming operation running and bring home that oil deal. Everything's in motion; we've got to be ready. You can't let me down on this."

Sergio sighed and continued, "In many ways, this prick has done us a favour. If this is the sort of person he is, he would have screwed us all sooner or later. It's better we found out about him now." Sergio paused before adding, "But, my friend, you have truly fucked up with this, you know that?"

Marco froze. His cousin had never spoken to him in such terms in all the time they had worked together, or as friends. Marco knew he would not have chosen a phrase like that without knowing the impact it would have.

"I am sorry you see it that way, Sergio. We will make it right. *I* will make it right."

"Let's not lose sight of the prize here. We're so close and I don't think this changes anything, for now. As long as we can get hold of Walker and make sure he doesn't start talking, we'll be fine."

Marco said: "I have Camilleri's people covering the passenger lists at the airports and the catamaran to Sicily. Nothing yet. I can check the hotels over there. I have all his financial details. I have told Hasan at Antayla Bank to freeze his accounts – suspected crime proceeds. I do not suppose that covers all his cash, but the balances are pretty high, so my guess is most of his money is now locked up.

"We have the boat in the marina and I am checking that as we speak. If he has taken it, we can pick him up on his approach to

Sicily. Camilleri will tell the Guardia di Finanza he is wanted for questioning on drugs charges, and get him put on the watch lists. The only other way out is on a fishing boat or a private yacht but, by this afternoon, the word will be out in ports and marinas that an Englishman is trying to get off the island. We have offered a good reward for information."

Sergio went along with Marco's response.

"Yeah, yeah. You couldn't have done any more, Marco. Look, stay calm. You've had a terrible shock, I know, but Natasha will be all right; she's tough. Now, get down to the office and make sure Nick's deputy, Greca, is onside – is that her name? Don't answer questions, just tell her how it is. Oh, and tell Simon to talk to my security guy. He'll handle any leads we get on the Italian side and he's checking incoming flights and boats, just in case."

With that, Sergio hung up.

His tone had softened a little towards the end. He had always been more a man of action and was never happier, or more energised than when he was executing a plan. Marco, by contrast, felt exhausted and a wave of emotion swept over him. Slowly, he started to sob, tears running unchecked down his cheeks. He cried for Natasha, with big shuddering bursts. He cried for all the lost time he should have spent with his long-dead wife and he cried for his years of loneliness and for the damage to his friendship with Sergio. The force of his grief rocked him for several minutes. It consumed him like a fire, expelling tensions, regrets, shame and failures. When the sobbing eased, and then finally stopped, he felt better. The release had done him good. He stood up, the outburst behind him, and concentrated on the anger and hatred he felt towards the man who had so callously harmed his daughter.

In his office, Marco called for Simon. Looking out of the window across the valley, with his back to him, to hide the redness in his eyes, Marco barked out instructions.

"Ports, marinas, Coastguard, the Harbourmaster, the airport.

Ten thousand euro for any information that leads us to that bastard. A bonus of the same amount for you, if you bring him to me in the next forty-eight hours from now! Tell the *Pulizija,* the military, the damn' Archbishop for all I care, but you find that man and do not sleep until you do! It is now almost ten a.m. He has at least twelve hours' start on us. Well, what are you waiting for?"

CHAPTER 33
INSPECTOR GEORGE ZAMMIT

MSIDA BASTIONS, MALTA

When Marianna had learned that George was going to Libya to help solve the migrant crisis, her reaction had surprised him. Rather than rant and chide him about going away, she saw it as an honour bestowed on all the family. She was quick to tell the shopkeepers, the nursing staff in Denzel's hospital ward, relatives the length and breadth of the island, of the great responsibility her husband had been asked to bear. She also did not hesitate to point out how she would have to suffer, single-handedly, all the additional burden at home, with Denzel still being in hospital.

On the day before his departure, she had hurried out to Muscat's, the gentleman's outfitters on Birkirkara's Valley Road, and returned with two heavy-weave, long-sleeved cotton shirts that took no account of the searing summer heat and humidity, which would no doubt be even worse on the North African coast.

"We want you looking your best, don't we? I've had your navy suit cleaned, express service, and I've checked your passport. It doesn't expire for another nine years. That means you've had that passport eleven years and you've only left the island twice, both times to go shopping in Sicily!"

George was feeling both excited and a little scared. It was true, he was not an adventurous traveller and he did not yet know much about Camilleri's private business, but he already knew he would never be any good at working under cover.

The other worry that was gnawing away at his peace of mind, was the phone call he had taken that morning from Nick Walker. He knew what Alphonse had found at the house and so much of what Nick had told him had turned out to be true. If that was the case, George reasoned, why would the rest be a lie? He had been trying to phone Camilleri all morning. His office said *'he was in meetings', 'he was out of the office', 'he was back in meetings'* ... and finally, *'not to phone again, the Assistant Commissioner had received the messages and would phone back in due course'*. George guessed Camilleri was avoiding him because he thought he might be trying to wriggle out of the Libya trip. He smiled at the thought.

He was due to fly out the following day and had to meet Camilleri to receive his final instructions that very evening. George decided to leave the subject of his phone call with Nick until then. Camilleri had sent a text, telling him to go to the military cemetery on the Msida Bastions, behind the main Police Headquarters. It was a small Protestant cemetery, in a sunken garden, situated on top of the fortifications surrounding Valletta. It was usually closed to the public, so he was surprised when he arrived and found the iron gates ajar.

Camilleri was at the far end of the narrow plot, sheltering from the sun under a mature cypress tree. He was smoking and looking out across Msida Creek, into the Marina.

"So, George, exciting times!" His reptilian smile did nothing to reassure his subordinate that this interview would go well. George's heart was beating faster than he would have liked.

"I hope your bags are packed and you are all set?"

"Yes, all ready," George said, half-heartedly.

"Come on, George, why the long face? Look upon it as a little holiday jaunt!"

"*Mela,* what is this private business you want me to do?" That part of the trip had been worrying him more and more, as the day passed by.

"Ah, yes, I am glad you have not forgotten about that." Camilleri pushed a black briefcase across the top of the tomb he was leaning against.

"In there are a few private papers and some other things, for a friend of Malta, working for us in Libya. He is doing important work of a secret nature and, from time to time, we have to send him information, laptops, phones, some money, that sort of thing. The only safe way of doing it is with a personal delivery. We do not want to attract attention to him, so we prefer to send a new courier every time. There is nothing illegal involved; just some housekeeping on behalf of a government agency."

Camilleri then raised his phone, to take a head and shoulders photograph of George. He examined the screen; then, satisfied, grinned a mirthless smile.

"Someone will meet you at the conference and ask you if you have seen the Arch of Marcus Aurelius. It is a famous tourist site, near the Port of Tripoli. You need to answer: *'Was it built in 166AD?'* Now, can you remember that?"

"Yes, Arch of Marcus Aurelius, 166AD. Think I can manage that."

"Good. The contact will pick you up and you will be driven out of town. There will be a rendezvous and you will meet a man to whom you will give this case. There is no need to speak to him – he has the combination; you do not. You will not, under any circumstances, open the case and never let it out of your sight. If you lose this case or it is not delivered into the right hands, you need not bother coming back to Malta. Is that understood? As far as your wife is concerned, I will activate her widow's pension."

George swallowed and nodded.

"How will I know he's the right man?"

"I think you will know! If in doubt, ask your contact to identify him to you. Do not contact me; as far as I am concerned, you are going to a conference and that is it."

Camilleri continued: "You will be collected tomorrow and driven airside at the airport. There will be no customs checks. You will be met off the plane at the other end and taken through the airport by friends of ours in Libya. There will be no checks at immigration or customs there, either. Once through, just get a taxi to the hotel. The bill has already been paid. Here is an envelope with three thousand Libyan dinars inside. That is about fifteen hundred euros, which should be more than enough. Do not go mad and do not attract attention to yourself. Remember, it is Libya; the place is awash with secret police and other villains. Play it straight and you will be fine. You are the pride of the Malta Police, George. Do not forget that!"

George wondered if that pep talk at the end was meant to inspire him. If it was, it failed!

"So, happy travels, George. We know we can rely on you. Remember, Superintendent Farrugia wants a full report on the conference, on your return!" His superior smiled.

George felt he could not stand Camilleri's patronising tone for another second. He wanted to wipe that smile off his condescending face. He also did not want to be burdened any longer by the information Walker had given him that morning, so spat it straight out.

"You know, I've been ringing you all day about something important. I heard something I thought you needed to know urgently."

"Really, George, what might that be?"

He had started so there was no going back.

"Well, I'm sure you've heard about the attack on Natasha Bonnici last night?"

"Yes, I am aware of it and that is what has been keeping me busy this morning. I was informed it was you who called the incident in. How did that happen?"

"The other day, I spoke with the people who have the villa near Denzel's crash site. I was just trying to find out a bit more about the circumstances of the accident and I left my card with the owner, a man called Nick Walker. Natasha Bonnici was his girlfriend or partner; she was there when I called. I didn't recognise her at the time, but, you'll remember, she was at the charity dinner we went to."

He saw Camilleri's eyes narrow.

"Walker didn't tell me much at the time, but then I got a call from him this morning, out of the blue. Sounded like he was in trouble. He was on a boat from the sound of it. He told me the *Pulizija* should investigate a betting firm called BetSlick, which he claims is engaged in money laundering. He also said there was a big Libyan oil smuggling operation happening soon. He refused to come in and give a statement, but said the Bonnicis were involved, along with a man called Sergio Rossi, from some Italian crime family. He also suggested the *Pulizija* were assisting, somehow. I don't know why he would call me about any of this. But as he wouldn't give a statement, and there's no evidence that I know of, I don't intend to take any further action. Unless you disagree, of course?"

There was a loaded silence. It stretched between them.

"Given the seriousness of the allegations, I thought you should know," George added, feeling uneasy.

"Why didn't you tell me this sooner, George? This is important!"

"*Mela,* I telephoned you seven times and finally your office told me to go away! Anyway, Walker also said there had been an accident involving his girlfriend, Natasha Bonnici. So, I called it in."

"Who else have you mentioned this to, George?"

"I told Alphonse to go to the house, because I was worried the girl might have been hurt in some way. And she had been. But the rest, I haven't told anybody. It could just be baseless allegations. You wouldn't take my calls and I didn't want to leave a message. I knew we were meeting today and this is more your area of expertise, so I kept it to myself, until I could tell you in person."

"Good thinking. Look, I already know about all this. Marco Bonnici phoned me about his daughter and there are enquiries ongoing. Between you and me, and I mean that, this Nick Walker is on the run. He has seriously assaulted his employer's daughter and it looks like he has stolen from Bonnici – embezzled the company's bank accounts.

"We are onto it but, as you can understand, it is a sensitive matter, which could affect business confidence on the island, so we are keeping it very hush-hush. I do not wish to start any rumours that adversely affect legitimate businesses. But it is interesting that you think Walker was on a boat. Where was he heading, did he say?"

"No. I did ask him, but he was about to go out of mobile signal range and refused to tell me."

"What time did he ring you?"

"I was shaving, so it would've been about seven-thirty this morning."

"Did he say why he was running? Give any reason?"

"He said he was involved with some dangerous people who wanted to kill him. I suppose that's a good enough reason to run!"

"George, I know these people. They are legitimate businessmen, not killers. Nick Walker is a lying thief who has been caught with his fingers in the till. You did the right thing coming privately to me. Now it is best you forget about it. Organised Crime are already onto it, but thank you for your discretion and assistance. You just go home and focus on our Libyan task, OK?"

George was pleased that he had given Camilleri something to think about. He could practically hear the cogs meshing as his superior lied his way through the conversation.

George took the briefcase from the top of the tomb. He was

surprised by how heavy it was. He shook it, but it felt solid; nothing moving inside it. Walking back to the car, he placed it on the seat beside him, swearing an oath that he would never let it out of his sight, no matter what. Camilleri's instructions had registered with him loud and clear. As he drove home, he wondered how much a widow's pension was these days.

CHAPTER 34
ABDULLAH BELKACEM
MARSABAR HARBOUR, LIBYA

THAT EVENING, Abdullah left the port, having spent more time aboard the *Malik Albahr*. Amr had shown him around the engine rooms and the pump rooms. Abdullah did not understand all the jargon and engineering shorthand, but he was eager to learn the basic principles of how a ship functioned.

The loading was going well and Abdullah was waiting for word that the courier had arrived in Libya. Once he had met him and taken the passwords and devices, he could get the banking arrangements set up and pay those who had to be paid. Then, they could set sail with the first cargo. Brave day!

As Abdullah walked towards his car at the end of the wharf, he noticed a man walking towards him with his head down. He wore a long black shirt and dirty grey jogging pants, sunglasses and a red keffiyeh loosely wrapped around his head. Abdullah looked at his guards, who had already pulled their pistols, holding them down by their sides.

"Peace be upon you, my friend," the man said with a smile. Abdullah recognised him as Abu Muhammed, the man he had negotiated with at the ISIL camp in the hills.

"And peace be with you. You will get yourself shot, creeping up on people like that." Abdullah moved to embrace him.

"There is never any danger when you are amongst friends!" replied Abu Muhammed.

Abdullah waved the guards away and they walked towards the Land Cruiser, stopping to lean on the bonnet. For a moment, Abu Muhammed scrutinised the *Malik Albahr*.

"You must be a proud man, Abdullah Belkacem. Not many people could achieve such a thing.

"I came to tell you – I think we have struck a very good deal, but word of this ..." he waved his hand to indicate the tanker behind them "... has spread and it has created jealousy down the coast. This is not good for us."

Abdullah curled his lips and shrugged his shoulders.

"This is your problem, my friend. What can I do, eh? You knew this would happen. That is why I share the prize with you. Where there is food, the hungry will always gather. The strong must protect themselves."

Abu Muhammed looked at him, with no trace of a smile.

"My problems are your problems, too. We will stop this nonsense but, I tell you, strengthen your men, buy more weapons. You are no longer a farmer with a few boats, shipping the filth across the water. This is Allah's fight and a fight for your country.

"Your weakness is too visible. Your clan needs to become an army. Many of the militia in Benghazi and Derna are fresh back from Syria. They have professional jihadi soldiers, Abdullah. They have fought in Iraq and, before that, in Afghanistan. They are believers like me but, unlike me, will not see the good in you. Be warned, they will not tolerate you. You are not one of them. They are dangerous people, Abdullah, and you have something they want. It is as well for you that I want it too!" He smiled through his teeth.

"We cannot be here in numbers, day and night – it is up to you to seal this area. Look what just happened here. I walked down this dock, without any challenge from you or your men. Where is your security? Do you want to be a dead man? If you do not have men with proper fighting experience, I will send you some. They will help you protect our business and your home. They will teach you how to stay alive in this rotten country. If we have a war with these people, then your money will have to be used to fight it."

"I can protect myself and my home, Abu Muhammed. What sort of man would I be if I could not? I have fought the government, I have fought the militias, and, yes, I have fought you and your jihadis in the past – and, every time, I have won."

"Those skirmishes were little boys' games. These are different times, Abdullah. Different times. Mark my words. These new men are battle-hardened and have even twisted the tail of the Americans, with all their power. Do not treat them lightly."

With that, Abu Muhammed patted him on the shoulder and began to walk away. After a few steps, he turned back.

"Friend, let me see your phone."

Abdullah showed him his five-year-old Nokia that had served him well enough. The other man glanced at it.

"I thought so. OK, tomorrow you will meet my friend Abdul-Lateef and he will help you. Abdullah, be sure to do whatever he asks!"

Abu Muhammed laughed then and clasped Abdullah briefly by the arm. "Go in peace," he said, and left, melting into the shadows by the harbour wall.

The day after the strange meeting with Abu Muhammed on the quayside, Abdullah got a text from him saying a friend of his would visit the compound in Marsabar, to help them with their defences. It said to take his advice as it was *'wise and well given'*. Abdullah wondered what that could possibly mean.

Later on, a scrawny youth arrived at the compound, tumbling out of a battered Toyota truck. He was carrying laptops, holdalls filled with cameras, cables and large lights on tripods. The youth introduced himself as Abdul-Lateef then told Tareq and Abdullah he was an expert in communications and social media.

"So, you got no YouTube, Facebook, Twitter ... nothing like that?"

Tareq looked at him.

"What do we need that shit for?"

The boy did not seem to notice their lack of enthusiasm and continued with his nonsense, explaining that managing how they were thought of by friends and enemies alike, was as important as raising crops, or gathering an arsenal of weapons.

"This is what ISIL do. It's not just about war-making. We tell the world how we follow Allah's word; we show them our schools, our hospitals and our mosques. We demonstrate we're the true believers, and how we treat our enemies and non-believers. We show them how many we are. It's how we get foreign fighters to come and join us; how we get money. It's this that makes people fear us and love us, as well. I do this for Allah and for Abu Muhammed."

He was on his knees fiddling with his equipment, when he turned to Tareq and said: "Get your best, newest weapons and as many men as you can find. Bring some trucks, too. As many as you have. Technicals, with the big machine guns. And I need someone who can ride a dirt bike for me."

Over the next hour, Abdullah watched Tareq, with forty of their men plus various family members, blaze through the scrub in the trucks. They brandished RPGs, automatic carbines with grenade launchers, assault rifles, and every other piece of hardware they could find. Abdul had all the vehicles in arrowhead formation charging across the semi-desert, sending plumes of dust high into the sky. Khaled was on his dirt bike, dodging and weaving between them, with Abdul sitting behind him, taking photographs and shooting video.

Later on, they went further out to lay a few land mines and smoke bombs, simulating a battle scene in the scrub. The men poured through ravines and climbed rocks, with live munitions and bomb blasts all around them. Abdul and Khaled videoed the action, taking positions both above and below the area of the fake fighting. The men seemed to enjoy the foolishness, shouting and screaming battle cries, charging through the gun smoke and dust clouds.

After several hours, Abdul announced he was satisfied and the men were released to go back to work. Abdul then went to a local school that Abdullah had helped, to film him sitting with children, reading a story to them. After that, they went to one of his farms, where Abdullah took a hoe out into a field of courgettes and scratched around in the soil. Finally, Abdul filmed the Imam and Abdullah at the local Marsabar mosque, looking at the roof and minaret, the Imam's arms extended high in the air, as if in thanks for Abdullah's benevolence!

He was still not totally convinced they needed to do any of this, but he could see the story that was evolving and was not entirely displeased. A protector of his people and his city, with a civic and religious duty to make life better for them. Maybe, he even quite liked it, although he would never admit it!

"I hope this does not come back and bite us," he said slowly. "Tareq, you had better warn our people, otherwise they will have a heart attack when they see those videos and pictures. They will think we have been overrun by some terrible devils!"

Then, he laughed aloud at the stupidity of it all.

CHAPTER 35
INSPECTOR GEORGE ZAMMIT

TRIPOLI, LIBYA

THE PLANE LANDED in Tripoli at ten in the evening, local time. The flight had taken just over ninety minutes and George had enjoyed the inquisitive looks, as he had stepped out of Camilleri's black chauffeur-driven police BMW, straight onto the airplane steps and into the business-class area at the front.

In the street at home, Marianna had been bursting with pride, prolonging his departure with hugs and kisses, not to mention unnecessary adjustments to his tie. She had ensured no neighbour missed the moment he climbed into the official car outside the house, the driver holding the door open for him.

He had yet to work out how he would deal with the briefcase. It was too heavy for him to lug around a conference for the next two days. It was bound to raise questions if he never put it down anywhere. He thought there had to be a place at the hotel where it could be left safely. Then again, Camilleri's words echoed in his head: *if he lost it, he could forget about returning to Malta.* Surely that was not meant literally? Probably more a figure of speech on Camilleri's part. At least that is what he hoped.

Stepping off the plane, he realised it was his first time on African soil. Mediterranean airports all tended to look the same and Tripoli International Airport was no exception.

A smallish man in a dark suit appeared from nowhere and took George's arm, steering him through a door marked 'No Entry.' He had brought an airport pass, with some Arabic script on a lariat, which he slipped around George's neck.

"Welcome to Tripoli. First visit?"

"Yes," George said, trying to be friendly. "It looks similar to Malta, so far!"

The man glanced at him. "It's very different from Malta, believe me."

He said nothing more, just walked ahead while George struggled to keep up, his bags and the heavy briefcase hampering his shorter strides. Some automatic doors swung open and they burst out of the back corridors, into the main arrivals hall.

"Taxis ahead. Pay only fifteen dinars, no more. They're all thieves here!"

With that, his escort turned away and left George alone with his luggage, and a brow beaded with sweat.

The large international hotel was much like any other, except that it was dry. George was not a big drinker but, at that moment, he could have done with a beer. Turning on the television, he stripped to his underwear and slumped on the bed, settling down to watch some random soccer game. Very soon, he dropped off into his usual deep, untroubled and uninterrupted sleep.

The conference was tedious. The large conference suite in the hotel was the same as those in the larger hotels in Malta. It occupied a windowless area with a low ceiling, under the main reception hall. It boasted gold-framed chairs with red mock velvet upholstery that tried, but, failed to create an air of grandeur and splendour. The coffee was thick and hot, the pastries fat and sticky, both of which delighted George.

During the coffee break in the afternoon session on the second day, a small wiry man with a drooping moustache, dressed in a Libyan police uniform, sidled up. Without a word of introduction, he asked George: "Have you seen the Arch of Marcus Aurelius?"

George hesitated for a moment, pondering the significance of the question. Then he remembered … 1066? No, that was something else. Finally, it came back to him.

"Was it built in 166?" he replied.

"I've no idea, but I'll meet you at reception at seven tomorrow morning. Be prepared for a journey of some hours."

"So, where're we going?" George asked him, in all innocence.

"You don't expect me to answer that, do you? And think about your clothes. Travel tomorrow in that suit and you won't make it through a single checkpoint. How much money have you got?"

George told him a slightly lower figure than he actually had.

"OK, give it to me tomorrow. We might need to pay at some of the checkpoints. Also, that briefcase: you hold it like it's about to explode! Find an old bag or whatever, put it in there and try to forget about it. Don't look at it, don't touch it, don't hold it unless you have to. Buy sunglasses as well; your eyes are shifty. You have a guilty look. Tomorrow you stare straight ahead. When we hit checkpoints, don't look left or right, only straight ahead. Don't speak, except to me. Got it? Is this your first trip to Libya? You must really try to look more Libyan."

George felt he did not deserve to be spoken to like that and pouted to show his disapproval. But the little man was right in what he had said. George had to make sure he did not stand out. At least it felt he was with someone who seemed to know what they were doing. George pulled at his waistband and tried his best to impose himself on the situation.

"*Mela*, so, tomorrow at seven. I don't know your name?"

The policeman stared at him in open contempt for a second or two, saying nothing, then turned and hurried away. George finished his coffee, put two pastries into his pocket for later and removed his jacket and tie. He looked down at the case. The policeman was right – he did not want to trail it through the streets of Tripoli. It was more likely to be stolen outside, than pilfered behind the hotel reception. He approached the concierge and ended up leaving the case high on a shelf, in the left luggage room. Happy it was safe there, he ventured out onto the streets of Tripoli, in a bid to improve his local credentials.

He walked through the busy streets of downtown Tripoli, the afternoon humidity settling on his skin. The city looked and felt like any other major Mediterranean city. It was hard to believe that this was a country in the middle of a civil war.

He went into a clothing discount store and browsed the multicoloured items on the rails. Marianna had never let him buy his own clothes and he was enjoying the freedom. He ended up purchasing a pair of light grey trousers and a blue short-sleeved shirt. A Moroccan street vendor sold him a hooded top, a Yankees baseball cap and some Gucci sunglasses for a handful of dinars. He slipped on the hoody, the cap and the sunglasses, checking out his appearance in a shop window. Yes, he was looking good and ready to go.

CHAPTER 36
NICK WALKER
GAMMARTH MARINA, TUNIS

Nick was guessing that, by now, the focus of the search operation would have shifted from Malta to the ports and marinas of Sicily. He was not wrong and his decision to head 170 kilometres west of there, to the Italian island of Lampedusa, had been a good one.

The eight-hour journey had been hard work. Forcing the Blue Cascade across the ocean at pace, he had hit every wave and trough with a force that jolted his bones. He developed aches in his arms, back and thighs. He started looking ahead at the pattern of the waves, anticipating the shuddering impacts as the Blue Cascade rose and fell over the corrugations of the ocean.

He would have liked to have booked into Lampedusa's marina, find a quiet stable berth on a pontoon and enjoy a night's sleep, uninterrupted by the rocking and rolling of the boat. However, that was never going to be possible, as skipper and boat details were always required on registration. All it would take was one phone call from Malta to the marina and they would be onto him.

He had found a spot on the charts on the south side of the island, where a steep-sided cove would shelter him from the worst of the waves and the rolling cobalt swell. That was where he dropped anchor. The events of the last twenty hours had drained him and, despite the lolling of the boat as the waters rose and fell, he had managed to grab a few hours of much-needed sleep. The next morning, he had raised the anchor and headed into Lampedusa harbour, where he refuelled and bought a few things from the quayside mini-market. In less than an hour, he had left the port and set off for Tunis.

The day passage from Lampedusa to Tunis had been equally tiring, but uneventful. He had plenty of time to think about what had happened at the villa. He had replayed the events of his last night there, forwards, backwards and sideways, trying to make sense of how it had all come about. The more he had thought about it, the more convinced he became that Natasha had largely been responsible for the wretched outcome of that evening.

She had blazed up about the problem with the coke, way beyond anything that was necessary. She had lied to him from the day she had met him. There had been plenty of chances to put it right, but she had persisted with the charade. Even if he had known she was Marco's daughter, would it really have made that much of a difference? Although he did not regret a moment of the good times or the sex, he had always been aware of her holding back from him. And now it was clear why.

Thinking back, she would never have sacrificed her involvement with her father's business to develop a relationship with him. She had used him purely to benefit herself and her family. Throughout their time together, she had systematically debriefed him on all the major aspects of BetSlick's operations. God, what a fool he had been! And to think he had been flattered by her interest!

That business was an organised crime concern, the size of which had only just become apparent to him. And, to cap it all, she had stalked him through the villa, with a gun in her hand. She had returned and crept into the house, shoes off, in the dark, with the intention of killing him! He had been lucky to get out alive and he was certainly better off out of it. So why then did he feel so bad about what he had done to her?

He could still feel the blow jar his arm, as the vase hit her skull. He could vividly see the way she lay huddled on the tiled floor, after sliding down the wall, unconscious. That was something he would never forget.

He had spent the time at anchor flicking through his phone, trying to find photographs of Natasha. He realised he had very few. He had found one selfie shot of the pair of them. They had been sitting at the table on the decking at the villa. Nick had held the camera above them, his other arm loosely slung round her shoulders. She was grinning, sunglasses concealing the upper part of her face. She looked radiant and was laughing at something that had passed between them. That was all he had left of her.

Nine hours later, he was tying up to a pontoon in the brand new, exclusive Gammarth Marina, just outside Tunis. He hooked the Blue Cascade up to the power and the water supplies on the dock, registered at the office, showing his passport, then went back to shower and smarten up. He was banking on being long gone by the time Marco thought of checking the Tunisian marinas.

During the crossing, he had found the Blue Cascade's Maltese registration papers under the chart drawer, which showed it was VAT paid, as well as the compliance papers issued by the boat-builder and an up-to-date owner's manual, recording all the maintenance and repair work. He had also found a bill of sale from the French shipyard that had built her five years ago. Nick prepared a realistic-looking authority on the letterhead of the Blue Cascade's registered owner, some Cypriot company, and put it on a USB stick. He was hoping it would be enough to enable him to sell the boat. The paperwork was all there to make the sale look legal, but it was not going to be easy, given it would have to be for cash, payable immediately.

The clerk in the office changed some money for him and told

him where to find the nearest yacht brokers, directing him to some offices near the port. The first broker looked at the photos of the boat on Nick's phone and the paperwork. He then looked at him and back at the papers and sighed: "We don't buy boats ourselves. We introduce buyers to sellers. We advertise boats in our window and catalogue them on our website. I should say, it normally takes at least three months to complete the process."

"What about if the boat is at a spectacular discount to market value?"

"Then we would have even more questions about such a sale. It is a nice boat, the papers are OK but, as I told you, we do not buy boats ourselves and neither will any other broker here. If you want to trade and bargain, I suggest you go to the *souk*."

After several hours of getting nowhere, Nick grabbed a chair at a roadside café and ordered a coffee. It was looking like he was running out of options to sell the Blue Cascade. Then, without any invitation, a large man dressed in battered brown pants, a stained off-white shirt and open-toe sandals, sat down at his table. He ordered tea, then grinned at Nick.

"I hear you try to sell a boat? A nice boat. A stolen boat?"

Nick furrowed his brow and looked him up and down, trying to get the measure of him. He did not look like a policeman, but neither did he look as if he could afford to buy a five-year-old, fifty-foot luxury cruiser! Still, Nick had nothing to lose.

"Yes. Well, yes and no. I've got a boat to sell, but it's not stolen."

The man patted the big round belly sitting above his pants, grinned and extended one enormous hand, which was hard and callused.

"You call me Bobby. I build boats and I also buy and sell boats. I have friends at the brokers. They ring me when interesting things come up, maybe ... how you say? Too hot for them! You understand? I don't care where boat comes from, if price is right. I can re-register a boat, change some colours, design, serial numbers, and no one will ever know. So, tell me about this boat. What makes it special?"

Nick thought for a moment. He was on the run, suspected of murder – nothing ventured, nothing gained! Hell, he could talk to anybody about anything!

They talked for an hour, while Bobby looked at the photos and the documents. He knew all about boats and Nick watched him build a mental picture of the vessel, the refurbishment work necessary to conceal its identity and the price he would offer.

"If what you say is true, it is worth at least seven hundred and fifty thousand euro, maybe one million. But, you know, if you want cash today or tomorrow, I can pay only one hundred thousand euro."

Nick immediately opened his mouth to protest.

Bobby held up his hand. "Don't bargain with me, friend. It's all the money I can get in one or two days. If you not interested, it's no problem for me. I finish coffee go do other business."

Bobby paused.

"So?"

Nick shrugged. This chubby, disreputable-looking man held all the cards. Nick had little choice at that point.

"So, if I come later, and if I like the boat, I give you as much as I can get in euros or US dollars, in cash. We meet here again tomorrow and I have legal bill of sale for you. We sign, I pay, and you run to wherever you're going. I sell this boat a long way from Malta or Cyprus. No one will ever see it again."

Later that evening, Bobby spent two hours crawling over every inch of the boat, torch in hand. After wiping his hands, he smiled and announced he liked the Blue Cascade. They agreed to meet at noon, at the same café, to complete the sale. Nick nodded in relief – one hundred thousand euros would take him a long way from Malta and Tunisia. He had hoped to get more, but what the hell? It was not even his boat! He thought about Marco's reaction, once he found out his beloved Blue Cascade had been fenced for a hundred grand. The thought even cheered him up a bit.

In the morning, he went into a local *souk* and sold some of his gold and all of Natasha's jewellery. It gave him a grim satisfaction to sell her stuff. He did not like the thought of carrying her personal items around with him. First, it was incriminating and made him feel like a thief. Secondly, as he handled the jewellery, the thought of those pieces nestling against her skin brought back emotions he was trying to keep in check. He was making a conscious effort to remember Natasha as the serial liar, who had arrived at the villa with the intention of putting a bullet in him. He had decided to try to toughen up and not let his own dark thoughts drag him down.

After a few minutes of haggling, he had traded the gold. It did not take him long with, a calculator, to realise he had been robbed by the dealers and made a note never to trade in North African *souks* again. But cash was cash, and that was what he needed right now.

Overnight, he had come up with an idea. As Bobby and he were in the back room of the café, behind a closed door, counting out piles of fifty euro notes, Nick asked if there was any way he could get hold of a fake UK passport.

"Well, UK passport is most valuable passport in the world, maybe second only to US. It's most difficult to forge. So, we don't do that. But I know a man who steal them, or he get blanks. Then no problem; if not, they must to be stolen to order. It's expensive, my friend."

"You surprise me! So, if I give you some of those fifty euro notes back, you could arrange one for me?"

"I need one hundred of these fifty euro notes and it take time to get, but yes. Maybe you also don't want to stay on the boat – not very private on the big expensive boat. People ask questions. Who is he? What he doing here? If you like, I can arrange a room, in a very nice house, in Sidi-Bou-Said, in Carthage? It's comfortable, clean and a nice woman, my aunt, will cook good food. Three or four days?"

"Bobby, I'm very pleased I met you. I suppose you need more fifty euro notes back to arrange this room for me?"

Bobby laughed again, which made handing over the money a little easier. Nick knew he was placing a lot of trust in this man. But, he had come up with the cash for the boat after all and had, so far, been as good as his word.

"Who knows?" Bobby continued, flicking through the folded wad of notes. "Perhaps you like it here, stay a little while?"

"I'll have no money left, if I don't get away from you soon!"

CHAPTER 37
MARCO BONNICI
CASTELLO BONNICI, MALTA

Marco returned from the hospital the night after Natasha had been injured, feeling better about the way her recovery was progressing. The injuries were not as serious as had first been thought. The doctors had assured him the swelling around her brain had begun to reduce and her condition was stable. Given the news, he was looking forward to getting home.

As he drove into the turning circle of Castello Bonnici, he noticed Camilleri's black police BMW parked to one side of the drive, under the portico. The Mercedes S series was also out of the garage, which meant Simon must have collected Sergio from the airport.

Sergio embraced him fiercely, the moment he walked into the salon. Camilleri hung back; he was there on business and he was not Family.

"She is good – better than I could have hoped for. She has had a small operation, to relieve the swelling, and that all went well. She is stable now and resting. The worst is over, I hope. It has been a difficult day."

"We will find him, Marco, he cannot run forever."

Marco asked Sergio: "Where are we with the search?"

"We know Walker took the Blue Cascade and we are

assuming he headed to Sicily, to make his way to the mainland and then perhaps back to the UK. That is my bet. He has limited money, no lead to speak of and no friends. We have checked all marinas and ports within his range that accept non-commercial vessels – nothing as of thirty minutes ago. He could be at anchor. We have three boats out, checking anchorages from Taormina to Agrigento. They will work throughout the night but, as you know, there is a lot of coastline.

Camilleri nodded his agreement, then said, "We do not believe he has gone south. The North African coast is difficult to navigate and there are not too many places he could have gone. Also, it is a long trip and he would have had to burn cash on fuel. You know how much a boat like that costs to run. We do not think he has enough money on him to waste it. He will have hit a few ATMs before he sailed, but he will not have got much. I agree with Sergio: he cannot run forever."

Sergio turned to Marco.

"I'm afraid there's some more bad news. Walker made a phone call to an inspector in the *Pulizija* from the boat, earlier this morning. He told him about BetSlick, the oil operation, about our involvement. Gerald has kept him quiet for the time being, but it's a serious concern. I had to tell the Wise Men. It's something that could compromise us all."

Marco paused and took time to let the news sink in.

"Personal grudge aside, this little shit will blow us all out of the water if we are not careful. We need to find him and shut him up *fast*."

Sergio sat in one of the large leather armchairs.

"Gerald has some interesting ideas about that." Marco sensed an uneasiness between them, as if something was going on that he was not yet unaware of.

Camilleri put his hands behind his back and closed his eyes, deep in thought.

"Yes, if you think it through, there are some interesting options. There are only two people who are of concern here. One is Walker – and we will find him – the other is my colleague Zammit, currently in Tripoli. I used a bit of leverage to get him to act as our courier. I assumed what he was carrying was valuable and guessed we would need a special courier; one who is too scared to do anything, other than what I tell him.

"But, now, he has to go too. Even if he swears to keep silent, that promise is only as good as the day he gives it. Another place, another time, he might step forward and open his mouth, when we need it least. It is a risk we cannot take."

Sergio nodded.

"I agree."

"So, what better place for a man to go missing than in Libyan bandit country? And that is exactly where he is going in the next few days!" Camilleri announced.

Sergio had already heard the plan and was keeping his gaze on Marco.

"Well, do not look at me! If you want to murder a Maltese policeman as a precaution, get on with it. Tell me, how exactly are you going to go about it?"

Camilleri looked perfectly comfortable with the conversation. He turned towards Sergio and raised his eyebrows, looking for confirmation. Sergio took a deep breath.

"He's carrying something very valuable – not just the down payment, but access to our European banking system, your banking connection in Cyprus. If it became known to certain parties that this was the case, and Zammit's location was disclosed, and we agreed to change our arrangements on supply in Libya, we could arrange it so we never see Zammit again."

Marco's eyes opened wide.

"No, no, no! This is all the wrong way round. We cannot just change our arrangements to cover up an assassination. Surely you are not suggesting we change our partners now? I have spent the past year putting all this together. It would be madness to change it at this late stage! The first shipment is ready to leave. It can sail tomorrow."

Marco looked at Sergio.

"There has to be a better way? Surely, we can offload this Zammit without changing everything else?"

Sergio got to his feet and held up a hand to silence him.

"There's a bigger picture here, Marco. I've got a Ukrainian contact, Danylo, who uses us for loans to stock build for weapon sales. This dealer has good connections in the Middle East and North Africa. Our minority partners in Libya have sent word they're not happy with the arrangement. They say this is too big for your guy over there to handle. They're questioning his experience and leadership ability. They say your man is an amateur and will soon become a liability. Someone will pick him off in a matter of months – which nobody wants. There're some serious people looking at what we're doing and getting ready to make a play. Remember, it's almost a state of war between the militias over there. They all need money and oil sales mean dollars!"

"So, tell me," Marco asked, "who is saying this? Our minority partners – you mean Islamist terrorists? Through some Ukrainian middle man?

"Are you seriously saying we should go into partnership with ISIL?" Marco's face said it all. "Sergio, are you crazy? They are madmen. We already have a good arrangement with some sensible people, who quietly get on with business and have what we need."

Marco counted off on his fingers.

"Supply, port access, shipping – all in place, ready to go! This Libyan ISIL militia you are suggesting we deal with, they hide in the desert, doing hit-and-run raids, not daring to break wind for fear the American satellites, or drones will hear them. They are dangerous lunatics and cannot be trusted."

At that moment, Sergio went to the desk and picked up his laptop.

"Take a look at this, Marco. Someone tipped me off about it being posted. Go on, take a look."

He beckoned Marco to come and look at the screen. Camilleri stood back; he had obviously already seen whatever it was.

A grainy YouTube clip appeared, covered with Arabic script. Arabian battle music was blaring in the background. Beneath the images, subtitles announced: "The rise of the Defenders of Marsabar".

They watched six minutes of what Marco guessed was Abdullah and some ragged riff-raff, charging around the desert, firing guns into the air and speeding about in trucks. They cut the footage with segments of Abdullah sitting cross-legged, talking to schoolchildren, then walking around a mosque with an Imam. The English and Arabic subtitles told the story of a regional protector, a martyr in waiting, an educator and a devout Muslim, prepared to sacrifice everything for his faith, his people and the town of Marsabar.

It was amateurish and, rather than being a display of the power and gravitas of The Defenders of Marsabar, it was a little pathetic. It showed rival militias that Abdullah was there for the taking. It had been badly filmed and badly edited. Some of the close ups made Abdullah's men look more like the extras in the *'Pirates of the Caribbean'* than fierce desert fighters. The sound mix was poor, with the cheesy background music drowning out the voice over. Abdullah leered out of the shots, the edit making him look furtive, unsure and self-conscious. His eyes swivelled left and right, never holding the gaze of the camera. The guns popped and crackled, but the timing in the fight scenes was out and looked like it was running on fast forward. The figures scurried around the mock battle field, like actors in a Chaplin movie. If Abdul-Lateef had wanted to deliberately embarrass Abdullah, he could not have done a better job.

Before Sergio closed the screen, he noticed the post had already been viewed over 7,000 times and it had only been up a day.

Sergio looked at him, gravely:

"Quietly going about his business, is he? That's Abdullah Belkacem, isn't it?"

Marco was lost for words.

"Yes, that is him. What the hell was he thinking?"

"I'm sorry, Marco. You've done good work here, but everyone in Libya now knows there's a new kid on the block and he's just announced, *'Come and get me!'* You know what? It's the wrong country to say things like that – because they will."

Marco knew when he was beaten and realised Sergio could be right. Over time, their oil business could get so big that Abdullah would not be up to the game. He felt deflated.

He turned to Sergio.

"And the Wise Men agree with this?"

"Yes, we've been on the phone, while I was in the air."

"OK, so how do we do it?" He did not like it, but he needed to understand the new plan.

"The Ukrainian, Danylo, will act as the middle man for the first transaction only. We've got to move fast, so we've got no choice. I need to ring him to confirm he can contact the minority partners."

"You mean the ISIL murderers?"

"Yes, Marco, that's who I mean. There's not much time, a day at the most. The deal still stands – we get the ship out to sea, our new partners will step up and Inspector Zammit will be a hero – or rather, a martyr – an unwitting casualty of a fire fight between two warring militias. He'll die acting in the course of his duty, while investigating a Marsabar-based people trafficking ring. The briefcase with the down payment and the banking stuff will be intercepted. Alongside him, the valiant Defenders of Marsabar will die in a flurry of bullets, which was always going to be their fate, if a little sooner than they'd expected."

Marco watched Sergio grin to himself, amused with his little speech. He continued; he had it all worked out.

"We'll transfer the banking arrangements to our new partners and we'll get contact details to set up new lines of communication. I don't see much else changing. They can assure us of all future supplies and we foreclose the marine mortgage we have over the *Malik Albahr*, so the ship legally becomes ours again. There's no doubt they've got all the technical knowledge to handle this. They've been stealing oil across the Middle East for decades.

They can easily move into the vacuum created with the death of your man, Abdullah."

"All very clever," Marco said. "So, we are bankers to ISIL now?" He shook his head in disbelief.

"You know, the Knights of St John have been fighting Islam since the twelfth century? There are some on the island who will not like this."

"Marco," Sergio put his arm on his shoulder, "the real Knights are all long dead and we live in modern times now. When you see Natasha, give her our love, will you? We all worry about her. Find out if she's got any idea where Walker might've gone. She knows him best. Gerald, thank you, you can leave us now. Your help is very much appreciated."

Once Camilleri had left, Sergio continued: "Look, Marco, I've got no agenda here, but leave us to handle this. We can focus on finding Walker and managing the changeover; you've already got your plate full. But, there's one other thing. The Navkov brothers have telephoned. They say there's money missing from their player accounts at BetSlick. Have you heard anything about it?"

"No, nothing. How much?"

"Nearly half a million euros."

"Jesus! Nobody has said anything to me about it. I will find out what the hell is going on!"

Sergio said: "You don't think there is a bit of a coincidence here?"

Marco thought it very strange indeed. Grozdan and Hristo Navkov were two of BetSlick's most important clients. Not only did BetSlick manage cash from the Family's activities, they also provided a similar service to a small number of select third-party clients. The brothers were Bulgarians: ruthless operators and Europe's biggest smugglers of counterfeit cigarettes. There were those in the Family who believed it should not be involved with them, but Sergio had argued that he was confident he could handle the brothers.

Marco felt beaten down and did not like the way his conversation with Sergio had turned out. He had taken the oil project off in a different direction, without talking to him first, and had gone to the Wise Men behind his back. On top of that, the theft from the Navkovs was disquieting. No, it was ominous.

CHAPTER 38
INSPECTOR GEORGE ZAMMIT

TRIPOLI, LIBYA

George woke early, excitement forcing him out of bed and into the shower. He went down to enjoy his breakfast, as best he could. Despite the nerves making his stomach churn, he filled his plate several times and, to be on the safe side, put several pastries into his pockets. It occurred to him, it might be the last chance of a good meal for some time. He idly wondered whether they would take him to lunch, during the drive.

Promptly at seven, he was packed and waiting, looking sharp in his new hoody, cap and fake Gucci sunglasses. As suggested, he had put the briefcase in a loose nylon zipped bag, to conceal it from prying eyes. It felt good to be out of the heavy, tight shirts and business suit he had endured for the last two days and, scrutinising himself in the mirror, he thought he looked appropriately dressed for some street action. He even wet his hair and tried to plaster it back, to complete the look. He was nearly done; one small trip and he could return to Malta, mission accomplished! At that moment, he was starting to quite enjoy his adventure.

He had slipped his Maltese Police warrant card into his breast pocket. He was not sure it would carry any weight, but it gave him some assurance that he had some official standing, no matter how remote.

At 7:00a.m. exactly, an Isuzu 4x4 pulled into the hotel car park and waited some fifty metres away. The vehicle's headlights flashed so George picked up the blue nylon bag, containing the briefcase, and his cabin bag, then walked over towards the car. When he was ten metres away, a rear door swung open, which he took to be an invitation to get in.

Inside, sitting in the back, was the policeman he had met the previous day at the hotel, in full uniform. The driver was a young boy in a tracksuit, eyes shielded by wrap-around sunglasses. George noticed the policeman had a service revolver holstered at his waist.

"Get in next to me," ordered the policeman. "Keep the bag on the floor and put the travel case in the boot. There's nothing stupid in it, is there?"

" I wouldn't think so." George replied.

He slung his case into the boot space and got in, pushing the nylon bag under the driver's seat with his foot.

"I don't expect trouble, but it's best to be ready. Have you got the money?" George handed over half of what he had left. In the rear-view mirror, he saw the boy smirk.

George was determined not to be pushed around, so he said, in his sternest voice: "If we aren't stopped, I want that back. It's Maltese police money."

The policeman just looked at him, folded the cash into his top pocket and secured the button.

"You can call me Yousef," said the policeman. "Call him Driver. We're going maybe two to three hours west, up the coast. We'll meet the contact – I've got a phone number – you hand over the briefcase, he checks it; then we turn around and we come back. I leave you at the airport and you go home. Easy plan, yes?"

With that, he put on some mirrored sunglasses and Driver pulled out into the traffic. Tripoli was a city with over a million inhabitants, so they spent the first thirty minutes driving west, along the dual carriageway that was the Coastal Road, sandwiched between the sea and the urban sprawl. The sea was flat and calm. Well-appointed villas and foreign embassies occupied the best positions, with north facing verandas and balconies to take in the beach view, while providing shelter from the worst of the sun.

After an hour wrestling with the Tripoli traffic, they drove through Az-Zawiya. The complex infrastructure of its oil refinery and terminal swamped the town, protected by high fencing and secure double gated entrances. This refinery handled most of the oil from the western oil fields and was one of the major legal points of export for Libyan oil.

They encountered the first signs of trouble beyond Janzour, a sizeable town a few miles after Az-Zawiya. The road had swung inland and the buildings had thinned out, giving way to stretches of agricultural land which bordered the road on both sides. Traffic was light in both directions, but Driver seemed to be aware something was wrong. He muttered to Yousef in Arabic, as he slowed the 4x4. There was a heightened sense of tension within the vehicle.

A large road bridge came into view, straddling the Coastal Road. It provided a good source of shade for a group of men carrying automatic weapons and wearing desert camouflage uniforms, who had parked two trucks in the shadow cast by the bridge, creating an impromptu road block. George noticed the car in front brake heavily, turn around and head back the wrong way, up the dual carriageway, towards Tripoli.

Yousef spoke, his voice steady: "Remember, say nothing and let me speak. This isn't a problem; they're SDF. I know them."

Driver approached at a crawl, keeping one hand on the wheel and the other hanging out of the car window, showing that he was unarmed. The soldiers looked unconcerned, lolling around and smoking. One came over to the car, rested his hand on the roof and stuck his head into the window.

Yousef spoke to him in Arabic and the soldier nodded along with him. Then he stood back and started pointing down the road, gesticulating. With a bang on the roof of the 4x4, he waved them on.

George had been staring straight ahead, but the Gucci sunglasses had large lenses, so allowed him the occasional sideways glance to follow the gist of the conversation. Even though it was cool in the jeep, he felt the perspiration forming on his hairline.

"What did he say?"

"There's been a bank robbery back in Janzour. There's an armed group active around here. They're robbing banks, killing many bank people and kidnapping. Now they're carjacking down there."

He pointed in their direction of travel,

"The Special Defence Force, these people," he jerked his thumb over his shoulder, "have closed the road and will hunt them out later, in the week. They're waiting for more soldiers from Tripoli."

"So, if the road's closed, how're we going to get through?"

Driver laughed and manoeuvred the car through the two parked trucks. Once through, it became clear the road on the other side of the blockade was empty of traffic. Driver accelerated and soon the Isuzu was flying down the road at its top speed.

Yosef sat straightfaced; Driver was grinning, enjoying gunning the vehicle.

"Now we see what this car can do!" Driver's window was down and a jet stream of hot air howled into the vehicle.

"They don't catch us on this part of the road and we don't stop for anybody," Yousef announced, "but the road is blocked fifty kilometres from here, so we'll go into the desert to avoid the problem. That's more dangerous. Remember, getting there is only half the journey – we need to get back, also. Maybe, if it's very bad, we'll come back after dark."

It was as if Yousef was talking to himself. At this point, he unholstered his revolver and checked the cylinders, ensuring the pistol was fully loaded. He reached under the passenger seat and pulled out a sports bag containing a Glock semi-automatic handgun, which he passed to Driver, who glanced at it and put it between the seats.

Even though the road was closed, there were farmhouses, businesses, mosques and even cafés on either side, all operating normally. Some larger towns along the way had small local militias out on the streets, to watch for trouble. They stood around in their military fatigues, in twos and threes, at junctions and in the central squares, but nobody tried to stop the speeding 4x4. The road was quiet and most inhabitants were avoiding using it, other than for local trips.

After an hour driving at full tilt, they came to an earth bank, about six metres high, blocking both carriageways. Around the earth wall, was a wellworn track in the scrub, where a succession of vehicles had created a detour past the obstacle and struck out into the open area to the south. There was a hand painted sign pointing down the track indicating 'Marsabar'.

Driver did not hesitate and pulled off the road onto the rough single track to the side of the earth wall. As he did so, six men appeared at the top of the banking, guns slung round their necks. They did not move; just stood perfectly still, watching them.

Driver turned and pointed towards them.

"Who are they? Don't look like SDF or local militia."

Yousef twisted his head one way, then the other, looking up and down the road, alert to danger. He ignored Driver's question. Instead he turned to George and said: "We're not far away now. Keep your eyes open; this is dangerous country."

He took a phone from his pocket and made a call, speaking in Arabic.

"It's OK. Our contact knows we're near. He's waiting for us. It won't be long." He seemed to be speaking to reassure himself, as well as George.

Just at that moment, a trials bike leapt out of a shallow valley to their left and raced alongside the 4x4. Driver panicked and grabbed the Glock, waving it at the motorcyclist, screaming in Arabic through the open window. The boy on the bike raised an arm and made the sign of a gun with his hand, pointing it back at Driver.

"What's happening?" George asked, his heart starting to beat at a crazy speed. Then, the biker suddenly peeled off and stopped his bike on the road behind them.

Yousef looked over his shoulder, while talking on the phone again and waved a hand, telling George to be quiet. He put the phone down.

"Hmm … I don't like this. Keep driving," he told Driver. "Look for a fork ahead, back onto the Coastal Road. There's a car park on the left, at a disused café. We're meeting there. They don't know who these people are. They say it might be SDF, following us to check our business, but I don't think so."

George did not like it, either. He was terrified and could hardly get his words out. This was the very situation he had dreaded; being stuck in the deserts of Libya, surrounded by armed men, with trouble bubbling all around. He felt a very long way from his yard and his chair in the shade.

"Can't we turn back and find somewhere safer to meet?"

Yousef looked over his shoulder again and saw a plume of dust rising about 800 metres behind them.

"No, look, the soldiers from the blockade are following us. They sent the biker to check us out: how many people, if we have guns; if we look dangerous. Our best plan is to get to the café and hope 'The Defenders of Marsabar' protect us!" He let out a hollow laugh.

Driver turned around, his head banging against the roof as the speeding car hit the ruts and potholes in the road.

"Did you see that 'Defenders of Marsabar' shit? What a joke!"

"Drive, faster!" Yousef ordered, gun in hand, staring out of the back window at the pillar of dust rising behind them.

CHAPTER 39
MARCO BONNICI
CASTELLO BONNICI, MALTA

It was early the next morning when Simon banged on the door of Marco's bedroom. He usually stayed awake until the early hours and then slept until six. That night, he had gone to bed as soon as had finished his conversation with Sergio and, despite his misgivings, had slept soundly until seven.

"Enter, Simon."

"Boss, we've got a lead on Walker! We have him in Lampedusa. When we started to draw blanks all over Sicily, Camilleri got in touch with Lampedusa's port security and we've got the Blue Cascade on the harbour CCTV. He tied up on the public wharf for an hour, refuelled and then left. After that, I'm afraid we don't know where he went."

"Right. Lampedusa! When did we find this out?

"I got a call, just now."

"Is Sergio in the Paceville office?"

"Yes, he should be. He left about ten minutes ago. He said he was sitting in on some staff meetings."

"I will ring him and see if he can make it back. Let me get a shower. In the meantime, can you go to the study and pull the Admiralty Nautical Charts for Lampedusa? And you may as well do the Bay of Tunis too. I will be down shortly. Oh, and can you, and whoever else is available, get ready to travel, as soon as possible?"

In the shower, Marco considered the new information and where Walker might have gone.

He thought back to previous conversations with Nick. He remembered he had spent some time in Gibraltar. There might be someone there he trusted, who could help him out on the next part of his plan. It would take a lot of fuel but, then again, if he had cash, he might be desperate enough to try it.

Camilleri had used Europol and Interpol to alert member bureaux that Nick Walker was wanted in connection with a transnational drug smuggling operation. He had requested any attempt by Walker to cross any border to be reported to the *Pulizija* immediately. It was one of the reasons Marco thought he might stick with the Blue Cascade, until he got back into mainland Europe and the Schengen zone.

His best guess was that Nick would refuel in Tunis and then do the crossing to Southern Sardinia.

Sergio returned within the hour and they settled in the study, the doors to the terrace open, letting in a lemon scented breeze from St Paul's Bay, to calm the midmorning heat. Marco briefed him. Sergio was perched on the mahogany library step ladders: "Let's call off the Sicilian search."

He jumped off the steps and came across to the desk. He peered at the chart and tapped at his laptop.

"There're only about a dozen marinas along the Tunisian Coast. That's not a lot of places to hide."

"Yes, but we do not have the same assets in North Africa as we have on the European side."

"How easy would it be to sell the boat, Marco? It's got to be worth a lot of cash?"

"Yes, but it is not the sort of thing you can just sell in a bar."

"Sure, so, can we get a team of two or three into Tunisia and have them check the marinas?"

"Already done, Sergio. Simon and one of his guys leave

tomorrow – first direct flight. We have another guy going to Lampedusa; a fast boat will take him this afternoon. He will be there this evening and will check out the CCTV, ask around, see if there is anything else we can find out. He will then join up with the others in Tunisia."

"OK. That all sounds good." Sergio was still looking at the map. "I'll see if there's any way we can cover the area between Tunis and Capo Spartivento. That'll be the place where he's forced to bear east for Cagliari or go up the west coast of Sardinia. D'you know,I think we're going to get this bastard."

CHAPTER 40
NATASHA,
ST JOHN'S HOSPITAL, MALTA

IT WAS four days before Natasha woke up. The sedation had been necessary to give the swelling around her brain time to reduce. Her first moments were disorientating. Her mind and body were only semi-connected. She lay very still, trying to make sense of where she was, and what had happened to bring her to this place.

First, she moved her fingers and felt the tight weave of the sheets. Then she flexed her toes to make sure her legs were still attached. A fierce thirst burned in her throat. She could hear a buzzing, like some insect beating against a window.

After a minute, the first sensation of discomfort started to filter through her waking state. She tried to raise her head but a crushing pain ran through her skull and she collapsed back down onto the pillow. She could feel the constriction of heavy bandages around her head and over her ears, explaining the muffled sounds around her.

Opening her eyes, she realised she was alone, in a darkened hospital room. Sunlight was pushing its way through the blinds, throwing thin bars of light and shade across the surface of the bed. She instinctively knew she would not be able tolerate that intense bright shaft hitting her eyes.

There was a call button on the bed, attached to the wall with a white plastic cable. She reached out and felt the smooth, cool plastic case. She pressed the large red button and somewhere, outside the room, she heard a faint buzz. Lying back against the pillow, she started to work through what had happened to her. She remembered hearing her name being called, then – nothing. She lay back, relaxing deep into the pillows, and felt her eyes closing, remembering nothing more of that first waking.

The second time, a nurse was in the room, adjusting the settings on a monitor. Natasha asked how long she had been asleep and was told she had been sedated for the last three days. The nurse scurried off to get a doctor, who tested her, scanned her and finally proclaimed himself satisfied. The wound had closed and would heal, the internal bleeding had stopped and the swelling had begun to subside. There was no lasting injury to the brain, except that she was suffering from a concussion and rest was the only treatment.

As she gradually pieced together the events that had brought her to the hospital, a sense of anxiety started to engulf her. It felt as though she had made a series of poor decisions, which had triggered a chain of events that were only now unfolding. She needed to talk to her father and find out what was going on. Whatever had happened with Nick, she had pushed him too far. It had never been part of her plan that she would end up lying in a hospital bed, with a headful of stitches.

She felt terrible; nauseous, tired and dizzy, but was determined to get out of there and back to Castello Bonnici, as soon as she could. She needed to know where the pieces had fallen.

She raised herself onto her elbow and managed to get a hand into the drawer of the bedside cabinet. Her watch was there, rings, earrings and the gold chain from around her neck. To her surprise, her iPhone was also there, with a small amount of charge still left on it. That was what she had been hoping for.

She cradled it for a while, deciding what to do and then

opened the text menu. She typed 'Nick' into the phone and wrote:

Where are you?

She waited on the off chance that there would be an immediate reply. Nothing. She flicked her emails and other messages, noting there was nothing that could not wait. She then saw there were seven unread text messages. They were all from an increasingly worried Elbasan, imploring her to contact him. She was not particularly concerned; he was an idiot and all his problems were most likely of his own making. She had no worries about the cash transfer; the money was exactly where she wanted it. She deleted the messages and gave them no further thought.

It was time for her to sleep. Tomorrow she would leave the hospital, even if she had to crawl out on her hands and knees.

CHAPTER 41
NICK WALKER

AUNTIE NESERINE'S HOUSE, TUNIS

On the face of it, life at Bobby's Aunt Neserine's turned out to be pretty good. Not only did she have a nice, well-appointed guest room that led to a small private courtyard, filled with potted lemon, tangerine and kumquat trees, but she ran a kitchen to die for.

Bobby had advised Nick to stay indoors and keep his head down. He told him there were not many foreigners in that area of Tunis, so it was best not to draw too much attention to himself. He passed the time in the pleasant surroundings, still haunted by feelings of guilt and uncertainty. He wondered whether it was the death of Natasha or the fear of reprisals, or possibly the weight of justice, that worried him the most. He did not know; all of those outcomes worked together to agitate and exhaust him. The only thing that roused him from his sloth and cheered him was the array of food. Aunt Neserine could certainly cook!

His quiet time at Sidi-Bou-Said ended on the second day, when a glowering Bobby burst into the courtyard.

"What shit do you bring down on my head?"

Nick put down *Moby-Dick,* the only English book Bobby could find for him, surprised by his tone of voice.

"What's up, Bobby?"

"Some East European man at the marina, asking about Blue Cascade and looking for you!"

Shit, thought Nick. It had to be Simon.

"Well, you said you'd move the boat to your yard! If you didn't bother, someone's bound to see it and start asking questions. Don't blame me for that!"

"Tell me, is it stolen? Who the hell you steal it from?"

"It belonged to a company owned by my boss. Don't worry. Just get it out of the marina and out of sight. He's not going to bother with the boat – it's me he's after."

"You? What does he want with you?"

"I killed his boss's daughter," Nick announced, matter-of-factly.

For the first time since Nick had met him, Bobby was speechless.

"Oh, fuck! *Ya salaam*! And you bring your troubles here?" Bobby's eyes bulged and he ran his hands over the rolls of fat on his jelly head.

"Look, let's go get the boat and take it to your yard. Then I'm gone, out of here. I don't want to hang around anymore than I have to. Listen, for what you paid, you knew that boat wasn't clean."

Bobby turned and paced around the courtyard. Then, spun on his heels to face him.

"I see you at marina in two hours. This man, he is going nowhere. The boat is what I want. I pay good money for it and I keep it. You go to the boat and you make sure this guy, he see you – then you run and you go. He chase you. Then, I move the boat. Tunis is a big city. You can easy lose him in backstreets of old town. Take the scooter to marina, then leave scooter in the car park. You escape on that – you can drive scooter?"

Nick nodded.

"Pack and give me your bag. I find an honest hotel, take a room and leave the bag there. You have phone, yes?"

Nick nodded again.

"OK, when I have boat, I will SMS you name of hotel."

He smiled grimly.

"This way, I keep your money safe and I am sure you be at marina in two hours." Bobby smiled. "You know you can trust me, yes? You no show, I keep your money!"

Nick scowled at Bobby, but it only took him a second to realise he had no choice but to leave the money with him, hard though it was. He could not outrun Simon, carrying a sports bag full of cash with him. Probably, he could not outrun Simon at all.

He went to his room and realised he was back to square one. He had more cash than before, but the airport was now of no use to him. There were no real land options, with Algeria to the west, the Sahara to the south and the closed border into Libya out east. Sardinia and Sicily were to the north, but the marinas and ports would now be well covered. The Blue Cascade was red hot, with Simon, or one of his henchmen, patrolling the marina and probably another team, either on the streets or about to arrive. He felt well screwed.

He was in Bobby's hands now. He had no choice but to play chase with Simon, to help Bobby get the Blue Cascade out of the Gammarth Marina and then hope he would keep to his end of the deal. Nick did not fancy being chased through the streets by the big Pole, but drawing Simon away from the marina was the only chance of getting the boat out and keeping Bobby on his side. He would have to check out the layout of the marina on Google and see if he could put a workable plan together. He went off to find an internet café.

Two hours later, Nick rode the blue Piaggio towards the marina, his head bouncing around inside Bobby's damp, sweaty helmet. In the internet café, he had studied a map and satellite photos of the marina. It had a circular layout, with an entrance in the breakwater to allow the boats access to and from the open sea. As the Blue Cascade was one of the bigger boats berthed there, he had moored it right at the end of the circular dock, furthest away from the main gate and nearest to the sea entrance.

His biggest worry was that, if he approached the cruiser and showed himself, Simon could cut him off from the exit and the scooter, his means of escape. The further he walked around the curve of the dock, the greater the distance to the entrance and the scooter. The other worry was that Simon might not be alone. Nick wondered whether they would really have a team hanging around the marina all day. Probably, given the Blue Cascade was the only lead to him they had.

Nick approached the marina through the new expensive whitewashed villas in the adjacent housing complex. The gate was open and there was a security point which was unmanned. He parked the scooter as near to the end of the dock as he could and took a chance by leaving the key in the ignition. He looked around for Bobby.

He soon spotted him. He was with two other men, dressed in shorts and T-shirts, sitting at a table drinking tea, outside the circular café next to the harbour office. Bobby put on his sunglasses and spoke, in an aside, to the other men. He then gave Nick a subtle nod and the plan was set in motion.

He approached the dockside, looking along each of the pontoons that ran out into the centre of the marina. People were cleaning yachts and one or two were wheeling trolleys of provisions from vans parked dockside. There were a few people about, but he was relieved it was not too busy. He kept making his way round the edge of the marina, alert and ready for action. His nerves were jangling and his heart rate was increasing by the minute.

A third of the way round, he could see the Blue Cascade, chrome and steel fittings glittering, its light blue trim resplendent in the afternoon sun. So far, nothing ahead, or behind him. He kept walking. He was almost at the boat when he noticed a figure step out of one of the delivery vans in a white, open-neck shirt and a dark suit. It caught his attention, as everyone else was wearing shorts, flipflops and polo shirts. Nick looked away, but he was sure this was it.

He pushed on more quickly now, towards the Blue Cascade. This was exactly the situation he had feared most. Simon was behind him; between him and his escape route. The only good news was he appeared to be on his own. But then Nick spotted a second figure, in tight fitting grey trousers, with black shoes and a long-sleeved white shirt, entering the marina at a run. The game was on.

Nick began jogging towards the Blue Cascade, letting them gain ground on him. He needed to draw them towards him. He jumped the metre gap from the pontoon onto the rear of the boat, clambered around the side of the cockpit and onto the front deck. Simon and his colleague were sprinting now, aware they had cornered him at the end of the dock, with nowhere else to run.

As Simon approached the boat, he yelled: "Walker, you're a fucking dead man!"

When they got to the berth, Nick stepped over the side of the handrails, dived off the prow, getting as much depth as he could under the water and started to swim with a powerful breastroke. Swimming fully clothed and with shoes on was hard. The distance to the other side of the entry channel was only fifteen metres, but it seemed longer. He was aiming for a slimy steel ladder back up to the dockside.

He held his breath for twelve strokes, but the effort was too much and he had to surface for air. He could see he was only a few strokes away from the ladder. Simon stood on the walkway, around the side of the Blue Cascade, shouting to his partner to run right back round the marina, counter clockwise, towards the entrance.

Simon pulled a gun and, before Nick could get back underneath the water, he sensed the whoosh of a silenced bullet, just to the side of his head. He ducked back under the water and made for the dockside. Climbing up the ladder in full sight of a shooter would be suicide. The bright sunlight helped him, giving him a full view of the yacht keels ahead, while the glare frustrated Simon's aim. Pulling hard against the water, lungs bursting, Nick made the inside of a pontoon, which gave him cover from any more incoming shots. He set about scrambling up onto the dock, hauling himself out using the mooring ropes and fenders of the nearest yacht.

Dripping wet, he started to run, his feet sloshing around in his sodden trainers. The other man was not that far from him now, moving at a full sprint. Within twenty seconds, he was astride the scooter. He turned the ignition key, twisted the accelerator and drove out of the car park, water flying from his soaking shoes and clothing. There was just enough time for him to raise a middle finger to Simon's accomplice, as he accelerated away.

At that point, he noticed the service road leading to the marina was blocked by a rusted white Transit van. The bonnet was up and two men in long white robes and skullcaps were peering into the engine. Bobby had brought help!

Nick briefly laughed out loud, before concentrating on part two of the plan. He needed Simon and his henchman to follow him, so he slowed, watching the side mirror until he saw a silver Peugeot SUV speed through the exit of the marina, its rear end sliding through the turn. Finally, he could increase speed and start the real 'get away', while they lost time, manoeuvring past the 'broken down' van.

He entered the sweeping roads of the upmarket residential area that lay between the marina and the suburb of Gammarth. Turning his head, he saw the silver Peugeot appear at the bottom of the road behind him. Pressing on, he weaved his way across the traffic at a large roundabout and entered the old town. Almost immediately, he found himself swerving and dodging pedestrians, vendors with hand carts and double-parked cars, which made the tight roads even narrower. At one point, he heard the faint incessant blaring of a horn. Hopefully, that was Simon, stuck behind some incident on the chaotic streets.

After twenty minutes of moving along, he started to relax and reduced his speed, letting his heartbeat slow a little. He was wet through, not just from the salty water of the marina, but from the work he had put into keeping the scooter upright and the adrenaline that had surged during his escape.

He noticed a café under a block of apartments, so he stopped and parked the scooter round the back, out of sight. Taking a seat away from the window, he bought a Coke and tried to look inconspicuous in his sopping clothes. He took out his phone to check for Bobby's text, with the address of the hotel where he could find his bag – and his money! It was a nervous moment. It would be very tempting for Bobby to take the cash and jewellery in the bag, and just leave Nick to swing!

His phone had been in a sailor's waterproof case, hung around his neck, under his shirt and, when he turned it on, he saw the message – a text from Bobby.

Sunny Apartments, Suite 12, Le Kram.

Then, a jolt, like a punch, hit him in the chest, right over his heart. He saw the name on the text below: 'Natasha'. He caught his breath and checked the date and time it was sent. Over twenty-four hours before.

Where are you?

Her voice rang in his head. A surge of emotion threatened to overwhelm him. Was she alive? Surely not! It was not her – it could not be! Probably that bastard Marco, trying to trap him. It had to be.

Still, he could not help himself, he had to know if she was still alive. It was a risk, but they already knew he was in Tunis, so there was nothing new they could learn, if he replied.

I never meant to hurt you. I was scared. You had a gun and I thought you were coming for me. Prove it's you.

Within thirty seconds, he received a selfie of Natasha in a hospital bed, with her head bandaged, but the trace of a smile on her lips.

See what you've done?

Thought you were dead. Been devastated.

You're in the shit.

Tell me about it. But will you be OK?

Got a hole in my head and trouble at home, but I'll live. Will miss you. Stay safe and keep this number?

Just so glad you're alive. Will txt again when safer.

OK. Our secret.

Nick fell back into the chair, struggling to breathe, tears of relief welling up in his eyes. He was not a murderer! He looked around the café with the dirty windows and empty glass counters, shook his head and laughed. In that instant, everything changed. He re-read the exchange of messages several times. There was still a chance it was a trap, but at least he could be sure she was alive, even if he did not know where her loyalties lay. She had a poor track record with matters of trust. To quell his euphoria, he kept reminding himself of that.

CHAPTER 42
ABDULLAH BELKACEM

VAI VAI CAFE, THE COASTAL ROAD, WESTERN LIBYA

Abdullah arrived at the car park of the Vai Vai Cafe within fifteen minutes of receiving Yousef's call. Yousef sounded scared, so he thought he had better get there first and take the best positions, ready to receive any unwelcome guests. There were many small groups of bandits who terrorised travellers along the lonelier stretches of the Coastal Road, but it was disrespectful of them to operate so close to Marsabar, and that made him angry! He was not worried about the call; he had dealt with such people many times and strong words, with a slap from Tareq, was usually enough to send them scurrying away, like the dogs they were.

The café itself had been closed and shuttered since the civil war broke out some six years before. It was near the scene of his big push to rid the area of Gaddafi's government troops, a move that gave rise to the name, *the Defenders of Marsabar*.

The car park was huge, compared to the size of the café. He remembered the times when big eighteen-wheelers would stretch across it and it was busy with traffic, flowing along the road towards Tunisia. The civil war and militia activity in Libya had led to the border between the two countries being closed, leaving the road empty.

The area was desolate, surrounded by low hills that protected it from the winds that blew in from the desert. The gravel plains stretched for miles to the south, broken only by the distant escarpment of the Nafusa Hills. Bunches of prickly pear and low shrubs segregated the car park from the road. He had Tareq and five other family members with him, more than enough to deal with a truck of road bandits! He was not expecting to be at the café for more than ten minutes. All he had to do was deal with the low-life militia scum in the truck, take the case from Yousef's passenger and get back to the strong room under his house.

The boys were kicking a football around the massive car park, when he heard Tareq shout. He pointed at the columns of dust rising up down a track to the south of the café.

"Vehicles, a few of them! Take positions!"

They all grabbed the semi-automatic weapons that had been cast aside, while they had passed the ball around the car park. Tareq was shouting instructions.

"Osama, Mussie, take the hill behind the café and cover us. You three, behind me."

Tareq stood, legs apart, with an RPG launcher over his shoulder and his M16 assault rifle hanging around his neck.

"Abdullah, what's this? I don't like it."

Abdullah peered down the road. There was only supposed to be one vehicle. He did not like it either. He had underestimated what they were dealing with.

"Give me a gun! This is not how it should be," he barked.

Tareq went to a vehicle and pulled out an Israeli Galil rifle. He loaded it and threw the gun, as well as a spare cartridge towards Abdullah. Then he raised the RPG launcher, pointing it at the Isuzu 4x4 that sped into the car park, skidding to a halt, showering stones and grit towards them.

The door flew open and three men got out, hands in the air. Abdullah recognised Yousef, the policeman; the others he did not know. There was a fat one, in strange clothes, clutching a heavy-looking nylon bag over his shoulder. They all looked at each other for a moment, then Yousef turned and pointed behind him.

"We're being followed. Eight men, two 'technicals' at least, with large-calibre machine guns or canons fitted on the back. There was also a boy on a trials bike. We don't know them! But, look, we have the case, here!"

He pointed to the fat, nervous man who, for some reason, was wearing women's sunglasses. He waved the case at Tareq, as if it was some terrible burden he was eager to be rid of.

Tareq and Abdullah ignored them and stood, listening intently. No signs of engine noise, just the sound of the wind blowing through the scrub. They looked at each other and Tareq shook his head. He then continued sweeping the area with the RPG held on his shoulder.

"So, Yousef, what is happening?" Abdullah asked. "Where are these bandits?"

Before Yousef could answer, a crackle of gunfire burst out from the low hill on the northern side of the car park. Bullets bounced on the compacted dust and sand. A youth who worked for Tareq at one of the migrant compounds was hit. He spun round screaming, as the bullet tore into his shoulder. Then the shutters of the café burst outwards, as they were kicked out of position, and a pair of automatic weapons opened up against them. Tareq hit the ground and pulled at Abdullah's legs.

"It's an ambush. Down, get down!"

Almost immediately, Tareq pulled the RPG launcher over his shoulder, sprang up into a crouch position and fired a grenade towards the café, blowing up the door and front window with a deafening crump. Broken glass rained down everywhere. Cheap panelling fragmented in the blast, leaving only half the facade intact. For a moment, there was silence, and Abdullah lay prone and exposed in the middle of the enormous car park.

Yousef and Driver had hand guns. They had raced for cover to the east side of the car park, shooting bullets behind them to cover their escape. Abdullah opened up his semi-automatic rifle and fired bursts into the café, while Mussie and Osama put down covering fire into the banking on the northern side. The fat man in the blue shirt lay face down in the dust, very still, with the nylon bag over his head. Abdullah glanced at him briefly and wondered if he was dead.

The deafening sound of revving engines and gunfire then filled the air. Three battered, Toyota 'technicals' flew through the entrance and into the car park, sliding across the loose gravel and stopping short of the café. They had been hiding from sight behind a bend in the road. The lead truck had a Browning heavy machine gun mounted on the back and the gunner, unable to aim from his unstable platform, was throwing large-calibre lead in all directions. Fortunately, the movement of the truck bouncing over the terrain meant most of the bullets were wide of the mark. Above the cab, Abdullah noticed the black flag of ISIL in Libya.

Abdullah reacted first, grabbing an anti-tank rocket from the quiver on Tareq's back and helped him reload the RPG. Tareq swiftly took out the lead vehicle, with a close range shot that blasted it into the air in a ball of flames. The man on the gun soared upwards, arms and legs flailing. The heat from the flash had burned Abdullah's face and beard, but he had felt nothing. With a massive crash, the burning truck landed metres away from them and another body fell out of the passenger door, smouldering where it lay. The truck then exploded a second time, as either fuel or ammunition went up. The policeman, Yousef, and Driver were pinned down, unable to make their escape.

George was scorched by the blast from the exploding truck, which burned his back and neck, but he was oblivious to the pain. He lay in shock, trembling, face down in the dirt. He was paralysed with fear, cursing Denzel's stupidity that had given Camilleri the leverage to put him in this place.

There were bullets flying in all directions. Shouts and cries filled the air. Yousef and his driver were now engaged in a battle with the attackers on the hill to the north side. The two other men Tareq had brought had hidden behind a low wall and were shooting rapid bursts of automatic fire into the ISIL vehicles. After thirty crazy seconds, the incoming shots seemed to stop. Then suddenly more shots came from the low hill behind the café, where Osama and Mussie had run to. Abdullah could not remember seeing them again and presumed they must also have been hit.

He reached for the last of their grenades and had just reloaded Tareq's launcher, when his brother was rammed back into him by a shot into the middle of his chest. He slumped. Abdullah caught him under his arms and felt his body shaking in spasm. Abdullah turned him and, for a moment, their eyes met. He realised he could do nothing for him, except bear his weight, as the strength flooded out of him. Abdullah laid him gently on the ground, his blood soaking through his shirt, mingling with his own sweat. He shook Tareq and shouted at him to get up. He put his arms around him and was about to give himself over to the shock of what had just happened, but realised he would not survive another minute, if he did.

A white rage built inside him, but he knew he had to control it or he would end up lying alongside Tareq in the dust. If that happened, all he had achieved for his family and his clan would be lost. He stood, automatic gun in one hand, and tried to wrestle the RPG from around his brother's body. The carrying strap was fastened tight and his brother's weight was over the weapon. He could not manage it quickly enough and, to stay out there, exposed, would surely make him the next target. He gave up and ran towards the wrecked café, seeking such cover as he could find.

Bullets had hit the second vehicle from both Abdullah's gun and those of the two men positioned behind the hill, on the east side. Its windscreen was out and there was steam and oil leaking from its engine block. The driver was slumped at the wheel. The third vehicle was still operational, the engine running and the doors open. Abdullah saw one of the two men who had been with Tareq lying awkwardly by the entrance to the café, blood pooling beneath him. Of the second, there was no sign.

Despite the crack, crack, of weapons being fired at him, he reached the café and burst in. Two men lay dead and a third was lying wounded on the ground, the result of Tareq's first grenade blast.

The injured man was defenceless, so Abdullah pushed his gun into the stomach wound that was oozing black bile and blood. The man screamed in pain.

"Who are you, you fucker?" Abdullah asked him.

"Go ask Abu Muhammed, dead man," he spat.

Abdullah paused, just for a second. Was he surprised? No, not really. He should have known it, as soon as he realised they were being attacked by a column of 'technicals' and not just some highway thieves out of Tripoli. The ISIL flag was just there to add insult to the fatal intent behind the ambush.

"This is for Abu Muhammed, then." Abdullah put the gun to the man's head and pulled the trigger.

Crouching low, he scurried towards where the window had been and looked out to see three figures in desert combat fatigues moving towards him, behind a row of low shrubs on the roadside. To his left, in the middle of the packed earth of the car park, the fat man was still lying on the ground. Abdullah assumed he was dead, but then saw him raise his head ever so slightly under the bag, to look around.

So, he was still alive, but only because no one had thought to shoot him. The man was either blessed or was being very clever. Abdullah shouldered his rifle and lined up a shot at one of the men creeping towards him, satisfied with the jolt the impact had on the target. He knew the ISIL raid had not gone to plan and they had lost a lot of men. He was starting to think he might just survive it. He owed it to Tareq so he could at least avenge him.

The hope was short-lived. One of the two remaining fighters had broken into a run and had reached the rear of the café. The second was pumping bullets into the front of the building, forcing him to take cover against the thin wooden walls. They were not thick enough to stop the bullets, but at least they hid him from sight. At some point, there was a sudden clatter. Abdullah thought someone had thrown a brick into the building, but he soon realised that it was a hand grenade. There were only seconds to react. Jumping to his feet, he charged towards what had once been the doorway. When he was nearly over the threshold, the explosion took him off his feet and threw him forwards, headfirst, out onto the hot earth.

George had been trying to work out what was going on. Terror prevented him from thinking rationally. He was shaking uncontrollably. The men waiting in the car park must have been with the contact, the one who was supposed to get the briefcase. They were the men Yousef was on the telephone to. The men in the trucks, who had chased them from the Coastal Road and then attacked them, were obviously trying to kill them.

He saw the dead body of one of the men who had been there to meet them, lying some ten metres away. He still had an RPG launcher around his neck and a rifle in his hand. The launcher was already loaded. He thought, if he could get close enough to reach those weapons, create some chaos, maybe he could get across to the third truck and make a run for it, away from the carnage. The truck was standing there, doors open, its engine still running. Or maybe he should just keep lying there, praying.

At first, his limbs refused to move. But, gradually, he crawled on his belly to where the dead man lay. He had spent plenty of hours on the police shooting range and the feel of a weapon in his trembling hands was reassuring. He had only ever used pistols and sporting rifles, but the military grade weaponry did not feel that different. He inhaled the smell of gun smoke in the air, took in all the blood on the ground and saw the burning vehicles, pumping black sooty fumes high into the desert sky. In a strange way, he felt the fear subside a little and was energised. He reluctantly realised, if he was to live, he had to play his part in what was happening around him.

George had watched the tall man in local dress, with the black beard, who had first met them, make a run for the café. He had then seen him dive back out, as an explosion inside threw more debris up into the air. By then, he had freed the grenade launcher from the dead body. As he had turned it over, the man's lifeless, dark brown eyes seemed to look into his and his mouth gaped open, as if to speak, whilst a trickle of spittle ran down onto his dark beard.

The weapon was heavier than he had expected, but he slung the long tube over his shoulder. Kneeling, as he had seen the dead man do, he felt for the trigger guard, pointed the weapon at the café and fired. The recoil threw him backwards but, when he scrambled back up, he was satisfied to see the café facade and some of the roof had totally disintegrated.

Abdullah's ears were ringing and the grenade blast had stunned him, but he still managed to see the fat man drop the launcher, pick up Tareq's rifle and throw himself down. He seemed to be smiling! He did not realise that what he was seeing was a desperate grimace on George's part. George quickly shuffled across the ground, taking cover behind Tareq's body, while he aimed and took a shot at the ISIL fighter who was still behind the low wall at the entrance to the car park. The first missed, but his second was a perfect headshot. Abdullah realised this man knew what he was doing. A shower of blood and brains cascaded down onto the light grey surface of the road. He did not know who the fat man was, but he thanked Allah for bringing him to them.

Abdullah tried to shake off the blast concussion that had disorientated him but, before he could gather his wits, he saw a familiar figure emerge through the ruin of the café building, although he was in an unfamiliar black and grey uniform, rifle in hand. He came towards Abdullah, who was happy to see he was walking with a limp.

"Samir, you treacherous dog!" shouted Abdullah, raising

himself off the ground, to a sitting position. "I should have killed you when Tareq told me to. Look!"

He pointed to where his brother was lying. He realised the fat man was lying next to Tareq, watching what was happening.

"He is dead. You killed Tareq, your own blood, your clan, your friend. So, you have joined the Beards, eh? They will cut your balls off within the month, when they find out what a treacherous, lying turd you are."

Samir gave him a sarcastic smile.

"You sent me away, Abdullah. You're to blame for all this. What's wrong, big man? Always telling everyone what's right, what isn't. Not anymore. You're finished, you're nobody, you motherfuck! Abu Muhammed's going to take everything: the migrants, the farms, your house, even your ugly wife and children, and that shitty old ship. He's fucking you, Abdullah, and you let him. Shame on you."

"You think Abu Muhammed will be pleased with you when you go back with ten men dead and three trucks burned out? He will think you hid in a gulley, while the fight went on. You are a liar and a coward, Samir, always were."

Samir's hands were shaking and, fumbling in his pocket, he took out a phone. Keeping his gun trained on Abdullah from a good three metres away, he set up the camera function and pointed it along the barrel of his rifle towards him.

"Well, Abdullah, this is it. First you and then the Maltese policeman. I'll find him, don't worry. Now, you smile for my camera, while I put a bullet in your face. The next photo will be of your stupid big brother, dead in the dirt. I'll make Abu Muhammed laugh with that." He steadied his hand. "So long, big man."

George had watched the man in black and grey camo appear, limping through the dust and smoke. He had scanned the car park, but somehow had not seemed to register George lying behind Tareq's corpse. George had looked around as well realising there was nobody else left alive, except the three of them.

The rest lay dead or had fled into the desert. The fighter was focused on the unarmed black bearded man. George slowly started to crawl, commando-style, to the edge of the car park, keeping one eye on the young fighter who was moving towards Blackbeard. There, under cover of some prickly spinosa bushes, he checked his weapon for bullets. He was thirty metres away. He watched the other two carefully.

He soon realised the younger man was about to execute Blackbeard and film it! Shoot him for the camera! George guessed Blackbeard was the man he was supposed to deliver the suitcase to. He had come so far to hand over the damned thing and that boy was not going to thwart him.

George heard the young fighter say, *'First you, then the Maltese policeman.'* He thought he had misheard at first, but no, that was what had been said. He wondered how the fighter knew he was going to be there. How could he possibly have known there was a Maltese policeman there? More to the point: why would they want to kill him?

He realised he had to act quickly. He slowly lifted his rifle and raised himself to a kneeling position. He followed the procedure he had learned on the police range, putting the stock to his shoulder, taking careful aim, breathing in, but then had to lower the gun and take a few deep breaths, to calm himself.

He was breathing hard, but had to try again. The second time, he aimed, held his breath and gently squeezed the trigger. He hit the younger man, catching him on the side of his head. The calibre of the bullet made up for what the aim had lacked. His head twisted as the bullet ripped across the side of his skull. George dropped the gun from his shoulder, took a gulp of air and raised a clenched fist above his head, in a triumphant salute!

For a moment, Abdullah was frozen to the spot. He turned his head to see the fat man shake his fist in the air. He watched, as George walked slowly towards him, with Tareq's gun pointing at him. Abdullah had no play to make, so he just knelt back on his heels and waited. He had no idea who this man was, only that he was no ordinary courier; probably special forces. Whoever he was, he seemed to be on his side. He watched as George got as far as Tareq's body and then stopped. He seemed to realise the link between them. He raised his eyes and looked towards Abdullah, questioningly.

Abdullah was exhausted. He stared at Tareq, lying there in the dust, and the realisation hit him that his elder brother was dead. At that moment, he could feel nothing, no emotion. He knew grief would take him later, closely followed by unspeakable anger.

He crawled over to his brother and took Tareq's hand in his. He closed his eyes and murmured a quiet prayer, rocking gently back and forth, on his knees.

"O Allah! Forgive him, have mercy on him, and cause him to enter Your Paradise."

He kissed his brother's forehead.

Tareq's body, so strong in life, was now crumpled and useless, lying on the hot, stony ground, his blood staining it black as it leaked out of him. Abdullah stood, looking down at Tareq for a while and aimlessly traced a pattern around his head with the point of his shoe. Then he turned to George, who stood watching him, and calmly said: "That is my brother. He is dead. I will be avenged for his loss."

George looked around, dazed and a little disoriented.

"I'm sorry," he said. "There seem to be a lot of dead people here." It was as if he had only just noticed!

"You were expecting me?"

"Yes. Well, I expect somebody."

George walked a little way behind him and fetched the blue bag he had held over his head. He returned and offered it to Abdullah, who had crouched down over his dead brother.

George, oblivious to the sensitivity of the moment, said: "I have something I must give to you."

Taking in the destruction and bodies in the dirt, he held out the blue nylon bag and waited for Abdullah to take it.

"Whatever's inside, I hope it's worth all this."

Abdullah stood and took the bag. He looked at the strange man who had saved him.

"My name is Abdullah Belkacem. I owe you my life."

George paused, before replying, "Yes, I suppose you do. You can call me George."

With that, he rummaged in the pocket of his hoody, took out a serviette that held the crumpled remnants of a breakfast pastry and started eating.

CHAPTER 43
AMR WARDA
MARSABAR HARBOUR, LIBYA

Amr Warda, proud new master of the *Malik Albahr,* was supervising the loading process and getting her ready to sail. The crew of ten were experienced seamen, but he still needed to run through his procedures for getting ready to put to sea. Every skipper had his own way of doing things and Amr was no different.

After several more hours, he was satisfied that the loading and ballasting was correct, as was the stability and trim – he had done the calculations himself. Amr had also prepared his ship-to-ship transfer checklist so that, when they reached Hurds Bank, he could set about moving the fuel oil and petrol to the smaller vessels.

The engine room was ready and all hands were at their posts. The pilot was on board and he was ready to sail the vessel out of port, through the small entrance, past the breakwater towards the open sea. He had already gauged the depth of the passage and was satisfied it was deep enough to take the loaded vessel's draught. The wind was light and the tidal range in the Mediterranean inconsequential, as usual.

Amr used the VHF radio to contact the Harbourmaster to say they were ready to unberth and leave. Two men strolled down the dock to cast off the heavy ropes that bound the ship to land. On board, the winches pulled the ropes in and free water started to appear between the dock wall and the side of the ship, as the thrusters pushed her out into the harbour. A small tug stood by, in case of trouble, but Amr was happy with the operation.

He was unashamed to feel a surge of pride, as the boat drifted out and began its journey towards Malta. He was, however, surprised he had not heard from Abdullah, who had said he would be there to wish them farewell on their first voyage. In any event, his orders were clear and the Captain saw no reason to vary them because of Abdullah's absence.

He waited until the *Malik Albahr* was clear of port, before telling his First Officer the route to Malta. He had turned off the automatic identification system and planned to sail east. That would take them along the Libyan Coast towards Benghazi, well away from the busy sea-lanes from Suez, at the head of the canal.

At Benghazi, he planned to alter course and sail north to join the main traffic heading westwards towards Malta. He would then activate the AIS system and the ship would appear on the commercial tracking systems. That way, if anyone checked their previous course, it would look as though they had come through the Suez Canal.

Passing through the Suez Canal was no easy matter, but he had received an email from a mysterious Italian address with all the necessary receipts and authorisations, which he would keep with the ship's papers. It would also fit with the fraudulent Certificate of Origin for the cargo that certified the oil was from Saudi Arabia. As instructed in the email, he had also altered the ship's log to record that the *Malik Albahr* had berthed for four nights in Jubail, one of Saudi Arabia's busiest ports in the Persian Gulf. Amr knew it was a criminal offence and one that could easily be discovered, but he was not worried, given the small chance of exposure and what he was being paid.

Once they were underway, he went to his cabin to catch up on more routine administration. He was sitting at his small folding desk, when he opened another email from another unidentifiable address, this time a mix of numbers and random characters.

Captain Amr Warda,

By operation of law and marine mortgage foreclosure, the ownership of this vessel, the Malik Albahr, has passed to Jakarta Logistics. Remains registered Palau. From now, all instructions will come from this email address. Complete current passage and transfer cargo as planned. All current instructions stand good. Then immediate return to Marsabar instructed. Further instructions to follow. No contact is possible with previous owners. Use this address if new instructions required or to report any matters. Ships agents, Mifsud, Malta will service on Hurds Bank if required.

Safe passage,

Jakarta Logistics

CHAPTER 44
MARCO BONNICI,
CASTELLO BONNICI, MALTA

IT WAS late afternoon and Marco was in his garden, just starting to feel the cool of evening descend. He was checking some of the pumps on the irrigation system. He had organised the plants into sections, separated by walkways, which played to their different combinations of colour and height.

The textures and shapes of the plants allowed him to create fascinating patterns, positioning the small, sharp, prickly ones next to round, bulbous ones. Large fronds curled and twisted over thick, textured leaf structures beneath. Pieces of jagged limestone provided centrepieces, around which circular patterns of small cacti were meticulously arranged.

Marco did not trust the gardeners to get the more subtle aspects of the design right; they all seemed to have a blunt, practical touch. He felt a personal responsibility for that thing of beauty he had created. There was an element of co-dependency; he needed it as much as it needed him.

A shadow appeared over his left shoulder and he was conscious of someone standing nearby, watching.

"Is gardening good for the soul, Marco?" asked his cousin.

"Yes, it helps with thinking and I fear we have quite a lot of that to do."

Sergio had his hands in his pockets and was staring off into the distance.

"I've just had quite an uncomfortable conversation with the Wise Men. They're very concerned."

"We are all very concerned, Sergio. We have two disappearances. Murderous Bulgarians are accusing us of theft, and my daughter nearly died. Yes, it is all most *'concerning'*!"

"They say we've got to fix this, and quickly."

"Really? Well, that is a useful piece of advice. Do you have anything in mind? I am all ears."

"Come on, Marco, let's not fall out about this. The Wise Men are sending someone to help us."

"And who might that be?"

"Raphael's on his way."

"Their enforcer ... You are joking?"

"No, that is exactly what we need. They say we're businessmen and Raphael is more of a tracker dog. He'll find Walker and the policeman and then they'll stop being a problem. He'll also look into the business about the theft at BetSlick. We're to give him full control of the hunt and provide all the help he needs."

"Sergio, I do not like the way this is going. You know the arrangement with the Family. What happens on the island is my responsibility. Here, *I* decide – not the Wise Men, not you, and certainly not a cold-blooded killer like Raphael. You can tell the Wise Men I will listen to what he has to say, but he does not go off on any enterprise of his own, unless I approve it in advance. Do you understand?"

Sergio smiled at him.

"I thought you might see it that way. The Wise Men also said they reserve the right to manage the cleanup in whichever way they see fit. And Raphael's how they intend to do it."

Sergio shrugged to show it was out of his hands.

"I suggest you don't cross Raphael. Tell him what he needs to know and stay out of his way."

Sergio wandered off and Marco turned his back, seething. He knelt back down, apparently to pick some dead leaves from a spiral aloe. As Sergio's footsteps faded away, he hurled his secateurs against a stone pillar in the central display.

It not only angered Marco, it shamed him to think Sergio and the Wise Men thought it necessary to push him to one side and usurp his authority in this way.

It was true, the episode on the dock in Tunis had been a disaster. News of the firefight in Libya and an early report from Abu Muhammed's people that the Maltese policeman had fled with Abdullah, was also disappointing. It gave Marco some satisfaction that the latter was Sergio's screw up and not his own. He did not feel quite so exposed, as that piece of the picture started to emerge. Failing to finish the policeman was one thing, but letting Abdullah escape to regroup and reassert himself, or at least interfere with their plans, was much more serious. He would be rabid for vengeance.

The sun had started to set, so Marco went in to wash and join his cousin on the terrace for an *aperitivo* before dinner. Despite everything, it was important to maintain appearances.

CHAPTER 45
ABDULLAH BELKACEM

MARSABAR, LIBYA

ABDULLAH PULLED HIMSELF TOGETHER AND, with George's help, lifted Tareq's body into the back of the ISIL Toyota flatbed. The car park was shrouded in smoke. The acrid bite of the propellant from the weaponry still hung in the air, rubber and oil from the two burning trucks creating a dense sooty cloud. Abdullah collected weapons and turned over the other corpses, checking for signs of life and going through pockets. He picked up a smartphone. Suddenly, he froze, then turned around and ran back to the Toyota

"You," he shouted to George, "now, get in! Hurry! Hurry! We must go."

He raced the truck all the way back towards his farmhouse, hitting the ruts and bumps at speed. George could hear the scarping sounds and dull thuds, as Tareq's unsecured body slipped around the flatbed. George had no idea what the panic was about, but stared resolutely ahead and braced himself against the impacts, as they buffeted the truck.

Abdullah had just realised where Abu Muhammed would strike next; the place closest to his heart. Rather than take a direct route home and risk being blindsided twice in one day, he took a track over the hills to the east. Time was important, but he could help no one if he was dead.

As the road crested a ridge overlooking the plain where his home stood, Abdullah braked, skidding to a halt in the dust. Black smoke rose from the distant buildings and he could see figures moving around outside the walls. He took the binoculars from under the dash and jumped out of the truck, his heart beating hard and fast. He had to find out what was happening around the distant homestead below.

He was too late, it was his house that plumed an oily black pillar into the powder blue sky. Tareq's Mercedes was burning in the compound. He was glad his brother did not have to suffer that insult. One part of the outer wall of the farmhouse had collapsed, due to a blast. It was obvious that a second group of Abu Muhammed's men had hit the farmhouse, while Abdullah was engaged in the fight at the café.

Abdullah reached into the leather case on his waist and pulled out his phone. Hardly daring to breathe, he checked his messages on WhatsApp. It was there!

I moved the goats to the shaded hillside.

It was a code he had agreed with his wife. It told him Rania and the children had escaped the attack and were safe, hiding somewhere or heading south into the Nafusa Hills. She and Abdullah had planned that, if the house was ever attacked, she would go to the cellars and through a short tunnel. The soft sandstone had made it easy work for the bodies who had done the digging. It exited into an old farmer's hut, well outside their walls. There, they kept an ancient, but serviceable Subaru 4x4. He only hoped Rania had remembered how to drive it!

Rania's family were wily Berber and would shelter her and the children in a village deep in the Nafusa hills, protecting them from harm. Abdullah understood only too well the power of taking hostages. Abu Muhammed had failed in that too! It was one less worry, in what was already a day of many misfortunes.

The depth of Abu Muhammed's treachery made Abdullah white-hot with anger; a rage that went beyond reason. He now realised the Beards must have done a deal with the Maltese to take over the oil supply business, behind his back. His grip on the binoculars tightened, as he watched the hated figures parading around what had once been his home. He had been humiliated. All he wanted to do was load all the weapons he had and race the truck towards them, blazing bullets at the bastards who had done this to him. But his head told him otherwise. He was not ready to die just yet.

The safety of his family was a blessing and he would give thanks to Allah for that in prayer. The gold and money in his vault were not so safe. The steel door was designed to look like a block stone wall, but Abu Muhammed was not stupid. Maybe he had already plundered the safe room and Abdullah would have to accept that his gold and money was gone; there was nothing he could do about it now. One day though, when he killed Abu Muhammed, as he promised himself he would, he would take back his money and more besides. Still, he had the heavy brief-case and there was some comfort in its weight.

He turned his back and left his smouldering home behind him. George was still in the truck, staring ahead, oblivious to Abdullah's gaze, an M16 carbine nestling in his arms. Without a word, Abdullah pointed the truck towards the coast.

CHAPTER 46
INSPECTOR GEORGE ZAMMIT

MARSABAR, LIBYA

George had been sitting quietly in the passenger seat, watching what was unfolding out on the plain. He could guess what it meant for his new friend. Friend? Accomplice? Captor? He was not sure what their relationship was. Abdullah could not hide the hard lines that had appeared on his face, the fierce set of his jaw. His eyes had narrowed, as he came to terms with the death of his brother, the havoc wreaked on his family and his inability to change or avenge what had happened. Abdullah thought he showed no emotion, but he might as well have thrown himself to the ground and howled. George would have thought none the less of him for that.

"Was that your home?" George asked bluntly.

"The desert is our home. That was only stones. But there will be a price to pay for this. My family are safe, but my house, my brother, my money and my ship have all gone."

"You have a ship?" George was surprised.

"Yes," sighed Abdullah, "the *Malik Albahr*. She is not a pretty thing, but how many men can say they have a ship, eh?"

The *Malik Albahr!* George was careful not to show a reaction to the ship's name. He had thought the day could not have thrown any more surprises at him. So, this man was the owner of the *Malik Albahr*? George shook his head, faintly amused by how ridiculously mad his day had turned out to be. He now had another piece of the puzzle – the vessel that had started all his troubles and had led him from the familiar quayside of the Grand Harbour to this empty, perilous place. He had a thousand questions, but was not going to bother about them now. All he could do was stare out of the window, at the barren landscape of bush and rock. A faint breeze blew the smell of burning rubber towards them.

Abdullah was silent for a while. Finally, he said: "I have heard it said that grief is like a hole. You can never fill it or forget it but, in time, you can learn to walk around it. So it will be with Tareq.

"He was older than me, but he always let me lead. Today, my mistakes caused him to die. I can never forgive myself for that."

George thought for a moment, choosing his words carefully.

"I'm sorry for the loss of your brother. I saw what happened today. You were ambushed. It's not your fault. You can't blame yourself. I didn't know your brother, but I'm sure he would not blame you."

"You do not know all that has passed. I was warned – but my pride and willingness to trust the word of a man who should never have been trusted, has caused all this. It is my fault and I must live with it. But thank you for your words – it is true, Tareq would never have blamed me. It is some small comfort."

With that, Abdullah choked slightly and then took a deep gulp of air. It was probably as near to tears as he would allow himself to get.

He drove on, lost in his own thoughts, until he pulled up at a ramshackle farmstead at the side of the road. Dogs ran out, barking at the truck. He got out and brushed them aside. An old man appeared and, after much embracing and some tears, they carried Tareq's body out of the truck and into the house. Abdullah stayed inside for about thirty minutes, presumably to follow the rituals of burial and to pray for his brother. When he came out, he got into the truck and sat for a moment in silence, staring vacantly out of the window with his head held high and a grimace on his face.

"We belong to Allah and to Allah we return. Tareq was a good brother and I will miss him," he said.

George had nothing to add, so he nodded, while Abdullah cranked up the engine and turned the truck down a track, northwards towards the sea.

When the coast came into sight and he was certain there was no threat for several miles around, Abdullah stopped the vehicle, smoothly for a change, without the usual clattering of rocks and spray of dust. He turned in his seat and looked at George.

"Do you have cigarettes?" he asked.

George shook his head.

"So, who are you? Special forces? What are you doing with my case?"

George could not help but smile at the question. His gaze remained locked onto the scrublands that surrounded them. He replied, speaking more to himself than in answer to Abdullah's question.

"I'm a Maltese policeman. A superior officer told me to deliver it to you. I've done that and now I want to go home."

"A Maltese policeman! No, my friend, you smell of special forces! My brave and dangerous comrade, there is no going back to Tripoli for you. You would not even reach the Coastal Road. In Allah's name, the Beards will be looking for you and will kill you, as sure as the sun will set tonight! You and I have to leave Marsabar, and soon."

In any other circumstances, Abdullah's intense stare would have terrified George. He could tell this man was assessing his usefulness, weighing it against the value of his life. George remained outwardly calm and continued looking out of the window, unintimidated by Abdullah's unblinking gaze.

"You had better tell your masters that ISIL have tricked us and taken our land, our ship and our oil. I will fight to take it back and avenge my brother but, for that, I need money and time. First, we must get away from here, or they will quickly find us. For now, my life here is over.

"So, if I help you escape too and get you back home, will you help me?" Abdullah asked.

"Help you how?"

"There is a way we can both get out of here, but it will not be easy. I can get us on a boat. Then, when we reach safety, we tell a story that I rescued you from the Beards and together we escaped. You will say I can never go back, because the Beards will kill me. That way, I can stay some time in your country. Maybe, because I rescued a policeman – if you truly are a policeman – you can get me a Maltese passport?"

Abdullah looked at George expectantly. He smiled back, thinking, *'It can't be that simple, can it?'*

"What about the case? What's the story there?"

"I do not know. Say the Beards took it? Say it got lost in the escape? Or, say you gave it to Abdullah because, from now on, I will call myself Tareq. I will be Abdullah's brother."

George looked at him and things started to fall into place.

"You're a people trafficker?"

He asked it matter of factly, without judgement.

"Yes, well, *'trafficker'* is an ugly word, but I help people cross the sea to find work and safety in Europe. For money, of course."

"You're a trafficker and you've got people waiting for a boat – a safe boat?"

Abdullah nodded.

"Explain to me how it works."

He ran through the mechanics of the voyage and the methods used to alert the humanitarian and naval vessels that patrolled the boundaries of the international waters. George was focusing more intently now. He felt there might actually be a chance that he would get home, after all. He looked up at the sky.

"Is the weather good?"

"It is now, but it will change later tomorrow."

A plan was beginning to take shape.

"*Mela,* I'm a Maltese policeman sent here to investigate trafficking. I've just been to a conference on it. I'm now going to steal a boat, rescue your migrants and get them to Lampedusa. You'll hide with the migrants in the boat. When we're picked up, I'll single you out, say you helped me, and then we'll see what happens. I promise I'll try to get you asylum in Malta."

George felt a momentary flush of confidence. The plan might just work. He had already completed a clandestine operation, fought off an assault by ISIL and survived. Next, he would single-handedly go on to rescue a boatful of migrants held by a gang of deadly traffickers. He wondered what Marianna would have to say about that! Plus, as a hero and a public figure, he would never have to put up with Camilleri's deadly manipulation of him again.

"Will ISIL follow us out to sea?"

"The Beards? Never. They come from Syria, Afghanistan, Iraq – places with no water. The sea frightens them. They are from the mountains and the deserts. They cannot swim, eh?"

"We must beware of the Coastguards though. If they stop us, they will bring us back and we will be sold on to the militias. Abu Muhammed will hear of it for sure. He is the bastard ISIL leader who has done all this to us … to me. But yes, this is what we will do."

George understood enough about Arab etiquette to realise a symbol of their arrangement was necessary. He reached into his pocket and fished out the remaining breakfast pastry. He broke it in half and gave a piece to Abdullah.

Abdullah looked at it and smiled. Without a word, he popped it all into his mouth, stroking the crumbs from his long black beard.

They drove down the hill to Abdullah's compound on the coast. It was silent. All the villagers and citizens of Marsabar were staying indoors, with their shutters closed, until whatever was happening was over. People knew ISIL militants were cruising the streets, in the mood for trouble.

The first thing they saw, as they drove onto the dusty forecourt in front of the compound, were two trucks, one with a formidable-looking, deck-mounted pair of Browning machine guns and both trucks flying the black flag of ISIL. George grabbed the dashboard with both hands. The last thing he wanted was another encounter with the ISIL militia. Abdullah, fearless, drove the pick up straight into the yard and parked next to the trucks.

"The scum are inside stealing more of my property! Come on, Maltese policeman, I will show you a trick or two!"

A fighter who was supposedly guarding the trucks, slid the large metal door open and stuck his head out, to see who had pulled into the compound. Abdullah took two steps forward and, without ceremony, smashed the stock of his rifle into the side of his head, leaving him stunned in the dirt.

Happy he had disabled the fighter, he pushed George towards the truck with the machine gun and gestured for him to climb onto the rear deck, where the guns were mounted. Two drab green metal boxes were attached to the sides of the barrels. Long ammunition belts snaked into the gun's oily breech, holding the bronze shell casings.

Abdullah grabbed the barrel of the machine gun.

"Make sure you lock the bolt down, like this, eh? It is an automatic firing pin and there are two squeeze triggers. Just fire and do not stop until there is nothing alive in front of you. There is no safety catch. If it is wearing black, blow it to pieces. And hold tight, eh? It is like walking a horny hound past a bitch in heat!"

He pointed towards the industrial unit.

"Remember, the first one out through that door will be me! Do not shoot until I am clear!"

With that, he ran around the side of the building. George stood there, on the back of the ISIL Toyota truck, self-consciously sighting the door with the huge gun and wondering what he should do if anyone came near him before Abdullah appeared.

It never occurred to him that he must have looked both ferocious and intimidating, his wild hair full of desert dust, his shirt soaked with Tareq's reddish-brown blood; not to mention the fact that he was holding a formidable twin-barrelled machine gun for use against armoured vehicles and aircraft.

There was a muffled crump of an explosion from inside the building, followed by the sound of shouting and screaming. The screams grew louder and then there was another shot. It only took a moment before the door flew open and Abdullah dived out, scrambled for cover by the first truck.

"Get ready! Do not wait, just fire!"

For a moment, time was frozen and George could not move. Three ISIL fighters appeared, looking left and right. Then, one saw him perched on the truck, pointing the heavy machine gun at them. They turned their guns towards him, but Abdullah fired a shot and one of them fell. Abdullah was screaming at George, who could not hear a word he was saying. He shut his eyes and pulled the triggers!

It was as if someone had thrown him in front of a train. The noise was like a hundred road drills hammering away at once. The recoil threw the gun about in his hands, as if he was holding a wild animal, yanking and pulling, in its efforts to break free. He did not see what happened when the first fighter was hit, but the short range and the size of the shells had cut him in half. Another lost his lower leg to a ricochet while, in the chaos caused by the Browning, Abdullah shot two others who tried to flee round the side of the shed.

The injured guard had managed to get to his feet and was leaning against the side of the shed, raising his gun, pointing it towards Abdullah. George swivelled the guns towards him, closed his eyes and looked away, as he pulled the triggers.

Within thirty seconds, it was all over. There was carnage in front of them; red hot, spent shells rolled around the bed of the truck and bodies spewing blood lay before the wrecked entrance to the building. The gunfire had punched holes all over the wall and the panelled sides had either collapsed or been smashed into pieces. The sweet, oily smell of the gun shells, mixed with blood, and the screams of the man with his lower leg missing, would stay with George for years.

Abdullah shot the screaming man in the head and the noise stopped.

"Good." he said, looking at the mess around them. "That was meant to be! Come on!" He led the way, walking straight through the puddle of smoking blood and gore, which was just about all that was left of the guard, trailing bloody footprints behind him. "Let's find a boat."

George stumbled around the horrible jumble of human parts, the sound of gunfire ringing in his ears like a bell. He noticed that the flies had already started to feast.

CHAPTER 47
NICK WALKER
SUNNY APARTMENTS, TUNIS

NICK ARRIVED at the Sunny Apartments, where he paid and collected a key from a bored youth at the reception desk. Dusty windows blocked out the burning sun. Worn, green mock-leather armchairs were strewn across the filthy hallway. A flea-ridden, old mongrel bitch lay flat out in the corner, mangy fur and droopy teats; it was difficult to tell if she was alive or dead.

The lift was narrow and dimly lit, which made travelling to the second floor feel like riding in a stiflingly hot, vertical coffin. A loose-fitting padlock secured the room on a flimsy hasp. Inside was a small chrome bolt that could be drawn, to protect against unwanted visitors. Nick locked himself in and started looking around for his bag.

There was no obvious sign of it anywhere. He swore and started to search in earnest, the concern swelling into panic. He looked under the bed and inside the grubby shower cubicle. When he pulled open the wardrobe door, there it was – a red Kappa sports bag. He exhaled and felt relief course through his veins.

He tipped its contents onto the bed. All the money and what was left of the jewellery seemed to be there. Bobby had been as good as his word. Now all he had to do was sit it out and wait for Bobby to get in touch when his new identity was ready. He thought about his plan. He would use the passport to book a ticket out of Tunis, get back into Europe, maybe Amsterdam. He liked Amsterdam; why not spend some time there? Take some time, lie low, eat well, enjoy some beers and think about the future.

Something jolted him from his daydreaming; a ping, the screen of his phone notifying him he had received a message.

Going home later today. Be safe. N. XX

Nick wondered what the point of wishing him safe was, knowing her father's men wished him anything but! The only good thing was there was no request for information, which meant this was not some fishing expedition from Marco or any of his cronies. And at least Natasha was still alive.

He picked up his phone and typed a reply.

Glad you're going home. Hope it doesn't hurt too much. Can we FT tonight?

If he could see her, he might be able to judge if she was being genuine or if someone else was pulling her strings.

IT'S ME! Trust me. But no FT. Too much going on.

Nick replaced the phone on the dresser and, almost immediately, it pinged again.

Got boat OK. Meet at café tomorrow for papers 10:00. Then you go.

It was Bobby. The passport must have arrived. He responded.

I want to go, but need passage on a boat to Italy – Sicily or Sardinia. Freighter or fishing boat. No customs. No police. Euro 5,000.

Will try for boat. Want nice cabin and also woman?

Nick smiled. Definitely no more women for him. After Natasha, he was not sure he would ever trust one again. He also decided he had had enough of the Sunny Apartments; he had not liked the place to start with, but the idea that Bobby knew his whereabouts unsettled him. It would be better to keep moving. So he levered himself up off the hollow in the bed, took his red Kappa bag and walked out of the hotel.

CHAPTER 48
MARCO BONNICI,
CASTELLO BONNICI, MALTA

In the afternoon, Marco went to the hospital to collect Natasha. When he arrived, she was already dressed and sitting in a wheelchair, with her long dark hair concealed under a heavy white bandage. She looked pale and vulnerable. He smiled and hugged her as tightly as he dared. The thought that he had almost lost her was unbearable.

"Let's go home," he murmured.

Once back, he fussed about getting her upstairs and into her room until Katia, their housekeeper, put a hand on his shoulder and politely told him to leave. The private nurse stepped forward and took over. The doctors had demanded strict bed rest, so Marco was surprised when Natasha appeared later on, dressed in shorts and a T-shirt, with a large gauze plaster covering the shaved side of her head. She sank into one of the wicker armchairs on the terrace.

"God, I'm so glad to be out of that bloody hospital – it's good to be home. I've got rid of the nurse; I'm really feeling much better."

The argument lasted five minutes, until, finally, Natasha sat there, arms folded, and refused to respond to Marco's entreaties. When he fell silent, she said: "Right, have you finished? Good, now tell me what's been happening? And tell me everything, please."

"Look, you have only just …"

She leaned forward in her chair and fixed him with an expression that brooked no objection.

"Tell me!"

Marco exhaled loudly in frustration, then recounted the chase after Nick across the Mediterranean, the episode in the Gammarth Marina and how he had made a fool out of Simon.

"I'd never have thought he had it in him!"

Natasha's reaction surprised and puzzled her father.

"Sweetheart, this is not funny. It has caused serious trouble for Sergio and me with Milan. You know little about the oil deal we are doing, but it is all tied up with that. There are tens of millions of euro at stake; three years of work at risk. It is a serious situation. That policeman who started all this trouble is in the mix as well and needs dealing with.

"Oh, and before I forget, it looks like Nick stole four hundred thousand euros from BetSlick, too. Unfortunately, he took cash belonging to the Navkovs. They have been to Milan and are throwing their weight around!"

"The Navkovs! Oh, God, that's not good! Are you sure it was Nick who did it?"

"We think so. He put a convincing paper trail together and diverted a player account into a bank account we think he controlled, then moved it on the day before he disappeared. He knew the systems; his signatures are on the paper authorisations. It has to be him. The Navkovs want his head. They have taken this breach of trust extremely personally."

"It sounds a mess, Dad. What can I do to help?"

"It is not your fault. You should never have been mixed up in it in the first place. I am really sorry that bastard hurt you."

"Why don't I just speak to Nick and see if I can get him to come back? I can tell him it's all been a massive misunderstanding. Will you talk to Sergio about it?"

"Sergio wants him dead, the Navkovs want him dead – hell, *I* want him dead! If he had not spoken out of turn to that policeman and stolen the Navkovs' money, it might just have been possible. But, not now. Anyway, how would you be able to contact him?"

"I assume he's still got his phone. I could send him a message – see if I can talk him round?"

"No! We are not using you as bait. You are not well enough and I refuse to put you in harm's way again."

"Dad, listen, I don't want Nick killed. He and I … we know each other well, understand each other. We've spent a lot of time together, you know – on your orders."

"What the hell are you talking about? Honestly, Natasha, you never cease to surprise me. You are not telling me that you are personally involved with him, are you?"

She looked him straight in the eye.

"Of course not, Dad."

"That had better be right. Nick told the police about the oil operation, the money laundering, probably all of it! He is a threat to the security of the Family, to Sergio and to everything we have built. Forget about him! Do you understand me?"

Natasha hung her head and nodded sheepishly.

"For the time being, Sergio has gone back to Milan, to liaise with the Wise Men and keep our oil plans moving forward. But I can tell you, there is a lot of concern over this mess, regardless of whose fault it is."

"And I'll tell you something, Dad. Something that might help. If BetSlick is so crucial, you need someone to take control there, someone completely trustworthy who understands the numbers, knows the Family and understands how the wider business works."

"Sounds like a perfect job description. Who are you thinking of?"

"Give me a week to get my energy back and I'll do it. I'm more than capable. Tell Signor Bruno you need me to step in for a while here and we'll see what we can sort out with the work in Milan. This is my chance to help the Family!"

"You are not being serious? How can you possibly do that? You know nothing about the gaming business."

"Try me! I've lived and breathed it for the last twelve months. Who d'you think Nick spoke to about BetSlick when he was at the villa? Who did he complain to? Who did he bounce ideas off? I know more than you think. I know the systems and I know Nick's plans to expand the operation. I understand the basics of compliance and regulation – and I know what goes on in the Albanian basement, which makes me uniquely qualified, wouldn't you say? I mean, tell me, who else is going to do it!"

Natasha's eyes gleamed, as they always did when she was excited. Marco watched his daughter carefully. He trusted her intelligence, there was no doubt about that but, at the back of his mind, there was that little voice that kept whispering in his ear: *What is she up to? What is she not telling me? Do I really trust my daughter?*

"What about your work for Signor Bruno?"

"Give me a month at BetSlick, then I can pick that up as well. The work currently on the table in Milan will only take a couple of days a week. Greca will make a good COO at BetSlick and I can manage the rest. I'm not afraid of hard work, you know."

"I had better have a conversation with Sergio, before we take this to the Wise Men. He is in Milan now, so we can ask him to take soundings. That way, we will at least have a feel for how they see things. I am not totally convinced they will go for it, but I never rule anything out on a first hearing."

He could not help thinking that the timing of recent events was convenient for her.

"Dad, why d'you never trust me!" she complained. "This is my big chance to step up. Say you'll support me?"

"It is not that I do not trust you, I am just worried it is too soon." he said at once, mostly to convince himself. "Give me a day or two and we can talk again."

Natasha said she was too hot. She went into the library and closed the door behind her. Ignoring her splitting headache, she opened her bag and took out the linen business card that Signor Bruno had given her. She looked long and hard at his personal mobile number.

CHAPTER 49
NATASHA BONNICI
CASTELLO BONNICI, MALTA

NATASHA THOUGHT about her conversation with her father and was pleased that her pitch to run BetSlick had not been rejected out of hand.

Her most pressing priority at the moment was the Navkov brothers. They could cause real problems, unless their loss was handled skilfully. It had not been part of her plan to be banjaxed by Nick, but the theft of the Navkovs' money had gone exactly as she had planned it, and now she was just the person to put it right – which would mean one last meeting with that idiot Elbasan.

She thought about the Wise Men and the power and respect they enjoyed. One day, they would no longer be able to call themselves the Wise *Men,* she would make sure of that. The Wise Ones? She had been thinking about that moment for a long time. At last, she could openly admit the scale of her ambition, not only to herself, but to Marco, Sergio and, in time, even to the Wise Men!

In London, she had worked with the traders and managers of the investment bank and, until that bastard tried to rape her, things had been going well. She had loved the excitement, the aggression and the battles with colleagues and clients. It was unfortunate she had had to leave. But sometimes things worked out for the best. Now, at long last, she was ready to get herself back into a real game.

Natasha had always needed the respect of others, to be noticed. It defined her and, without it, she felt worthless. She sought attention, power and influence, and did not care how she achieved it.

Relationships were necessary, as was sex, but, to her, they were rarely enjoyable for their own sake. She knew men always underestimated her. They saw the beauty and charm first. Then, if they looked carefully, the intelligence – but never the ruthless ambition and her willingness to act on it. Her inability to give anything of herself and basic lack of interest in her partners, soon saw an end to any longer-term romances. Strangely, the person she had felt happiest with was Nick Walker.

As the evening drew in, she finished a light dinner and was heading upstairs to her room, when the front door opened and her father ushered in a tall, dark man, in a black suit. He was pulling a small, expensive-looking cabin bag that clicked over the stone flags in the hallway. She watched his entrance, out of sight, from the shadows of the gallery overlooking the front door.

He was maybe two metres tall, with thin dark hair and a high brow. He had low eyebrows over almond-shaped eyes. His high cheekbones and smooth pale skin gave him a Slavic look. The man must have sensed he was being watched. He stopped and stood still for a second or two, then turned his head upwards and searched the shadows, looking for whoever might be there. Natasha pushed herself back against the wall, but still felt his gaze land on her. His expression did not change, but his eyes lingered, appraising her, searching for something, perhaps sensing her guilt.

Knowing who he was, Natasha did not wait for an introduction. She turned away and went into her room, shutting the door behind her. Instinctively, she found herself turning the key in the lock. Maybe it was because the visitor now knew which room was hers and, for some unknown reason, that bothered her.

She set an alarm for after midnight and, when her phone vibrated on the bedside table, woke and lay still, listening to the sounds of the house. The *castello* was built of stone, so there were none of the creaks and groans of flexing timbers, common in old wooden-floored buildings. At night, the air was cold and still. Her years of living there had attuned her to the mood of the place and she often thought she could feel the pulse of hundreds of years of history, gently throbbing through the old walls. After waiting and listening for a while, she felt sure there was nobody lurking in the gallery or softly creeping down the halls. She took her phone and messaged Nick.

R u awake?

Yes on beach sleeping rough tonight.

Not good. Are you safe?

Not really. Hope to get out of here soon

What's the plan?

To get away, stay safe and start again

Wish I could help but things are bad here too. Wise Men sent a hit man down. He's after you. Better get moving fast. You still in Tunis?

Stop asking where I am! Not telling

You need money?

No. Sold Blue Cascade!! Your dad will be pissed

He's already pissed. Sorry about the Dad thing. R we gonna see each other once all this settles down?

No idea

Let me know where you end up – it's me – you can trust me

She was getting nothing back from him, apart from the fact he was sleeping rough somewhere, so abruptly ended the message. She felt a pang of disappointment that things had ended as they had with Nick. She felt a sadness and found herself missing him, an emotion that was new to her. Maybe something could have come of it ... if he had not had the job she wanted.

As the light of her phone faded away into darkness, she lay back, conscious of the silence that enveloped her, dense and impenetrable. She replayed the conversation in her head and concluded that it would probably be the last time she would message Nick.

As she lay there, she sensed a change in the atmosphere. She felt a presence, a strange feeling or intuition – more mental, than physical. Was it the smell of another person, or the sound of one of the cats prowling the corridor? No, it was more than that; it made her uneasy. She strained to listen, focusing her senses, concentrating her mind to heighten her awareness.

Her door was locked. The room was familiar, with its dense shadows and dark recesses. She concentrated some more. There was absolute silence for several minutes but, still, her senses tingled. Finally, she heard something – several soft footsteps and the careful closing of a distant guest room door.

CHAPTER 50
INSPECTOR GEORGE ZAMMIT

ABDULLAH'S COMPOUND, MARSABAR, LIBYA

Abdullah jumped onto the truck and removed the firing pins from the machine gun. Then he led George into the back section of the shed, where the bodies lived, avoiding the scattered remains of the Beards.

Inside, cowering on bunks and mattresses laid on wooden pallets, paralysed by shock and fear, were several dozen people: men, women and one or two children. Families were huddled together, while the single men pressed themselves against the back wall of the shed. One lay dead, face down on the floor, a huge hole in his back. A shell from the machine gun must have gone through the dividing panels and ripped into him. George muttered a prayer, asking God to forgive him for another soul he had taken that day. Abdullah saw him looking at the corpse.

"Forget it, he is with Allah now. We have bigger worries to deal with."

It was easy for him to say that, but George felt physically ill, as much by the sight of the ripped and shell-torn body lying on the dirt floor, as by the terror he had inflicted on these people. He wanted to tell them he had not meant to do it, that this was not who he was. He was a policeman! He could not find the words to speak to them and, even if he could, he would not have been able to get them out.

In Malta, the migrants were vilified in the press, in the bars, even in the churches. They were blamed for every ill the country suffered, real or imagined. Their boats were turned away by the government. The NGOs helping those in mortal danger on the waves were prosecuted and had their rescue ships impounded. Rumour had it, the Maltese government had granted Italy oil exploration rights in its waters, in exchange for being able to wash their hands of helping in the humanitarian rescue endeavour of *'Mare Nostrum'* – 'Our Sea'!

The Maltese and Italians largely resented this generation of African and Middle Eastern migrants. Their presence changed the character and culture of those Catholic countries and few believed they deserved a place in their Christian world. People understood the hardship of their journey, but few understood the perils they had fled from, why they should be extended protection, or even hospitality. And now, here they were, frightened, confused and helpless, in the middle of a gunfight between murdering ISIL and the traffickers, in whose uncaring hands they had placed the last remnants of their hope.

Abdullah had his automatic rifle trained on the huddled mass crowded at the back of the shed. He scrutinised them. A child was crying incessantly. George saw the resigned expression on Abdullah's face and, for a terrible moment, thought he might silence the child with a bullet.

"Any man speak English?" Abdullah shouted.

There was no response.

"If you speak English, we go. No English, you stay, eh?" He waved his gun at the group.

A large man in his late twenties or early thirties stood up. Beneath his hooded top, it was obvious he was bulky. He looked Abdullah straight in the eye, with no fear. Abdullah smiled and waved the gun at him. The man spoke in a sonorous voice.

"Me and my brother speak English."

"Nigerian? Can you sail a boat, work VHF, read GPS?"

"We were fisherman on Lake Chad. We can do this."

"What do they call you?"

"I am Abeao and that is my brother Mobo. His name means freedom. Good joke, eh? We are from Kano. Place with a lot of bad men."

Abdullah nodded.

"There are bad men everywhere."

Despite the hardship of a journey from Nigeria, the brothers had kept their impressive physiques. George privately doubted fishing on inland water was anything like making a crossing of the southern Mediterranean, but said nothing.

"OK, you will both be captains," Abdullah decided. "You sail free. No money. You are my men. You work for me but, when we get to the other side, you keep your mouth closed very tight and tell no one. If you talk, I have people in the camps who will kill you for fifty euros. Yes? "

The bigger of the two Nigerians, Abeao, nodded and spoke briefly to his brother.

"Tell the others we leave in half an hour. The first thirty to pay one thousand US each. You also collect any money owing. I will give you a list. No money, no go. I count the total. If you steal, I shoot you. Understand?"

With that, he let loose a shot past the head of the standing Nigerians, who threw themselves to their hands and knees.

Some women in the group started screaming in panic. More children started crying, clinging to their mothers. Everybody shrank further back against the wall of the building.

"OK?"

Abdullah pointed his gun at Mobo, who twisted the amulet he kept hidden in his jeans pocket. The small wooden figure had been given to him as a child and had been baptised with him, soaking up the holy water. It had protected him from evil and misfortunes so far and he silently prayed its power was strong enough to preserve him in the coming days.

"OK? Yes?" the Arab demanded.

Mobo murmured, "OK. Half hour. One thousand US"

Mobo had promised himself to do whatever it took to leave this blood-soaked place and move onwards, to Europe.

George guessed most had already been stripped of their money or had earned a right to the passage through work, or other darker services. But Abdullah was clever. He wanted to keep the group occupied and together for thirty minutes or so, while he prepared the boat. The Nigerians would be kept busy with thirty different arguments about who had paid what and to whom. George knew that Abdullah needed most of these people in his boat anyway, so he could hide amongst them when they landed, or if they were stopped by the Libyan Coastguard or another militia boat.

Abdullah pulled at a large metal sliding door and locked them all into the living quarters. He then opened a small back door that led out onto the slipway.

A melee was already forming around the Nigerians. He beckoned George to follow him through the door and headed to the adjacent store buildings in search of water, food and the electronics that would be essential for their journey. The store had been forced open by Abu Muhammed's men but, apart from some rifled boxes, the supplies seemed to be largely untouched. Their sudden arrival must have disturbed the thieving. George sorted through some boxes and began to make a pile in front of the building, starting with life jackets, twenty-litre plastic jerry cans of water and stolen military ration packs.

In an office at the back of the store, Abdullah started a separate pile with a charged satellite phone, a GPS compass with an extendible antenna, two twelve-volt battery packs and a box of flares. As an afterthought, he threw some first aid kits onto the pile and a marine signal lamp that operated from the twelve-volt battery. He tested each electronic item and once satisfied, unlocked a drawer in a desk, and took a small hand gun and some clips of bullets.

Abdullah had bought racks of Chinese-made inflatable dinghies from the Alibaba website. The dinghies were in crates piled four high and the shelves ran the length of the shed. Each boat could hold up to fifty people. George had seen the glossy, high-powered RHIB that sat covered in a store house at the top of the beach, but Abdullah had told him all of Marsabar knew that boat. There were not many like it. They would not get five kilometres offshore without the Coastguards and Abu Muhammed knowing. Also, they needed to hide with the bodies so, when we landed there are no questions. Abdullah insisted it had to be that way.

George went back into the shed and grabbed Abeao, who was arguing with a crowd of people around a cardboard box, half full of dollars. Abeao took the box to Abdullah, who started counting and wrapping the notes into thick rolls. He shouted to Abeao to send three of the younger men to start moving the supplies to the slipway on the beach.

Abdullah held his rifle and pointed out one of the large stacks of crates containing the rafts. Three men pulled one down and took a crowbar to start prising the wooden panels apart. Inside was the flimsy, grey, plastic dinghy that was going to take them across the sea to Italy, Malta, Lampedusa, who knew where? George's knees went weak for a moment, the fear surging through him. Fighting it back, he tried to concentrate on the task at hand.

They laid the raft on the scrubby beach, smoothing out its plastic tubes. George found the valves and attached the air hose Abdullah had given him. Abdullah went back to a nearby shed and started a compressor, that forcing air into the tubes that made up the sides of the raft. He watched the tubes fill, fidgeting and pacing around the ballooning plastic. Once the raft had taken shape and become semi-rigid, Abdullah stopped the compressor and listened. He poured water over the tubes, looking for bubbles that would show an air leak in the raft. He then fitted the flimsy floor panelling and the back frame, which would take the outboard motor.

At first sight, George thought the vessel looked pretty robust and a much better proposition than he had expected. But, then, he turned to look at the waves, crashing up the beach and the huge expanse of turbulent water ahead of him, and realised his optimism was misplaced.

Abdullah seemed to have no such doubts. If he did, he had banished them from his mind as he applied himself to getting things ready.

They carried the sixty horsepower outboard motor and locked it to the boat's backboard. Six twenty litre jerry cans of petrol completed the loading. The smell of the petrol, the crying and keening of woman and children, came to define George's experience of the miserable hours that followed.

Abdullah walked around the raft one last time, holding his ear close to sections and rubbing spit along the seams. Finally, he stood up straight and resolutely said:

"Yes, we will get the bodies on now. We need thirty. No more. I do not care who has paid and who has not; it is time to be gone. Get your gun, George. This is the most dangerous moment– when they realise I will leave some behind. Shoot them if you need to. Desperate people do desperate things, eh?"

George was appalled at the thought that there could potentially be more bloodshed. He knew he was not going to shoot anybody else that afternoon. They were all desperate people.

He waited by the frail dinghy, Abdullah's assault rifle in his hand. The Nigerians led the first ten people out of the shed. They donned their life jackets, struggling with the ties, then took off their shoes and pulled the dinghy down the slipway, into the shallow water.

"No dragging," screamed Abdullah, "do you want to make holes?"

The plastic dinghy looked totally unsuited to its task, as it bent and bucked over the foaming waves that rolled up the beach. Four men, waist-deep in the water, held it firm as the Nigerians went back to get more people from the shed.

They emerged through the back door with a family of four men, two women and a small child, who also put on their life jackets and clambered onto the boat. Meanwhile, Abdullah kept the muzzle of his gun pointing through the door into the shed. He was shouting in Arabic. When the loading was complete, with a sudden movement, he slammed the door and fixed a padlock to a hasp. Cries and shouts came from within, followed by the sound of fists banging on the metal door. Abdullah let loose a flurry of shots high into the top of the door. The shock of it quietened those inside. It occurred to George, with Abdullah gone and Tareq dead, there was no one who would let them out.

Abdullah motioned him to the boat and, from behind, pushed his backside over the tubes, as he clambered in. Abeao pulled Abdullah up and into the raft and started the motor. Two of the boys, waist high in the sea, had been holding the ropes to steady the dinghy. As the boat surged forward into the deeper water, they lost their grip, leaving them splashing and shouting in the surf. The other two kept holding on, struggling to keep their heads above the bow wave, and were towed out towards the open sea, more under, than above the warm, salty water.

Once Abeao was certain they had cleared the beach and would not be pushed back by the incoming waves, he eased back the throttle. Eager hands pulled the two half-drowned youths aboard. The other two were left screaming and waving on the beach.

Without a backward glance, Abeao handed the throttle to Abdullah who opened it up and started setting up the GPS. They had finally left Libya behind them.

George watched, as Abdullah cast his eyes upwards and

opened his palms towards the sky. He was mumbling a quiet prayer, no doubt for his family, for a safe journey, for Tareq and for his speedy return, so he could ensure the slow and painful death of Abu Muhammed. George thought prayer could never hurt, so he closed his eyes and started invoking the Blessed Virgin, St Christopher, St Michael the Archangel and anyone else he thought might be listening.

CHAPTER 51
NICK WALKER

TUNIS

WHEN NICK HAD FLED the Sunny Apartments, he had jumped onto Bobby's scooter and headed south, to Hammamet, on the coast. It had taken him an hour, the scooter buffeted by the speeding traffic on the main trunk road.

In the early evening, he slid into the Hammanet Beach Palace hotel, an enormous place, filled with package sunseekers, dressed in their holiday best. His own wardrobe was by now more shabby chic, but his good looks and fair complexion gained him access and acceptance amongst the crowds. He took a seat at a poolside restaurant, where the lights were low and he could watch the entrance from reception. He ate well, listening to a time-serving English singer crooning ballads and pop anthems, and even enjoyed some beers. When the singer took a break, he telephoned Bobby.

"Hah, my friend is missing! You are tired of Auntie's cooking?"

Nick was more tired of Bobby's fake bonhomie and phoney charm.

"So, Bobby, how d'you know I'm not lying on my bed at the Sunny Apartments?"

"Because I go there and you have gone! You not at Auntie's and not at luxury apartments! The big Polish man is looking for you, I came to tell you. This is not my doing. You believe me? I see you tomorrow and we do our business. We meet at Auntie's house – it is more safe."

"No, Bobby, it's not *'more safe'*. We meet at the café, as before. Did the big Polish man offer you money to give me up?"

There was a silence on the phone. Nick continued.

"Of course, he did! But, tell me, Bobby, does Simon know you have the Blue Cascade? You see, I don't think he does."

"What are you saying, my friend. You don't trust me?"

"No, Bobby, I don't. No offence, but I can't trust anybody right now. What d'you think Simon will do, if he knows you stole a million euro boat from his boss?"

Silence.

"I'll tell you what, Bobby. We'll meet tomorrow and do our business at the café, quietly, just you and me. Then, you get me on a boat out of here and I'm gone. I'll pay you the five thousand for the boat trip. Simon will never know anything and you'll have made yourself a lot of money. He can keep running around in circles and we're both happy. Then, when I'm on the boat and sailing away, I'll ring my friend."

Bobby was confused.

"What friend? Why you ring a friend?"

"I will ring my friend and tell him not to call the big Polish man to tell him you have his boss's boat, and also not to give him Auntie Neserine's address in Sidi-Bou-Said."

"No! Auntie knows nothing! It's not right!"

"I know she doesn't and I don't want that nasty Polish man to hurt her, trying to find out. But that's what'll happen, if I don't make that call. And there's a special word I've got to use to prove no one is forcing me to do it. So don't think you can grab me and make me, because it won't work."

There was another silence on the other end of the phone.

"OK, we meet at the café. 10:00a.m. I have passport. You bring money and I try to get you on a boat. It will be safe."

"If I see anything suspicious, anything I don't like, I'll disappear and you'll lose the profit on your nice new boat and make Auntie Neserine very upset."

Once the cabaret had ended and the waiters had finished clearing the last of the glasses, Nick wandered down to the far end of the beach and pulled a sunbed from the stack. The security guards walked past and he gave them a cheery wave; a half-cut guest, enjoying some quiet time under the stars. After that, they left him in peace and, despite the growing chill of the evening, he managed to fall asleep, until Natasha's message roused him a little after midnight.

The message left him no further forward in understanding whether it was actually her making contact, or if her phone was being used by Marco or his people. It caused alarm bells when the messages repeatedly asked him where he was and what his plans were but, in reality, it did not matter. They already knew he was in Tunis and Simon was already on his tail.

The early morning chill and damp woke him before the sun came up, but he felt good, well-rested and strangely calm. He walked through reception, passing the bemused hotel staff, and out into the car park. Fifty minutes later, he was negotiating the early morning Tunis traffic.

After half an hour figuring out the Arabic street signs and seeking directions from non-English speakers, he found the café and deliberately rode straight past it, without turning his head. He spent another thirty minutes circling it via various side streets, watching it from different angles, checking on the comings and goings of cars, trucks and especially, people.

He still did not trust Bobby. The fact he had left the bag as planned, with the cash untouched, went a long way, but Nick knew Simon was around and Bobby had as much resistance to a wad of cash, as a Labrador had to a plate of warm sausages.

When it was nearly time for them to meet, Nick walked down a narrow side street, past an array of fresh fruit and vegetables, spilling out of a shop and onto the street. The café was on the opposite side of the road. All seemed quiet and people hurried about their business, as usual.

Suddenly, he heard a loud voice behind him that made him spin on his heels.

"Hello! You secret agent, eh?"

Bobby's meaty fist slapped him on the back and he laughed his big laugh. He was ridiculously conspicuous, in a patterned canary yellow shirt, shiny green jacket and mirrored sunglasses.

"I see you, looking here, looking there, sticking your white face around corners! Come, my friend, we go inside, it's getting hot."

They crossed the street and sat down at a window table. The sticky sweet tea and almond pastries arrived. Bobby took half a pastry in one bite and Nick watched him, as he chewed.

"So, you swim like fish? Marina people very cross with me. Guns bang, bang, in the expensive marina. Bad men run here, run there, upset the rich people. All bad for business."

"Did you get the boat out?" Nick asked.

"Sure, we get the boat. Also, we get big trouble from police, they say I steal boat. Huh! I show the papers, but it cost a lot of dinar for police. Then marina manager bring big foreign man to meet me. He want to meet you. I tell him many lies and make me frightened. I don't like him but I want you go now; you bring me too many troubles and expense."

"Well, Bobby, if you buy a stolen boat, at a very cheap price, you have to expect to do some work for it! The passport, have you got it?"

"Wait a minute, my friend. Enjoy a pastry."

Nick soon got where the conversation was going. Bobby's greedy eyes were locked on his, as he chewed the pastry, flakes stuck to the stubble on his cheek, calculating how much more he could get out of him.

"No, Bobby, no more money. I've paid enough already and you robbed me on the price of that boat. Have you got the passport or not?"

"I have passport, but I need more expenses. Marina manager, policemen, the scooter. I need another five thousand. You famous – many people want to talk to you. Everyone wants to talk to you! All ask me and promise big money. But I tell them you are crazy Englishman. I don't know where you are or where you go. Maybe Cyprus, then Ukraine or maybe Russia. I am saying I look for you, too. I am saying you owe me money. When you go, I go for holiday. Come back when quiet. Five thousand more expenses and everybody happy. We must all be happy, yes?"

Bobby raised his eyebrows and Nick took a pastry, to give himself some more time to think. There was not a lot he could do, he had nothing more up his sleeve. The fact Bobby was squeezing him for more cash was reassuring in a way. If he was going to just hand him over, he would have done it by now. Reluctantly, Nick gave a nod. He hated a shake down.

"Yes, Bobby, we must all be happy."

Bobby reached inside his green, synthetic jacket and pulled out an envelope. Inside was a worn, dark red, UK passport. Nick opened it and checked name, details, expiry and the photo. There were stamps from several visits to the far east, Japan, the US and one for Argentina. It felt right and the weight and pliability of the pages were good. The name on it was Harry McDonald and the date of birth was within a year of his own.

"Is it stolen?"

Bobby looked hurt.

"So what? It is good job, yes? The cobbler is best in Tunisia. And you no worry, when the real Harry MacDonald uses passport – he has big problems, not you!"

Bobby boomed a laugh across the café.

"It looks good. Thanks. You've been a massive help. Now, about a boat?"

Bobby leaned back in the chair, pleased with himself.

"You like to fish? I know a man who likes to fish. We drive to Kelibia, maybe two hours by car. He has nice boat. Well, maybe boat is not so nice! But he fish two, three days, go to Lampedusa and sell his fish. You show nice new passport and you just walk down quay. From Lampedusa, you can fly to Italy. In Lampedusa, Hotel Neptune is very good. Well, in Lampedusa it is only good hotel. And for you, only five thousand euro."

Nick thought about it. To double back might not be such a bad plan. Simon and his henchmen were wandering the streets of Tunis, probably concentrating on the airport and the commercial ferries. They would not expect him to go back to Lampedusa.

In fact, it would actually work a lot better, he reflected, because if he left Tunis by air, he would need a 90-day entry stamp on the new passport, to show when he had arrived in the country. That would mean more delay, more money. Once in Lampedusa, he was then in Italy, so in the EU's Schengen area, where there were no identity checks on movements between EU states for a UK passport holder. A lift out of Tunis was also an appealing prospect – Nick did not fancy bumping into Simon!

"OK, three thousand euros and it's a deal."

"You rob me! You tell me five thousand! No, no, no, you behave like Arab!"

And so it went on for a bit until, begrudgingly, Bobby conceded a discount – to four thousand euros.

"Don't sulk. You people like bargaining! OK, when do we go?"

"What is this *sulking*? I have car waiting. You have everything? Then we go now."

Nick slid the scooter keys to Bobby and they set off for Kelibia, a town perched on the furthest northeast point of Tunisia. The peninsula reached out, like the tip of a finger, pointing the way back to Malta.

Eventually, they entered the pretty 'old town', having driven along the coast, past the idyllic white sand beaches and large empty hotels. But, when Bobby drove Nick down the bumpy concrete road along the quayside and pointed to the stinking heap where he would be spending the next few days, his good mood faded.

The *Eye of Osiris* was a dirty, fish-encrusted mess of a boat. At twenty-six metres long, it was a good size for a local fishing boat, but plastic boxes, ropes, nets and marker buoys created a deadly jumble on deck. Washing lines trailing T-shirts, underwear and shorts hung from every piece of the communication antennae. The hull was rusted and patched with steel plate. It was definitely a working boat. A collection of commercial truck tyres as fenders hung over the sides from blue nylon ropes and black oily smoke came from the exhaust, indicating the old diesel engine was banging away below deck. A faded, green tarpaulin had been strung over the aft deck, to shield the crew from the worst of the sun, whilst busy laying lines and nets.

The skipper was Nasim, a stocky, middle-aged, bearded man with dark, curly hair and a John Deere tractor baseball cap pulled low to shield his eyes. His dark skin was burned red on his cheeks and nose, where the sun had blazed through the wheelhouse. He wore long denim cut-off shorts and a white singlet stained with oil, sweat and fish scales. He looked at Nick, ignoring his outstretched hand, and spoke to Bobby.

Bobby smiled and then turned to explain to Nick, "He no like you! You go down below. When out at sea, you come up. No one can see you in port." He pushed a bundle of cash at Nick. "I pay half now; you pay half in Lampedusa. That way, he no kill you and throw you into the sea when I go."

Bobby laughed heartily at his own joke. Nasim glared at them both.

"Does he speak English?"

"Not much. But he not want to talk to you anyway. Stay away from him. He is not so bad – but the crew, yes, very bad!"

Bobby gave a big guttural laugh. He thought this was even

funnier and slapped Nick hard on the shoulder. The flesh on his neck wobbled and shook.

"It's OK, my friend. Just no let them cut you up like fish! Now, you no forget – telephone your friend! We do good business, so this last job is important. Yes? Think of kind Auntie! You have battery on phone?"

Nick assured him that he had and, with that, Bobby vigorously shook his hand with his big ham of a fist. Chuckling to himself, he wished Nick luck and left.

The crew were a team of three surly, sinewy youths, wearing bandannas over their heads as protection from the fierce sun. They were all barefooted and sported the same cut-off shorts as Nasim, together with faded, dirty singlets. They smoked and watched with wary, suspicious expressions.

He looked around at his companions, gave them an unacknowledged smile and followed the skipper down a short companion way to a noisy, fetid cabin with two bunks. The diesel engine thrashed away, causing everything to shake and rattle. The smell of fumes intensified, as he entered. A small, open porthole seemed designed to let the hot air leak inside. With a sigh, he set about trying to hide the Kappa bag amongst a pile of boxed foodstuffs. Some of the rolls of gold coins and watches he kept in his pockets, just in case.

After an hour, the revs of the engine picked up and he felt the boat move away from the quayside. He stuck his face up to the small grimy porthole; they were underway. As instructed, Nick waited for about twenty minutes and then went topside.

The boat was ploughing into the Bay of Tunis, in perfect blue water, with a cloudless sky above. They were long-line fishing for tuna, the crew smoking and chatting, while live baiting the hooks with anchovies, skipjack, squid and other small fish they had netted on returning from their previous trip. These were hooked onto the miles of lines that the boat would feed into the waters. The bait scraps were being thrown overboard, to the delight of the gulls and terns, swooping and calling above the wake of the boat.

The breeze from the forward movement cooled the deck. Nick found a quiet spot, in front of the wheelhouse where he sat down, leaning his back against the steel structure, letting the rhythmic heave of the boat lull him to sleep in the afternoon sunshine.

CHAPTER 52
NATASHA BONNICI
CASTELLO BONNICI, MALTA

AT CASTELLO BONNICI breakfast was being taken earlier than usual. As Natasha walked onto the terrace, she saw Marco sitting tight-lipped with the man she had seen arrive the night before. Raphael looked even more unpleasant close up, with that low brow and those cat-like green eyes. His white shirt, black suit and thin grey tie gave him the appearance of an undertaker. He was calm and watchful, exuding an air of confidence, that bordered on authority. There was a tense atmosphere, as if he and her father had already exchanged words.

Natasha was surprised when the new arrival did not even bother to stand up as Marco introduced him. He merely pointed to a seat opposite him and said: "Would you care to sit down, Natasha?"

She bristled. Who did he think he was? This was her home, not his. But, she did as he suggested at a nod from Marco. Raphael gave her a thin-lipped smile.

"I will need to talk to you at length today about your relationship with Mr Walker. We must work together to understand his motivations, his strengths and vulnerabilities. Also, as I have said to your father, I will need your laptop, tablet and mobile phone, please."

Natasha looked at Marco, mouth open in surprise.

"It is routine. Your father objected too, but he has just spoken to Signor Rossi and now understands the necessity. It is nothing personal, just the way I work. He has agreed to permit me access to all his communication records: email, telephone, WhatsApp, Messenger, etc."

Marco looked at Natasha, with a worried frown on his face. He was not enjoying this. He said nothing, but did not order her to comply, which suggested to her she could push things a little further.

"No. I'm sorry, I'm not giving you access to my private messages. You can talk to me first, see how far we get. Then, if you're still not satisfied, you can make the case for scrutinising my data."

Marco studied the crumbs on the tablecloth. Raphael smiled and edged a little closer.

"I thought you might say that. It is not an unreasonable position to take but, given the nature of your special relationship with Signor Walker, I feel I must insist."

"I'm sorry, Raphael, there's no *'special relationship'*, but it's still a *'no'*."

"Can I make a suggestion? Let me refresh my coffee, so you can speak to your father alone. When I come back, we can resume our conversation. It will also give you a chance to tell him who it was you were texting in Tunisia, just after midnight last night. Anyone else for more coffee? No?"

With that, he unfolded himself from the chair and left the terrace. Marco looked at Natasha with a disappointed expression on his face.

"Well, what can you tell me that I do not already know? It was Nick, was it not?"

Natasha could see Marco would not be able to make this problem go away. He had always been able to do that for her before. She had brought this on herself and part of her hated that her father was paying the price for her reckless behaviour. But she saw something else in him, maybe for the first time: fear, even weakness. And that changed the game.

The other part of her recognised that, played correctly, Raphael was someone who could be helpful in furthering her ambitions within the Family. She was wary of him, it would be stupid to be otherwise, but she could see the possibilities. She was so distracted by these thoughts, she did not even realise Marco was speaking to her.

Raphael had come back out onto the terrace with a cup of coffee and a plate with a Danish pastry. She knew she had to buy more time to get this lizard off her back.

"Well, Natasha? How is this going to work?" He pressed her. "Are we on the same side or are we not? I am a very black and white sort of person. Those who are with me, have my unswerving loyalty. Those who are not ..."

Marco sat still, arms folded, and watched his daughter. It was her move.

"A big part of me wants to tell you to go and fuck yourself. But I respect Sergio as well as my father and I'm totally committed to the Family, which has my absolute loyalty. I deeply resent any insinuation that I'm a threat to any part of it.

"I won't give you my phone or my laptop because there'll be no need. I'll tell you everything I know about Nick Walker, including the messages we sent each other in the last couple of days. But I'm warning you now, I can't tell you where he is, because I told him not to tell me. I don't know whether he's out of Tunis. All I know is that he met someone who was going to help him.

"Here's what I'm offering. Listen to what I've got to say and work out how big a threat he really is. Then, if you like, I can try and bring him to you."

Raphael looked at her for a moment, weighing her up. He turned his gaze to Marco.

"I am glad to see she is as clever as they say she is. Can we use your study this morning?"

Marco waved his arm, giving his permission.

"Shall we start in thirty minutes?" Raphael suggested.

He crossed the terrace behind Natasha's chair as he left.

"I hope you are not playing games with him, Natasha?' Marco murmured. "Trust me, if you are, you will lose. If you are planning to warn Nick, do not even think about it. Raphael will monitor all communications to and from the *castello*."

"How? Don't be silly, Dad. He's only one man."

"He brought two assistants; they're in the cottage. That's how they knew about the text messages. And, in case you missed it, he has just taken your phone from your bag."

"Shit! You're kidding?"

"Sorry. No, I'm not. And please do not use that sort of language."

Natasha looked down from the terrace, across the small farming enclosures nestling in the valley. Her mind was working overtime. It took all her will to contain her anger, but it burnt white hot.

"I hate that man. Hate him." She shook her head and let out a short yell of frustration. "Don't worry, we'll get out of this, Dad. You'll see."

Raphael and Natasha settled down in Marco's study and stayed there for most of the morning. First, Raphael returned her phone, apologising for the deceit, but warned her to be discreet about using it in the future. He had proved his point; communications were being monitored.

Raphael had a small digital tape recorder, the size of a cigarette lighter, which he placed on the table between them. They sat back in a pair of soft leather armchairs, either side of the enormous fireplace. They were surrounded by tall mahogany bookshelves, filled with medieval manuscripts and endless leather-bound books, all carefully indexed, but never read. The books and the centuries-old fireplace filled the room with an aroma, thick with tobacco, leather and smoke.

Then they talked; or rather, Natasha talked. Raphael listened intently. Natasha began to relax. There was nothing to hide; the truth was a complete exoneration of both Marco and herself. The drugs and the dealer were the catalyst to the argument, but she spun a picture of a man becoming more dissatisfied with the rewards he was receiving for the increased risk he was being asked to take, and seeking release in his drug dependency.

Yes, there had been a time she had become too friendly with Nick, but she had cooled it down. Her strongest loyalties were not to him, they were to Marco and the Family. She explained her ambitions to develop a role for herself within the Family and said she would never risk all that in misguided loyalty to someone intent on bringing down everything she held dear.

Natasha was familiar with Stockholm syndrome: the bond of empathy that develops between some captors and captives. She knew Raphael would understand it only too well, so she pretended to become more open with him, offering confidences and affecting a growing intimacy. She sat further forward in her chair, bringing herself nearer to him, as she spoke.

She had deliberately revealed a lot about herself, things she would have told few other people. She drew Raphael into the conversation, leading him, letting him feel he was in control.

The interrogation ended at last and he turned off the recording device, slipping it into his pocket. He sat for a while, quietly contemplating what he had heard over the past few hours. Finally, he spoke, slowly and formally, as if making a speech to assembled dignitaries.

"Natasha, thank you for your cooperation and your candour. I am impressed with your resilience, given how tired you must be feeling. This has been an important conversation and will go a long way to making sure the trust within the Family remains healthy. Yes, you have made mistakes but, all in all, you are an impressive young woman."

"Thanks," she replied, through gritted teeth. "Preserving the tight bonds that exist between my father and the Family in Milan is the most important thing to me. I hope you believe that."

"Yes, I believe you have told me the truth today. You know, my role in the business is often misunderstood. I see my real value in being able to talk to people, as we have done today. My job is to understand, clarify situations where there might be animosity and mistrust. It is so much better to handle things this way. If you are going to progress in the business, our paths will no doubt cross again, and I would like you to think of me as your friend. I do hope you think that is possible?"

Natasha smiled widely at him.

"As for the delicate matter of Signor Walker, I do think it will be hard to reach an understanding with him, but we require him to return to Malta. I will need to have a long conversation with him, so we can account for the missing money amongst other things."

He looked at Natasha pointedly. She held a neutral expression, while looking directly into the almond-shaped eyes of a killer.

"You're right, I guess. I'll help convince him the best thing for him is to come back, but I think we both know that won't be easy. He doesn't trust me and I don't think he'll take the risk. But I'm happy to try. I think you should also know, I'm putting myself forward as the person to take over at BetSlick."

Raphael looked at her, his face showing no reaction to the suggestion.

"Well, I can see the opportunity there, but that is not for me to decide."

"I already know a lot about how the systems work, as you know. If you want me to have a look at the accounts, I might even be able to find out where the Navkovs' money went."

"You mean, you think you could do what Greca and the finance team have so far failed to do?"

"I don't know, but I'm willing to give it a go. I've got a few ideas and there's nothing to lose, is there?"

Raphael stood there, wondering if Natasha had any motive, other than being helpful. After a moment, he said:

"Well, you are right. There is nothing to be lost."

"I assume you've changed Nick's login, so I'll need access codes to get into FinBet, the accounting software and FinSlick, the shadow accounting system."

"You know Nick's login?"

Natasha bit her tongue at this slip.

"No, but he might have hidden files that only he can access and his passwords would be a starting point."

"I see. Do you need to go into the office or can this be done remotely?"

Raphael looked at her, his eyes narrowing slightly.

"I can do it from here and I've got an idea where to start. Nick often worked from home and we both took an interest in how the public and private accounts packages interfaced. For obvious reasons, there weren't many people he could talk to about how the dual accounting worked. I'm a good listener and a fast learner."

Nick had established two sets of accounts: one that could be shown to the regulators, the accountants, and was used by the majority of the employees; then, a shadow set of accounts that recorded the monies received and returned into the bank accounts established by Elbasan and his Albanians. That was the cash transferred to and from the Player Accounts at BetSlick. Those accounts reconciled back to the various operations undertaken by the Family and formed part of the underlying business architecture Natasha would be working on with Signor Bruno.

Natasha had frequently sat with Nick on the loggia at the villa, when he was working on the two systems, drafting lists of improvements he wanted the Mumbai-based developers to make. Natasha had a clear and logical approach to anything related to numbers, so had frequently made suggestions, and even recommended solutions to tricky technical difficulties. Nick had never realised how much knowledge she was absorbing during those sessions.

Raphael decided there was no harm in seeing if Natasha

could do what the others had tried and failed to do. At worst, she would learn a lesson humility. At best ...

"Well, if you are happy to try, I will have a time-limited login emailed to me and you can work from the study. I will need to see all your work, of course. We will also have to put a message together for Nick Walker. I will give this some thought, but it can wait until tomorrow morning. You are looking pale, perhaps we should call it a day for now?"

But Natasha's work was not done yet. After a brief rest, she had one more loose end to tie up.

CHAPTER 53
INSPECTOR GEORGE ZAMMIT
SICILIAN CHANNEL, ABOARD THE INFLATABLE RAFT

On the boat, Abdullah had kept a low profile, leaving the brothers to manage the passengers, while he held the throttle and navigated a course due north of Marsabar. It was one thing to point the raft north, another to know how to allow for the position of the boat in the mass of water being moved by the currents. Abdullah would periodically consult the GPS and adjust his bearings to try to keep a true course.

It took the best part of three hours to clear the twelve nautical miles and get outside Libyan territorial waters, but they would have to wait many more hours before a call for help could be made. If they were picked up too close to the Libyan coast, they would just be taken back, because that was the agreed protocol. There, they would be held in some hellish militia-run detention camp. It was not an outcome Abdullah was prepared to contemplate.

The next day, conditions improved and they were making about five knots. Allowing for currents and wind, the GPS told them they were over fifty miles away from the coast of Libya. Anyone who tried to cross the Mediterranean in an inflatable dinghy knew that waves could be killers and Abdullah had deliberately not overloaded the boat to avoid it being swamped.

Even in the current benign conditions, water lapped over the sides and spray continually drenched those sitting on the tubes. Those inside were constantly having to bail water out of the raft. After the first night at sea, several passengers began to suffer from exposure and dehydration. George calculated they had sufficient food for another day or so but, despite rationing it out, they had badly underestimated the water requirements.

The Nigerian brothers strictly administered the rations and tolerated no protest. Abdullah had chosen them well. Abeao had found a short piece of knotted rope that he swung around threateningly, while Mobo had a short, but substantial, length of timber he used to prod and poke people. Abdullah and George both had hand guns, but these were kept out of sight of the others. Abdullah had told George that, if they had to use them, he had to squat low and fire upwards. There were too many tales of rafts getting punctures when firearms were used.

For George, the first night had been terrible. Within an hour of setting out, he had become horribly seasick and felt like he was edging ever closer to death. He was listless and disorientated. Despite having had his pick of the weather proof clothing, he was freezing cold, as the wind blew through his marine waterproofs. In the early hours of the morning, a man, who introduced himself as Bilal, asked George if he had any spare clothing he could give to his nursing wife and child, who were terribly cold.

Bilal told George he had been made homeless in Syria and had driven his wife and newborn, in the family Peugeot, through Jordan and then across the Sinai to the Libyan-Egyptian border town of El Salloum. There, families could cross into Libya without passports and register with the charities which provided accommodation, medical care and even the chance of education. They had settled in Tripoli but, since the war between the government and Boutros's militia had spilled into the city, his wife had become ill with stress and anxiety. She could not face the trauma of being caught up in another civil war and begged him to get the family to Europe. The boat from Marsabar was his answer.

Few of the passengers were protected from the spray which, together with the persistent north-westerly wind, slowly and gradually sucked the last reserves of warmth from them. To George's shame, he was not inclined to part with anything that was going to keep him warm. He realised there was no room for chivalry or good manners on the boat. They were all in a fight for their lives.

George saw Abeao watching the conversation and called him over.

"Have we got anything to protect people from the wind and the cold? Any more clothes? "

The spray ran in rivulets down Abeao's face and George could see he, too, was shivering in his soaked hoodie and track-suit bottoms.

"Maybe. I look."

He rummaged in some plastic sacks at the front of the boat and brought out two clear plastic bags that held some thin tarpaulin sheeting. He shouted to Mobo and, together, they rigged the sheets over the heads of the passengers, securing them onto the ropes that ran around the tubes, by putting cable ties though the grommet holes in the tarpaulin. The result was a flapping blue bubble that shrouded the raft and added a new intermittent banging noise, as it flexed and braced in the wind.

George had already taken a towel from a sack and said to Bilal: "Wrap the child in this. It's something, at least."

Abdullah watched George and the Nigerians from the rear of the raft, shaking his head at their efforts.

"My friend, I see what you do, but now you make a sail. The wind, it comes from the north-west and will blow us back to Libya. Is this what you want?"

"Just until morning. Let's try and keep people dry, until we have some sun. Then, we can take it down."

Abdullah grimaced.

"Such kindness will kill us."

The huddled mass pulled the shelter closer and sat on the tarps at the front of the raft, trying to prevent the wind and spray howling straight underneath. Mobo fashioned some more cable ties into straps that the passengers hung onto, to drag the tarp down into the raft and stop it billowing above them

Late in the night, George had just recovered from his latest bout of retching over the side of the boat, when he noticed Abdullah looking at him, intently. He beckoned George to sit beside him. George pushed his way to the rear of the boat and squatted down against the tube next to the purring outboard. Looking ahead, over the rippling tarpaulin, all he could see was the black of night and the tops of the waves, as they rushed towards the raft.

"That is a very good sail you make. Our speed is now two knots slower. With the current against us, we are just standing still in the water. But, they are all warmer and cannot see the danger of the sea, so that is good."

George bridled at his sarcasm.

"If we hadn't done something, we would have had no one left alive by morning. They'd all be dead of exposure. This must happen to everybody you send out here. Doesn't it bother you?"

"My job is not making pleasure cruises. I get people across to Europe and my boats are the best, most make a safe journey. You can see, we have the phones, the GPS, the life jackets – what else should I do? Look, this boat is full; all my boats are full. People need to go to Europe."

"Maybe, but it's still not safe, is it?"

A sudden gust of wind lifted the tarpaulin and the nose of the boat rose up, causing screams from those under the blue sheeting. It fell dramatically, as the next wave passed and the trough pulled the frail craft down.

Abdullah adjusted the line of the motor and smiled, shaking his head at the naivety of the question.

"Is it safe in Kano? Ask Mobo or Abeao. Is it safe in Syria, where Shia and Russian bastards barrel bomb the cities? Ask your new friend, Bilal. Or in Yemen, where you can be killed by Saudi drones, Al Qaeda or ISIL guns – you choose. You do not know what *'not safe'* means, Mr. Maltese policeman."

George pressed on.

"But it's not safe for them in Europe, either. These people are not wanted there; in fact, in my country, they're hated. There aren't any jobs waiting for them, like they think. It's not easy to make a new life. I see refugees everywhere, waiting by the road for day work, at day rates. They're exploited, they've got no money, no right to be housed. Everybody blames them for any crime that happens. It's not a good life for them."

"I know what you say is true. But they do not get bombed, shot, starved – it is you who do not understand. Now listen, I want you to hear a new story."

Abdullah began speaking in hushed tones. He told George about his life in Marsabar and events there since Gaddafi's death, ending with the deal he had made with the Maltese businessman, Bonnici. He explained about the purchase of the *Malik Albahr*, the death of Mahmoud Mansour in the Grand Harbour, Samir double crossing him, the role of the Beards, right down to first seeing George in the car park of the Vai Vai Cafe. George sat in silence and listened.

Once he took into account what he knew about Camilleri and the garbled tale he had heard from Nick Walker about the money laundering operation, the picture suddenly became very clear. George reckoned, if he was right in piecing the jigsaw together, the sheer scale of the enterprise was staggering.

Throughout their conversation, it was obvious that, although Abdullah had contravened every law in a civilised country's statute books, he genuinely believed he had acted honourably. He told George he lived in a broken country, where the rule of law had ceased to exist and society belonged to those who were the strongest. Those who could enforce the law, made the law.

The events of the past few days had created a strange bond

between the two men. Despite everything George had witnessed, he decided he would use whatever leverage he had to ensure Abdullah made his way to Malta and avoided an Italian detention camp. He grimaced when he reflected just how far his moral compass had swung, over the past few days.

The truth was, George was no longer sure who was right and who was wrong. The old boundary between right and wrong had changed for him, irrevocably. Knowing what he did, and having survived a serious attempt on his life, he was not even sure how safe he would be, once he returned to Malta. The attack in the car park, and what the ISIL boy had said, troubled him. The young fighter had known about George's presence in advance and had been ready to kill him. There was only one other person who had known exactly where George would be that day and with whom, and he was currently sitting safe behind a desk in Police HQ, Floriana.

George pulled himself together and tried to plan a strategy for his return. Abdullah still had the briefcase with him and had tied it to a lug on the outboard, to stop it being washed away or snatched from his grasp, while he dozed over the motor. George guessed the contents of that case would be a help to them both, once they reached land. Having come so far to give it to Abdullah, George swore he would do his best to make sure he kept hold of the damn' thing.

At daybreak, Abdullah told him they were far enough away from Libya to call for rescue. The sea had calmed and was a gentian blue. The tarpaulin had been removed and George sat studying the gentle waves. The early morning sun provided a warmth, strong enough to dry them out but, looking up at the clear sky, he could imagine how hot the summer sun would soon become.

The lack of water worried him. He desperately hoped that the rescue would be quick. He was constantly thirsty. The twice-daily cup the Nigerians allowed them was simply not enough, but he had told Abdullah they had to take the same ration as everybody else. He could feel his lips beginning to crack under the assault of the wind, sun and salt. He knew it could take another twelve hours for a boat to reach them, even from Lampedusa. If they sent a Maltese Naval vessel, it would be even longer.

Looking around the boat, George saw the expressions on people's faces. The early excitement and exuberance had long gone. One of the babies had cried long into the night, but had now, thankfully, fallen silent. It occurred to him it might have even died, but its mother still held it clasped tight under her life jacket. To his surprise, he noticed the mother was wearing a heavy and voluminous yellow weatherproof jacket, similar to his own. At the back of the boat, hands still on the outboard, Abdullah sat with a blue tarpaulin wrapped around him. George realised Abdullah must have given the woman his own jacket in the early hours of the morning, to try to preserve what little warmth she had left.

Apart from his nausea and fatigue, it was the terrible sense of abandonment that got George the most. Miles of emptiness above and beneath the flimsy raft, the enormous green ocean rumbling and belching, spitting spray in their faces. There was never silence; the constant sound of the wind rattling, flapping and whipping any lose item it could find.

The raft was so low in the water, their horizon seemed to be only a matter of metres away. George was losing his sense of time and perspective. After a day and a night at sea, he knew he was less able to focus and he could feel his daydreams starting to become hallucinations. Abdullah broke into his waking dreams, thrusting the satellite phone handset towards him.

"Ring," he demanded, "it is time."

George shook himself awake and gathered his thoughts, before taking the phone and dialling the familiar number for Malta Police HQ. He pictured the imposing stone entrance of the building in Floriana, his colleagues arriving for the day shift, chatting and joking, coffees in hand, ready to get on with their morning.

As he began dialling, his pulse quickened with his rising anticipation. He thought about the reception desk and the duty desk officers, bellies straining their too-tight uniforms. Behind the reception desk, in the walk-in cupboard, the telephone switchboard panel would be humming and clicking. The call, a digital sequence, waited to be de-coded and processed, all their hopes relying on a few chips of silicon and cobalt, while, around them, the enormous sea endlessly swirled and churned.

Abdullah held the GPS screen to his face, to show he had the co-ordinates ready.

"Make us safe, Mr. Policeman!"

The phone rang, and rang, and rang.

Abdullah looked at George, frustrated, and snatched the phone, holding it to his ear.

"It is working. Why is there no answer?"

"Don't worry. It's normal," he replied, "nobody's in a hurry in Malta, especially the *Pulizija*!"

After a minute, a female voice picked up the phone.

"Malta *Pulizija* HQ. Good morning."

With huge relief, George quickly started talking.

"Inspector George Zammit for Superintendent Farrugia. It's urgent."

There was a pause. Just for a moment, he feared they had lost the connection and were doomed to float the ocean, until their time was up. Then he heard: "He's out this morning. Can you call back?"

"NO! Absolutely not! This is an emergency! I'm in mortal danger! Please get a senior officer to talk to me, RIGHT NOW!"

It sounded as if the operator had dropped the hand set onto the desk. George heard her heels clattering along the tiled floor, disappearing off down the corridor. He held the phone for what seemed like an eternity, but finally heard the muffled speech and the crackle of somebody picking up the receiver.

George could not believe it when he heard the smooth tones of Assistant Commissioner Gerald Camilleri come down the line.

"George? What on earth is going on? Where are you? We have all been beside ourselves."

George felt anger building inside. He drew on the same strength within him that had helped him to pull the triggers on the machine guns at the compound in Marsabar; the same strength that had enabled him to fire the RPG at the Vai Vai Cafe. He shouted: "Take down these coordinates and read them back to me. I want these passed on to the Coastguard in Lampedusa. Do it *now*, Gerald."

There was a pause, but he heard Camilleri repeating the location, as he scribbled down the numbers and then read the coordinates back.

"Where exactly is this, George?"

"I'm on a migrant raft, escaping from Libya, where you sent me. I've got your man with me, and he's got his bloody briefcase, in case you're interested. We escaped from an ISIL ambush and we're travelling together.

"You know, there's a lot of dead time on a raft, Gerald, and there's not a lot to do but talk and think. I know all about the *Malik Albahr*, about the oil smuggling; I know where it's going next and that you gave the man with me gold. I can also guess that the story Walker told me is true and his gaming business is somehow involved. Oh, and I met an ISIL terrorist, someone who knew exactly where I'd be and had orders to kill me – until I shot him. Who could have told him where I'd be? Am I onto something here, Gerald?"

He spat out his superior's name contemptuously.

There was silence on the other end of the phone. George knew, whatever Camilleri had been expecting from this call, it was not calm defiance. George pushed on, before his nerve failed.

"I've got a satellite phone, with plenty of charge left. I want a call on this number in fifteen minutes from the Italians in Lampedusa, telling me a boat is on its way. If that doesn't happen, Gerald, I swear my next calls will be to the *Times of Malta*, *La Republica* and Internal Affairs. I know everything and I'll make sure you become famous for all the wrong reasons. So, Gerald, read this number back to me."

Camilleri read it back.

"Don't overthink this, Gerald. I can't begin to tell you what I've been through; what you've put me through. I'm going to call my wife. I'm going to tell her to go down to the station and see Superintendent Farrugia, to ask him for updates on our rescue. Have you met Marianna? She makes a lot of noise when she's upset."

"OK, OK! Officer in distress, I am onto it. I will ring your wife and tell her we have found you and you are coming home. Do not stir things up. Try to relax – we will get you home. Then we will talk.

"But first, one question. Think carefully, before you answer. It is very important. Are we still friends?"

"Friends?" George screamed.

"Friends, George. I know you are angry, but it is important that I know. Are we still friends?"

George felt his anger and defiance drain away. He knew he would have to compromise. He would not put it past Camilleri to leave them adrift – Abdullah and all the innocents were depending on this phone call to secure their rescue. He knew it would suit his superior far better if they arrived, blue and bloated, in Italian Navy body bags.

He said, through gritted teeth, "Yes, Assistant Commissioner, yes, we're still friends."

"Good, George, that is what I needed to hear. It is important to me that we stay friends. There will be many people who are very pleased with what you have achieved. I will call Marianna and we will arrange a proper homecoming for you. Sit tight, help is on its way."

CHAPTER 54
NICK WALKER
SICILIAN CHANNEL, ABOARD THE EYE OF OSIRIS

In the Mediterranean, the longline bluefin tuna season runs from January to the end of May, but the *Eye of Osiris* was twenty-six metres long, so she was small enough to fish all year round. And that was what she did. The big commercial vessels fished with complicated fixed-cage systems, luring shoals of migratory tuna into extensive traps, anchored to the seabed. Once the fish swam into them, they would be towed to large fish farms, where they were fattened on sardines, squid or mackerel, before being cropped for the European and Japanese markets.

Nasim told Nick, in his broken English, he was just a regular long-line fisherman, but it did not take Nick long to realise he cared little for regulations, be they to preserve fish stocks, benefit his crew or for the safety of others at sea. The moment they had cleared coastal waters, he turned off his automatic identification system, having heard too many Mayday calls from migrant boats, struggling off the shores of Libya. He was a fisherman, so getting the catch in and sold was his only concern.

The young crew worked hard, baiting lines and feeding miles of barbed nylon out into the ocean. They smoked continually, shouting and singing, happy to be working and waiting to see what luck the trip might bring them. The *Osiris* travelled at a quarter of the speed of the Blue Cascade, rolling and lolling in the swell. Nick kept his eyes fixed on the horizon to keep sea sickness at bay.

They were some fifty nautical miles south of Lampedusa and the crew were busy collecting in an endless line of fish, when the shout went up. Everybody on the boat stopped work and Nasim throttled the engines back. Nick joined him, as he left the wheelhouse to examine what looked like a migrant raft, through powerful binoculars, some 800 metres away.

"Nasim, can I see?"

He passed Nick the binoculars.

"We no go near. Raft can move very fast and people no good. We must catch fish."

Nick could see some of the occupants on the raft, standing and waving, although they were quickly forced to sit back down. He noticed the outboard motor, a powerful inshore affair, that could probably reach five or six knots without swamping the rubber dinghy.

Nasim was looking at the sky, checking the wind and the wave conditions, in case he needed to make a speedy getaway.

Curiosity made Nasim edge the *Osiris* a little closer for a better look at the vessel and its hapless passengers. The wind was light and there was a one-metre swell, with waves of about half a metre. For the moment, it was nothing the raft could not handle.

There was what looked like a VHF radio aerial protruding from the stern of the boat.

"Look, Nasim, they've got a radio. Call them, check they're OK?"

He hesitated, squinting at the raft.

"Why? Not my business."

"Come on, Nasim. What if it were you out there?"

"Am I so stupid to fish in boat like that?"

He continued staring at the raft and eventually spun on his heels, saying:

"OK, I try. But they no come on my boat."

Nick followed him back to the wheelhouse and watched as he picked up the VHF handset, which he tuned to Channel 16, the calling channel for all non-commercial craft.

"Osiris to raft, over"

"Osiris to raft, over"

He waited for about thirty seconds and then heard a reply, in accented English.

"Raft to Osiris, six eight."

Nick thought it was interesting that they had a VHF radio and knew the protocols of how to use it.

Nasim tuned the channel to sixty-eight, so they could begin to speak.

"This is Osiris, no pick up. We call Libyan coastguard if you like? Over?"

"No Libyan Coastguard. Italian Coastguard in Lampedusa coming. They know our position. Repeat, no Libyan Coastguard. We hope Italian ship arrive soon. We need water, over?"

Nick could see Nasim did not like the sound of that. It meant getting close to the raft and that could be dangerous. Bobby had already told Nick all fishermen were wary of the migrants and there were frequent incidents of smaller vessels, trying to help the rafts, being taken over by force. The raft turned towards them.

Nasim spoke into the VHF handset, "Hold position. We drop water. Collect when we go, out."

With that, Nasim closed the channel, shouting at one of the hands to fill some twenty litre containers and rope them to a large buoy. The raft could pull them in, while the *Osiris* made its escape.

Nick watched the proceedings, straining his eyes, fascinated by the encounter. He picked up Nasim's binoculars again and took another look. He had seen pictures of the rafts before, but actually seeing a real one, with real people, bobbing around sixty or seventy miles offshore, was a lot for him to process.

He saw various people sitting on the tubes and squatting on the floor in the middle of the boat. It did not seem too crowded and most were wearing yellow life vests. Many were dressed in ordinary street clothes. A few had woollen hats, some had hoodies, others wore tracksuits. Amongst them were women and even some young children. The more excitable of them kept jumping to their feet, shouting, waving at the *Osiris*; others sat passive, simply watching.

The raft continued its progress towards them. He guessed the speed at between three to four knots. Two of the *Osiris* crew brought four plastic jerry cans filled with drinking water onto the deck and lashed them to a one-metre buoy.

"Hurry up," Nasim shouted, "I don't want to go near them. Let's go."

They threw the containers over the side; the buoy disappearing from sight, before it bobbed back up to the surface. Nasim returned to the wheelhouse and pushed the throttle to full ahead, sending the boat surging forwards. The raft carried on heading towards them, although still some two hundred metres away. At that speed, they would end up sailing close past each other, but the raft would have to slow and turn, if they wanted to board the *Osiris*. Nasim seemed confident that they would rather stop to recover the water, so avoiding any risk of them being boarded. Even so, Nick nticed he had produced a pistol from a locker behind the helmsman's seat and was busy checking the cartridges.

Nick watched, as Nasim lined up to pass the raft, port side to port side. He needed to make a smooth turn away from it as he was still towing fishing lines and did not want them fouled up. The people on the raft were pointing at the large red buoy; that was their target. They were less interested in making for the *Osiris*, which was already moving at speed. Nasim glanced behind and throttled back a little to reduce the size of the wake, so as not to swamp the raft.

The boats were moving towards each other, about twenty

metres abeam and fifty metres apart, but closing. Everyone on the Osiris was on deck, fascinated by the scene unfolding ahead. On the raft, two large black guys appeared to be in charge. They were organising space to lift the buoy and pull up the water. Two Arab types stood by the outboard, at the rear of the raft, one of them in full sailing waterproofs, the other, bearded, his head wrapped in a traditional *djellaba,* guiding the raft towards the buoy.

When the boat passed the raft, the man in waterproofs made a telephone gesture with his hand and fingers, shouting across in English: "Radio Lampedusa Coastguard! Please! Tell them we're still waiting! Give our position."

Nasim gave him a thumbs up sign from the wheelhouse, before spinning the wheel to finish his turn away from the raft.

As he did so, Nick noticed something familiar about the battered figure who had shouted at them. It was not the full waterproofs that made him stand out. Nick could tell he was corpulent beneath the yellow one piece, but that was not it either. He was looking directly at Nick, shading his eyes to get a better view. Nick thought he recognised the man, but could not quite place him. Then, it came to him in a flash; he was that bloody policeman from Malta! The one he had phoned that first night, from the Blue Cascade. Inspector Zammit! Nick could only stare and wonder what the hell he was doing there – was he somehow involved in all this as well? That moment of recognition shocked him and he watched as the man turned to keep his eyes on him, whilst the boats slid past each other. It seemed that the policeman had also recognised him.

Open-mouthed, Nick raised a hand in recognition.

CHAPTER 55
INSPECTOR GEORGE ZAMMIT
SICILIAN CHANNEL, ABOARD THE RAFT

George grabbed the VHF radio from Abdullah.

"I need to speak to the skipper of the fishing boat."

"Why?"

"Please, Abdullah, just do it."

Abdullah took the handset and powered up the unit. He hit channel sixty-eight and started calling.

"Raft to Osiris, over."

"Raft to Osiris, over."

"Osiris receiving, over"

He passed George the handset.

"I need to speak to the Englishman, over."

A long pause followed.

"There is no Englishman aboard, over."

"Yes, there is, I've seen him. Where're are you heading? Over."

"We unload fish in Lampedusa. Over."

George thought about the places he knew in Lampedusa.

"Tell the Englishman to wait at the Hotel Neptune. If I get there first, I'll wait. Tell him I'm a friend and we need to talk. Over."

"OK. I tell him. Out."

The boats then moved steadily apart until the *Osiris* disappeared from the raft's limited view.

Abdullah looked at him, askance.

"What is that about? Who is this Englishman?"

"*Mela,* it's very strange; but it's OK. I know a man aboard that boat. Maybe he can help us. Let's hope the skipper gives him the message and he waits for us in Lampedusa."

Abdullah grimaced.

"You meet friends here, in the middle of the sea, eh? Remember, we must get to Lampedusa first and I think tonight will be bad weather." He was looking at the darkening sky, noticing how the wind blowing in from the north-west was strengthening.

Just then, the satellite phone rang, the sound commanding the attention of all those on board. Abdullah gave it to George and watched intently.

It was the Italian Coastguard, out of Lampedusa. George listened, nodding along.

"What? *How long*? Can't it be sooner?"

Abdullah looked across at George, lines of exhaustion etched on his face.

"How long until the boat arrives?"

"Six hours."

Abdullah looked at the heaps of dense, towering, vertical clouds, forming in the purple light to the north of them.

"We are not safe yet, my friend."

CHAPTER 56
NICK WALKER

SICILIAN CHANNEL, ABOARD THE EYE OF OSIRIS

As the *Eye of Osiris* pulled away from the raft, Nick stared in disbelief at the figure on the back of the frail vessel. It was clearly the fat Maltese policeman, whose card he still had in his wallet, the one he had telephoned from the Blue Cascade – was it really less than a week ago?

Nick had waved at him, but he had not been acknowledged. It did not matter; there was no doubting who he was. Nick made his way up into the wheelhouse to talk to the skipper. Nasim was still holding the VHF radio when he barged in through the door.

"You have funny friends." He waved the VHF handset in front of Nick.

"The man on the raft?"

"Yes. He your friend?"

Nick thought for a second.

"Yeah, he is, what did he say?"

"I no go back for him, no way," Nasim said.

"I don't want you to. I think he knows what he's doing, but what did he say?"

"So, we in Lampedusa by morning and you go to Hotel Neptune. He come. Maybe tomorrow."

"Why don't you go back for them and help?"

"What can I do? If Tunisian, yes, I help, sometimes. In Tunisia, no work, prices go up and more up so people leave. Government say go, go Germany, Italy, yes! Always this way. In Germany and Italy, plenty work for Tunisian Arab people. No work for black African. When I see them, I no stop. They bring AIDS and no good people."

Nick had heard these sentiments before. The universal prejudice against black Africans ran deep in the Arab countries, as it did in southern Europe.

"Your friend lucky. Maybe he live and see tomorrow." Nasim looked at the sullen, swollen clouds, piling up on the northern horizon. As he smelt the sharp, fresh aroma of ozone, that he knew preceded the arrival of the rain, he felt the first drops of salty moisture on his face. "Maybe not so lucky."

The tuna catch had been good and the enormous beasts were thrashing about in the fish hold, as the crew went about killing them; pushing metal spikes through the top of their heads into their brains. They bled the fish by cutting them just below their fins, venting a stream of thick dark blood to get rid of the lactic acid that had built up, as the fish fought on the line. The boat was awash with the acrid smell of blood and fish. The flake-ice machine churned away and the crew shovelled the ice over the catch, some over a metre long. It was a bloody affair and neither man nor fish looked the better for it.

The crew finished the slaughter and were hosing each other down from a high-pressure saltwater pump. They took little notice of Nick but laughed and joked, as they went about rinsing down the decks and collecting the lines. A good payday was waiting for them, if they could get to Lampedusa and meet the buyers who sold to the Japanese markets.

When all the lines were in, Nasim pushed on for the island. Nick could tell he did not like the look of the rain clouds gathering on the darkening horizon. When the storm struck, the poor souls on the raft would not have much chance of making land. Nasim eased the throttle forward and turned to face him, seeing the concern on Nick's face.

"The Coastguard boat coming – not your problem."

Nick turned his back on him.

CHAPTER 57
NATASHA BONNICI
THE AQUARIUM, ST PAUL'S BAY, MALTA

NATASHA HAD LEFT in the early afternoon, following her meeting with Raphael. She had pleaded with her father that she needed a change of scenery, to clear her head. Marco was sceptical about her motives, but knew there was little he could do to stop her. Before she drove to St Paul's, she had sent a message to Elbasan from the Albanian Basement. She had arranged to meet him in the Aquarium, a new tourist attraction on the edge of the resort. She looked and felt terrible. She had spent some time applying make up to conceal her deathly pallor and a loose-fitting woollen hat was pulled low, to conceal the bandage that protected the wound on her scalp.

It was early summer and the Aquarium was busy with young families and school parties, watching a wide variety of fish swimming in giant Perspex tanks and through transparent tubes that ran above their heads.

She had told Elbasan to wait in the shark tunnel, which was a connecting tube, twenty metres long, through the biggest tank in the Aquarium. Visitors could walk through the tunnel and have the experience of being within a few centimetres of the ultimate predator. Natasha watched Elbasan who was standing in the tunnel, from the other side of the Perspex tank. Her eyes settled on him as he stood there, fascinated by the fish. He was transfixed by the blue-grey torpedo shapes, as they effortlessly slid past, their dull lifeless eyes revealing nothing of their intentions.

Natasha stood back in the shadows, her body tingling with anticipation. She watched Elbasan intently and noticed he had slipped on a cheap leather jacket over his stained working singlet. She pursed her lips in distaste at his appearance, turned off her phone and, with one last glance in his direction, slipped out of the Aquarium.

Less than thirty minutes later, she returned to the *castello* and flopped into an easy chair on the terrace, beneath a broad striped sunshade. She was tired and her head was pounding. She closed her eyes for a moment and almost immediately fell into a shallow sleep. It was not long before she was woken by Raphael's appearance. He silently emerged from the house, in his usual funereal garb, but she sensed his presence immediately.

"I am sorry, did I wake you?"

Natasha roused herself and sat up in her chair.

"I hear you have been out for a drive. A little early in your recuperation, I would have thought?"

"Possibly, but I'm fine, thank you. I can't sit about doing nothing all day. I'm not that sort. A little drive, to enjoy some sea air for half an hour, was just what I needed."

"Very good. If you are feeling up to it, I have that login we talked about, but I do not want your father to think I am over-tiring you."

"I'll have a coffee and then we can sit down in the study, say at three?"

Natasha had a coffee, drank plenty of water, took her painkillers and readied herself for the next few hours. She knew exactly where she was going with her investigation into the BetSlick systems, but the secret was to take longer, try more convoluted routes to lose Raphael in the process. To jump immediately to the solution would compromise her entire plan.

The familiar, intimate atmosphere of the library encouraged

concentration and she took a seat, with her laptop, at the large eighteenth-century Tuscan writing desk. Raphael was waiting for her and pulled up a second chair, alongside her, so he could watch her interrogate the systems. She could sense him sitting close by and had to block out the smell of the cigarettes, mingled with his expensive musky scent. She booted up her laptop.

"I have Nick's login and password."

He slid his phone towards her. The login was the standard BetSlick protocol, with CEO@BetSlick.com. She paused and looked more closely at the screen when she saw his password, 'Na7a54a!!'

Raphael saw her hesitate.

"Yes, it surprised me too! 'Natasha'. *Che romantico.*"

Natasha ignored the comment. For the next half hour, she logged into the two accounting systems and started a predictable search pattern through all transactions relating to the Navkovs' transactions with BetSlick. She made a show of finding nothing of interest. The money came in and the money went out. Nothing much more to it than that.

She then started searching the FinSlick accounts, which were the second accounts behind the BetSlick business system. She tracked the Navkovs' money coming into the system from Antayla Bank, a business owned by the Family, and its transmission to a second account in the name of a long dead Turkish teacher from Ankara. The money then went from that dummy account into the BetSlick player account, but disappeared and never returned.

Raphael watched and understood the logic of the search so far.

Natasha then instigated a search programme of all accounts within a certain set of parameters. A long list of player account numbers appeared and she started opening the client details for each account. After forty minutes, she sat back in her chair and pushed her spectacles up, on top of her hair.

"Well, I know where the money went and I know where it came from."

Raphael looked at her.

"Dimmi."

"Look at these player account numbers." She highlighted two thirteen-digit numbers. "See the difference?"

Raphael peered at the numbers.

"Yes", he said pointing at the screen, "those two digits are transposed, the two and the seven."

"So, I don't think Nick ever meant to steal the Navkovs' money. He meant to steal the cash from the other account, but screwed up the player account numbers!"

"Well, who owns the other account?"

"The Family."

Natasha sat back, arms folded, smiling in satisfaction.

"So, what you are saying is, he meant to steal the Family's money, but slipped up and took the Navkovs' by mistake? I can see how that could have happened. Well done! But it does not really help us, does it?"

"Well, maybe it does, because I think, in a day or so, I can reverse the transaction and get the cash back into the Navkovs' account. I've got to make a few calls, but it's a mistake, so we should be able to reverse it via the banks."

"I do not know what to say. If you do achieve that, it would be impressive work! The Wise Men will be glad it is not coming out of their own pocket and it might go some way to persuade the Navkovs it was an accounting error, so they haven't been disrespected."

Natasha knew very well that the four hundred thousand euros had been transferred out of BetSlick and, after a series of onward transfers, was sitting in a trust account in the First Bank of Mauritius, where she was the sole beneficiary; a fact that would never be disclosed. The trust company was located in a modern and efficient office, above a shabby two-storey shopping arcade in Port Louis. All she had to do was make a phone call to a nice Indian lady, called Mrs Jingree, confirm her identity and the cash would then be transferred back into the late Turkish teacher's account with Antayla Bank, and onward to one of the Navkovs' player accounts with BetSlick.

Elbasan had set up the dead Turkish teacher's account and then given her the passwords to allow her to operate it. Nick's misplaced trust had given her the knowledge to access, renumber and operate BetSlick player accounts. She had easily established the Mauritian trust account and that was all she needed to do. There had been no mistake, she knew exactly what she was doing and what it would look like. She understood the implications for Nick and the powerful signal it would send to the Wise Men in Milan when she managed to put it all right.

As she and Raphael sat in silence, working through the implications of what they had found, Marco knocked and entered the study. He said nothing, but went and sat on an overstuffed leather sofa. The two of them looked at him, waiting for him to speak.

"Well, I have two pieces of news – both troubling," he announced.

Raphael left the desk, taking an easy chair by the fireplace and beckoned Marco to continue. Natasha turned her chair to face him, the heavy legs scraping against the polished stone floor.

"Camilleri has just phoned to tell me that the Maltese policeman and my Libyan contact have been found, drifting on a migrant boat, eighty kilometres south of Lampedusa and that the Italian Navy is on its way to pick them up! Can you believe it?"

For the first time, Natasha thought Raphael looked rattled. He put his hands behind his head and scowled.

"*Che cavolo …?* How has that happened?"

"I have no idea. Apparently, there was a clash between the Marsabar militia and our new partners. Our old friend and the policeman escaped, leaving a trail of bodies behind them. Our new partners now control the town, the port and the refinery.

They have also taken control of the tanker and its cargo. However, Abdullah Belkacem and Inspector Zammit slipped through their fingers and took to the high seas."

Raphael was decidedly unimpressed.

"They are heading for Lampedusa, presumably?"

Marco nodded.

"Camilleri assumed we would want to contain the situation so has got a message to the Lampedusa police, ordering them to wait on the island. The Assistant Commissioner will arrive first thing tomorrow, on an Armed Forces plane, to start the debrief personally."

Raphael nodded.

"That is good thinking. If we have the policeman and the Libyan on Lampedusa, why not tempt Walker there as well? I will see what I can organise to neutralise them all. Natasha, it is time we sent our message to Nick Walker and asked him to change his travel plans. We must try to tempt him with the prospect of a reconciliation in Malta."

She nodded at Raphael and then turned to her father.

"Dad, you said there were two pieces of news. What's the second?"

"Yes." He paused, shifting in his seat. "This is equally distressing. Camilleri has just returned from St Paul's, where a man he believes to be Elbasan was killed in a traffic accident. Except, Camilleri does not believe it was an accident."

Natasha put her hand to her mouth in shock.

"Oh my God! You mean our Elbasan? The Albanian? Why doesn't he think it was an accident? Were there witnesses?"

"Apparently not, but it happened in the Aquarium car park, a place not known for high-speed driving and, from the state of the body, Camilleri thinks the car ran over him three or four times."

CHAPTER 58
INSPECTOR GEORGE ZAMMIT

FORTY KILOMETRES SOUTH OF LAMPEDUSA, MEDITERRANEAN SEA

Conditions at sea were deteriorating fast. The increased wind speed was generating two-metre waves, on top of the two-metre swell, that crashed over the sides of the raft. There was a sense of panic amongst the weary travellers who were at the limit of their endurance, whilst still maintaining a frantic bailing operation. Had the raft been overcrowded, as most migrant rafts were, they would certainly all have perished.

The temperature had dipped, the wind tore at their soaking clothes and the sixty-horsepower engine was all but useless, in the face of the rushing waves and headwind. Abdullah struggled to keep the bow of the boat into the wind and waves. If the waves caught the raft beam on, he was fearful it would be flipped.

Never had the sky seemed so dark; the sea so big and merciless. The horizon disappeared from sight, as the raft rose, then plunged into the troughs between the waves. The vivid blue of the water had turned grey, purple and dark green, while the pale azure sky had become tumbling stacks of bruised clouds. Like all those on board, George was absolutely terrified. Everybody knew this was a fight for survival and there was no conversation, just prayers and urgent shouts about waves, wind, bailing and the hope of rescue. Abdullah knew that if the storm did not abate, or they were not picked up before nightfall, they would not survive the night.

Late in the afternoon, when they had nearly lost all hope, their prayers were answered. The masts and communications tower of an Italian corvette became visible, just for a moment, above the crest of the waves. Screams from the other end of the raft and frantic pointing alerted George, who scrambled for the waterproof bag, containing the flares. Watched by anxious eyes, he lit a smoke flare and threw it into the water. Within minutes, the corvette *Corraggio* approached them, ensuring its bow wave was low and did not add to the chaos of the waves and swell that threatened to swamp them.

The corvette turned to come abreast of the raft, sheltering the flimsy boat from the waves and the wind. After ten minutes of low-speed manoeuvring, it cut its engines and drifted alongside them. The crew threw lines to the raft which were secured to the front and rear cleats. They were then pulled towards a scramble net that had been lowered, to allow the exhausted travellers to clamber aboard the corvette. Crew members climbed halfway down, lending a hand to the most weary and weak.

George made sure Abdullah and he were the last aboard, to show that they took responsibility for the whole sorry enterprise. The ship's officers had already been alerted to the special status of one passenger and the crewmen helped push him up the net and over the side of the rail. George collapsed in a heap on the wooden deck and lay panting on his back, eyes shut and breathless. The officers and ship's medic had started a medical assessment process of everyone who had been rescued. One knelt down beside George and started loosening his life jacket, which he had pulled so tight in his panic, it was constricting his breathing.

"Inspector Zammit? We were told you were on the raft. I'm First Officer Sabelli. Welcome aboard. You're safe now. You must have quite a story to tell! Please, let me help you up, I'm sure the Captain will want to meet you."

George had been preparing for this moment.

"Thank you. This is my colleague, Tareq Belkacem. He's with the Libyan Police, Tripoli, seconded to work with the Maltese *Pulizija.*" George grabbed Abdullah, who was slumped at the rail next to him and pushed him ahead, making it clear wherever he went, his colleague came with him.

"We were on a joint operation, investigating trafficking in Marsabar, but we were taken by ISIL fighters. He helped me escape. I owe him my life."

"Well, Mr Belkacem, welcome also. You both make our life at sea seem very unexciting. Please, both come this way."

The Captain was charming, but already had plenty to worry about, taking on board extra passengers in the middle of a storm. George showed him his *Pulizija* identification card, which he glanced at in a cursory fashion. Abdullah had hauled his brief-case up the netting and was clasping it tightly. The crew gave them a change of clothes, coffee and hot food. Once they had dried and calmed themselves, George and Abdullah they were shown to a quiet corridor, where there were two thin mattresses on the floor and two light quilts.

Once they were alone, Abdullah and George looked at each other. Abdullah chuckled, while shaking his head.

"Well, Mr Policeman, we live to fight again, eh? I swear, those last hours, I never thought we would live through this day!"

"*Mela,* I know." George shook his head. "I didn't think I'd be quite so happy to realise I'll be seeing my wife again soon! Maybe I'll introduce you to her. You can come and eat with us – she makes good food."

"Yes, I would like that. My home seems far away now, but it would please me to be your guest." Abdullah grabbed George's hand momentarily and both men realised an unlikely friendship had been forged, in the desert scrub of Libya and on the rolling seas of the Mediterranean.

The pair relaxed back onto the mattresses and Abdullah pulled the quilt over his head. In a muffled voice, he said: "Now I must try to sleep and put this terrible day behind me."

"Yes," George replied, "that's a very good idea."

The relief quickly brought deep, but not peaceful sleep. George dreamed he was back on the raft. He felt the rolling pitch of the boat and the violence of the force eight wind, throwing water into his face and stripping the shouts from his mouth. He was woken up with a jolt and realised he was being shaken by a rating, who told him he had slept for four hours and that they were expecting Lampedusa to be within sight soon.

The corvette sailed into the harbour, past the statue of the Madonna and Child that watched the ships come and go, and berthed quickly, without fuss. George stood at the rail with the others. They were expected. The quayside was alive with medical staff, border guards from Frontex, the EU border and coast guard agency, with their interpreters, public health officials. Charity workers had laid out boxes of clothing, energy bars and bottles of water were on a series of trestle tables.

The migrants were taken off the corvette and led to a large marquee on the quayside, where the Frontex officers screened them. Basic details were taken, where children and vulnerable people were identified and taken to one side. Then, they fingerprinted everybody. An officer from Europol took the screening reports and watched the migrants as they filed out of the tent, watching for any sign that further questioning might be needed, if he suspected any connection to human trafficking, organised crime or terrorism. The medical officer undertook a cursory examination of all new arrivals, before, they were handed over to the charity workers.

George and Abdullah were ushered straight past this procedure and into a small police Portacabin. George was taken to one side by an officer and told he was to be debriefed by a Maltese police official, who was expected to arrive shortly. He pulled Abdullah towards him and announced they would both wait for the officer together. George guessed it would be Camilleri. The pair of them were led to a police compound on the other side of the harbour, which had a comfortable room with some sofas and a coffee machine.

As soon as they were left alone, Abdullah asked, "Well, Mr Maltese Policeman, what now, eh?"

"I don't really know. *Mela,* let's see what happens. The worst they can do is throw you in a camp and you can then plead for asylum. I'll help you. I can prove your life is in danger if they send you back to Libya. You're a Berber and ISIL have tried to kill you."

"But I want to go to Malta. I will be good and, maybe, open a small shop." Abdullah patted the case. "But, for now, I give this to you."

He handed George the case with the gold and the bank papers. "The papers are useless, but the gold, not so!"

"What am I supposed to do with this?" George asked, a little taken aback.

"Keep it safe and give it back to me in Malta. If there are expenses, I will understand. If you steal it ... well you know, eh? The combination is 1511. That is my birthday, day 15 of November – you can remember that, no?"

George took the case and dialled the combination. He and Abdullah then took the valuables out of the case and wrapped the bars of gold with their sopping wet clothes, taken from a blue plastic bag the Navy had provided.

"This'll stop them clinking. If anyone asks you, you can tell them the case was lost at sea. I hope I don't get searched getting on the plane!"

Abdullah laughed: "If you do, just make a bribe to a policeman!"

"That might just work," said George, thinking of Camilleri.

"Listen, I'm going for a walk to look for my friend and I'll find somewhere to dump this case, while I'm out. I've got a feeling the person coming to talk to us might recognise it."

The last thing George wanted was Camilleri demanding the return of the case. He walked up to the desk sergeant and told him he needed some air, promising to be back in good time to meet the Maltese police. The sergeant shrugged his shoulders and George left the compound, dressed in his new Italian Navy tracksuit.

He felt ridiculous. The tracksuit top they had given him aboard ship was too short for a corpulent man like him and he had to constantly pull it down to cover his bulging belly. The bottoms were for a man considerably taller than him, so he had rolled them up to stop the ankle cuffs trailing in the dirt. Nevertheless, he strode out of the port, asking for directions to the Hotel Neptune. Basically, there was one main street, Via Roma, and the hotel could be found at the northern end of it.

George found an overflowing skip outside the shell of a half-built shop and pushed the case deep into the rubbish. It felt good to be finally rid of it, after what seemed like weeks. He wandered for another ten minutes, until he saw the whitewashed facade of the Hotel Neptune, at the end of a curved gravel drive. He walked through the reception, as confidently as possible, and moved out onto a terrace overlooking the swimming pool. Nick Walker was already sitting there, reading Moby Dick, a beer in his hand, looking as relaxed as any other guest.

He guessed that Walker's motive for showing up was to cut a deal, to provide information in exchange for immunity from whatever crimes he had committed in Malta, and protection from whoever he had crossed. George had no authority for those sorts of conversations, but he wondered what Assistant Commissioner Camilleri would say, when he arrived. He was beginning to realise Walker's and Abdullah's fate lay in the Assistant Commissioner's slippery hands.

George made his way over towards the Englishman. Walker was sunburned but looking clean and tidy, in fresh jeans and a slightly creased, pale blue shirt. With his tousled blond hair and tightly trimmed beard, he looked as if he had just stepped off some multi-million dollar yacht in the marina at Portofino. It made George even more conscious of his own dishevelled appearance and ill-fitting tracksuit.

Walker rose to greet him, taking off his sunglasses and flicking back his blond hair.

"Well, surprise, surprise! I'm pleased you're in one piece, Inspector. Last time I saw you, I wasn't so sure you'd make it. There was no way the fishing boat's skipper was going to pick you up. I'm sorry, there was nothing I could do. I was just an item of cargo myself."

George waved away the apology and stroked his thick growth of stubble. Nick gestured towards the bar area.

"*Mela*, let's sit down and compare notes. I don't really know where to start with it all."

"Hang on, before we begin, you didn't send me a WhatsApp message just now, did you? I've only just charged my phone and I got a strange message, telling me it was in my interests to come to Lampedusa. Bit weird. Was it from you?"

George shook his head.

"Nothing to do with me. I told the fishing boat skipper and he must have told you, or you wouldn't be here."

"Yeah, that's right. The WhatsApp's strange but, then again, nothing surprises me these days!"

They left the terrace and headed inside to the empty bar. George made a detour through reception to find a gents and spotted a very tall, thin man, standing at the desk, dressed in a black suit, with sunglasses perched on his angular face. He turned to glance at George, but looked straight through him, dismissing him as some scruffy-looking tradesman, working in the hotel.

George thought the man looked out of place in his suit and tie, which made him hover nearby, to listen in on his conversation with the receptionist. The man leant over the counter towards her, speaking in a cultured Italian accent. There was something about him … a sense of menace.

"Do you have a Mr. Walker staying with you? I am due to meet him here."

George watched the clerk shake her head in reply. The man then pulled out several 10cm x 15cm photographs and laid them on the counter. He took out his wallet and placed a fifty euro note on top of them. Nothing was said, but the clerk took the note and pointed towards the terrace.

The man smiled and removed his sunglasses, returned them to their case, picked up the photographs and sauntered towards the entrance to the terrace. George lurked behind a pillar along the corridor and, like a sleuth in a movie, peeked around the corner.

The man ventured out onto the terrace and that was George's cue to move – taking the opportunity to dart into the bar and grab hold of Nick Walker's arm.

"Quick, quick, come with me. There's someone on the terrace looking for you and I don't think you want to meet him. Seriously, move, now!"

They walked briskly through the lobby and out into the parking lot.

"Let's wait a bit and see if he comes out," hissed George.

Like a couple of schoolboys, they hid behind a large white van, with signage on the side showing air conditioning services available across the island 24/7. They watched the entrance and waited. After ten minutes or so, the man in the dark suit appeared and stood under the portico, lighting a cigarette. He looked around attentively.

Walker whispered to George: "I've no idea who he is, but you're right, I don't like the look of him either. Wait here, I've got to go back to my room for a minute. I won't be long."

Before George could stop him, Walker started moving towards the back of the hotel, hiding behind the cars. He disappeared onto the terrace, leaving George behind the van, his heart pounding. After a couple of minutes, the man crushed the cigarette with his heel and walked across the car park towards where George was standing. He was sure he had been spotted.

Deciding attack was the best form of defence, George banged the van door with his fist, as if to lock it and made a show of noisily spitting on the tarmac. Then he confidently swaggered out into the other man's path. The man sidestepped him, a disgusted expression on his face. George gave him a loud, throaty '*Buongiorno*', as he walked on past.

When Nick re-appeared, he was carrying his red Kappa branded sports bag. The two of them checked the front car park, then scurried out of the front door and walked towards the port.

"Shit! What the hell's going on?" asked Nick.

"Don't worry, I've got an idea. *Mela,* you trust me, don't you?"

"I don't even know you but, right now, I don't have a lot of choice, do I?"

They settled into a brisk walk, along the quay, towards the police compound, with George keeping one hand firmly around the waistband of his sagging tracksuit bottoms.

As they turned into the police station, Nick started to become uneasy.

"What're we doing here?" he demanded, unease turning to alarm.

George was not quite sure himself.

"You're assisting me with my enquiries. Can you think of anywhere safer to hide? What're you calling yourself these days?"

The desk sergeant raised an eyebrow when they came in and asked them both to sign in. George entered his name and that of Harry McDonald.

The desk sergeant said to George, "There was a call for you. A senior Maltese officer is coming to collect you but, I'm sorry, there's been a delay, it won't be until early tomorrow. You're welcome to stay here tonight, with your colleague. It's not the

Neptune, but it's better than where you spent the last few nights."

George could not have wished for a better outcome.

"What about Mr. McDonald?" the desk sergeant asked him.

"Put him in the cells. He's assisting me with my enquiries. I'll be taking him back to Malta tomorrow or releasing him, depending on what my senior officer decides."

George grabbed the red Kappa bag from Nick and gave him a push towards the desk.

"You bastard!" Nick struggled for a moment, but the desk sergeant quickly came around the counter and took a firm hold of him. Nick's expression was one of genuine fury, mixed with disbelief. The desk sergeant held on and snatched a bunch of keys from under the desk. It was business as usual to him.

George just had time to raise an eyebrow at Nick, in an attempt to reassure him, before he disappeared behind the metal door leading to the cell block.

CHAPTER 59
SERGIO ROSSI

SIGNOR BRUNO'S PALAZZO, BRERA, MILAN

It was late evening when the five Wise Men gathered at Signor Bruno's palatial home in Milan. The area was pedestrianised in part, but a fleet of Audi A8 cars were occasionally spotted, weaving their way up via Brera to the arched entrance of the *palazzo*, near the Piazza Simpliciano. Local law enforcement and retailers waved them through, with deferential bows and smiles – after all, Signor Bruno and his family before him, had owned many of the properties on the street and he was a person of some importance.

It was unusual for them to meet in the evening, as three of the five were in their eighties and not at their best after dinner. However, Signor Bruno had insisted there was an operational matter they needed to be aware of.

So it was that Sergio Rossi was left sitting alone in the Palazzo's 'large' dining room, at the end of a long table, with the remnants of dinner still in evidence at the other end. He had only met with the Wise Men as a group occasionally, usually when they were celebrating a religious festival, or to dine with them when something had gone particularly well. This was not such an occasion.

Before long, staff appeared and, without a word, removed the plates, glasses, table linen and fruit bowl. They then busied around with a silver crumb scraper before stripping the table, polishing the cherrywood tabletop, then returning the chairs to their position, tucked under the table. He noted he had not been offered any refreshments, or been given any indication of how long he might be expected to wait. Signor Bruno usually showed his guests exceptional courtesy and its absence tonight left a hollow feeling in Sergio's stomach.

After forty minutes of waiting, the doors opened and Signor Bruno entered, taking his seat at the head of the gleaming table. The other four Wise Men shuffled in, two carrying drinks, the third puffing a cigar. Not a word was spoken. Sergio had never been received in such a fashion. No eye contact was made with him, except by Signor Bruno, who kept his watery pale blue eyes locked firmly on him.

Sergio was aware that Signor Bruno was a man of few words and did not speak without carefully considering the implications. Sergio was ready to listen carefully to what was to follow.

"Tonight, I speak for us all. We have discussed what you have told us and I assume there is nothing new we should know?"

"Signor Bruno, you know everything that I know."

Sergio desperately wanted to speak, to explain himself, but knew that it would do him no favours to speak out of turn. So, straining every fibre of his body, he sat still, hands clasped tight in front of him, and held his tongue. Quite a feat for a Sicilian!

"We have two words for you to consider – risk and accountability."

Signor Bruno paused, as if something of great importance had just been said. Sergio nodded along, not understanding where the conversation was going.

"The frequency of risk in the current situation is high. That means a loss will probably be incurred. The severity of the risk is also high. That means the extent of that loss will also be significant. So, it is highly likely we will suffer a significant loss, if the current circumstances prevail. That makes this a matter that warrants our urgent attention.

"What is at risk is the energy project, which is central to our future plans, and the cash management operation in Malta, another necessary component of our ongoing business. To fail to deliver the first is a major setback; to compromise the second, by failing to deliver the first, is disastrous.

"We are agreed, I take it, that both these operations are under your direct control?"

Sergio could hardly deny the fact.

"Yes, Signor Bruno."

"You are rewarded well for what you do? You have adequate resources to recruit the people you need? You have had the time to implement the plans we agreed? So, the strategy was correct and the plans were good?"

Sergio sat silent under this rebuke, which was harsh and direct.

"But now we have a failure to implement the agreed plans. A situation where events have occurred and their consequences have not been properly managed, despite all the resources at your disposal. We are not here to help you in your operational management of our plans. We do not have the energy and drive to do things like that; we are old men."

There was a shuffling, with some smiles and nodding around the table.

"We think, we plan, we trust others, younger and more vigorous than us, to be men of action, to deliver the results. We plan for the future of this Family. Our work will benefit your generation, not ours. We do not lament this failure because of any loss we will suffer. We lament it because, thanks to you, we have failed to deliver our promises to the wider Family. It is they who will suffer the losses.

"That brings me to the second word we have asked you to consider tonight: accountability.

"Events are moving fast and we urge you to seize control of

them, otherwise we will need to speak more about that second word."

Sergio made to speak but, as his mouth opened, Signor Bruno's hand shot up to silence him.

"I have finished speaking. I believe you have work to do. Good evening."

CHAPTER 60
INSPECTOR GEORGE ZAMMIT

POLICE RECEPTION CENTRE, ISLAND OF LAMPEDUSA, ITALY

Early the next morning, the Armed Forces of Malta Islander plane taxied onto the apron at Lampedusa's small, but efficient, air terminal. Assistant Commissioner Gerald Camilleri stretched his cramped limbs and breathed in deeply, enjoying the fresh breeze on his face and the smell of the clean salt air.

He had mixed feelings about the task ahead. He had leaned hard on Zammit and the poor man had endured an exceptionally rough time, over the past few days. It was hard to throw one of your own under the bus but, at times, it was necessary. He did not know what the group in Castello Bonnici were planning, but he was certain it would not end well for George Zammit. Unfortunately, Gerald Camilleri had sold his soul to Marco Bonnici a long time ago and would do anything to ensure their mutually beneficial arrangement continued.

The whole episode with George Zammit had been a major headache for Camilleri. He had not managed to keep George's involvement with the Libyans and his brush with ISIL quiet. His family had been told that he was involved in an undercover operation in Libya and attending the conference was merely a cover story. Like all the best lies, it contained a grain of truth. It had taken quite some time to calm Marianna, who had reacted much as George had predicted – hysterically. By the time Camilleri had left the house, she had calmed herself and was starting to see the upside of the situation, namely that this was a fine opportunity for her to become the centre of attention for some time to come. Camilleri was sure that, within thirty minutes of his departure, half of Birkirkara would have known George, on some clandestine operation, was missing in a war zone in North Africa.

The Maltese Prime Minister had been alerted and messages sent to what passed for the government in Tripoli. Camilleri had been forced to call in favours and make threats at the highest levels, to prevent it all becoming a big media story. It was not every day that a Maltese police officer was captured, and possibly killed, by ISIL.

Camilleri's relief when he took George's call was profound; not because of any concerns for his welfare, but because he had been imagining George, once he had escaped the ISIL ambush, sitting in a newspaper office somewhere making allegations, amongst other things, of corruption in the Maltese Police! However, the relief was short-lived, as Camilleri realised the job ahead of him was to keep George on the right track and prevent him from misusing the leverage he had undoubtedly acquired.

A waiting police Fiat took him the short distance towards the harbour and, sooner than Camilleri had expected, they arrived at the police station on the quayside. He was shown into a large interview room, with five chairs and a Formica topped table. The walls were unplastered and unpainted cinder blocks. Camilleri took a seat at the head of the table, adjusted the creases in his suit trousers and brushed the dust off his brogues. It was warm, but appearances were important and, no matter how intense the heat, Assistant Commissioner Camilleri never took his jacket off and never broke into a sweat. He was looking forward to the debrief and was certain it was going to be an interesting morning.

George, on the other hand, looked dishevelled, as he entered the conference room. His hair was still wet from the shower and his heavy stubble threatened to soon become an unruly beard. He was still wearing the ill-fitting tracksuit and immediately felt a hundred times worse, when he saw the immaculately presented Gerald Camilleri, not a grey hair out of place, facing him across the table.

Camilleri stood and held out both arms, as if to offer him an embrace. George remained standing in the doorway.

"George, I never thought I would be so pleased to see you. But, here we are."

Camilleri dropped both arms, but then extended a soft white hand, with manicured nails. George kept his arms at his side, avoiding the handshake. Camilleri ignored the snub. With all the sincerity of a Medici, he pressed on.

"I cannot tell you how relieved we all are to have found you and, I have to say, you are looking none the worse for your adventures."

"You didn't find me, Gerald. I doubt whether you even bothered looking for me. But it doesn't matter, because I'm back and I'm afraid things are very different now."

"Oh, George, I was hoping it would not have to be like this. I can understand you are upset but, surely, we can have a civilised chat about things?"

"No, we can't."

George found that his voice was firm and strong. He felt none of the fear that usually accompanied conversations with Assistant Commissioner Camilleri. So, he pushed on.

"First, you need to meet two friends of mine."

George pulled the door to the conference room wide open.

Abdullah and Nick walked into the room. Gerald Camilleri sat down in silence. He appraised the men, as a snake would two small rodents, judging which to take first. But, he soon realised any control he thought he might have had over the situation, was gone. A twisting of his mouth and a shifting in his chair told George Camilleri was out of his comfort zone and clearly confused.

"Well, I must say, I am surprised. You are Nick Walker, I know. And you, sir, are ...?"

"Abdullah Belkacem, people and oil smuggler, now known as Tareq Belkacem." Abdullah bowed, as he introduced himself.

To Camilleri's obvious discomfort, George added with a smile, "He's also known as '*the Defender of Marsabar.*'"

Abdullah nodded, sagely.

Gerald Camilleri's eyebrows rose so high they were about to disappear into his hairline. He looked at George in apparent defeat.

"Well, George, what can I say? I am speechless. The floor is yours."

George took a deep breath and began. "For different reasons, three of the people in this room belong in prison. That's where you'll all end up, Gerald, if you don't do as I say. My two friends here have agreed to what I'm suggesting. Now, it's up to you."

Nick Walker and Abdullah looked at George and then at each other. They had no idea what his plan was, but had the good sense to keep quiet.

"Quite frankly, I don't care whether or not you go to prison but, right now, I need you to hear me out, or I and these gentlemen will bring you down," George continued, on a roll.

It was not the first time Gerald Camilleri had been up against it and he, too, knew when to bide his time and listen.

"*Mela*, on my own, all I could prove was that you sent me to Tripoli, with a bag of gold and some bank documents. Mr. Belkacem here can verify the contents of the case, which I gave to him on your instruction. But, you see, I also know that you tried to have me killed, in the same ambush you planned for my friend, Abdullah. The gunmen were looking for a Maltese policeman. Who else could that have been? That makes even a mild-mannered man like me really cross, Gerald. You were part of a conspiracy to murder me. That's a crime."

Camilleri did not flinch or blink, his poker face remained expressionless. His mind was racing.

"Why did I go to Libya, anyway? I could say I did it because you blackmailed me. OK, Denzel might get into some trouble but, to be honest, what I've seen over the last few days has toughened me up no end. I can live with that. So, we can add to all your other crimes, a charge of blackmail or, at least, one of obstructing the course of justice.

"Let's carry on, shall we? Mr. Walker, who paid you a sizeable retainer for favours and services rendered to BetSlick, places you at Castello Bonnici, with Marco Bonnici and Sergio Rossi, from the Milan crime family. Abdullah knows the Bonnicis and the Milanese are at the heart of the oil smuggling operation. In fact, Sergio Rossi told Mr. Walker that you had *'the knack of making problems go away'* and you agreed with him. A court could draw their own conclusions from that conversation.

"Mr. Walker is prepared to make a full and frank confession, implicating all concerned. So, on top of conspiracy to commit murder and blackmail, we're talking fraud, bribery, false accounting, tax evasion, perverting the course of justice, conspiracy to breach money laundering regulations and more. *Mela,* an impressive list of charges, so far."

Nick looked at Camilleri and casually said: "Be in no doubt, I'm prepared to tell an honest policeman all that I know, if I can find one."

Camilleri shot him a glance, but maintained his silence. George continued: "Of course, he'd prefer to make peace with the Family and not compromise their operation, in exchange for the promise of a long and happy life, without having to constantly look over his shoulder.

"My friend, Abdullah here, or Tareq, as he now likes to be known, can confirm the payment of gold and cash to him and knows that it was the Maltese police, meaning you, who were sending it. That corroborates my story and, I'm sure you see, directly implicates you, Gerald. Mr. Belkacem has full knowledge of the Bonnici organisation's role in establishing the oil smuggling operation. He's seeking asylum in Malta. He'd better get it, or he'll have a very interesting story to tell the Maltese *Pulizija* and the *Guardia di Finanza* in Italy. He's very keen to do a deal. Information in exchange for asylum. Sounds like something they might go for."

George had hit his stride. He spoke without faltering or hesitation. Camilleri was thinking as fast as he could, realising he was being offered a way out of this.

"It also occurred to me that, with a word in the right ears, your bosses in Milan might be inclined not only to dispense with your services – but also with you! So, it all looks potentially very messy, Gerald, doesn't it? *Mela*, you're a practical man and you can see that all this is best avoided. Let's see how that can be managed, shall we?"

They continued talking for several hours and eventually arrived at a position that Camilleri thought he could live with.

After phone calls to Marco in Malta and Sergio in Milan, Camilleri left the building for a smoke and to clear his head. While looking out over the sea wall, he felt his phone vibrate. It was a text.

Walk to the end of Pontoon G.

Camilleri looked back into the marina, along the pontoons holding the medium-sized yachts and cruisers, until he worked out which was G. He saw a tall, slim, darkly dressed figure standing at the end of the far pontoon. Just at that moment, almost as a signal, the figure lit a cigarette, turned towards him and blew a cloud of smoke in his direction. Camilleri slowly walked to the pontoon. As he threaded his way over the mooring lines, ropes and service cables, strung between the boats and the floating jetty, he saw the figure standing ahead, his back towards him. He had a slender build but, judging by the width of his shoulders and the way he easily shifted his weight from one foot to another, there was strength and speed in the man.

Camilleri drew closer. The other man slowly turned to face

him. He moved forward and pushed his face close up to Camilleri's. Camilleri recoiled, as he felt the man's warm breath and took a step backwards.

"Camilleri? Listen, we work for the same people and I need you to tell me who you have got inside there?"

"Who the hell are you and what do you think you are doing?"

"It is best that you do not know, but please help me do my job and we will get along fine."

The man smiled, his mouth a thin line, incisors just visible, protruding over the bottom lip

His confident intrusion into Camilleri's body space oozed aggression. The Assistant Commissioner struggled to regain his composure.

"I am afraid that is just not good enough – and I do not take kindly to attempts at intimidating me. If we are on the same side, behave like it, and we will see where that gets us."

"OK, have it your way. Let me make some educated guesses. Number one – Nick Walker?"

"Yes."

"Two – Inspector George Zammit?"

"Yes."

"Three – the Libyan trafficker?"

For some reason Camilleri could not fathom, he replied, "No, he didn't make it."

"Excellent. Now, this is what we are going to do. You finish up here, get them in a car and take them to the airport. If you are going to be more than an hour, ring me on this number. Here is my card.

"Tell them you are all leaving from a private terminal. There is a hanger marked D56, next to the DHL hanger. Drive in and get out of the car. Tell them to wait inside. Then turn around and walk away. Whatever you do, do not look back."

The man in the black suit grinned mirthlessly and then pushed past Camilleri, flicking his cigarette into the oil-stained water. Gerald Camilleri immediately thought about George's comment that the men in Milan might want his own demise, now his cover was blown. The man on the dock did not look the type who could be trusted or reasoned with. Camilleri, known as the man who did not sweat, looked pale and shaken, as he headed back towards the police compound.

CHAPTER 61
AMR WARDA

HURDS BANK, OFF MALTA, ABOARD THE MALIK ALBAHR

TWO DAYS after setting sail from Marsabar, Amr could finally bring the *Malik Albahr* onto the shallows of Hurds Bank, fifteen kilometres outside Maltese territorial waters. Once they had joined the main sea lanes, the passage had been smooth and trouble-free. They had caught the tail end of an unseasonal storm that had ripped across the southern Mediterranean, but the *Malik Albahr* had taken it in her stride. Amr enjoyed the familiar feeling of the ship rolling beneath his feet, the fresh sea air and the routines of days at sea.

He was determined to forget the horrors of Abdullah's cave, the gangster owners and the chaos of sailing in the southern Med. As soon as he could, he had promised himself to give up his command of the *Malik Albahr* and return to work in the Pacific or Indian Ocean, getting as far away as possible from all those crazy people.

His orders were to arrive at Hurds Bank at dusk, so that the ship-to-ship transfer of the cargo could take place at night. Although they would be outside territorial waters, and could rely on the Maltese to look the other way, it was not unknown for Italian naval ships to show up and start asking questions.

The risk with a ship-to-ship transfer was always spillage and consequent pollution, which all the captains of the local bunkering vessels took seriously; accidents happened. It was why any ship making a transfer of fuel had to notify any local port authorities likely to be affected by a spill. Amr had messaged the owners about this and they confirmed it had already been taken care of. Somehow, he doubted that.

It was nearly 23:00 when the lights of the first bunkering tanker approached. Amr had been watching the blazing ribbon of light along the Maltese coastline; glittering high-rise buildings, streams of traffic and, that evening, a spectacular fireworks display. The bunkering tanker towed the massive six-metre primary fenders that would be positioned between the vessels, to prevent them bumping and scraping together. Sparks were to be avoided, at all costs, during the transfer of the oil. So, the first job would be to secure the fenders, before pulling the vessels close together.

He had already turned on the heating coils around the holds, to warm the fuel oil – the thick oil was more difficult to pump when cold. The crew on the derricks were waiting for his orders to lift the cargo hoses for connection to the manifolds, so they could pump the oil between the two vessels.

It took at least an hour to set up the transfer operation, which was expected to take most of the night. As it happened, Amr did not need that long to finish the evening's work.

He did not remember the exact time the assault on the ship by the Italian *Guardia di Finanza* began, as he was busy concentrating on getting the hose connections correct. The first thing he saw were two helicopters racing low across the sea from Malta, circling the bows, with high-powered searchlights that raked the decks. A moment later, men were fast-roping down from them onto the cargo decks. Others, from three Armed Forces of Malta RHIBs, had already scaled up the side of the *Malik Albahr* and had the confused crew on their knees, with their hands on their heads.

It was all over in a matter of minutes and Amr had to admit

he was slightly relieved events had been taken out of his hands. He co-operated with the *Guardia di Finanza* as completely as he could. They ordered the crew to disconnect the hoses and the vessels de-moored. A pilot arrived from the Grand Harbour and the *Malik Albahr* was taken into the custody of the Maltese authorities.

After a few weeks in a Sicilian jail, Amr was released without criminal charge, but with a firm warning that he should stay away from the coast of Africa. To his relief, he was not found to be part of the conspiracy to smuggle embargoed or stolen oil. He produced a carefully prepared trail of paperwork to prove his instructions and his belief that the cargo was legitimate. There were some sticky moments when the ship's log was examined and the stop at Jubail in Saudi Arabia was proved to be false. Amr's explanation was that someone had forged that entry and, feigning anger, he pointed to the clumsy rubbing out, where the alteration had been made.

He knew he was lucky to get away so lightly. Numerous breaches of regulations were noted on his Captain's record, including the falsification of the ship's log, improper use of the automatic identification system and failure to notify the competent authorities prior to affecting a ship-to-ship transfer of potential pollutants. None were fatal to his chances of getting another command with the more flexible ship owners.

Nowadays, Amr sails medium-sized tankers owned by a reputable shipping company, out of Port Moresby, in Papua New Guinea. He makes regular trips to Japan and Australia. Occasionally, he still has nightmares about his time in Abdullah's cave and his experience working in the southern Mediterranean.

CHAPTER 62
ABDULLAH BELKACEM

POLICE RECEPTION CENTRE, ISLAND OF LAMPEDUSA

ABDULLAH, Nick Walker and George sat waiting for the return of Camilleri. Nick had been highly impressed by the way George had handled him and was enjoying running through the conversation.

"You've played a blinder mate! I think we're going to walk away from this! You're one tough cookie. God, I could do with a drink! Do you think we're nearly done here?"

George thought about it.

"*Mela,* I don't know. I hope there's something in it for everyone. I've given it my best shot and Camilleri seems to be on board with it all – but people can be bloody-minded, you know. God knows what the Italians are really thinking?"

Abdullah was rocking his chair on two legs and had his back leaning against the wall of the conference room. He turned to Nick.

"My friend is a fighter and a soldier. I have seen it with these eyes." He turned to George. "But, yes, you have scared that policeman badly. I thank you, but ask you why you do this for us? You are not in trouble. You do not need more problems. Now you know your boss's secrets, are you safe or do you have more problems? I think you have more problems."

George pondered.

"I just want to go home. I want us all to go home and I don't want any more trouble. You can't fight Camilleri and the Family. They're bigger than us and they're everywhere. You take one down and another knocks on your door. That's how it is. They're businessmen. The politicians and the police are also businessmen at heart. Look after their business, keep trouble away from their door and they're happy. I'm making peace and trusting they'll be grateful for it."

"Well, if this all works out, I'm gone for sure. You won't see me for dust. I always wanted to be successful and have money, but it doesn't have to look like this. I'll find a different way."

Nick pushed off from his chair and went to look out of the window.

"He's on his way back. He's on the phone and he looks worried."

Camilleri came into the conference room and took off his jacket, carefully hanging it on the back of a chair. George had never seen Camilleri in his shirt sleeves and was surprised how much it aged him. He looked paler and thinner –vulnerable even.

"Well, gentlemen, we have a new problem. I am happy with the deal that we have reached, but it seems there is someone outside who is not. I have spoken to my associates who decide these things, but they say I should hand you all over to a man who is waiting outside. I suspect he wishes to do you harm."

With that, he looked around the group, gauging their reaction. George's mouth dropped open and Nick spun on his heels, putting his hands to his head.

"I knew it was too fucking good to be true."

Camilleri described the Italian who had spoken to him on the pontoon. He told them he had been instructed to take Nick and George to a hangar at the airport, where Camilleri believed they would be killed.

George and Nick immediately recognised the description of

Camilleri's Italian, as that of the man looking for Nick at the hotel the previous day.

Abdullah broke the silence.

"So, this Italian, does he know that I am here, too?"

Camilleri shook his head and said: "For some reason, I did not confirm that. So, no, he does not know you are here.

"Well, then, this is easy for us. No sad faces necessary."

Abdullah took George by the arm.

"Friend, I thank you for what you have done for me and for your courage. Now it is my turn to do some good thing for you. I will go and do what I must do!"

George looked at him, confused. Camilleri understood perfectly, and nodded his head, saying: "If you think you can, you should. Be warned – he looks strong and fast."

"We will see who is stronger and faster. So, Mr Policeman, I need one hundred euros."

Camilleri took out his wallet and handed Abdullah a bundle of notes, without counting them.

"If you are going to do it, you need to go now."

Camilleri gave him the instructions about where Raphael had told him to go.

"You have forty minutes – then we will be on the Armed Forces of Malta plane back. If you are there, I will help you at the other end. If not, we will have to go without you. Yes?"

George was still confused about what exactly was happening.

"Do not worry, I will deal with this the old Berber way," Abdullah told him.

He pointed to the blue plastic bag in the corner of the room.

"George, do not forget our things! And you, Mr big Chief Policeman, you, who caused me to lose my brother, my home and my fortune – do not touch that bag or I will upset this nice party. If that bag is not as I left it when we meet again, one night, I will come for you. I will gut you and your friends who have cost me so much. That, I promise."

Then, Abdullah left, much amused by the expression on Camilleri's face.

George was concerned.

"If Abdullah gets rid of this man – won't the Italians, or whoever, just send another hitman?"

Camilleri looked out of the window, thinking.

"I am not sure. They are practical people. Once we are back in Malta, they will see the deal we are offering for what it is. Anyway, at this moment, there is no alternative, is there?"

Abdullah's first call, after leaving the police station, was to a general boat supply shop which sold marine goods, including boat fenders, ropes, marine paint, nuts and bolts and a range of wicked looking fisherman's knives. He selected a long thin filleting knife and asked for it to be loosely wrapped in brown paper.

The runway in Lampedusa ended almost in the centre of town. As there was so little flat land on the island, everything was concentrated into the south-east corner. But, in the interests of speed, Abdullah took a cab and paid the ten euro fare to travel along to the *Villaggio Aeronautica.*

Once there, he quickly found the hanger marked D56 and entered it, without challenge. Inside, it was full of pallets of cargo, some stacked three or four high. There were many places an assassin could conceal himself. Abdullah did not have long to wait, before he saw a shadow pass across the hanger entrance. A tall figure moved quickly from one side to the other. As Camilleri had observed, the man did not make a sound and was light on his feet. Abdullah realised he would have to take extra care.

There was no sound in the hangar until a departing plane manoeuvred across the apron, in front of the entrance doors. Abdullah took advantage of the noise to change his position. He removed his shoes and went to the back of the building, moving along the walls, looking for the Italian man. He lifted a clipboard from a hook and used it to conceal the filleting knife. Knowing the assassin would be looking in front of him, towards the main doors, Abdullah reasoned he would have his back turned.

Finally, he saw a dark figure standing in the shadows, behind a stack of crates, looking at his phone, with his gun and silencer resting on top of a nearby box. Abdullah was close, maybe five paces away from him, when he broke cover and breezily walked towards him, holding the clipboard up in front of him.

He gave a wide smile and, when he got within two paces, said:"*Telbeh sane al-khas beck*!"

Meet your maker!

The clipboard fell to the floor, distracting the man for just a second, long enough for the knife to flash across his throat. A red ribbon of blood gradually turned into a stream. The man did not even have time to reach for his gun. In seconds, he had fallen to his knees and was choking to death on his own blood.

Abdullah carefully wiped the knife on a cardboard box, as Raphael thrashed about on the floor, then shoved it between some boxes on a pallet. He put his shoes back on and left the building. He had killed many creatures that way – chickens, goats, sheep – but killing an enemy, with one stroke of a knife, was always the most satisfying death.

CHAPTER 63
MARCO BONNICI
CASTELLO BONNICI, MALTA

IMMEDIATELY ON HIS return to Malta, Camilleri went to the *castello* to speak to Marco. He was flustered, but took some deep breaths and sank into one of the old leather armchairs in the study. Marco also seemed distracted and unfocused. He stood nearby, fiddling with a pipe cleaner he had found in a wooden box on the desk, whilst glancing out of the window. Natasha, meanwhile, was totally relaxed and reclined in an easy chair, her grey knitted beanie pulled low over her head and a large pair of dark sunglasses shielding her eyes. Headaches, she told him. Camilleri wondered why Natasha was present at all, but he did not have the energy to debate the point.

He began by explaining how Zammit had ambushed him in Lampedusa and how the tables had been turned against them all. He had made a judgement call, he told them.

"Marco, it was plain that not everybody could walk away from this without consequences. Zammit and the others demanded a price for their silence. Let me be candid, my first concern was for yourselves, and those of us here in Malta, although I do not think Milan need to be made aware of that fact. There is going to be some fallout, but I hope I have kept it as limited as possible. If they want to, Zammit, the Arab and Walker could easily bring us all down. They have enough to do significant damage but, this way, you can demonstrate to Milan that we have contained the problem."

It was apparent that Marco had to sell the deal to Sergio who, in turn, had to sell it to the Wise Men. Camilleri was emphatic this had to be done immediately, before anyone involved got cold feet and backed out. Marco thanked him for his hard work and said he would be forever in his debt. Natasha thought those were big words to say to the policeman. He might start to get ideas above his station.

After walking Camilleri back to his car, Marco returned to the study, where his daughter was sitting quietly in her chair, knees drawn up to her chest. To her surprise, her father said he would speak directly to the Wise Men. She realised cutting out Sergio was a bold move for him and not one he would take lightly. But he had read the way things were going and knew Sergio's head was going to be the one to roll.

Her father turned to face her, leaning against the desk. He looked worn out, the bags under his eyes and a day's stubble making his appearance uncharacteristically unkempt.

"Natasha, I have had enough of all this. I really cannot handle it anymore. You should know, I am probably going to visit Milan and then I will leave Malta for a while. I do not have the stomach or the allies for a long fight. I have done what I can to save us both. Once this is sorted, I am taking a sabbatical."

"But Gerald says you won't be implicated in the fall out – there's no reason for you to leave!"

"I know, but I think a bit of distance between us at this time will not hurt. You can continue with your plans here, uninterrupted. You have a lot going on and, frankly, from what I have seen, I do not wish to be involved in any of it."

Natasha looked at him askance.

"I don't know what you mean? What're you talking about?"

"Do not forget who you are talking to! I raised you and I have watched you just about every day of your life. Camilleri has told me he asked Walker about the Navkovs' money and Walker says he did not know a thing about it. Gerald is inclined to believe him. He said Walker had nothing to gain by lying, with everything else out in plain view. It looks like the disappearance of that cash was set up to discredit him.

"And, I checked the Audi the other day, after that killing in the car park at St Paul's. I felt terrible doing it and hated myself for even thinking you could be involved in something of that sort.

"But then, I started looking around and noticed the old Land Rover looked like it had been valeted. No one has cleaned that vehicle for years. I had forgotten we even had it. I asked a few questions down in the vineyards and old Paolo told me you had asked him to clean it, after you had hit a dog."

Marco put up his hand to prevent any interruption.

"I do not wish to hear any more lies and I do not wish to know the truth – I do not think I could handle it right now."

He reached the door and turned back, saying, "You know, Natasha, there was a time when you used to worry me. But now, you actually frighten me."

CHAPTER 64
SERGIO ROSSI

MILAN

THE FIRST SERGIO knew of the clusterfuck in Lampedusa, was when he was summoned by the Wise Men, at midnight that same night. Signor Bruno's driver, Toni, collected him from his girlfriend's apartment and drove him to the *palazzo* in Brera. If Sergio's last meeting with the Wise Men was frosty, this time it was glacial. Sergio was escorted – there was no other word for it – into Signor Bruno's study and shown a chair. Signor Bruno did not even bother to rise and shake hands. For the first time in Sergio's experience, Toni did not leave the room, but stood behind him, just outside his field of vision.

"Accountability, Sergio. We talked about that word last time we met. This is what concerns us. You want to know why you are here? Of course, you do.

"First, you broke the deal with the Libyan and brought in ISIL. It was an act of madness to partner with the Islamists – when have Catholics and Muslims ever worked together without bloodshed? You then failed to deal with the Libyan and the Maltese policeman, even allowing the pair of them to conspire together to blackmail us, compromising both the energy operation and the gaming business. You took control of the hunt for the whistle-blower, Walker, and let him escape. To cap it all, one of the Family's best resources had his throat cut, while trying to rectify your mistakes. These actions have attracted attention from financial authorities and police in two countries. It is an unprecedented catastrophe, one of the most serious in the Family's recent history.

"So, what can I do? You are the accountable one, Sergio, and you will help put this right for the Family – by paying with your time.

"I am handing this matter over to Salvatore Randazzo, who will liaise with you from now on. Be sensible, Sergio, and we can meet again, maybe in a few years, to discuss your future. You are still young. You have time ahead of you. Meanwhile, I suggest you do as he says."

Signor Bruno nodded at the driver, who went to a side door and ushered in a smartly dressed, dark-haired young man, in his early thirties, who took a seat by the door. He was classically good-looking, with a chiselled face and high cheekbones. The most striking thing about him was the piercing blue of his eyes. Sergio had heard of Randazzo. He was a banker by training and had been part of the financial team behind the Family's businesses for some years. He had always been a backroom type and it surprised Sergio to see him getting involved in operational matters.

Signor Bruno rose, took his ebony-handled stick and, without a backward glance, left the room.

Salvatore Randazzo took his cue and moved to sit behind the desk, vacated by Signor Bruno.

"Well, Sergio, it's a shame we meet in such circumstances. I've always heard good things about you. I'm sorry for this situation, but I need to know what you want to do about it?"

Sergio was taken aback, but realised, if he was going to take the fall for this, the Family would allow him to state his terms. He sat for a moment and considered his position.

"OK, you can tell the *Guardia di Finanza,* or whoever else is chasing this, the fuel smuggling was my operation. Nobody else need be involved. We will agree a statement and I will stick to it. Keep my wife in the manner to which she is accustomed and get me a good lawyer, who can do a deal on a plea. But I want looking after on the inside – privileges, protection, you know the score. Then Carlita, my girlfriend, will need some money and you need to keep up the subscription on my box in the San Siro. I had to wait years to get one. As a special gift from me, you can even use it, if you want to. When I come out, I want reinstatement and payment for money lost during my time inside."

Salvatore Randazzo looked at him, blue eyes ice cold.

"Most of that can be arranged but I'm not sure about the girlfriend – you know how Signor Bruno is about family."

Sergio's patience snapped. He did not take kindly to being lectured about his morals by a little shit like Randazzo.

"Fucking pay Carlita, Salvatore, and do not piss me about!"

"Hmmm, if you put it like that, I suppose I can find a way. OK, that's all for now. We'll call it a day. Tomorrow, we can meet with the lawyer and start preparing the details. Maybe, tonight would be a good time to say goodbye to your girlfriend?"

Sergio left the *palazzo* and quickly found a bar away from the tourist area on the Corso Garibaldi, where he drank, while he considered his future. He was still a young man and time in prison was sometimes the cost of doing the business they did. Everybody in 'operations' knew that. He might serve five or six years, but there was plenty of time left for him after that. While he was gone, they would realise what they had lost. Hell, with some luck, the Wise Men would all be dead by the time he was released and Marco and some of the others could be running the show. Then, they would really have some fun!

He did not see his girlfriend that night. By the time he finished drinking, he could only just crawl out of the car and make it to his own bedroom at home.

The next day, he met with Salvatore at the offices of the *avvocato*, near the Porta Venezia. Sergio had a stinking hangover, so Salvatore and his chummy lawyer friend soon started to become seriously annoying. It was obvious the two of them knew each other well, as they laughed and joked their way through the morning. Sergio felt he should have been the centre of attention, rather than gate-crashing their private reunion.

Salvatore did not seem in the least embarrassed or fazed by the situation. He was 'strictly business'. It was only then that it hit Sergio how much trouble he was in. Salvatore and the lawyer talked about how to handle the *Guardia,* the PR aspects of the trial, the likely plea bargain that could be struck … all as if he was not even in the room. If Sergio had not felt so shocking, and shocked, he would have intervened; even demanded his own choice of counsel, but he allowed the day to drift by, without staging any protest. He knew he needed Salvatore Randazzo, who was now his only access to the power and strength of the Family. Without him, he would be left with nothing. He tried to remain calm and sought comfort from the distant future he had seen in the bar the night before, knowing his day would come again.

He listened to the details of the fallout from the arrangement under discussion with the Guardia. The management of the Maltese branch of their bank, Antayla Bank, was surrendering its Maltese banking licence, having found it had been the victim of several money laundering schemes. The offices of BetSlick had been raided and closed. The *Malik Albahr* had been intercepted, outside Maltese waters, and the cargo seized. Numerous small-time officials involved in issuing false documentation had been arrested, along with several port officials. A person had been found dead in Lampedusa, killed by unknown assailants.

Apparently, Gerald Camilleri had fed a doctored version of events to the *Guardia di Finanza,* noting that most of the criminal activity seemed to have occurred in Italy and had been committed by Italian citizens – namely, Sergio. In his view and that of the Maltese Commissioner of Police, there was little of interest to the Maltese, other than some corrupt junior civil servants and the money laundering operation, undertaken by BetSlick.

In due course, it was agreed that Sergio would serve no more than four years in an Italian prison. Through Salvatore, the Family thanked him for his sacrifice and promised him adequate compensation, following his release. In fact, the open prison where he would be sent allowed mobile phones and had some limited internet facilities, as well as a decent kitchen. Salvatore assured him he could pass the time there without too much bother. He was allowed home one weekend a month and, while his wife was too ashamed to visit him in prison, Carlita was allowed to visit his private cell, on a fortnightly basis.

The *Guardia* hailed the conviction as a major step in the fight against organised crime. The raid on the *Malik Albahr* was widely televised across Europe. The ultimate humiliation was the choreographed trial, with pictures of Sergio, in cuffs and an orange overall, sitting in the courtroom in a glass cage. That had not been agreed and it had upset his wife more than anything else. The cooperation with the Maltese Police was also widely applauded, with extensive quotes from Assistant Commissioner Camilleri stressing the good relations and excellent teamwork that existed between the Maltese and Italian agencies.

The Family promoted Salvatore Randazzo and he became de facto head of the day-to-day business operations – Sergio's old position. They gave him three months to restructure the organisation, a challenge he set about with gusto. Once Sergio started his sentence, at Sant' Agata prison in Avellino province, Salvatore sent his apologies, saying it was imprudent for him to visit too often, as it risked bringing him to the attention of the authorities, who would no doubt be logging visitors. As it turned out, other than Marco, not a single member of the Family ever visited the prison.

As time moved on, Sergio gradually realised he had been hung out to dry and forgotten. His humiliation had been witnessed on national television. Once, he had aspired to become a Wise Man and enjoy untold respect and riches, as the head of the Family. He believed he had earned that. But it was not to be.

He was now a convicted criminal and his family shunned by polite Milanese society. It had taken a little time for him to register the full extent of his fall and then he started to regret having rolled over quite so easily. As Marco was all but out of the picture now, living in Serbia, apart from brief trips to Italy, Sergio had written to Natasha at the *castello* and asked her to intervene on his behalf. She had replied, wishing him well and saying those in Malta were looking forward to his release. She promised to speak to Salvatore.

Some weeks later, he received an A4 envelope, postmarked Milan. Inside there was just a single, large photograph. It was evening; Salvatore wore a dark jacket and a white shirt, top three buttons undone. He was raising a glass of champagne to the camera, as if in a toast. By his side, smiling widely, with one arm loosely draped around his waist, was Carlita. There were other well-dressed people in the background of the photograph, but the most prominent among them was Natasha, looking over her shoulder at the camera, also raising a glass and smiling. It was clear that they were in Sergio's box at the San Siro.

Carlita never visited Sergio again after that and Sergio never tried to find her. Bitterness and resentment burned inside him. Salvatore had shown him what he already knew deep down. As far as the Family was concerned, he might as well be dead.

CHAPTER 65
NICK WALKER

GIBRALTAR, FOUR MONTHS LATER

AFTER ARRIVING IN MALTA, Nick had done what needed to be done with Camilleri. He had met with a new face, Salvatore Randazzo, who had been brought in from Milan, *'free from any historical baggage'*, to clear up the mess caused by the collapse of BetSlick and the oil deal. He had promised Nick, if he stayed in Malta and helped wind up the company without too much fuss, it would go a long way towards mending fences with the Family.

George, Nick and Abdullah had all given statements to Camilleri about their knowledge of the oil smuggling business and the money laundering operation, omitting any mention of the name 'Camilleri'. The Assistant Commissioner had copies, which he held in his private safe at home, as did each of the others. Salvatore had seen the documents and had made certain guarantees as to the safety of all concerned, in exchange for their silence. George, Nick and Abdullah all swore to him that, if any harm came to any one of them as a result of the Family's actions, the statements would be made public by the others.

They did not know it, but it had been a tight vote amongst the Wise Men to let them escape with their lives. One vote fewer and an arrangement would have been struck with some East Europeans, who specialised in removing problems such as a trio of potential whistleblowers. There had even been a suggestion that an Assistant Commissioner of Police should be added to that list, but the idea was vetoed by Signor Bruno.

Nick Walker had resigned from BetSlick and wound up the company, as he had promised, rather than clearing out the cash and leaving a string of debts behind. That meant all the money in the Family's player accounts could be released back to them as clean gambling winnings, which had kept them happy. Once that had been done, Camilleri had swooped in, with half a dozen squad cars and some handpicked journalists, to take the plaudits for exposing the extensive money laundering operation. Nick publicly maintained that he had been conned by criminals on his staff and their maladministration.

As soon as he was able, he had taken a plane out to Heathrow, and then transferred onto a flight to Gibraltar. He had thought long and hard about where to go and had decided he needed somewhere he could quickly put down some roots, so he could establish a new business. He knew the Rock, having spent a few years there before going to Malta, and he still had some business connections. After a few weeks catching up with those in the industry, he realised he could start again and build himself a legitimate business, avoiding all the nonsense that he had got himself into with BetSlick.

He had tried to avoid any contact with Natasha, following his return from Lampedusa. His priority had been to sort out the business with Camilleri and Salvatore. He had no contact with Marco, who he understood had left the island. All formal business documents were handled by Salvatore, as Marco's attorney. Once that was all done, he had just wanted to leave Malta, as soon as he could.

Natasha had known Nick was around, but did not contact him, either. There were things happening with the company formerly known as BetSlick, she would rather not get into with him.

The truth was that, as soon as he had left the island, the shell that was BetSlick was resurrected. The staff were rehired, the accounts recapitalised, a fresh lease concluded and the large illuminated sign that ran the length of the first floor was replaced with the new name, BetHi. The only thing that really changed was the name of the CEO: Natasha Bonnici.

CHAPTER 66
INSPECTOR GEORGE ZAMMIT

THE GRANDMASTER'S PALACE, VALLETTA, MALTA, FOUR MONTHS LATER

Every Maltese child knows Valletta was built in the sixteenth century, after the Great Siege of 1565. The Throne Room of the Grandmaster's Palace is the centrepiece of one of the first buildings commissioned by Jean de Valette, Grand Master of the Knights at the time. It is one of the largest halls in Valletta, its walls covered in golden palm damask and the ceiling decorated with frescos, telling the story of the Knight's victory over the Ottomans.

It was in that very room that George was to receive his Medal for Bravery from the President of the Republic. The front left row was filled with dignitaries from the government, including the Minister for the Police, the Justice Minister and the Attorney General. Also in attendance were representatives from the judiciary, the Libyan Embassy, the *Guardia di Finanza,* and various EU institutions. Behind them were the massed ranks of senior police officers, in full dress uniform. The first face George registered amongst the sea of uniforms was that of Sergeant Major Chelotti, the officer who had called him the 'use it or lose it' inspector, scowling at him. George smiled broadly and gave him a wink, as he took his seat.

Marianna sat in the front row, to the right, hardly able to

contain her hand-wringing excitement. Sitting next to her was Gina, wearing a too-short pink affair with four inch, wedged matching shoes. Denzel sat on the end of the row, to stretch his injured leg. He was still on crutches, but was presentable in a dark suit and tie. Behind them were his extended family, neighbours and a host of other people he barely knew, all of whom had been invited by Marianna.

George felt the whole period immediately after his return to Malta had passed in a blur. He had been physically and emotionally exhausted. On occasions and for no particular reason, he had been prone to bouts of tears. Marianna suggested it was probably Post Traumatic Stress and she said she had it all the time and you just had to learn to live with it.

After a couple of weeks of sleeping, eating and thinking through all he had experienced, he felt more relaxed and was ready to be seconded to the *Guardia di Finanza,* in Catania, to help prepare the case against Sergio Rossi and others involved in the oil smuggling racket. Camilleri stayed close to him, phoning him daily, to ensure he retained *'a positive state of mind'*. He need not have worried – the deal they had struck in Lampedusa suited everyone.

George had realised, while floating around on the raft waiting to be picked up, that to use what he knew to bring down everyone involved, would make him a pariah in the police. Also, it would make him a target for those wanting revenge or to dispose of evidence! He was pretty sure he would be on someone's hit list the minute he returned to Malta, unless he showed he could be trusted.

On arriving in Lampedusa, he had decided to try and use Camilleri as a fixer so he could get the best deal available for everyone. It was not justice, but it was a result and, if everybody was happy and nobody got hurt, what was the problem with that? It was a task Camilleri was admirably suited to and, once it was all over, the world kept turning, as it had done before.

And so, here he was, promoted and about to be decorated!

Colleagues were generous in their congratulations and he had become a bit of a celebrity in the force. They had started to include him in after-work beers and he had even received invites from other officers to one or two social occasions.

During the ceremony, the Commissioner of Police recounted the tale of Inspector Zammit's trip to Libya – or, at least, a sanitised version of it: how he had taken on an undercover operation, aimed at bringing down a dangerous gang of people traffickers, and how he had attacked and neutralised the operations of a highly armed band of ISIL fighters.

He told of the single-handed rescue of thirty refugees from modern slavery, battling another troop of ISIL fighters, using heavy machine guns, and then sailing a raft over one hundred kilometres of stormy seas to safety. Added to that, he highlighted George's exemplary police work in identifying the oil smuggling gang that had led to the raid on the *Malik Albahr*, as well as bringing down a major money laundering operation. The President added how it was the most gallant story of police service she had heard and, if she had been told it was the plot of a Rambo movie, she would have dismissed it as fanciful! Sergeant Major Chelotti rolled his eyes upwards and sighed deeply.

The nickname stuck for a while after that – Rambo Zammit. It did not displease George.

Marianna clapped her gloved hands together feverishly, as her husband rose to receive his award, pushing out his chest and hoisting his trousers. He bowed to the President and they shook hands.

Camilleri sat quietly watching the medal presentation, his stork-like legs folded over each other, congratulating himself that he had succeeded in finding a way of making everybody happy. He knew he had to keep a close eye on George – a very close eye indeed.

After the ceremony, George and the family took drinks with the President and other dignitaries. The Prime Minister briefly joined their group and personally thanked George for his contribution to the fight against the evils of people trafficking. He told him his name would always be associated with bravery and dedication to the force. George nearly burst with pride when he said he would remember the name Zammit and follow his future career with interest.

As the proceedings were winding down, Camilleri approached them, accompanied by Superintendent Farrugia, who held out his hand to him jovially.

"Well done again, George – you've certainly done alright for yourself with this escapade. Medals, this reception ... and congratulations on the promotion, Superintendent Zammit! From now on we'll be equal rank, so you'll have to call me Mario."

Camilleri patted George's arm.

"George, Mario and I have been talking. Obviously, there is not room for two superintendents in the Immigration Section. How would you feel about coming to work for me, as a Super in the Organised Crime Command? You have already proved yourself to be very useful in that area. I would say it is a big step up, but I am sure you can handle it. I can always do with a man who has a nose for the way things work on this island. What do you say?"

George swallowed hard. It was not what he had wanted or expected. The Organised Crime Command was forever in the thick of controversy and had a reputation for using questionable methods. They had some of the pushiest officers around and always considered themselves a cut above everybody else. The meaning behind that comment about understanding *'the way things work'*, was clear to him. Camilleri really did want to keep an eye on him and now saw him as an insider, someone who would do his bidding, without asking too many questions. George felt he had stumbled into a carefully constructed trap.

"Well, it's a great offer, Assistant Commissioner, but I really don't know. Can I have some time ..."

To George's surprise, Marianna then jumped in to speak for him, face flushed with excitement.

"Of course, he'll take it. You know George, never pushes himself forward, but he's more than capable. The President said so! Didn't she, George?"

"Quite!" said Camilleri with a checkmate smile. "That is settled then. See you on Monday, George. Remember, it is business suits in the Organised Crime Command Squad – your days in blue are over! Behind every successful man is a strong woman and I can see your wife is a force to be reckoned with, George!"

Marianna glowed with pleasure, wringing her hands with the thrill of it all, an enormous smile spreading across her face.

On the way home, George was silent, fuming about his wife's intervention. He knew he had little choice but to accept Camilleri's offer, but Marianna's behaviour had really annoyed him. He realised she was aware she had got carried away, from the way she tried to steer the conversation to other, more mundane things. Denzel and Gina sensed trouble and sat quietly in the back of the car.

After a few more minutes of listening to prattle, George could not hold back any longer.

"Please don't ever forget yourself like that again, Marianna. It's not your place to meddle in my work. I would've agreed to take the job, but not because you pushed me into it. In this new job, we'll be invited to all sorts of events and get to meet some very important people. I don't want you embarrassing me again, do you understand? *Mela,* you'll have to learn how to behave properly, if you want to be a senior officer's wife."

Silence fell. The kids stared fixedly out of the side windows. Marianna looked at her husband in shock. George had never spoken to her like that before and certainly not in front of the children. All she could find to say was: "Yes, George, I'm sorry."

He dropped his wife and the kids back at the house, giving Marianna and Gina a kiss and patting Denzel on the back. He then announced that, because it was his special day, he would like pasta with rabbit and peas for dinner. That was enough to restore the normal balance of their relationship. A request for a simple plate of food, a symbol of equilibrium, of routine. He smiled and drove off, leaving Marianna standing on the pavement, all in a fluster. Secretly, George believed she quite liked this stronger, more authoritative superintendent husband.

CHAPTER 67
ABDULLAH BELKACEM

BIRKIRKARA, MALTA

George drove a mile or so down the road and went into a small hardware store, double parking outside on the yellow lines, placing his *'Police Business'* card on the dashboard. The pavement was cluttered with sweeping brushes, lengths of pipe, ladders, stacks of plant pots, a jumble of plastic tubs and bins. Inside was even worse, with tools hanging from the ceiling, shelves stacked with tins of paints and resins, the floor covered with lengths of wood and plywood panels.

The back counter had wooden shelving and drawers with nails, hooks, screws, bolts and fixings of every size and type. Behind it, was Abdullah, in a pair of jeans and a sweatshirt, emblazoned with the New York Yankees logo. He had scrapped the ragged dirty turban, trimmed his beard right down and cut his black hair short. He had a joiner's pencil pushed behind his ear and was wearing some designer spectacles. He looked every inch a Maltese ironmonger.

Abdullah finished serving a trade customer and was perched on his high stool behind the counter.

"So, my friend the hero! You in the paper tomorrow, eh?"

"I should think so."

"Is the lady wife much pleased? Is she in the picture also?"

"Yes, Abdullah, the lady wife is very much pleased. The pictures will show she is the one getting the medal, not me!"

"That is good. If the lady is happy, we are all happy! You will drink tea with me or is my tea not good enough for you now, Mr Chief Policeman?"

"Your tea is always good enough for me, my friend."

After killing the Italian, Abdullah had calmly left hanger D56 and met Camilleri, Nick Walker and George just outside the security point, ready to go airside. George had no doubt Camilleri would have boarded the plane and instructed it to leave without Abdullah, if he had not showed up when he did.

Fortunately, it was an Armed Forces Malta plane, so no one bothered to look in the carrier bag George was holding or Nick's red Kappa bag, as even Camilleri would have had trouble explaining away the contents! On landing in Malta, Abdullah had been taken into custody by the airport police, where he put in a formal request for asylum. He had been released a few days later, pending the decision, on assurances received from Camilleri.

Some weeks later, George persuaded Camilleri to put the squeeze on an Egyptian businessman to buy one of the gold bars from Abdullah at a reasonable, but not extortionate, discount. With the proceeds, Abdullah had leased the small shop and the business, on busy Birkirkara High Street, with two living rooms upstairs, and had set about becoming a Maltese shopkeeper.

He quickly settled into his new role. His English was not bad and his Arabic adapted well to the Semitic-based Maltese language. He had even started to acquire an Italian vocabulary, particularly useful when selling to the many Italian tradesmen working on the island.

He had tentatively deposited five hundred euros into the Antayla Bank account, using the codes, passwords and keypad supplied in the briefcase he had taken from George, at the Vai Vai

Cafe car park. To his surprise, the account was still active, all the transactions completed, and he had found a way of transferring money from Turkey, to a bank in Tunis. There, a member of his wife's family would visit monthly, across the closed border, to make withdrawals.

If his asylum request was accepted and, given the support of Camilleri, there was no reason it should not be, Abdullah could apply for a Maltese passport. Then he could ask his wife and family to join him in Malta and they, too, would become citizens of Europe. He and his wife spoke regularly, but she was reluctant to leave the security of her family home in the Nafusa hills. Abdullah tried to persuade her of the benefits to their children of a Maltese education, in English, so they could go and work anywhere in Europe. What a thing that would be! The irony of holding such dreams was not lost on Abdullah.

Destiny is one of Islam's six articles of faith and Abdullah knew that Allah had a plan for him. That plan was that, one day, he would return to Libya, wipe Abu Muhammed off the face of the earth and regain what was rightfully his. He was as certain of that, as he was of anything. How it would turn out, only Allah knew, but that had always been good enough for Abdullah.

They often spoke of events in Libya and Abdullah called George, *'the brave one'*, *'the soldier'*, *'the hero'*. George got tired of telling him it was not like that, but his friend would reply, laughing and poking him with his long, nicotine-stained finger: "Looking at you now, I too would not believe it, if I was told this story. But I saw it all, with these eyes, and these eyes do not lie!"

In the back room, the kettle had boiled and George pottered around, assembling the pot and the little glasses in which they took their sweet mint tea.

Abdullah locked the front door, turned over the handwritten sign that said *'Me return in 20mins'*. It was not perfect English, but people got the gist of it.

George thought about the medal ceremony, only an hour or two before, in the Grandmaster's Palace, the congratulations from his fellow officers, from Presidents and Prime Ministers, from his family and Marianna's friends in the street. He had to laugh. If they could only see this – the warlord and the Superintendent of Police, happily taking tea together, in the shaded courtyard of an ironmonger's shop in Birkirkara.

EPILOGUE

MADLIENA, MALTA

DRESSED IN LOW-SLUNG JEANS, heavy sweatshirts and knitted woollen hats, Abeao and Mobo ignored the heat of the midday sun and manoeuvred heavy stone flags onto the extensive patio area. They were working in front of a stylish, modern bungalow, high on the Madliena ridge. The residence had commanding views over the whole of the east coast, from St Paul's, in the north, almost all the way to Valletta, at the mouth of the Grand Harbour.

They had spent the morning plastering an extension to the garage and the fine dust had given their matt black skin a peculiar light grey patina. The rivulets of sweat that ran down their cheeks further textured their faces, washing away the dust and creating a lattice of delicate black lines. But it was easy enough work and the pay was good; they had a rhythm going and the slabs were falling into place, quickly and accurately.

Abdullah had signalled to the brothers in the compound on Lampedusa and promised them help, if they kept their mouths shut about who and what he was. With Camilleri's intervention, all three of them had ended up together at the Hal Far migrant camp, in the south of Malta. Abdullah was the first to be allowed to leave and had told the brothers to find him, once they were free to look for work. They had agreed to keep in touch through a priest who worked in the camp.

Abdullah felt he owed the brothers, not only for their help on the crossing, but for their silence upon arrival in Lampedusa, keeping his true identity secret from the authorities. Through contacts made in the shop, he had found them work as general building labourers and, later, as sub-contractors to some of the larger building firms. He always received good reports on the speed and quality of their work.

The brothers lived with four Somalis in a two-bedroomed flat, near the Marsa end of the Grand Harbour. They had enough money for food and rent, and Abeao had got himself a driving licence. They had bought a small battered van, which they filled with a collection of basic tools they were buying from Abdullah, on weekly instalments. They had a business they could only have dreamed of in Nigeria. They slept at night without fear and, on Sundays, went to their church free from the watchful eyes of their neighbours. As young men, with no family or obligations, they soon forgot the hardships and perils of their journey. At times, they found themselves laughing at their good fortune – if they had known it would be so easy, they would have done it years earlier!

That was how they ended up laying the stone flags on Assistant Commissioner Camilleri's new patio, at his luxury hilltop bungalow. There was no Mrs Camilleri and they rarely saw the man himself. Abdullah had explained who Camilleri was and the need to complete the job, without drawing attention to themselves. It amused him that the Chief Policeman had come to see him to find casual labour for his home improvements. Abdullah had no hesitation in pushing the brothers to take the job and, all in all, he considered it a fair and just thing that Camilleri pay them bundles of euros for their honest work.

It was true, Europe really was a special place, full of opportunities.

ABOUT THE AUTHOR

AJ Aberford is a former corporate lawyer who moved to Malta several years ago. He is enthralled by the culture and history of the island that acts as a bridge between Europe and North Africa. Its position at the sharp end of the migrant crisis and the rapid growth of its tourist and commercial sectors provide a rich backdrop to the Inspector George Zammit series.

To keep up to date on AJ Aberford's fiction writing please subscribe to his website: **www.ajaberford.com**.

Reviews help authors more than you might think. If you enjoyed *Bodies in the Water,* please consider leaving a review.

You can connect with AJ Aberford and find out more about the upcoming adventures of George and Abdullah, by following him on Facebook or, better still, subscribing to his mailing list.

When you join the mailing list you will get a link to download a novella, *Meeting in Milan,* a prequel to the Inspector George Zammit series.

ACKNOWLEDGMENTS

The Inspector George Zammit series is my debut work and I have too often been blind to my many mistakes. I thank my wife, Janet, for gently pointing them out, the time she has spent working on the various drafts and for her encouragement and support. I also thank my editor, Lynn Curtis, who has worked patiently with me, giving sage advice, steering the plots and refining the prose.

AJ Aberford

THE GEORGE ZAMMIT CRIME SERIES

Meeting in Milan (short-story prequel)

Bodies in the Water
Bullets in the Sand
Hawk at the Crossroads

MEETING IN MILAN

Short-story prequel available for free: www.ajaberford.com.

What is a family?

Two very different cousins, one from Malta and one from Sicily, are brought together to embark on their university studies in Bologna.

While spending time with their uncle and dying aunt in Milan, they learn some truths about themselves and realise that family is not what it seems.

In the space of a few short weeks, they have a decision to make. It is a choice that could change their lives forever and, once made, there will be no going back …

BULLETS IN THE SAND

George Zammit returns in *Bullets in the Sand*

Pre-order now.

When Inspector George Zammit, of the Maltese *Pulizija,* reluctantly agrees to help his old friend, the former Libyan militia leader, Abdullah Belkacem, his quiet life is turned upside down. George is reluctantly thrown into an adventure in the wilds of North Africa, encountering American special forces, Russian mercenaries and warring militias, all with their own complex agendas.

Natasha Bonnici is part of *The Family,* a sophisticated, organised crime group, based in Milan. Ambitious and ruthless, she sets her sights on a share of Europe's energy market, as well as control of *The Family* itself and there are no limits to how far she will go.

Abdullah Belkacem wants to win back his lands and his money, as well as avenging his brother's death. He cannot do it alone and so turns to powerful forces, dragging George – the only person he can trust – with him.

In the southern Mediterranean, nothing is what it seems.

Here follows a taster …

Warning: contains spoilers – do not read until you have finished Bodies in the Water.

PROLOGUE

SANT'AGATA PRISON, AVELLINO, ITALY

The correctional facility of Sant'Agata was hidden away in a wooded area of Avellino province, in the Campania region of Southern Italy. As it accommodated a good number of senior organised-crime figures and other wealthy white-collar prisoners, its governor and his crew provided a menu of special privileges, on a pay-to-stay basis, to help their guests pass the time more comfortably.

Over the previous four years Sergio Rossi had enjoyed the full range of these concessions, from specially prepared meals to, initially at least, fortnightly visits from his girlfriend, Carlita. His wife, when she was inclined, only visited on his name day and religious holidays. He received an ample supply of cigarettes, DVDs, and even had access to a sports streaming package, direct to the TV in his cell. It was true, he had it better than most, but other more important promises had been broken and that had gradually eaten away his trust in his former associates, to such a point that he now harboured feelings of profound ill-will towards them.

He had been sentenced over four years ago. This morning, his term was up. At 08:00, he was free to go. He had paid the price, and anger at his treatment by those he had trusted had helped him survive the physical confinement. During that time there had been plenty of opportunity for him to plan how to avenge himself on those associates who had persuaded him to take the fall for their criminal enterprise, only to abandon him once he was inside.

The buzzer sounded and the steel gate swung open – he was free. Before he crossed the threshold to freedom, he spat on the floor in front of him. Unless a person had survived confinement, they could never understand that no revenge would ever be sweet enough to compensate for the loss of four years of normal life. No revenge would ever be harsh enough to redress the humiliation and insult of standing trial, displayed in a glass box. All because of what had turned out to be a misplaced sense of loyalty. Sergio had agreed to accept sole responsibility for an oil-smuggling conspiracy so that others could remain free.

The prison was set in open countryside. A double wire fence separated the inmates from the fields and forests beyond. Sergio walked out into the sunlit car park and paused to view the facility from an outsider's perspective. It was a stylish three-storey building, with tasteful grey and brown cladding on its lower fascia. Only the undersized windows spoke of its true purpose. It looked more like a heavily protected junior school than a prison. Turning his back on Sant'Agata, he immediately spotted the immaculately clean black saloon with heavily tinted windows, parked at the edge of the car park.

Sergio was short, with a barrel chest and long grey hair that he wore swept back behind his ears. The time inside had taken its toll, but he still looked good for a man in his mid-fifties. The occupants of the car recognised him and the doors swung open. Two men got out. Both were wearing black suits, white open-necked shirts and sunglasses. One was holding a silver tray, with a glass and a bottle of champagne on it. Sergio walked towards them, pinning a big Sicilian smile to his sallow face.

"Signor Rossi, Salvatore Randazzo sends his regards and is looking forward to meeting you." The man held out a brimming glass as he spoke and gestured to the back seat while his companion, smiling broadly, bowed slightly and held the door open for Sergio.

He hesitated, one hand on the door, the other around the stem of the glass. He drank some and felt the entire four-year experience begin to recede. He allowed himself to smile, as some of the accumulated anger and hurt started to subside, but his words were still pointed.

"So, he couldn't be bothered to come himself? A big man now, *sì*?"

"Please, Signor Rossi." The driver bobbed his head and waved him into the back of the car.

When it had become apparent that someone would need to go to jail and Sergio had been informed that he should be that person, Salvatore Randazzo had replaced him as head of operations within the Family. Though the Wise Men of their organisation favoured Randazzo, who was clever, good-looking and hungry for success, Sergio had found him arrogant and disrespectful. Salvatore had never visited him once in the four years he had been inside, preferring to send messages through intermediaries and grudgingly conduct the occasional brief conversation with Sergio by mobile phone, until it seemed he started to find even these irksome and left further calls unanswered. It had been agreed that Sergio would be *distanced* during his time inside but, nevertheless, it still hurt his pride and he thought the behaviour of the younger man, at best, discourteous, at worst, insolent and short-sighted.

The rear passenger door shut behind him, with a solid clunk; the driver and his partner got into the front seats. He sank back into the comfortable leather upholstery, taking another long swallow from his glass. As he refilled it from the bottle left in a wine cooler beside him, he noticed a glass screen between the front and rear seats and rapped on it.

"Where're we going – what's the plan?"

To his surprise, the men did not drop the screen, but

continued to look straight ahead, while the one in the passenger seat replied through an intercom.

"We're going to Naples, Signore. It'll take an hour, so relax, drink champagne and enjoy the journey. There, we'll meet Signor Randazzo."

Sergio realised his phone was in his bag, which the guys had put into the boot of the car. He banged on the screen again.

"Hey!"

"Signore?"

"I need my phone, it's in the boot. Pull over."

There was no reply from the men in front, who continued to stare at the road ahead. The intercom went dead. The car rolled on, with no change of pace. Sergio banged on the window again.

"Hey, pull over, I want my phone!"

The silence from the front started to unnerve him. He tried once more, banging frantically on the glass.

"I'm telling you, *stronzi*, pull over – now!"

He put his hand on the door handle and was not entirely surprised to find it locked. Starting to feel uneasy, he sank back in the soft leather seat.

"Listen, you dickheads – let me out now. You don't know who you're messing with."

The intercom crackled.

"Signor Rossi, we know exactly who you are and we've got our instructions. Please, sit back. Everything is fine. There's nothing to be concerned about."

There was nothing dignified Sergio could do in response, other than set his jaw and stay silent. His body tensed, his heart rate began to race. He acknowledged to himself that he was afraid. The only weapon to hand was the champagne bottle. He put it to his mouth, half-full, and took a long draught.

The single-carriageway road from the prison ran through countryside for a while, before it joined the state highway to Naples. After only ten minutes, however, the car slowed. To Sergio's increasing alarm, it pulled off onto a rough, unmade track, leading up a gentle slope bordered by a thick scrub of willows and poplars. Beyond this, they found themselves in an area of reforested pines and cypresses. Not that Sergio noticed the details clearly – his mounting sense of unease was now verging on panic. His breath was coming in short sharp bursts, sweat beading on his brow and upper lip.

He shouted and swung at the glass screen with the base of the champagne bottle. It bounced back at him each time he lashed out until, with a gasp of despair, he realised the screen was not glass, but a thick sheet of acrylic – probably designed to be bullet-proof. The car turned off the track and slowly edged its way towards a small clearing amongst the trees. He could not believe what was happening. This was it. The Family wanted him dead. The intercom came on. The man in the passenger seat turned to look at Sergio. His face was completely calm and relaxed, no sign of tension.

"Signore, they told us you'd be a fighter, so we can do this in one of two ways. We're professionals. It can be handled quickly, with respect and without pain. Please, consider that option. It's the best way. Or you can fight and we'll keep you in the car, with the doors locked. We have ten litres of petrol stored behind those bushes and we'll use it to burn you alive. That won't be so quick and there'll be much pain. It's up to you. Either way, the end will be the same."

These chilling words put the matter beyond any doubt. Sergio slumped back in the seat and took a very deep breath. Despite his efforts to appear calm, his voice was shaky and his words garbled.

"I've got money. More money than you can ever imagine. I'll pay you both and then I'll disappear. Tell them it's done and there'll be no trouble. You'll be rich. We're all businessmen, *yes*?"

"I'm sorry, Signore. I have to deliver proof of death, otherwise it'll be me in the back of the car next time. Now, which way is it going to be?"

Sergio was not going down without a fight. There was no

way he was going to sit there and allow the Family to arrange his disappearance. He had one last play left and nothing to lose.

"Do what you have to do."

The men got out of the car and stood well back. With a remote, the driver unlocked the rear doors. After a second, the one behind the driver's seat flew open and Sergio leaped out, head lowered, and charged like a bull towards the men in black suits, champagne bottle in hand. Anticipating exactly that response, the assassins were ready. One raised his Russian PSS silent pistol.

HOBECK BOOKS – THE HOME OF GREAT STORIES

We hope you've enjoyed reading this novel by AJ Aberford. To keep up to date on AJ Aberford's fiction writing please subscribe to his website: **www.ajaberford.com** and you will also be able to download the free novella *Meeting in Milan.*

Hobeck Books also offers a number of short stories and novellas, free for subscribers in the compilation *Crime Bites*.

- *Echo Rock* by Robert Daws
- *Old Dogs, Old Tricks* by A B Morgan
- *The Silence of the Rabbit* by Wendy Turbin
- *Never Mind the Baubles: An Anthology of Twisted Winter Tales* by the Hobeck Team (including many of the Hobeck authors and Hobeck's two publishers)
- *The Clarice Cliff Vase* by Linda Huber
- *Here She Lies* by Kerena Swan
- *The Macnab Principle* by R.D. Nixon
- *Fatal Beginnings* by Brian Price
- *A Defining Moment* by Lin Le Versha
- *Saviour* by Jennie Ensor

Also please visit the Hobeck Books website for details of our other superb authors and their books, and if you would like to get in touch, we would love to hear from you.

Hobeck Books also presents a weekly podcast, the Hobcast Book Show, where founders Adrian Hobart and Rebecca Collins discuss all things book related, key issues from each week, including the ups and downs of running a creative business. Each episode includes an interview with one of the people who make Hobeck possible: the editors, the authors, the cover designers. These are the people who help Hobeck bring great stories to life. Without them, Hobeck wouldn't exist. The Hobcast can be listened to from all the usual platforms but it can also be found on the Hobeck website: **www.hobeck.net/hobcast**.

OTHER HOBECK BOOKS TO EXPLORE

The Rock Crime Series by Robert Daws

The magnificent Rock crime series from acclaimed British actor Robert Daws – includes free bonus story *Echo Rock.*

'An exciting 21st-century crime writer.'
Peter James

'A top crime thriller.'
Adam Croft, crime writer

Detective Sergeant Tamara Sullivan approaches her secondment to the sun-soaked streets of Gibraltar with mixed feelings. Desperate to prove herself following a career-threatening decision during a dangerous incident serving with London's Metropolitan Police, Sullivan is pitched into a series of life-and-death cases in partnership with her new boss, Detective Chief Inspector Gus Broderick. An old-school cop, Broderick is himself haunted by personal demons following the unexplained disappearance of his wife some years earlier. The two detectives form an uneasy alliance and friendship in the face of a series of murders that challenge Sullivan and Broderick to their limits and beyond.

The Rock crime series transports readers to the ancient streets of the British Overseas Territory of Gibraltar, sat precariously at the western entrance to the Mediterranean and subject to the jealous attention of neighbouring Spain. Robert Daws shows his mastery of the classic whodunnit with three novels rich in great characters, tense plotting full of twists and turns and breath-taking set-piece action.

The Rock

Exiled to Gibraltar from London's Metropolitan Police after a lapse of judgement, DS Tamara Sullivan feels she's being punished – no matter how sun-kissed the Rock is.

But this is no sleepy siesta of a posting on the Mediterranean. Paired with her new boss, DCI Gus Broderick, Sullivan will need all her skills to survive the most dangerous case of her career.

A young constable is found hanging in his apartment. With no time for introductions, Sullivan and Broderick, unravel a dark and sinister secret that has remained buried for decades.

Are they prepared to face the fury of what they are about to uncover?

Poisoned Rock

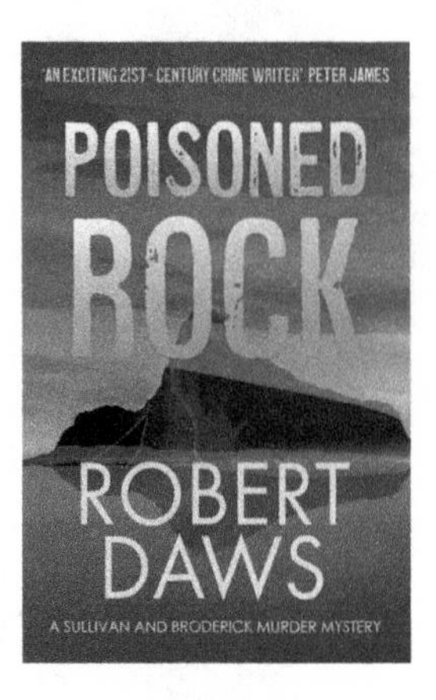

As the bright lights of a Hollywood movie production shine into the dark recesses of Gibraltar, murky secrets emerge from the shadows of the Rock's past.

It seems the legacy of wartime spying, sabotage and treachery runs deep on the Rock.

Past and present collide plunging detectives Tamara Sullivan and Gus Broderick into a tangled web of intrigue and murder, and their skills and uneasy working relationship are about to be tested to the limit.

Killing Rock

A wealthy household massacred in Spain.

Unidentified mummified remains found at the foot of The Rock.

A US Congressman's run for President hangs on events in Gibraltar.

What's the connection?

Detectives Tamara Sullivan and Gus Broderick face the most dangerous and elusive murder investigation of their lives, and for Broderick, it's about to become all too personal, with his career in real peril as his past comes back to haunt him.

Will Sullivan and Broderick's partnership survive this latest case, as killers stalk the narrow streets of Gibraltar?

CPSIA information can be obtained
at www.ICGtesting.com
Printed in the USA
LVHW041043290622
722312LV00003B/8